Morrighans Weave

Magical Girl

by

C. C. Martinez

They came from somewhere—some parallel dimension that they would never talk about. These days, they are called Faeries. Back then, when everyone feared them, they were the Good Folk, the Fair Folk. Their true name is the Fae.

They liked it here on earth. Really liked it. At one point, they got humans to fight for them, to conquer territory for a sort of Faerie colony. But the humans they contracted were no more trustworthy than the Fae themselves. No one involved acquitted themselves with honor, but the ones who really burned them worst were the Morrighan. In the final betrayal, it was the Morrighan who led the fight to expel the Fae, and the Fae never forgave them.

Eventually, the Faeries retreated to the woods and shadows. They lived on the fringes of the world until a time came when the woods were cut down and the shadows washed away with artificial light. Having nowhere left to hide, they gave up and tried to return to their own world, only to discover that it had become unlivable. The Fae were within a generation of being annihilated.

Desperate Faeries make desperate plans. Complicated, crazy, dangerous plans. They decided to secure a new home in the world of the humans by waging war against humankind.

But times had changed. The humans were now organized and well armed. Perhaps no wiser, but better informed. Ordinary help was not going to suffice. So, being Faeries and in desperate straits, they devised a more complicated plan—one involving the Morrighan.

These new players were oblivious. They had no idea that they were the Morrighan. They didn't know how much the Fae hated them, or why.

And the one now known as Andrea Melman didn't even know what to wear to school.

Chapter 1

Andrea looked down at the clothing options on her bed, trying to make the least bad decision about what to wear.

"Andrea Melman, get down here! You're going to be late for school!"

"No, Mom, I'm not!" she yelled through the door. "I do this every day! It's a twenty-minute walk!"

"No! I'm driving you to school today!"

Andrea froze. Why was her mom driving her to school? This never happened. And today of all days. This was the day her mother, the archaeologist, was leaving to join her father, the cultural anthropologist, at a dig in central Turkey for the better part of the year. Hands-on parenting had never been the Melman way, and suddenly her mom wanted to drive her to school?

Half opening the door, she shouted down the stairs. "Why?"

Up until now, the Melmans had never been the sort of family who conducted conversations by shouting between floors.

"I just want to talk to you about a few things."

Alarm bells went off in Andrea's head. Conversation was one thing, but "a few things"? This was spiraling dangerously out of control.

Her brother, Dion, never had to submit to parental interrogations. Sure, he was seven years older than her, but when he had come back from his year abroad announcing that he was switching majors—essentially moving him from pre-law to pre-living-at-home-forever—no one questioned that.

Ten minutes later, Andrea was sitting in the passenger seat of the family Subaru, staring straight ahead as her mother tried to make small talk. Then, a few blocks from school, quite out of the blue, she pulled over and killed the engine.

Andrea was too surprised to speak. Her mother was staring at her hands on the steering wheel, fumbling for a way to open the conversation.

Andrea was looking at her—up close—for the first time in a very long while. Partly because of how seldom either parent was home, but also because the Melmans functioned more like a collection of satellites than as a real family.

Ever since the move to Brooklyn four years ago, face time had become increasingly rare. Back in Cincinnati, at least there had been family dinners and outings. New York had sped everything up, and the resulting centrifugal force had flung the four Melmans into equidistant orbits around a world of careers and interests. Now Andrea was studying her mother's 46-year-old face and wondering whether she would look like her at that age.

Fat chance. Her mom was beautiful—had always been beautiful. Captivating green eyes and reddish-auburn hair of unusually vibrant color. Even stressed out and middle-aged, she looked terrific. *Genetics have failed me,* Andrea thought. *Mouse brown hair and unremarkable hazel eyes. A future growth spurt might possibly bring me up to five foot two if I live long enough.* Meanwhile, her mother's thought collecting pause was growing intolerably long.

"Mom?" she prompted gently.

"Oh, right." Her mother turned to face her. "Honey, this isn't the best moment to bring this up but... I..." She shook her head as if annoyed at her own hesitancy. "Okay, two things. I'll keep this to two things. The main thing is, and I don't know how to put this..."

"Oh, God! Am I in some kind of trouble? I can't believe I've done anything interesting enough to even *get* in trouble."

Her mother laughed. "No, it's nothing like that. It's just that I'm still getting used to the idea that your father and I are going to be away for so long, and—"

"Mom, we've been through this. Chance of a lifetime, remember? Career-making excavation. Big sweat-bonding opportunity with the Turkish director of antiquities. Dion's in charge here at home. Good grades, no boys. We're fine."

"I don't know, Andrea." Her mother was facing straight ahead again, clearly struggling to organize her thoughts. "Now that I'm leaving, I'm not so sure—not about trusting you. If anything, you're *too* self-sufficient."

She laid her hands back on the steering wheel and tried to take a slow, calming breath, but halfway through, it collapsed into a gasp. "Andrea, I'm sorry I haven't been a more focused mother with you. I mean, a more... 'there' mother."

Andrea wasn't ready for this much emotion. Hoping to keep her mother from continuing, she launched into a flurry of words.

"Mom? Where is this coming from? You're a *great* mother. And Dad's a great dad. *I'm* the difficult one here. I'm sorry I'm such a loner girl. I'm sorry I don't make friends easily… or at all. But I'm really happy. Not all smiley-happy but—you know—an *inner* sort of happy. And that's because I don't have you guys constantly pushing me to be something I'm not."

"Okay, okay." It was obvious her mom didn't know how to approach what she wanted to say, and time was short. She had to let it go.

"All right, then. Moving on. Witchcraft."

"Whoa!" Andrea lurched upright and faced her. "What about witchcraft?"

"No! No!" Her mom was frantically waving her hands. "Not criticizing witchcraft. No witch issues here. Your choice, your path, all good. Calm down."

Unconvinced, Andrea sank back into her seat.

"Honey, we never talk about it. And it is *your* business. Your father and I are clear about that. We read what you gave us. We did our own investigations."

Andrea's head snapped up.

"Okay, wrong word! We *looked into it further,* and we both think it's a beautiful, positive thing. No problem on the home front."

"Then what?" Andrea said, feeling more and more uncomfortable with where this was going.

"Honey, we're fine with it. *Brooklyn* is fine with it. But it's a big world out there. A lot of people have no understanding of things like Wicca. Or the perspective they have is really... skewed. A lot of places, places I've worked, they actually *fear* witches. They kill them. And even here in America, there are people who really... I don't know what to say. I don't want you to give anything up, but I'm really worried about what you might run into out there."

Andrea began to relax as she absorbed what she was hearing. Unlike the terrifying prospect of discussing her mother's parenting skills, this was an issue she had previously considered. Even better, just behind them, a New York City Sanitation truck had come around the corner and was making collections. According to the City of New York's laws regarding alternate-side-of-the-street parking, either this conversation was wrapping up really soon or someone was getting a fifty-dollar fine.

"Okay, Mom. I hear what you're saying. You realize I never talk to anyone about this, right? I don't go to witch stores. I'm not in a coven. No midnight rides, no standing outside school recruiting fledgling witches. Honestly? This is where my complete indifference to humanity really pays off."

She was glad to see her mother smiling at this, but she didn't know how else to put her at ease. "Mom, I am what's known in the Wiccan community as a solitary practitioner. And believe me, I am the most solitary witch you are *ever* going to meet."

"Okay, honey." They both seemed to realize that this was as close to "dealing with the issue" as they were likely to get. "I accept what you're telling me. But I'm sorry, I'm never going to stop worrying. It's a mom thing."

It seemed like a good moment for a hug or something, but the shrieking air brakes of the huge white garbage truck behind them combined with what sounded like some pointedly violent trash-can handling suggested that the moment had come and gone.

Before they knew it, they were in front of the school, exchanging rushed good-byes. The car pulled away, and Andrea walked into Brooklyn Preparatory High School K290.

Chapter 2

"The best time to get to Andrea is right when she walks in the door," a tall slender girl with shoulder length auburn hair named Gaylen said to the fidgety fashion victim buzzing around her.

"And she'll help me?"

"Look, Marion," Gaylen said flatly. "She'll do what she can. She's not a magician."

Andrea heard this much as she was walking in, before she even saw them. She knew Gaylen. Kind of. They weren't quite friends. It was more a relationship based on nods in the hallway.

Gaylen played bass in a variety of bands and had an easy manner about her that people were drawn to. Andrea envied her confidence. It was something you could read from her clothes: easy, functional, cool. Gaylen was her own girl. The other girl was… *wow*.

There was leather. And vinyl. Black denim. Glitter. Buckles. Chains. Safety pins. Even paperclips. And stripes—both vertical *and* horizontal. It was as if someone had tried to incorporate a random sampling of every Goth look since the 1980s forward into a single outfit—and then added stripes.

"Hey, Gaylen," Andrea said casually while her eyes were asking *What the hell…?*

"Hey, Andrea. This is Marion." She mouthed the words *Hot Topic* while Marion's eyes were on Andrea.

"Hey, Marion, that's a strong look there." The look of gratitude in the girl's eyes was both sad and a little creepy, but Andrea understood. Marion fit the profile.

Another kid whose junior high school career had been one long humiliation. For boys, it might be the result of a pathological ineptness at sports. A girl could achieve the same result by failing to parse the subtle distinction between fitting in and sticking out in her fashion choices.

Determined to reinvent herself for high school, Marion had apparently decided to double down on sticking out. Chances were good she'd gotten nothing but crap ever since. Eye-rolling critiques from old friends, parents asking her if there was "anything she'd like to talk to them about." Yep. This girl wanted a strong look. She was just trying too hard.

Gaylen nodded a *see you later* and let herself be carried off by the noise and chaos of a high school hallway at flood tide. Edging Marion and herself into a trophy alcove, Andrea assessed the mission.

At first glance, Marion appeared to have been seduced by the economics of acquiring mascara in bulk, but that wasn't her biggest problem.

"Marion, let me share some stuff with you that a lot of stylists say about stripes…"

By the time they came to Andrea's homeroom, she was wrapping up. "… And so, honestly, there really are a lot of other, you know, even *better* options for you out there, especially in this direction. I'll send you a list of sites if you'd like."

It was gratifying to hear Marion's gushing thanks, all the more because Andrea knew she had hit the right balance. Make an accurate assessment of intent, lay out the critical areas for immediate improvement, and limit everything to what the girl could handle without making her head explode. It was a satisfaction that evaporated the second she sat down and caught her own reflection in the window.

Oh, look, there's that girl in the witness protection program again.

By any sane reckoning, Andrea Melman was an attractive, popular girl with a wicked sense of humor and a legendary grasp of fashion and style. Everyone seemed to understand this except Andrea Melman. It was her curse to possess a sharp, critical mind capable of compassionate analysis of anyone but herself. The girl who could gently persuade the fashion-challenged into "appropriate options" was helpless in the face of her own looks.

Andrea had somehow arrived at the opinion that everything she wore made her look like either a potato or a slut—"and not much of a slut at that." So she kept herself out of the clothes that expressed her personality and wore what she referred to as "preppy camouflage." Hiding in plain sight while committing an act of cowardice in the face of fashion.

The first-period bell abruptly interrupted her parade of dark thoughts and launched her into the familiar chaos of the school day.

Originally, Andrea had resented the complex, impersonal environment of a New York City high school: the large class sizes, the crush in the halls. Her teachers seemed to be well-intentioned, but always on the verge of overload. Trying to grab a moment of their time between classes just made her feel guilty.

But Andrea didn't really need a lot of help, and she began to take a certain pride in working out her own solutions. Over time, she even began to appreciate the delicious sense of anonymity that K290 provided.

Back in Ohio, lunchtime was a minefield of cliques and personal histories to be carefully navigated as you picked (or were rejected) by different tables of kids in the cafeteria. New York was freedom. No one cared.

She had once overheard someone say, "Thing about Brooklyn is, you don't *start* nothin', you don't *get* nothin'."

It was true. You just kept your head down and minded your own business, and that was that. It was the day Andrea Melman truly embraced being a New Yorker.

* * *

Before she knew it, the school day was over and it was time to go home. The hall near the third-floor stairwell was deserted as Andrea tried to shoehorn another study guide into her already overloaded backpack. From down the hall, an alluring glimmer caught her eye. A vision of something that didn't belong in a Brooklyn high school—a girl with the poise of a runway model, dressed for a Manhattan gallery opening. In the middle of her fumbling, Andrea stopped dead in her tracks.

It was *her,* that girl from the videos. A head of blonde hair with two huge ponytails shooting out sideways and curving down to her waist. Natalya. From that band with the cellos… Black Swan Brigade! No drums or guitars, just droning but intricate textures and Russian lyrics.

10

The videos were always recorded in the same poorly lit space with a low-resolution cell phone camera. Darkly uncompromising, but just daring you to look away. Andrea was fascinated by them… well, by *her*.

Some girls had style. They read about it in magazines, bought it in stores, hoarded it in their closets. Natalya, though—she *was* style. Technically, her look was a variant of Elegant Gothic Lolita, but that was just a starting point. She was a walking art installation, always in flux. On the rare days when Andrea might see her from across a crowded hallway, she couldn't identify half of what the girl was wearing. Where did those clothes even *come* from? Did she make her own accessories?

At first, Natalya seemed to be on her cell phone, but no. As the distance between them closed, it appeared that she was talking to a point slightly above her and to her left. It seemed crazy, but Andrea could have sworn that Natalya was referring to *her,* at one point looking straight at her and then back to the side. The Russian accent completely captivated her.

"No! Don't waste my time. Mind yourself and behave."

That was all she caught. Andrea tried to gather up her stuff and move away from the stairwell that Natalya was obviously making for, but she was transfixed by the sight.

Suddenly, the other girl was right there, bearing down with a hard, blue-eyed glare.

"Out of my way, little girl!"

Andrea froze. Her backpack dropped and books shot out like shrapnel in every direction.

Panicking, she held out her now free hand and started babbling an introduction.

"Oh, hi! I'm Andrea Melman and—oh, you don't know me, but… I mean, I've seen your videos and I think—"

"*AHHNDRAAYYA MELLMAAHNN*," Natalya interrupted with exaggerated warmth and a broad smile.

Taking the bait, Andrea basked in Natalya's attention for one clueless instant.

Then, swift as a guillotine, the smile dropped, the eyes froze, and, she let out a low growl. "Out… of… my… *way!*"

Andrea collapsed to the side. Natalya picked a path around her books as if they were roadkill and stormed down the stairs.

Andrea was still trying to collect her things when she heard Gaylen's snarky cackle behind her. "Oh, *AHHNDRAAYYA*, I see you've met *NATAALLYA*."

"What is her problem?"

"Hmmm. Near as I can tell, *everything* is her problem. Oh, and apparently that now includes *you*. Have a nice weekend!"

* * *

Walking home was Andrea's favorite after-school activity. Ever since her family had uprooted her existence in Cincinnati to drag her halfway across the country, walking around Brooklyn had been her consolation prize.

With their simultaneous hiring by New York University, Mom and Dad had become the archaeological equivalent of rock stars. The move had given her brother Dion the opportunity to accept, and subsequently squander, a scholarship to Columbia. Andrea though, received a more subtle benefits package. She got the chance to explore a place where worlds collided, overlapped, or ignored each other, sometimes all at the same time. Grand parks and plazas from the Civil War era standing next to abandoned industrial sites backfilled with endless brownstones, all of it filtered through the cycles of American capitalism. Farms to mansions to row houses to slums to hipster hangs, every boom and bust destroying the previous beloved old neighborhood by letting the next group in to ruin everything all over again.

Andrea was halfway home before she remembered a certain timely fact. *Oh, God, my birthday's tomorrow.*

Turning fifteen was a big deal for most girls, but Andrea was certainly not "most girls." No one besides her family and the State of New York had any inkling that it was her birthday, and she was happy to keep it that way.

Andrea knew of only three kinds of birthday celebrations. You had your big parties, where the birthday girl, in a tragic bid for popularity, invited multitudes of people she barely knew. And then there were the small parties, with one's friends creating a lot of drama about the guest list—to Andrea's way of thinking, an argument for not having friends in the first place. And, of course, there were family parties held in restaurants with a humiliating cake moment and gifts like a savings bond for college, or a twenty-five-dollar gift certificate to a store where twenty-five dollars bought one glove or a third of a sweater.

At home, she found two envelopes on the kitchen table that her parents must have left for her. The first had a hundred-dollar savings bond in it.

If not for his scholarship, Dion's tuition would be around forty thousand a year, she thought. *Were their parents trying to tell her something? Was she being prepped for community college?*

The second envelope was so perfect, she actually laughed aloud. A twenty-five-dollar gift certificate to Hot Topic, with a note saying that they were "trusting her to act responsibly" and treat herself to something "age appropriate."

Oh, sure, she thought. *What age would that be? The Victorian? Babylonian? Jurassic? Just once, I'd like to do something irresponsible, just to mix it up a little.*

Waiting for her on her bed upstairs was a third envelope, with her name written in magenta crayon. Inside was a fifty and a note: "Get whatever you want. Happy birthday. Dion."

Dion was cool. He didn't believe in making anything any more complicated than it needed to be. His wing was down a long hallway, and the isolation was such that they could do pretty much whatever they wanted without bothering each other. In Dion's case, this meant playing some very loud electric guitar and even having the occasional band rehearsal.

Andrea's wing was situated between Dion's and their parents' areas, and since the family custom was not to barge in on anyone without warning, it was an ideal arrangement for an independent girl.

Home was where Andrea could be Andrea. Researching fashion trends and reading cookbooks, working on the singing and guitar
playing no one knew about, exploring dance moves she wouldn't
dream of doing in front of others. It was where the Andrea Melman of
the future lived, and tonight, on her birthday eve, home was where she
could celebrate the witch within.

Chapter 3

Andrea hadn't gone looking for witchcraft. It just seemed to find her. It was a bit of a surprise, actually. The popular wizard and vampire trends had rolled over her without leaving a mark. But a passing reference to Wicca in a school assignment ignited an internet search that never ended. The more she read, the more it resonated, and a few weeks before her fourteenth birthday last year, she had simply declared herself a witch, and that was pretty much that.

Celebrating the moon cycles, following the wheel of the seasons, the solstices, and equinoxes, she felt connected to the natural world like never before. The fact that everyone else was oblivious to things like that just confirmed her belief that most people were oblivious.

That Andrea would be a solitary witch had been a foregone conclusion. The idea of being social enough to join a coven was inconceivable to her. In fact, her lack of interest in explaining or justifying herself made Wicca almost too perfect for a girl so good at keeping her life hidden. That said, most of her interest was in plain sight. She had shelves of occult books in her room, and the table by the window always had a seasonal display of plants, gemstones, and other items that any other witch would immediately recognize as an altar.

But she never wore pentagrams or ankhs or any other sort of, in her words, *witchy-kitschy crap.* Andrea tended toward extreme positions on many things, and to her, any form of advertising or accessorizing one's religious beliefs was just "sad." Also unacceptable: heavy eye makeup, angry lectures about the burning times, and big, pointy wizard hats (even though she was secretly dying to wear a big, pointy wizard hat).

The Birthday Eve ritual was an annual event—or it would be after tonight, since this was the second time it was being performed.

Andrea had found a lot of magical rituals to be elaborate and time consuming. Early on, she had developed a few simplified routines for the usual occasions. But the Birthday Eve ritual was the big one, and it captured her complete attention.

Lots of Wiccan rituals were about "celebrating the goddess" or "giving thanks for the harvest," but every once in a while, when witches wanted a specific thing, they worked up something with a little spell casting in it.

Spell casting was the glamorous bad boy of the witches' tool kit. People loved it, hated it, feared it. The "official" Wiccan policy on spells was sensible enough: Don't do things to people without their permission. On a moral level, it was questionable, and from a practical standpoint, it tended to spawn social disorders that were bad for other witches. But spells you cast on yourself—personal magic—were fine. Some witches might do a lot of these over the course of a year, but Andrea had saved up her requests for one big ritual.

The first step was to cleanse herself with an herbal bath. Then she swept out the ritual space with one of those witchy-looking besom brooms. After that she cast a circle by marking north, east, south, and west, before calling in the elements earth, air, fire, and water with candles, incense, and a ritual knife called an athamé.

17

Every step of the way, there were lots of invocations and incantations. Andrea being Andrea, she inevitably ended up with a pile of reference books and printouts to read from while inside the circle. After a while, it was traditional to make an offering of "cakes and ale"—in her case, cookies and grape juice—to the gods.

In many languages, the word for *witch* also meant "wise ones." Andrea had acquired some of her wisdom last year, when she forget half the things she wanted to say due to low blood sugar. This year, she had written the whole thing out and brought a bottle of grape juice and a full box of cookies.

As spells went, Andrea had produced a pretty serviceable one. A bit long, and somewhat derivative in a British sort of way, but in a Wiccan context that wasn't an altogether bad thing.

Boiled down to the essentials, she was asking for help in four areas:

1. To find the courage to express herself honestly and openly (i.e. to let the upbeat girl inside get equal time with the deadpan snarker);

2. To help and protect people (with a side request to not make things worse in the process);

3. To manifest her creative side in the world (basically, to wear the kind of clothes she dreamed of wearing); and

4. To make some real friends.

And at the last moment, she threw in…

5. To wear a big, pointy wizard hat.

That last one seemed to come out of nowhere and wasn't in the written spell, but since she worked it in before the concluding "As I will it, so mote it be," technically it still counted. She decided to think of it as four aspirations and a cool hat.

One of the disadvantages of the Wiccan ritual, compared to rituals found in movies and cartoons, was the way things didn't simply conclude with a smoke puff and a sound effect. It was almost midnight by the time Andrea finished putting things away and removing candle wax from the wood floors with a trick involving a hair dryer and a paper bag.

Finally she dropped into bed, tired and happy, right at the start of her birthday, and fell into a deep sleep. The next thing she knew, the sun was up, the birds were singing, and something really weird was in her bed.

Chapter 4

It's not every day that a fifteen-year-old girl wakes up to find three super-sized Easter eggs in her bed. But there they were: six inches high, colorfully decorated, and nestled right by her pillow. Easily overwhelmed under the best of circumstances, Andrea's mind went straight to meltdown.

What are they? Where did they come from? Who put them here?

Gradually, the frantic buzz of panic gave way to the simplest of observations. Each egg had a basic color. "Red, blue, green." She said it out loud just to anchor the words outside of her spinning thoughts. It was a start. Then there were the egg specific graphics. "Hearts, diamonds, stars."

Andrea began easing into her safe place. The place where she could keep the world at bay by analyzing it to death. Reaching out to touch the red egg, she felt an unexpected warmth.

"Warm. Okay... I can do this," she thought. *"A little more information and..."*

Then it wiggled.

Choking back terror, she fell back over the side of her bed and onto the floor. Scampering across the room on her hands and knees, she knocked over her besom. In one motion, she jumped up, grabbing the broom in both hands like a medieval pike, and glared at the eggs on her bed.

As the moments passed with no further movement, Andrea began speculating.

Who did this? (Aliens?)

What is this? (Retribution for bending the laws of the universe?)

What should I do? (Cook them?)

After a bit more useless mind spinning, she calmed down again and resumed her analysis. From the way they were decorated, they appeared cartoonish and childlike.

Could this be a birthday present? From Dion?

No. He, of all people, would know not to pull something like this on her. Andrea's history with things small and creepy mostly involved a lot of screaming and breaking things. A single water bug, down in the basement ages ago, had terrified her into getting a really big can of bug spray for protection.

Oh! The bug spray! Yes!

Still brandishing the broom just in case, she turned to grab the big red-and-black aerosol can from the floor next to the window. Immediately, she regretted taking her eyes off the eggs. When she looked back, the red eggshell lay open by her pillow. It had hatched, and now something was going to kill her and leave its spawn to nest inside.

A pink blur flew into her field of vision.

Oh-god-oh-god-oh-god…

She swung blindly with the bristly end of the broom and hit something just as it made a high-pitched sound.

"Konichi." [*Thunk*] "Wa-a-a-a…"

It bounced off to the left, behind her guitar amp. Andrea sprang into action. Circling warily around the amp, broom in one hand, bug spray in the other, she could feel her warrior spirit rising within.

There! Behind the pile of guitar cables. Wham!

"O-o-o-o-o… yamero yo yamero yo," it wailed.

She could see some sort of pink rodent scuttling about in there.

Fire bug spray!

"A-a-gh-h-h-h!" The misaligned nozzle shot a line of poison straight up Andrea's arm. "Ew, gross!"

Suddenly, the creature flew straight over her shoulder, making her duck. She dropped the bug spray, grabbed the broom with both hands and spun around. The broom smacked into a floor lamp, knocking it over and shattering the bulb in a bright flash.

"Wakarimasen-n-n-n-n…"

Andrea tried to talk herself through the situation. "Okay, by the window… carefully. Watch where you're going." *Thunk, crash.* Another lamp. "Watch where the *broom* is going. There, on the sill. Nice and easy. Okay. Broom or bug spray? Broom or bug spray?"

"Wakarimasen… Ai-i-i-i!"

"Okay, bug spray again."

"Ai-i-i-i…"

"Point nozzle *forward*."

"Ai-i-i-i…"

"Wait… what was that?" Something was digging its way up through the layers of fear and adrenaline that Andrea was operating under. Something not appropriate for alien predators to be doing. Something sounding suspiciously like…

"… a-a-a-ai-i-i-i-i…"

Was that crying? Did bugs cry? Shaking with fear and excitement, she sneaked up to the windowsill, ready to be disgusted and horrified… ready to kill or be killed. Ready for just about anything— except the sight that greeted her.

"Watashi o korosanaide."

Whatever that meant, it was coming out of what appeared to be an adorable five-inch-high cheerleader in an all-pink outfit curled up in a ball and sobbing her heart out.

Andrea was stunned. Dropping the bug spray and the broom, she edged closer and felt her own tears welling up. She moved to touch her, then—realizing she was using the hand soaked in insecticide— switched hands.

"Watashi o korosanaide," the cheerleader pleaded.

"Okay. I'm really sorry, but I don't know what you're saying," Andrea said, brushing up against her with her index finger.

"Please don't kill me," the cheerleader said in perfect English.

"I'm not going to kill you. I'm so sorry I... wait, what?"

"Please don't kill me."

"What?"

"Please don—"

"No, no. Not that. The English. You're speaking English now?"

"I'm your guardia—"

"Wait. What are you? What is this? I don't..."

"I'm your guardian—"

"You're my guardian angel?"

"No. I'm—"

"I'm no expert on this, but shouldn't you be a bit bigger? With wings? And isn't—"

Frantically waving her hands and shaking her head, the tiny character tried to slow down Andrea's runaway train of thought. "No. Just listen..."

"It's the spell. Did I summon you?"

"No. It's ... Uh, what spell?"

"I must've messed something up. You're from Satan, right? No, wait. I don't believe in Satan. Are you an alien?"

"Listen to me!"

"This is a sign from the universe, isn't it? Are you from the universe?"

"No. Stop it! I'm from Japan. I'm your guardian character, Rei."

"Japan? I didn't order anything from Japan. Wait. You're my guardian character and... *what?* Ray?"

The tiny pink cheerleader rolled her eyes, gave an exasperated gasp, and started over.

"I'm... your guardian character... and—"

"Oh, my God! Am I the chosen one? Is that it? Do I have a destiny, or something? I mean, I thought things went pretty well last night, but I had *no* idea..."

"*Andrea!*" The creature floated before her, shaking with aggravation. After a deep breath, Rei seemed to find an inner calm, and she began again in a quiet, almost gentle tone of voice. "Andi-chan, I'm not sure what you did last night, and I'm not trying to suggest that you're not, like, a really good witch and all..."

Andrea could sense the faintly patronizing tone. Her face fell.

Rei scrambled not to lose her. "I mean, I'll bet you're a *super* witch..."

25

As if realizing that Andrea wasn't buying any of this, Rei stopped and switched to a different approach. "Look, Andi-chan, I don't know anything about witch things. What I *do* know is that you're a special girl and you asked for help bringing out that specialness, and that's why I'm here. I'm your guardian character. Certain children get one." Gesturing at the other eggs, Rei looked perplexed. "You have three. I don't know why that is. Honestly, I don't know a lot about what's going on here right now. *Something's* not right…"

Andrea had gone quiet. Nothing she was hearing lined up with her expectations, and she was trying to back up and reassess what had happened up to this moment. Finally, she said sheepishly, "So you're saying that most people who get a guardian character don't usually try to kill them?"

At that, Rei flew up, hovering a few inches from Andrea's face, and started in on her. "No! As a matter of fact, *no*, they don't! What's the *matter* with you? Is this how you treat guardian characters in America? You almost *killed* me. And *poison*? Chemical weapons? Really? There are laws against these things. What about the Geneva Conventions? Where is the United Nations when you need it?"

"Rei?" Andrea called out.

"This would *never* happen in Japan."

"Rei?" Andrea said more quietly.

"People *respect* guardian characters there!"

"Rei?" Andrea practically whispered.

At that, the umbrage seemed to drain out of the little character. Pointedly refusing to make eye contact, she settled into an annoyed simmer to hear the girl out.

"Rei, I'm really sorry I reacted that way. I didn't mean it and I swear it'll never happen again."

"Well... all right."

"Before we do anything else, maybe you'd like something to eat? And then maybe you can tell me what a guardian character is and why I have one—or three."

Rei's sense of righteous anger seemed to evaporate at the mention of food. She floated down onto the window sill and pondered for a moment. "Uh, do you have ramen noodles here in America, Andi-chan?"

"I'll go check."

Chapter 5

Nothing. No ramen. No nothing.

Rei had actually seemed more freaked out after the excitement of cheating death wore off, so Andrea made the extra effort to go to the Japanese supermarket.

During the walk, her mind drifted back to yesterday's run-in with Natalya. She was torn between shame and excitement over the girl's treatment of her, and the delicious memory of the image she made striding down the hall. A swirling wash of silver jewelry over the mostly black outfit, topped with that insane feral blondness. How did she get those ponytail things to stay up?

The corset, the flared skirt, the short stiletto boots. Most girls would just be begging for attention dressed like that. On Natalya, it was shock and awe. People kept their distance from her. Rumors abounded. Stupid things. Crazy things.

She was a Russian-mafia princess. A supermodel. A descendant of the Romanovs. Of Rasputin. Of Vladimir Putin. She always carried a gun. Her nails were coated with cyanide.

One thing was certain: In all Natalya's time at K290, no one—from the hottest guy to the boldest lesbian—had ever worked up the courage to ask her out. Everyone was too intimidated.

The Japanese supermarket took some interpreting. Andrea wasn't entirely unfamiliar with Japanese foods and graphics. She just had never been completely surrounded by them, and the effect was disorienting. So many fluorescent colors. So many happy branding cartoons. So many things the embarrassed staff were unable to give English equivalents for.

In the end, she was gently steered away from the notion of preparing soba from scratch and, instead, walked out with a week's supply of instant noodles and an assortment of frozen mochi.

* * *

Turning the corner to her street, she ran into Kyle. Actually, she walked right past him, sitting on a car almost as though he'd been waiting for her to come by. Being a ten-year-old boy, Kyle read Andrea's distracted state as a personal challenge. He jumped up, positioned himself directly in front of her, and began waving both hands while walking backward, chanting "Andy, Andy, Andy, Andy, Andy," until she finally gave up and acknowledged him.

"Hey, Kyle," she said with a smirk. "Did you want something?"

"What? Oh… Andrea! Where'd *you* come from? Why, yes, hello. Nice to see you."

"Little preoccupied here, Kyle."

"As usual, Andy. Hope you didn't get sushi in there."

"There's more to Japanese food than sushi, Kyle."

"Parasites, Andy. Giant tapeworms and poisonous bugs from the ocean. It's all over the internet. I'm just trying to save your life, Andy. You should be grateful."

Andrea stopped short and laughed. "I'll be grateful when you stop believing everything you read on the internet."

If nothing else, Kyle was always good for a laugh. With his discount skater clothing and aspirational sneaker choices, he gave Andrea a sense of being connected to Brooklyn. Their history had begun four years ago, the day her family had arrived here.

Her first memory was getting out of the car and seeing the gothic monstrosity of a house her maternal grandmother had left them and Kyle, slouched against their moving van, critiquing everything that came out of it. "Nice table! You gonna *eat* on that?"

At that point, Kyle's criticisms were stronger on tone than content. He immediately latched on to Andrea. "So did you know your grandmother was a witch?"

Eleven-year-old Andrea's first instinct was to ignore the little troll. "Whatever."

"I'm Kyle."

"Whatever, Kyle."

"This is a total witch house. That's how I know."

Andrea didn't dignify this with a reply.

"Is that your bike? It's a total girl bike!"

"Kyle, look at me. I'm a girl."

"Whatever." He snorted and laughed as though he had scored big points in the exchange. "I live right across the street, in a *normal* house."

"How is it normal, Kyle?"

"Well, for one thing, we don't have, like, a hundred acres of land."

"More like an eighth of an acre." Still a vast tract of land for Brooklyn, but the fact that Andrea felt as if she was making progress showed just how little she understood about arguing with an ten-year-old boy.

"Whatever. You gonna raise corn like back in Kansas?"

"What? *No!* And really, it's *Ohio*, and Cincinnati—a *city* in Ohio. Is that all you think happens in the rest of the country, Kyle? People just sit around raising corn?"

He was laughing so hard he could barely answer. "Yeah! And cows! And tornadoes! Okay, Dorothy. Good luck in the big city."

"It's Andrea."

"Okay, Andy, whatever you say."

Since then, four years of interactions had built a serviceable relationship between them. Kyle, as it turned out, was not really evil or anything, just a little brother without a sister to torment. He had recently revealed the interesting fact that he had dreams of designing superhero costumes. And while the first things he had shared with her were hard to picture on actual humans, he had taken an art class over the summer and was getting better. He loved to show stuff to her, and at least one of his goofy outfits always made her laugh.

They were approaching Kyle's house when it occurred to Andrea that the boy had something on his mind beyond messing with her head. She tried to prompt him. "Hey, Kyle. Got some new stuff to look at?"

"Oh, yeah. Always. Not on me but, you know, later. Listen, Andrea?" Upon hearing him use her real name, she slowed her pace. "Like... you know about, like, *fashion,* right?"

"A bit."

"Okay, so, like, I mean, do you think... could a guy like me ever, you know, make a *living* coming up with costumes and stuff?"

"Sure. Why not?"

"Really?"

"I mean, it's not easy, but it's possible. Why?"

"Oh, nothing."

Andrea stopped, laughed, and turned, making him stop, too. "Kyle, you used my real name. You called me 'Andrea.' It's not nothing."

This cracked him up. "Well, everyone in my family says coming up with costumes and stuff is, you know, stupid and, like, it's not a real job and that I gotta get 'real' and all." He was looking at his feet now. "And my brother says I've got no talent anyway and I should be an engineer like he's gonna be, but..."

Andrea had a sense that the situation went a lot deeper than career advice from Mark, the college boy. "Look, Kyle," she interrupted, "you can't give up on your dreams just because they're hard or impractical. Or because other people—even your family—don't think you can do it. It's like…"

She paused, trying to find a sports metaphor. Kyle seemed to get ideas better when they came wrapped in sports jargon. "Like a football team at the, uh, goal line. If you get the ball, then you know everyone is going to try to tackle you, and, I mean, they probably will, but you don't *not* do it—you know, run the ball, and… well, you still try."

She looked up to see Kyle barely suppressing a laugh, which burst free as soon as they made eye contact. "What?" She had thought the sports thing was going pretty well up until then.

"You're all right, Andy. You're totally clueless about sports, but I get it: No guts, no glory, right?"

"Well, yeah, I guess." Actually, she had thought she was laying the groundwork for something a lot more subtle and inspirational. "Yeah. No guts, no glory."

He seemed relieved to have the question addressed in terms of his personal toughness and not something about his soul or any of that "girly crap." "Hey, thanks," he said. "That's good. I just gotta keep all that stuff from bringing me down."

He had already started up the walkway to his house when Andrea thought of something. "Hey, Kyle? The thing is, sometimes, in football—and in lots of stuff—they *do* get you down a lot, and you know, you gotta get back up again. That part can be, like, really hard. And I think maybe that part's more important than talent—the getting-up part."

"Okay, coach!" He laughed. "Catch you later."

"Later."

* * *

On her return, Andrea found her brother Dion sitting at the kitchen table eating a sandwich, a guitar case on the floor next to him. Tall and lanky, he looked like he should be playing in some sort of alt-Americana band and living in Texas. His lackadaisical medieval poetry studies and secret love of 80's hair metal bands, however, made this a case of fraudulent branding.

"Dion! Why are you here?"

"Why, hel-*lo,* Andrea. Yes, it *is* nice to see you, too. Why, I'm doing *fine. Thank* you so much for asking."

"Sorry. Just surprised. You're practically never here, you know."

"Yes. I hear that about myself a lot."

"So why *are* you here?"

"Assuming you don't want a long, detailed philosophical rationale for my existence…"

"Which I do not…"

"My latest girlfriend is no longer my latest girlfriend."

"Wait. Wasn't this the lead singer in your latest band?"

"Which is also no longer my latest band."

"Sorry?"

"Oh, it's cool. And anyway, I needed to be here to be your parental substitute. Mom left yesterday, didn't she?"

"Yup."

He noticed the neon-pink bag. "When did you start eating Japanese food?"

"Oh, this? Just some instant noodles and ice cream—well, mochi… mochi ice cream, I guess."

"For breakfast?"

"Oh, you know…"

He threw her a skeptical glance. "Don't make me have to issue dietary guidelines Andrea. Ice cream and noodles doesn't sound like a properly balanced breakfast to me."

"Firstly, it's lunch. And secondly, you of all people are hardly qualified to be setting dietary guidelines for anyone."

He laughed and got up to leave. "So what are you doing today? Anything special for your B-day?"

Andrea was at the sink, filling the kettle, and didn't look up. "Oh, you know. You never know."

Dion paused, started to say something, apparently thought better of it, and walked out.

Chapter 6

Back upstairs, Andrea shared the noodles and tried to communicate with her guardian character. It wasn't easy. Rei was still one agitated little creature. Perhaps Andrea's near-lethal welcome was to blame. Maybe the trip from Japan had left her with a lot of… egg lag? Whatever the reason, the story Rei was trying to tell tumbled out in incoherent fragments.

Rei had been in Japan. No, the *three* of them had been in Japan. For years—decades, maybe. She wasn't sure about the time frame. Anyway, there were these magical girls in Japan. No, *cartoons* of magical girls. Well, actually, both real girls and cartoon girls and… it was kind of complicated. Maybe that could wait till later.

Then there were these "eggs." Eggs that looked a lot like the eggs on her bed, but were actually quite different, and, well, they were going to play a game with these eggs, sort of.

Andrea was going to be in charge and they would go out and find eggs that had gone "bad," and then "clean" them and give them back to the kids they originally came from.

Oh, and eventually—well, hopefully soon—there would be other kids, like Andrea, with their own guardian characters, like Rei, who would get together and hang out and support each other. That would make it all a lot more fun.

Andrea appeared on the verge of a migraine but Rei persisted, trying to outline the fundamentals of what a guardian character was and how they were supposed to work together. "We're a team! We go around saving artifacts that hold the creative potential of children, and return it to them! The artifacts are called 'heart's eggs,' and…"

"Wait, what do you mean, 'artifacts'?"

"Well, I guess you could say they're the physical manifestations of a child's creative energies, which emerge when they lose faith in themselves."

Andrea was trying to focus, but Rei kept zooming around her bedroom in a pink blur. Each new location seemed to trigger a new topic or a different aspect of a previous topic. It was simply exhausting, and eventually Andrea buried her face in her hands and moaned. "Rei!" She pointed at the windowsill. "Sit there. Explain eggs."

Rei floated over, sat down, and took a breath. "Every child starts with an egg that holds their potential. Think of it as a tangible manifestation of their creativity. Most kids eventually grow out of it, and it fades over time and finally disappears. That's sad but quite normal. The problem is with kids of high potential who fall prey to feelings of fear or hopelessness. Without realizing it, they can poison their egg with doubt and negativity. Then it transforms into a dark egg. A dark egg turns black. We're going to find them, fix them, and return them to those kids' hearts! Isn't it *great?*"

"Kind of. That is, maybe. Wait…" For one thing, two other eggs were sitting on her bed, their mere presence raising a host of questions. "So are these guys part of this 'team,' or do they do something else?"

"I don't know. I mean, I know *who* they are, but I can't understand why they aren't with their own girls."

"Wait! Girls? So this is some kind of gender stereotype thing?"

"No! Well, yes, I guess it usually is, but I'm not sure it *has* to be. I don't really know about that, actually."

"Are you on the internet? Can I look this up somewhere?"

"What? *No!* We're just here, with you."

"Are you all from Japan?"

"Well, the three of us are. I know that at least."

"So will they be speaking Japanese when they come out?"

"Probably not." Rei looked somewhat embarrassed. "I was supposed to take care of that before we… Anyway, I reset myself to speak English."

"From when I touched you?"

"Yes."

Andrea seemed skeptical. "How would that even work?"

"It's… it's complicated…" Rei began fussing with the pom-poms that normally hung from her waist. "I don't really think about things like that." Brushing out imaginary tangles in the strings, she was starting to look distinctly annoyed and distracted by the endless questions as Andrea pressed on.

"So you're invisible to anyone who doesn't have their own guardian character?"

"With a few exceptions, yes."

"Exceptions such as…"

"Um, I don't know. Sometimes, other people can see us. It's rare. The important thing is, normal people can't see or hear us."

"So, I'm not *normal* now?"

"No! Wait… What do you mean?"

"Never mind. How do you fly?"

"Huh? I don't know. How do you walk? You just do. How does anyone do anything? And why does any of this matter?"

"Am I going to have to wear a uniform or something? Do I have any say in what I wear?"

Silence.

"Can anything be changed or swapped out?"

More silence. Rei was done answering questions for the moment. In fact, she was quietly freaking out. Andrea was so hard to read. She seemed so… *suspicious.* The longer they talked, the more it felt like an interrogation. Rei was so busy fielding questions, she hadn't really had time to be herself yet. She was supposed to be pumping Andrea up and cheering her on, but so far, she couldn't get a single cheer in edgewise.

* * *

The solution for so much thinking turned out to be the same for both of them. They fell asleep. It was just before sunset when they woke up, refreshed and apologetic.

Rei insisted that they go to an area outdoors where she could start Andrea's training, and after another round of noodles, they set out for one of the deserted factory yards nearby. Andrea, worried that the other eggs might hatch at any moment, padded a messenger bag with an old cashmere sweater and brought them along.

Rei was surprisingly quiet during the walk. For a time, Andrea worried that she had gone too far with her endless concerns and questions. Gradually however, it occurred to her that, not only were her concerns and questions perfectly valid, but, if anything, she wasn't being concerned enough or asking tough enough questions.

"Did I ask for this?" she wondered. *"Did I really summon this with my ritual? A five inch tall pink cheerleader zipping around my bedroom? This is my connection to the goddess and the awesome majesty of nature? I've never seen any mention of anything like Rei on the Wicca forums. And what is with her anyway?"* Andrea stole a glance over at her new fashion challenged friend. *"She looks like a cartoon. Does she even know what she's doing?"*

"Rei?" she said cautiously. "Do you, ummm… Do you know what… is… going on?"

It wasn't a very well framed question but Rei, intentionally or otherwise, didn't really answer. "We don't know why, but in the last year or so, activity for heart's eggs has gone up to unprecedented levels in this area."

Which answered nothing, but she persisted, "Rei, I'm sorry, but how does all of this relate to me?"

Rei stopped in her tracks. "You don't see? You have the power to *save* them. You can restore dark eggs and return them to the children they came from. That's what the guardian does. You're the heroine in all of this!"

Andrea was having trouble visualizing herself as any sort of heroine, but since they were coming up on the industrial site, she decided to let it go for now and see if things sorted themselves out.

Chapter 7

Even though she herself lived in an area of single family houses, Andrea had originally believed Brooklyn to be mostly made up of brownstones. Over time, she came to see just how big a place it really was.

Aside from the residential areas, there were vast commercial districts. Miles and miles of junkyards, factories, and warehouses—both active and abandoned. Andrea's neighborhood was located close to a particularly blighted section of industrial real estate.

A short walk brought them to a boundary road. They passed through a line of trees and the remnants of a chain link fence to find themselves in a wide, weed-choked parking lot across from an enormous empty warehouse. A chill wind swept small clumps of trash around the broken asphalt as the sun hung low on the horizon. It was not a particularly uplifting environment and—even by Brooklyn standards—it didn't seem especially safe.

"Is this a good idea?" Andrea wondered as she set down the egg bag.

Rei, by all appearances, was either unconcerned or unaware that huge abandoned industrial sites might have a down side. Rising up and moving closer toward Andrea, she made eye contact and began her lesson. "Miss Melman?"

Andrea smiled tentatively and stood a little straighter. "Yes Rei?"

"Miss Melman, I think we can agree that things have not started out as smoothly as might have been hoped for. In my opinion, we have gotten bogged down in too many theoretical issues, so I intend to focus on practical instruction and keep this brief."

Having no idea what Rei was talking about, Andrea nodded vigorously.

"Okee dokee! There are two kinds of changes: your basic magical-girl transform and the more extreme magical-girl Excellion transform."

"*Excellion?*" Andrea asked. "Is that even a word?"

Rei froze midfloat and blinked. "Of course it is. It means... ah, 'ultimate.' Anyway, the point is that the Excellion transform is more powerful, but it involves what we'll call *overshadowing* you. The guardian character initiates the change and shares control, giving you the strongest powers and enhancing your regular personality. In your case, that means I would overshadow you and bring out the perky, athletic cheerleader within."

Andrea suppressed her reaction to that, but Rei seemed to catch it anyway. She sank slightly and floated off to the side. "As it is, your resistance to giving up control is so strong, I'm actually afraid to do that right now. Maybe, when we know each other better, we can try that."

Andrea gave her a look that suggested this might be a very long time coming. Rei pushed on. "The basic magical-girl transformation involves you inviting and accepting me into your heart and manifesting your unique expression of the magical-girl powers. Everyone has their own version of the powers, depending on which guardian character they transform with. My transformation with you would be called 'Luminous Heart.'"

"Luminous Heart," Andrea repeated, trying not to sound too dubious.

Apparently believing she had now covered the fundamentals, Rei zoomed back in front of Andrea and beamed a brilliant smile at her. "Okay, Andi-chan! Here we go! Hold out your thumb and forefinger at a right angle with both hands, and place them together to make a diamond. Then reverse one of them to flip the diamond as you say 'Crystal Bright Heart Lunation, unlock!'"

Picking up on Rei's enthusiasm, Andrea made the shapes with her hands and gave as spirited a recitation of "Crystal Bright Heart Lunation, unlock!" as she could. Then she waited, expecting this to be the first step in a long, intricate ritual with lots of incantations and gestures. Thus, she was quite unprepared for…

Wham! Suddenly, Andrea was surrounded by a swirling light show, with the disorienting sense of sliding forward while simultaneously falling backward. Was that *music?* She could sense Rei in front of her, without really seeing her there. Andrea's arms reached out of their own accord to bring Rei toward her chest, and she was oddly unsurprised when the little pink character passed straight through her.

She heard Rei's voice call out from behind her, "Crystal Bright Heart Lunation!" And then, quite spontaneously, Andrea found herself executing a short series of poses, each with a different-colored flash of light, before settling down, legs akimbo, back in the dreary, industrial parking lot.

Rei darted excitedly back and forth before her. Thoroughly disoriented, Andrea was still blindly following Rei's instructions when the little cheerleader thrust her pom-poms up over her head and yelled, "*Jump,* Andi-chan!"

And so it came to pass that the same Andrea Melman whose paralyzing fear of heights had kept her off of Ferris wheels now launched herself straight up, twenty stories into the air. Hanging there, two hundred feet up, she felt conflicting emotions.

On the one hand, she wanted to scream from looking down at the ground, so very far away.

On the other hand, she wanted to scream about the outfit she now found herself wearing. Somehow, the screams canceled each other out and came out as an angry, high-pitched whimper.

Apparently sensing that things had not gone as hoped, Rei flew up to guide the shaking girl back to earth.

"*Whaaaat is thisss?*" Andrea wailed, staring down at the garish pink-and-white getup.

"Your wonderful new magical costume?" Rei suggested optimistically.

Now, a hot-pink cheerleader outfit with coordinating pleated skirt, pom-poms, leg warmers, sneakers, and translucent sun visor, featuring a bare midriff and a hair decoration shaped like a giant heart,

45

might be well within the normal range of magical-girl fashion options; indeed, students of the genre could consider this arrangement a bit on the conservative side. But Andrea didn't see it that way.

"Rei! What is this cosplay nightmare?"

"But, Andi-chan, it's kind of like *my* outfit, don't you think?"

"*You* are a guardian character from Japan. *I* am a fifteen-year-old girl from Brooklyn with her whole life ahead of her. What if someone I know *sees* me in this?"

"Uh... They'd be jealous?"

"Where are my clothes?"

"They'll come back after you're done being Crystal Bright Heart Lunation?"

"Oh, believe me, Rei, I am *done* being Crystal Bright Heart Lunation."

Rei fell back as if she'd been kicked in the chest. "Andi-chan?"

Still shaking from the experience, Andrea was walking away from Rei to where she had put her bag, when a dark figure slipped out of nowhere, picked it up, and looked inside. "Do I smell eggs? I think you have something for me, my little cheerleader."

Instantly, embarrassment gave way to fear and a whole new set of concerns.

Andrea was furious with herself. *This* was what she should have been worried about. Running around at night in a deserted industrial parking lot, doing all this stupid guardian nonsense, and now someone wanted to steal her two giant eggs, and she hadn't even gotten a chance to meet the other characters.

Wait a second. Even in her agitation, she managed to think to herself, *Who the hell steals guardian character eggs?*

She pushed aside her fear and got a good look at the figure examining her bag. Young, slender, male. Black hair. Black jacket with white trim and a few randomly placed buckles. Slim-cut black pants. Blue-black cat ears, matching tail. A few silver crosses.

He smiled a wicked grin at her and flashed cool blue eyes that, under different circumstances, might have held her attention. But there was the matter of that tail… Moving in a very realistic fashion. And the ears were really, well, *catlike*. And twitching. Again, very realistically.

Andrea was yanked out of her musings by a new voice coming from near her leg.

"She's quite an exhibitionist, this girl, don't you think? I mean, we don't see this sort of getup around here every day, do we, now?"

She looked down, and at first it appeared that there was no one there. Then, what seemed to be a cat-themed guardian character floated around from behind, fingering the hem of her skirt. With a similar set of cat ears and tail, Andrea quickly noted that the character was wearing an outfit of basic black with silver accents that seemed to intentionally mirror the intruder's getup. The simplistic coordination sparked annoyance within Andrea's core fashion values. *So this is it? Characters get paired off with humans like a matching handbag?*

"Nyanka! Pretend you have manners," Cat Boy chided.

Up to this point, Andrea wasn't sure what to make of things. Too many strong feelings had assaulted her in too short a time to make sense of it all. But some smart-ass little guardian character getting familiar with her, calling her an exhibitionist, *touching* her clothing? That was the final straw.

In reaching her breaking point, Andrea Melman discovered that she was not a screamer. Nor was she a pleader or a berserker. In fact, to her great surprise, she learned that a warrior dwelt in the territory just beyond her last nerve. Pushed past the edge, she fell into a kind of desperate practicality.

The pressure of near panic focused her, and within that focus, time seemed to gear down. The spaces between the seconds expanded, providing a clarity against which the tactical and strategic options presented themselves for her scrutiny.

One of these options was surprise.

Cat Boy thought she was a scared little girl. But she could see now that he wasn't all that much older than she was. Maybe eighteen—but still a boy, really. And nothing undermined a teenage boy's game like a fearless, confident girl.

Andrea knew, of course, that *she* wasn't a fearless, confident girl. But *he* didn't know that. And he wasn't expecting anything of the sort. Meanwhile, Nyanka was still hovering around her waist. *Okay,* she thought. *Fearless, confident girl, unlock!*

"Hey, Cat Boy!" The change in tone immediately caught him off guard.

"Huh?"

"Control your monkey, or I will." *Thwack!* The back of her hand caught Nyanka like a tennis ball and sent him spinning off to the side. "Ai-i-i-i!" he wailed, quickly recovering and flying back to a position safely out of her reach.

Cat Boy was moving toward her, but she could see in his eyes that he didn't know what to do to regain control of the situation. He tried turning on the charm, but in response to having his guardian character slapped by a girl in a pink cheerleader outfit, it came across as weak.

"Actually, he's not a monkey. He's a guardian character. Umm… I would have expected you to realize that. His name is Nyanka. You can call me Illya."

"I can call you 'Here, kitty, kitty.' Is Illya your name or not?"

He stopped in his tracks. "Most girls… I, ah…"

Fixing her eyes on him, Andrea drew upon some very real anger. She started advancing on him, holding his gaze while assessing her options.

"Most girls? Really? *Most girls?*"

It seemed to be working. He couldn't quite manage a response, even a feeble one.

Andrea was walking on a wire. At the same time that she was presenting this fierce persona and delivering precisely modulated intensity with her voice, she was simultaneously trying not to slip into a panic. Assessing the geometry of the situation helped.

49

She determined that three more paces would put the bag within reach. In the darkness behind him, the trees were barely visible, but she figured they couldn't be any higher than her original jump with Rei. It was time to act.

He looked puzzled when she accelerated toward him. In the next two steps, she grabbed the top of the bag. He seemed too surprised to resist, and on the third step she jumped.

A forty-five-degree angle had seemed about right, and she was clearing the trees and wondering how to land when Rei suddenly reappeared beside her. "Your weight is much reduced in this state, Andi-chan. Just let your knees absorb the landing. You don't need to roll or anything. You'll see." Rei flew ahead and waved her down. As predicted, the landing was no problem.

Andrea couldn't quite tell when, but it seemed that Rei worked the transition out of Crystal Bright Heart Lunation the moment her feet hit the ground. It seemed to happen in the blink of an eye, with none of the drama of the original transformation. And thank God, her regular clothes had returned from wherever it was they had gone.

Luckily, the street was deserted. Andrea was in a state of happy shock, and Rei flitted about her madly as they escaped into the Brooklyn night, laughing all the way home.

Chapter 8

"'I can call you "Here, kitty, kitty'"—how did you come up with *that?*" Rei asked, doubling over in laughter. It was almost midnight, and Andrea and Rei were treating themselves to green tea mochi ice cream with chocolate syrup.

"I don't know. How did *any* of that happen?"

"You stopped worrying long enough to let your true nature come out—that's how."

"*That's* my true nature?"

"Sure."

Andrea was lying across her bed, with Rei buzzing back and forth, swooping down occasionally for mochi.

Rei was giddy with relief that things had worked out, but she knew that Andrea was still very much on the fence about everything. She raised her pom-poms and floated in front of the girl chanting, "Andi-chan, Andi-chan, you really rock!"

Andrea's face displayed mild annoyance, but she seemed resigned to having her own personal cheerleader. "I still don't understand what you were saying about me being a heroine. And who was that Illya guy? And his monkey—I mean, his character. You didn't recognize either of them?"

Rei settled down on the bedspread. "No. I've never seen an *animal* character. I mean, Nyanka was definitely a guardian character, but he felt really… off. Like, a little unbalanced, you know? And Illya— the ears and that tail. What was that all about?"

"You mean I'm not going to grow cat ears and a tail?"

"Oh, no! I've never even heard of that... oh, wait, Andi-chan, are you disappointed?"

"What? No! I mean, they were cute on him and all."

Rei floated up to Andrea's eye level with an inquisitive smirk. "Really, Andi-chan? Just how cute *were* they?"

"Stop that. I'm just saying, with the outfit and the silver cross thing, the whole kind of Elegant Gothic Pirate look made the cat stuff seem a bit less girly. Wait. Would that just be his normal transformation outfit? I wonder if he dresses himself."

"Would you like to apply for the position, Miss Melman?"

Andrea blushed and threw a pillow in Rei's general direction. "Shut up! You know that's not what I meant. I just don't see why he gets the cool bad-boy outfit with matching cat accessories, and I look like a pink lollipop."

Rei shot her a look.

"Which looks great on you!" Andrea added quickly. "But, seriously, you're five inches tall and from Japan. This look doesn't exactly say 'modern American girl,' you know. And I still don't get it—where did my clothes go?"

"Andi-chan, for the last time, I don't know where the clothes go during a character transformation. No one does. No one else but you even cares."

Rei could sense that Andrea was drifting back into interrogation mode.

"So, I wasn't really flying tonight?"

"No. You will fly, but that wasn't what happened tonight. You were actually jumping and then floating to maintain altitude. It's complicated."

"Complicated?"

"I'm sorry, I don't really know how these things work. They're easy and natural to do, but as for how it happens? I mean, how do you ride a bicycle without falling over?"

"Would it really make you any happier to know this stuff?" asked a new voice from behind them.

"Well, probably not, but…" Andrea began, and then whirled around toward the egg bag.

The blue egg had hatched, and floating above it was a guardian character wearing a blue jacket, black boots, and a blue beret. She was carrying what looked like a messenger bag, and the beret had a big blue diamond on the side.

"Um, I'm Andrea and—"

"Yeah, I know. I'm Masa."

If Andrea had been expecting all guardian characters to be bright and cheery, this was a corrective. Masa, it seemed, would barely look at her.

"Oh." She wasn't sure what to say. Did she need to introduce herself? Introduce Rei? Were there protocols for these things?

"Masako! Why are you being so rude to Andi-chan? Give a proper accounting of yourself. What's the matter with you?"

"Oh, right, Rei. Like you can't see how ambivalent she is about all this."

"That doesn't matter."

"It *absolutely* matters."

"She's just different."

"You mean the whole trying-to-kill-the-guardian-character thing? Well, yes, I guess you do have a point there."

"That's not my point, and you know it."

"Her heart is divided."

"She has many aspects."

"Maybe she's crazy. Have you considered that? Do we really know *anything* about her? I mean, other than the homicidal tendencies."

"Stop it! You don't know her. I won't stand for thi—"

"Stop arguing! Both of you!"

The three of them turned to the egg bag, where a third character wearing what looked like a poufy green chef's uniform floated in the air, glowering at them. The top of her chef's toque sported a five-pointed star. "This is supposed to be *my* entrance! Masa, why are you showing up so *late*?"

"Why are either of you even here at all?" Rei asked.

"I wasn't going to come out, Sumi," Masa growled. "She can't handle the responsibility, and she doesn't want us."

"You don't know that!" Rei yelled.

"It's obvious!" Masa yelled back.

"My entrance!" Sumi yelled even louder.

"Stop it." Andrea's voice was barely audible above the din. What brought the three characters to heel was the undertone of ragged breathing, and the sob that broke on the next inhalation. Andrea didn't know why she was crying, but hearing them argue about her as if she weren't there had suddenly become unbearable.

It was just too much. An insane cosplay makeover, a twenty-story jump, escaping the clutches of some creepy cat boy, and now *this* was the part sending her over the edge?

Looking around at the three characters floating in front of her, Andrea saw that they had gone from argumentative to penitent in a heartbeat. As if keying off her emotions, they now looked close to tears.

So, they're willing to dress me in humiliating outfits, risk killing me by dropping me from dangerous heights, and God knows what else, but they don't want me to feel bad. What on earth do they want?

Hoping to dial down the drama, she tried to find a conversation starter. "So… You're all from Japan?"

"Yup!" Rei chirped.

"Sort of," Sumi hedged.

"Not really," Masa grumped.

An uncomfortable silence followed. Andrea waited to see how they would resolve it.

After a minute of watching the three diminutive characters stare daggers at each other while throwing the occasional worried look her way, Andrea stepped in. "Wow! This is it? You guys are 'yup, sort of, not really' from Japan? And you want me to sign on and do *what* with you?"

Drawing on a heretofore untapped dramatic instinct, Andrea sensed that a strong exit would go well at this moment. She stood up and moved toward the door. "Okay, tell you what. I'm going to go heat up some ramen for whoever wants it, and maybe while I'm gone you can cook up a plausible story you can all agree on. Okay?"

Her last impression of the characters as she closed the door was of three rather stunned faces floating in the center of the room. She almost burst out laughing at the sound of them all yelling at each other on the other side of the door.

Ten minutes later, she could still hear them arguing as she approached her room with a tray. Intrigued, she parked it on a table and leaned in to see what she could pick up.

"And *technically*, we're not from Japan."

"I think she gets that. But we've lived there since before she was born."

"What do you want to tell her, then?"

"I don't care about that part. Why are our memories of things so different?"

"The programming. We had it erase certain memories."

"*Shared* memories. Why are we missing different memories? Masa, what do you remember about that?"

"I'm not sure. The fact that we're all recalling different things and forgetting different things—that can't be right. We would never have agreed to that."

"So, what are we telling her? Masa doesn't trust her at all, and you seem to trust her too much. You're sure she's who we're looking for?"

"You didn't see her back there. The only thing I'm sure of right now is that she's the real thing. But why are *you* two here? And where are the others?"

"I told you we shouldn't submit to the programming again. Now we're—"

"Not now, Masa!"

"Oh, crap. It's *just* like home: flying around in circles and never getting anywhere."

"How long does it take to make noodles in a cup?"

"Maybe she's right outside, listening to us argue."

"And maybe she decided not to trust us after you two introduced yourselves with your stupid, pointless arguing. Maybe she's never coming back. Maybe—"

"Maybe she can hear you from all the way down the hall," Andrea said as she worked the door open with her shoulder and brought the tray into the room. "Really, guys. Fifteen minutes and you're still at it?"

Rei put her face in her hands and moaned.

Masa folded her arms and looked out the window.

Sumi sniffed. "Is that curry? Is one of them curry? Dibs on the curry!"

Even though she hadn't understood most of what she'd heard, Andrea's spying had left her feeling a lot more empowered. She decided to set the tone as they ate. "Okay. I know there's probably some ritual introduction or speech or whatever you normally do, but since we've already screwed that up, why don't we just keep things simple? You all know that I'm Andrea."

Rei and Sumi threw pointed looks at Masa who then floated forward to address Andrea. At first she seemed to be struggling to overcome a desire to fly back to her egg and stay there. Finally she began with a listless, "Hi Andrea. I'm Masa." For a moment she seemed content to leave things at that until motivated by a sharp poke in the side from Rei. "Okay, so I'm supposed to be helping you with your artistic and musical aspirations. Oh, and also to reflect some of your innate levelheadedness, but that may be coming off as rude right now, so I'm going to try to… not be that way."

It was a minimally sincere approach but somehow Andrea seemed to get that, under the current circumstances, it was as good as Masa was going to be able to summon today. In response, she allowed Midwestern good manners to trump East Coast bluntness and chirped out, "Hi, Masa, I'm really glad to meet you. I could use a lot of help in the artistic and musical areas. And please," she said, looking at them all, "let's agree to be as real and honest as we can be in this situation. I think we're all better off with an occasional apology for going too far than we are with not trusting the things we're saying or hearing."

This seemed to make an impression.

She looked over at Sumi. "And you?"

"I'm Sumi, and I reflect the nurturing, cooking, and cleaning aspect inside you—the domestic goddess within."

Andrea hadn't been sure what to expect from this character, and yet, this really threw her. "Ah, Sumi?"

Sumi patted her outfit and looked up with a big smile. "Yes, Andi-chan?"

"This is sort of awkward, but I don't *have* a domestic goddess within. I mean, I'm really not that into feeding people and nurturing and all."

59

Masa started laughing. Sumi looked crestfallen, and Rei had her face back in her hands.

"Yes, you do," Sumi insisted simply.

"We have so much to work on," Rei said.

"You are *so* lying to yourself," Masa said.

"But you *love* those things," Sumi pleaded.

"Everyone has many things to learn about themselves," Rei babbled. "I mean, who can really say what they are or aren't?"

"So this is you being real and honest?" Masa snarked.

Andrea stared at them, trying to come up with a response to the steady stream of chatter coming from the three creatures that, apparently, she was not going to be able to lie to.

"Wait!"

All three voices came to a dead stop.

"Let me talk."

For the next fifteen minutes, Andrea told them a tale of ancient horrors. A tale of third grade. About an obsessive little girl with a fixation on Martha Stewart. A story of young friendships and violated confidences. How she was cruelly taunted on the school playground as "Martha Melman" by the boy with whom she had shared a winter cranberry-apple tartlet in a 'seasonally appropriate presentation.' How she was shamed for her insistence that there was a "correct" way to do anything worth doing.

Andrea was on a roll. Her words escalated from long-rehearsed grievances to deeply suppressed frustrations, until she wound up with a passionate "Oh, damn you, anyway, Martha Stewart!"

"Wow!" Masa said. "What does that even mean?"

"Aren't you overreacting just a teensy bit?" Rei asked.

"I mean, this really seems like the sort of thing you should be able to get over by now," Sumi added. Andrea stared at Sumi for a long moment. "I'm just saying. I mean, you're *fifteen*. Maybe you need to just let it go."

Andrea pondered that for a moment. "Well, maybe. But this is Brooklyn, and if anyone hears about this, what little life I have is over. For now, we keep this between the four of us."

They all solemnly nodded agreement without bringing up the fact that they really had no one else to tell.

"So, now that you're all here, when do I get to go out there and save some dark eggs?"

"You already *told* her?" Sumi gasped.

"I'll bet you didn't tell her *everything*," Masa said.

"Yeah," Rei mumbled. "About that…"

Chapter 9

Like many twentieth-century institutions, K290 had been con-
ceived with a host of optimistic assumptions. The school's cafeteria was an apt example. The original "Statement of Design
Intent" described "an open environment encouraging the free flow
of interactions between students of all grades." That dream died
sometime during the first minute of the first lunch period, when
the seniors and juniors grabbed the north wing and conducted a
purge of any underclassmen. Thereafter, the "free flow of interactions" was restricted to upperclassmen inflicting retribution on
border violators.

The cafeteria, like the rest of the school, was overcrowded.
The problem had been addressed by adding extra tables directly across
from the central "food acquisition area." In effect, a space between
the two wings of the cafeteria, previously left uninhabited for reasons
of noise and smell, became a new low-rent district for kids not cool
enough for the normal areas. To no one's surprise, this was instantly
and forever to be known as Loserville, and from her first day at K290,
this was where Andrea sat.

Andrea had no quarrel with the status quo and felt no stigma in
eating lunch by herself. Actually, she preferred it. Listening to music
while catching up with homework was far easier than trying to maintain any semblance of small talk with her peers.

It was hardly surprising, then, that she should tense up at anyone making their way toward the table she had long ago staked out.
She was, however, quite surprised to see Gaylen, lunch tray in hand,

homing in on her. "Hey, Andrea," she said, banging down her tray and sliding over.

"Oh… uh, hey…"

"Gaylen. We've never really met. I hope I wasn't out of line dropping Marion on you the other day."

"Oh, no! Not at all. I'm glad to help people if I can."

"That's what I'd heard."

Andrea was surprised to hear that anyone had heard anything at all about her, never mind the idea that she was glad to help people. "Really?"

"You're known as the 'fashion monk'—wise in the ways of fashion, but sworn never to use it for your own benefit."

Andrea couldn't help herself and burst out laughing. "*Really? And who, exactly, says this?*"

"Oh, I just made it up right now. But it might be true, you know." She reached for Andrea's phone. "What are you listening to?"

Under normal circumstances, Andrea would have a minor meltdown at the thought of someone touching her stuff or looking at her current playlist, but Gaylen's audacity was hard to resist. She confidently accessed the playlist and scrolled through with fierce interest. "Sorry, rude musician thing. I can't trust anyone until I've gone through their music. Oh. Look at *this*. You like you some dark, droney music, some hard-rocking music *and* some… oh, my God! You not only *have* Black Swan Brigade; you actually *listen* to them?"

"Wait, how do you know that?"

"This phone tells you how many plays there are on a given track."

"I can't believe I didn't know that."

"Here, look at mine."

"Oh, wow, you have her, too. And you've listened to it more than I have."

"We have different stuff, but a similar breakdown. Very dark. Very light."

"Don't most people?"

"I wish. Not to get all 'negative,' but most people wallow in the same stuff."

Andrea smiled at Gaylen as she made air quotes around the word negative. "But reality *is* dark and light. You'd think people would embrace that."

"Yeah, but... no. Andrea, most people use music as wallpaper to cover a shallow worldview. Marion's playlist, for instance: an angsty, angry soundtrack for her endless resentments. Those jocks over there? An endless 'gettin' pumped and humped' soundtrack. Different people, different styles, but the same rinse-and-repeat soundtrack thing."

"Wow. All I'm trying to do in life is balance the aspects."

Gaylen laughed. "Tell me about it." The period bell rang, and she handed Andrea her phone. "Back to the living hell we call high school. Try to stay in touch."

"Uh, I…"

"Andrea… It's cool. Just wave to me in the hall. And smile once in a while. Things are probably worse than you know, but you don't know that *yet*. Do you?"

"Okay." Andrea laughed. "See you around."

* * *

At day's end, Andrea had two objectives. The first was logistical in nature: She needed to secure stocks of ramen and mochi for the group. The employees of the Japanese supermarket were outwardly pleased and privately a bit concerned to see her buying prodigious quantities of what were essentially snack foods, but Andrea was too preoccupied to pick up on their polite suggestions to consider the rest of Japanese cuisine.

The second objective was subtler. Something fundamental was bothering her about her relationship with the characters, but she couldn't pin it down.

As much as she might ask, and as much as they might say in response, very little real information was getting passed along. And every time she tried to focus on a particular statement or issue, her mind would wander and some new thought would distract her.

Andrea had a lot of issues, but attention deficit had never been one of them. So why couldn't she analyze this? Were they affecting her focus? And if so, how? She had to figure this out.

It was dark outside, and another round of noodles consumed when Andrea tried to interrogate her pint-size new roommates. But once again, she could get only the sketchiest of details about them and where they came from. Any personal information was completely out of the question—the one exception being their views on Japan. Getting them to talk about Japan was easy. *Too* easy.

Andrea was aware that she had viewed Japan through rose-tinted eyewear based on her feelings about the fashion scene there, but to the characters, it was heaven, and anywhere else was a dreary wasteland. Japan was safer. Smarter. Deeper. Funnier. More delicious. Andrea found herself starting to seriously resent the place for being so damned perfect.

The magical-girl idea was a hard one for her to wrap her mind around, too. Some quick research suggested that a lot of mixing and mashing was going on between various kinds of superheroes, fairies, princesses, aliens, wizards, and—especially galling to her—witches.

But to her color-coded companions, the only kind of magical girl that mattered used her powers to collect, cleanse, and return these "heart's eggs" to the children who had somehow lost them.

Andrea was starting to realize that she had no idea where the characters got their information. Basically, she was accepting everything they said on faith.

That aside, some persistent prodding revealed that the story was a bit more complicated than the original picture of going around rescuing the creative potential of the K-through-twelve set. For one thing, certain heart eggs weren't just turning into dark eggs simply because a child was feeling depressed.

"We've become convinced that someone is manipulating the situation and forcing heart egg transformations." Sumi said. "Something is being done to trigger the process in a lot of kids in this area."

"Why here?" Andrea asked.

"No one knows." Masa said. "All we know is the numbers around here are comparatively huge. It's almost as if someone wanting to obtain a large number of dark eggs had developed a sort of "farm system" to create them—right here in Brooklyn."

It occurred to Andrea that if somebody had gone to this much trouble to set this up, they just might be opposed to her interfering. *How* opposed wasn't clear, but as a rule, Andrea was not comfortable with confrontation.

And as far as being some kind of heroine went, right now her total skill set for fighting evildoers—if, in fact, any of this was actually evil—consisted of being able to transform into a pink cheerleader and jump really high.

Rei had tried to outline what her other powers were, and how they might work, but the concept of theoretical powers facing off against theoretical threats left Andrea with some very practical concerns for her nontheoretical well-being.

In the meantime, Andrea's bedroom was slowly being transformed into Base Camp Guardian as the characters made themselves at home. Given the size of the space, this wasn't immediately apparent. One of the perks of living in a nineteenth-century mansion was having an immense bedroom.

Essentially the attic above a wing of the house, it was twenty-five feet wide and over fifty feet long, with a high peaked ceiling. She suspected that her room had more square footage than the average New York apartment.

The "adjustment therapist" hired by her worried parents after the move from Cincinnati had insisted that Andrea's issues were solvable with a kind of color therapy/feng shui approach. The legacy of that diagnosis was a bright yellow paint job that Andrea had originally hated but never got around to changing. Now it provided a useful contrast to the red, blue, and green blurs that constantly flitted about.

Each character had staked out an area by moving her egg there. Andrea wasn't sure whether the characters actually slept, but they did retreat back to their own eggs at the end of the day.

Sumi, whom Andrea suspected of latent diva tendencies, had settled herself inside the linen closet at the far end of the room, away from everyone else. Masa staked her claim on one of the bookshelves next to Andrea's altar. Rei originally seemed to want to stay on Andrea's bed, near the door to the room, but compromised by building a nest from old sweaters behind the music gear nearby.

Considering how deep an incursion this was into Andrea's jealously guarded private space, she was surprised to find herself not completely upset and even slightly amused at their casual invasion of her world.

Chapter 10

Later that evening, Andrea was trying to attack some math homework when Masa suddenly flew up in alarm. "A dark egg! Do you feel it?" Rei and Sumi looked around them as if reading the air for clues.

"Oh, yes! I can smell it." Sumi said.

"You can *smell* these eggs?" Andrea asked.

"Not really smell," said Masa. "It's a feeling. A sensation, I guess."

Rei threw a look at Masa. "What should we do? She's not ready."

Masa pondered the question. "How about we just try to observe things tonight, without getting involved?"

"But Andi-chan is—" Sumi began.

Rei cut her off. "No. Masa's right. We need to get an idea of what we're dealing with first." Turning to Andrea she asked, "Does that make sense to you?" Andrea wanted to state for the record that pretty much nothing was making sense these days but she kept it to herself.

So the four of them set out into the night, looking for a dark egg. Masa indicated that it was in the direction of Kyle's house across the street. A pathway next to his house ran through the block to a park that was usually entered from the next street over.

It was the kind of standard-issue small park the New York City Parks Department squeezes into certain residential areas. Swings and benches and bathrooms, but no ball fields or handball courts. During the summer kids would hang out there all evening but at this time of year it was empty.

Moving along the hedges at the back of the park, Masa heard the music first. "Hush. Listen."

Haltingly, then with growing confidence, a lone violin was laying out the long tones of a melody in a minor key. Being outdoors, it was almost impossible to fix the location of the sound's origin. It seemed to be coming from everywhere and nowhere. They stood in the shadows as the music got louder. As their eyes adjusted to the dark, Andrea thought she could see someone on a park bench facing in from the street.

"Characters." Sumi whispered urgently.

"You can sense other characters, too?" Andrea whispered back.

"Within a certain range."

"More than one?"

"Maybe. I don't know"

The violin's tone seemed to be changing, but then Andrea realized that a female voice was now singing in unison. The effect was hauntingly beautiful if a bit creepy. She thought the sounds were coming from the stands of trees that hid the park from the houses on either side. The person on the bench hadn't moved, though. Were they listening? Asleep?

Andrea was feeling cautious, but she also had a burning curiosity about what was going on. Curiosity won. "I'm moving in closer to see who that is. Wait here."

"What?" Rei said.

"No way!" Sumi declared.

It seemed that guardian characters were *not* inclined to take orders.

Masa flew up in front of her. "Look, Andi-chan, anything that involves dark eggs is our business. If you go, we go."

Andrea smiled. "Okay, but just keep it down. Someone out there can hear you, right?"

"Someone's guardian character already knows we're here, even if they don't know exactly who we are," Rei reminded her.

"Food for thought. Let's go behind the bathrooms and see who our mystery guest is."

They moved quietly and peeked around the bathroom entrance to see.

"Kyle!" Andrea's loud exclamation brought on a round of annoyed shushing. "I told you about him. Why would he be out here?"

The music was rising in volume. Kyle seemed to be in a trance. In the air above him, a disturbance was gathering. At first, it shimmered like a mirage, but then it started filling in with a dark, angry purple mist that swirled with menace. Andrea was so focused on what was happening over Kyle's head, she almost missed what was emerging from his chest.

"What is *that?*" she whispered.

A black egg with a white band around the center had emerged and was rising up into the night.

"That's a dark egg," Rei said.

"Is that music how they're getting the eggs to change?" Masa wondered.

"Do you think…? Sumi began.

"Wait!" Andrea interrupted. "They're taking Kyle's heart egg right now?"

If the characters responded, Andrea didn't hear them. Time, for her, had just stopped. Up until this point, everything had been a series of concepts and theories about kids and potentials—stuff that Andrea felt she could consider, then put aside to work out later. But now, right here and in this very instant, Kyle—*her* Kyle—was having a piece of his existence teased out of him and removed. *Which* specific part of his creative potential that was being taken was still fuzzy in her mind, but the fact was, her mind was having less and less to do with things.

Waves of righteous anger were flooding over her rational impulses, and the Andi-chan who now turned and confronted the characters was hot-blooded and spoiling for a fight.

"Oh, no. I am *not* letting this happen. Rei! Transform with me. What do I do again?" She desperately tried to remember the thumb-and-forefinger diamond arrangement. "Oh, come *on*! What is it? Heart, Crystal…? Rei! Help me!"

"Andi-chan, we weren't going to do any more than watch, remember? You're really not ready."

"Rei!"

"Okay. Invert the diamond and just say, 'My heart *unlock!*'"

"Right. My heart *unlock!*"

Once again, Andrea fell into the colorful slipstream. Moving in multiple directions simultaneously, finishing with the same series of poses, and dressed in the Crystal Bright Heart Lunation cheerleader costume. Any chance of keeping a low profile went out the window with the transformation, since anyone who could see characters could see this light show. As Kyle's dark egg rose to almost twenty feet above him, a familiar sight bounded from the trees on the left side of the park.

From thirty yards away, Illya made a series of dazzling ten- to fifteen-foot leaps. Within seconds, he was right in front of her, with Nyanka buzzing madly about, checking out her characters.

The leaps were a surprise. Andrea hadn't really considered what sort of powers his transformation might have. "Illya?"

"So you *did* remember my name," he said, with a suggestive leer. "I'm really quite touched."

"Leave that egg alone!"

"Hm-m-m, well…" He pretended to ponder her demand. "No, I think I'll take it. Now, you just run along like a good little girl, and nothing unpleasant will happen."

Andrea hadn't a clue how to respond. Other than anger and attitude, she really had nothing to oppose him with. Meanwhile, the situation around her was slipping into chaos. Nyanka, with so many females to act up in front of, was bouncing around like a lunatic. Masa, Sumi, and Rei were trying to ignore him, but he kept popping up everywhere. "Oh, Illya," he gushed. "I have three good little girls to play with. I hope they're not *too* good."

Just then, Andrea noticed that Nyanka's hands and feet were really oversize cat paws. *How could I have missed that?* she thought. *Wait, it doesn't matter. Don't get distracted.* A host of questions were demanding her attention. How could she grab Kyle's egg? What was Illya up to? And why had she started this without a plan?

Illya moved in on her, just inches from her face. "You need to get your priorities straight," he said. "Your little friend Kyle isn't going to miss his egg, but *you* are risking a great deal by interfering in *my* business."

Andrea couldn't help herself. "Business? You're *selling* the eggs? But to who? Why? For how much? What could anyone possibly want with the heart's eggs of children?"

Illya fell back and threw her a look of pure exasperation. "What part of 'keep out of my business' wasn't clear, Miss Melman? At what point did you take that to mean 'please feel free to ask me all manner of inappropriate questions'? You don't *seem* stupid. Are you just stubborn? Why can't you simply accept my gracious offer not to hurt you, and let it go at that?"

"Were you playing the violin just now?"

Illya went from stunned disbelief to laughing out loud. "Unbelievable! Listen to me, little girl. I am your *enemy*. You can't just demand that I stop collecting eggs. You can't ask impertinent questions about my business, and you can't ask about my playing the violin."

"But you're really good. How can you use a gift like that in such an awful way? Oh, and you just answered my question. Thank you."

Standing there in the lamplight of the cobblestoned park path, Illya looked irritated and uncertain. Suddenly, an exaggerated stage cough came from a voice somewhere off to the right, and he abruptly turned and executed a perfectly targeted leap up to where Kyle's egg was hovering. He swept it into a bag, and touched down again, facing Andrea. "You've been warned. This is none of your business, and your interference will *not* be tolerated."

Andrea was trying to figure out what to do, but all her options seemed weak, and Nyanka was still zipping madly around the others, making it hard for her to focus. "I know there's only one of me and three of you, but we can learn to share," he said suggestively.

The characters were trying hard to ignore him, but Sumi couldn't quite stop giggling, which undermined the whole effect.

"Nyanka! We are gone!" Illya shouted, launching himself toward the street.

"So maybe I'll catch you girls around." Nyanka said, floating sideways, posed as if leaning against a lamppost and tipping an imaginary hat. Andrea had to admit, it was a cute move. Then she snapped back into the moment and realized she was coming away from this encounter with nothing. No egg. No information (outside of the knowledge that Illya played the violin—and rather well, truth be told). She saw Illya land over near the sidewalk, where the unknown person must have been hiding. Then he bounded out into the street, with Nyanka in tow.

Andrea was thoroughly frustrated at how badly things had gone. Indeed, she was so angry at being this weak and ineffectual, she actually stamped her foot and launched herself a few feet into the air. This unintended effect riled her at first, but as she floated down to the grass, it occurred to her that the only power she had any experience with might be useful for at least one thing. She was dying to know who the mystery voice belonged to. Running after the pair wasn't very practical, but maybe she could learn something from aerial reconnaissance. "Rei, I'm going to jump up and try to see who that was."

"Okee dokee, Andi-chan."

She launched herself upward to what she hoped was a suitable height, and caught a break. The pair weren't even trying to run away. They had crossed the street, making it easier to see them. And the woman with Illya wasn't exactly hiding her identity. That slender frame, the flawless ensemble, and the huge mane of blonde hair with ponytails sticking out sideways.

Natalya.

Chapter 11

That flirty, egg-stealing cat boy's girlfriend was *Natalya*? Odder still, the cold night air carried a sound she would have never associated with Natalya.

Laughter. *Normal* laughter. From Natalya.

Andrea had a moment to consider this as she floated back to earth. To her right, she noticed Rei floating in formation with her. The evening's activities had been a painful lesson in the importance of training. As of tonight, playtime was over.

Rei kept her tone relaxed but precise. "Toe to heel at forty-five degrees. Knee flex on the landing, Andi-chan, nice and easy."

Andrea followed the instructions and was rewarded with an elegant landing. She started to walk over to Kyle's bench, but then stopped, turned, and gave a small bow. "Thank you, Rei."

Kyle was fuzzy but functional. "Whoa. Hey, Andy, what's up? Why am I out here?"

"Oh, hey, Kyle," a post-transformation Andrea said casually. "How are you doing?"

"Uh, I don't know. Fine? Whatever."

She hoped that maybe nothing had happened. He seemed to be acting pretty normal for Kyle. But maybe a test was in order. Sitting herself down at the other end of the bench from the still woozy boy, Andrea probed for evidence of some kind of "creative potential" deficit. "Listen, Kyle, I met this guy at school who's into comics and anime and all, and I was thinking maybe, you know, he seems to know a lot about the whole industry and…"

"Oh, yeah?"

Kyle's face lit up, and Andrea felt a spark of hope.

"Yeah, wow, Andy. The thing is, I'm, like, really over that whole stupid art thing."

Andrea froze. "Oh?"

"Oh yeah. I was all, you know, worrying about stuff, all that art crap and, you know, like, having talent and all, but I feel like I'm over it."

"Really?" She almost managed to bury her disappointment.

"Look, why waste time on anything you can't really do, you know?"

"But, Kyle, you haven't really *seen* what you might be able to do."

"Yeah, yeah, but come on, Andy, we both know I'm not exactly a natural or anything."

"Kyle, plenty of people have to work really hard to do the things they're passionate about… the things they love."

She wanted those last words back the moment they slipped out.

"Oh yeah, 'The things they *love!*' Good one, Andy. That's just what Mark was telling me."

Kyle's brother had something to say about art and love? Andrea restrained herself.

"He says life is a grind, and you never get to do what you really want anyway. He says dreams are just a big scam to keep you from getting anywhere real. Like, making money or getting a car or… you know, stuff like that. He says being an artist is just another name for being a loser, and that chicks don't want some crybaby with a lot of questions. They want a real guy with… I don't know, a car, I guess."

Andrea's usual approach to people was pretty "live and let live," but for Mark, she was willing to make an exception. He was an idiot, and he deserved to suffer for inflicting his miserable perspective on the innocent.

Kyle was continuing to ramble on, but it was a wall of words that she would never break through at this point. She was in a daze as she got up to walk back home.

Kyle's "'Night, Andy, keep it real" seemed genuine but empty. It reminded her of the meaningless things the jocks at school were always saying. *Oh, God,* she thought. *Kyle's turning into a lunkhead. How did this happen?*

Everyone was quiet coming into the house. The characters were exhausted and looked as though they needed a meal and a hug. She fixed them up with some mochi and then surprised everyone—including herself—with the decision to go back outside for a walk alone.

The wind had picked up and given the night air an edge. She briefly considered going back for a warmer jacket, but her feet weren't interested and she looped around the neighborhood aimlessly.

If she'd expected to process the evening's events on the walk, it wasn't working. Everything was a blur with a nauseous undertone. Dense emotions were swimming around inside of her: fear, shame, disappointment, depression. She could feel each one for a moment, but nothing would stick. She was just turning down her street on the way back when a colorful bit of trash caught her eye. A piece of a drawing.

She stopped dead in her tracks.

Things started to churn inside of her. A line of torn pictures led up the street to Kyle's house. She began picking up the fragments, at first in a calm, deliberate way, then frantically, dashing back and forth across the street, reaching under cars and running onto people's lawns. Eventually she was standing in front of his house, pulling illustrations out of the garbage and sobbing.

It was around ten that night when Andrea threw the remains of Kyle's career as an artist onto her desk. That gave her the rest of the evening to torture herself over how she had handled things. She didn't waste a second.

All night, she huddled on her bed, silent and isolated. A mind, capable of deep and powerful analysis, turning on itself, hacking and slicing into everything she had done or failed to do. After hours of bearing witness, Rei, Masa, and Sumi retreated into their eggs.

Andrea noticed nothing. Everything was compressed into a single point of failure, and that point was her. Her inability to focus. Everything the characters had tried to teach her that she had been too lazy or distracted to understand. Her clueless rescue attempt. How she had gorged herself on the righteous anger of the moment and how that indulgence had handed everything over to Illya.

In this dark world of self-recrimination, she had only herself to tear apart, to blame, and to punish. By the time it started to get light out, her lungs and stomach were aching from crying, and she looked like hell.

Then suddenly it got a little better. Not *a lot* better, but sort of a "Pandora seeing the Hope fairy at the bottom of the box" kind of better.

Andrea had come to some understandings about herself and made a lot of promises to the Goddess that night. But what dragged her out of bed and got her to school that day was a plan—not the best of plans, but a workable one, and one she needed to act on while time might still be on her side.

* * *

Makeup would go only so far in hiding the difference between eight hours of crying and eight hours of sleep. Dion took one look at the result over breakfast and offered to call her in sick, but she declined. Today, good enough was going to have to do.

School sharpened her. She kept a low profile in her classes and avoided human contact even more than usual. Fifth period was her first opportunity to act, but conditions weren't favorable. That really left only last period, and she carefully scouted positions and a handful of secondary options.

The first bit of luck was a gift. Natalya was alone in the hall. She was walking at a normal pace, not looking up or paying any attention to her surroundings. All the luck after that was of Andrea's own making. She had been keeping track of the girls' bathroom. Now it was empty.

Natalya was on that side of the hallway. Andrea approached from the other side, pulled deep into herself, head down.

Natalya was now four steps from the bathroom. Andrea kept her pace but angled sharply toward the door.

Three steps, and Natalya was still oblivious. Andrea's arms looked as if she was carrying books, but they were all in her backpack.

Two steps and closing. Arms out, Andrea entered Natalya's field of vision.

One step.

"Hey!"

Offering no response, Andrea had her arms around Natalya and deflected her into the door.

"What are you...?"

Door open. Natalya pushed into bathroom. Door closed.

"You!"

"Yeah, me."

On any other day, Andrea would have been terrified. Natalya, cornered, was ferocious. Breathing heavily, nostrils flaring, she resembled a very pissed-off jungle cat. And Natalya wasn't the sort of girl who believed in sensible nails. She had talons like a raptor.

"We need to talk."

Whatever Natalya was geared up for, it didn't appear to be talk.

"What do you want?"

"Tell your boyfriend I want to buy Kyle's egg back."

Andrea never saw Natalya's response coming.

She giggled.

Chapter 12

Natalya giggling was just weird. Andrea was too frazzled to handle the abrupt change gracefully. "Did you hear me? I want to buy back his egg. You sell them, and I want one. *That* one."

"My boyfriend?" Natalya wasn't quite focused on the issue at hand.

"I don't want to buy your boyfriend. Pay attention!"

But it was no use. Natalya seemed off in a dream world.

Andrea pushed ahead anyway. "How much?"

"Eh?"

"How much?"

"How much…?"

"For the *egg*. What is your *problem?*"

"Oh, that. We get five hundred dollars for each one. So, let's say, for you… a thousand?"

"A thousand?" Andrea's face fell and she started to tear up. Where was she going to get a thousand dollars?

Natalya caught the look and abruptly turned to check her hair and makeup in the mirror. "Well, we need to be compensated for the Andrea Melman aggravation factor. It is a business, you know. We're not out there so you can flirt with my boyfriend. Okay, say… six hundred? But that's a one time offer."

"*Me,* flirt with *your* boyfriend?" Andrea noticed that every time the word *boyfriend* came up, Natalya seemed quite amused. "*He* has been flirting with *me!* And I'm pretty sure that is both inappropriate *and* illegal in the State of New York."

"Oh, dream on, little girl. Now, we're talking cash here, yes?"

"Yes. Should I bring it to school tomorrow?"

Natalya stopped, turned, and just stared at her as if at a slow shop girl. "Oh, yes. *Please!* You bring a bag full of money here, and I'll hand you a mysterious package. Sound good? I wouldn't want to be, oh, merely within a thousand feet of a New York City public school. That would just look like your average narcotics felony. No, let's do it *right here in the school.* We'll find a surveillance camera to stand in front of, and that way we can guarantee ourselves a spot on the evening news. Do you have a side you favor being photographed from?" Moving back and forth with her hands held up as a frame, she made a show of trying to ascertain Andrea's "good" side,.

Maybe it was just the lack of sleep, or maybe getting a price she could afford relaxed her, but Andrea couldn't help but laugh at Natalya's antics. "Okay, okay, I'm not used to doing anything like… this."

Natalya's eyes hardened. "Miss Melman, this 'this' you speak of is not illegal. It's not covered by any laws any more than trafficking in lost baby teeth would be. I don't know why you are so upset by what we're doing. These eggs have a life cycle. We come in near the end of that cycle and collect them before they disappear or go bad. The children aren't hurt. Only the most minute percentage of these eggs would ever become anything."

"But, it's *theirs*. It's *their* possibilities for—"

"We will do this exchange this one time." Fierce Natalya was back. "After this, we will fight for every egg. We did not choose this life, but it is our livelihood, and, mark my words, we will protect it." She walked to the door and turned. "Tomorrow night, then, at the park. Ten o'clock. Oh, and no guardian characters."

* * *

By the next night, everything was in place. Andrea had most of the six hundred already, and Dion lent her the balance without a question. Predictably, the characters were not happy about being excluded.

"So now we trust her?" Masa snorted.

"Andi-chan, is this wise?" Sumi asked.

Rei wasn't saying anything, but she obviously had concerns. The question of how to handle the egg was discussed. The dark eggs didn't just float about. They had their own distinct personalities and would fly off if not cleaned immediately. The thought of giving up the money and then losing Kyle's egg gave Andrea a minor panic attack, but the others were confident she would be able to clean the egg without a problem. And since a cleansed egg always returned to its owner, that was all she need do.

Andrea left the house at five minutes of ten. The compromise they had worked out was to leave the bedroom window open. If there was any hint of a transformation, the characters could be there in less than a minute.

The walk was uneventful, and Natalya was waiting on the bench. By way of greeting, they exchanged nods, and Andrea sat down and handed over the envelope of cash. She wasn't surprised when Natalya started counting the money, but then, after peeling off five twenties, she suddenly stopped and handed them back to her.

"But... it's all there," Andrea said.

"I know it's all there. We get five hundred for them. I was not serious about the aggravation tax. It was... a joke."

Andrea had a hard time picturing Natalya joking. Why wasn't she taking advantage? Or at least making more of a profit from the situation?

"Uh, thank y—"

"Don't thank me for this, Andrea Melman. Thank me for warning you to stay clear of our business. You are an innocent on dangerous ground."

Natalya handed her a black plastic bag inside a string net webbing. "This is your responsibility now. I assume your characters know what to do."

She rose and started to leave, then turned back to face her once again.

"I will not lose to you, Andrea Melman. Not one more egg, and not Illya, either."

Andrea knew better than to cross Natalya by stepping on her dramatic exit line, but she couldn't stop herself.

"*Oh, my God.* As *if* I were interested in Cat Boy." Which got a smile out of Natalya. "And really, on what planet would I be considered competition to you?"

Andrea stood up with the bag, and they faced each other for an awkward moment.

"Well, okay, then. Thank you for… uh, warning me to stay out of your business and pointing out my being innocent and stupid… and—"

"I never said stupid."

"Oh, right. And the egg… an-n-nd…"

"Good evening, Andrea Melman!"

"Okay. See you in school. Bye."

* * *

Ten minutes later, they were gathered in the backyard, an area enclosed by high, dense hedges. Andrea was nervous, but Rei was beaming and radiating confidence. "This is the fun part, Andi-chan."

Andrea had to suppress her vision of five hundred dollars flying away and concentrate. "Okay, let's do it." She and Rei transformed into Crystal Bright Heart Lunation as Masa and Sumi worked the bag from around the egg. The egg floated up, apparently disoriented and uncertain.

Andrea positioned herself a dozen feet away and brought her hands up, making a heart shape between her thumbs and fingers. She cleared her throat and, aiming the shape at the dark egg, confidently intoned, "Dark Heart, lock on!" A heart-shaped outline of sparkling light shot up from her hands to the egg, freezing it in place. She almost stopped to look, but she was nervous about completing the ritual. Centering herself, she took a deep breath. Calm settled over her as she felt herself connecting to the inspiration at the root of her own magical rituals. She intoned the words "Bright Heart!"

A column of white light enveloped the egg, and inside she could see it changing: a quick shimmer of color initiating a shift from black to glowing white. The luminescent egg hung in the air for a few long seconds, and then shot up and over the roof toward the street. Andrea jumped up with the others right behind her, clearing the roof just in time to see the egg go into the room she knew to be Kyle's.

As they settled back to earth, Rei was cheering. "An-di-chan! An-di-chan!"

Masa actually looked proud, and Sumi was getting weepy. Andrea had to wonder if it was always like this, or if they were just relieved that she hadn't screwed it all up. By the time she transitioned out of Crystal Bright Heart Lunation, those questions were gone. Andrea Melman had rescued her first dark egg, and she was pumped. "We did it! That was amazing. I want to do another one right away. Let's go out and get some more. I could do this all night."

"But of course, you realize, it isn't always this simple," Masa suggested gently.

"Oh, I know, I know, but look what we did. Tomorrow we'll start training, and I'll learn everything there is to know about saving eggs."

Sumi and Rei exchanged a long look.

Chapter 13

In the following days, Andrea learned a lot about the capture and saving of dark eggs, and also a bit about living with roommates.

Her characters began settling into what she assumed were their "normal" personalities.

Early on, Masa unearthed an old smartphone with internet access. From then on, she spent much of her time doing research on topics she never discussed.

Masa's artistic leanings were hard to fathom. She was usually off on her own, with a large sketch pad in hand. At first, Andrea assumed she was, well… *sketching*, but anytime she caught a glimpse of what she was doing, it always seemed to be dense writing in an alphabet similar to Celtic runes. No one ever said so, but Andrea always sensed that questions about the sketch pad were not welcome.

Sumi came across as lighter and easier on a superficial level. But her tendency, under stress, to pull rank on the others made Andrea think she was at least "first among equals" if not actually highest in some unspoken ranking.

Beyond that, Sumi seemed to be hiding the most behind her airy guardian-character facade, but Andrea understood implicitly that she was being kept out of a number of loops. Somehow, it never felt personal, and she never took it that way.

Rei seemed to enjoy being the ditzy, energized athlete—every bit the cheerleader she was dressed to be. Andrea felt a little bit wistful that there weren't more opportunities for Rei to express herself. She could see that Rei was dying to pump her up with energy and enthusiasm, but there were limits on how pumped up a girl like Andrea could get.

Still, Rei's tender feelings toward her were no obstacle to a tough-love approach in the training regimen. Rei's basic theory seemed to be that theory was overrated. To her, the only thing better than twenty-five jumps to a precise height was fifty jumps to that same height.

Floating got the same approach. Andrea got so sick of hearing "Eyes open, Andi-chan!" that it actually made her keep her eyes open.

Actual flying involved her first "accessory": the Star Lifters—essentially, a pair of in-line skates with little wings on the back in official Crystal Bright Heart Lunation pink.

Andrea being Andrea, the first roadblock was the idea that you just called for them and they showed up, on your feet and ready to go. "But where do they come from? How is it that they fit me perfectly? How do they *work?*"

Rei had learned to deflect any questions that had no useful answers. "They work by leaning in the direction you want to go. Let's start by leaning 'up.'"

Clearly, after her terrifying initial twenty-story jump, Andrea was now taking a rather more cautious approach to first steps. A slow, timid rise of a few feet gave her the confidence to try a series of forward, backward, and lateral leans. "Okay, this isn't so bad," she said tentatively.

Rei had learned to hide a lot of her initial reactions to Andrea's way of getting around to things, but this time it took real effort to stifle her disappointment. "Andi-chan, they're for *flying*. Let's take them up for a spin. I'll be right next to you."

Andrea eased forward and up and started to pick up some speed and altitude. "You realize I've never even used *regular* skates before, right?"

"No problem. Let's just practice a stop-and-float. Center yourself and pull to a stop."

Rei just couldn't understand it. Back in Japan, kids went crazy over the Star Lifters. It was love at first sight, dreams come true. You didn't have to encourage them; quite the contrary, you had to warn them about running into buildings and trees.

Andrea's first approach to everything was to stand off and analyze it to death. She was able to work through a lot of basics quickly, but it really bothered Rei that she should be so tentative about such a fundamentally joyful activity. They were practicing abrupt changes in direction when something came up.

"Uh, Rei?"

"Andi-chan?"

"Um, not to overthink this, or anything, but, uh, what happens to the skirt when I'm up in the air and going sideways and all?"

"What? The *skirt*? Ah! I didn't realize. Fly with your body horizontal and look at the skirt."

Andrea tried the move, but something seemed odd.

"Now try floating in place and angling your whole body downward."

"Oh, I don't know about that…" Andrea seemed on the verge of quitting then and there but a tentative attempt at the move showed something was very unusual. Try as she might, no matter what angle she took, the skirt stayed put. It was as soft to the touch as ever, but somehow the skirt's orientation and form always remained, for lack of a better phrase, "modestly positioned."

"Rei! It's… *magic!*" Andrea started engaging in more radical flying maneuvers, both delighting and scaring Rei.

"Buildings and trees, Andi-chan! Buildings and trees!"

* * *

Happy as she was to see Andrea's enthusiasm for the Star Lifters, Rei was starting to worry about what else was getting swallowed up in the cultural divide. The properties of the magical skirt were such second nature to Japanese kids; it had never occurred to her to have to point it out. And yet, Andrea couldn't possibly have known about it.

Rei called a meeting with Masa and Sumi when they got home. "All I'm saying is, this isn't going away. It could come up in a million ways."

Masa had already considered the problem. "We need to take her training slow. I think we should go in sequence and build up her skills around the central mission. Since I'm teaching her the dark-egg-immobilizing technique, I should train her next, Sumi."

Sumi was clearly unhappy to be coming last again. "Okay," she said, "but I think we need to engage her in more ways than just the powers."

"*Or...* Maybe we could include her in any meetings we have about her." Andrea chimed in from her bed across the room.

Rei and Sumi babbled embarrassed nonsense for a moment until Masa spoke up. "Did you hear the whole discussion?"

"It was a little hard to miss."

"Then you understand the concern. A number of things are not what we had expected. *You* are not quite what we expected."

Andrea showed a flicker of hurt. "Oh."

"No, no." Masa flew over next to her. "*You're* not the problem. We seem to have not adequately prepared for this. It's actually got nothing to do with you. Our understanding of your world is flawed."

"But, I mean, this whole thing of you talking about me is really uncomfortable—especially when I'm right here."

"Actually," Masa said, "that's just another example of the cultural confusion. We think it's rude to make you watch us argue, and you think it's rude not to include you."

"So, we need to find some middle ground?" Andrea offered helpfully.

Masa seemed to consider that carefully before replying. "No. That sounds very balanced, but I don't think so. The middle ground between two islands is not a good place to land. Sometimes, you need to surrender to a single viewpoint. You're not here for us. We're here for you. I think we need to acknowledge our foreignness in this situation and take the responsibility for learning your view of things as best we can. Sumi has the right idea. We need to engage in more than just the area of the mission, and the powers. We represent aspects of your would-be self. We need to engage in that with you."

"Okay, so what would that actually mean?"

Masa flew to Andrea's electric guitar in its stand, and floated just above it. "Andi-chan, you want to play in a band, don't you?"

"Yeah. So?"

"So why haven't I heard you practice your guitar once in the entire time I've been here?"

"Well…"

Apparently sensing a theme developing, Sumi dashed over to Andrea's computer workstation. Gesturing at a stack of printouts and the overloaded corkboard above the monitor she added, "And you never try any of these recipes you're always reading."

Andrea fidgeted self-consciously. "I'm not really—"

"And you never do any exercise!" Rei piled on. "You need to think about the future. You're not going to be fifteen forever, you know. You need to start running. Or dancing. Do they have *Dance Dance Revolution* here?"

"Can't we just have a snack right now?" Andrea suggested hopefully.

"Oh, yes!" Sumi gushed. "Let's learn to make mochi! Do you have a really big mortar and pestle? This will count as exercise, too!"

"Or I could just go back on my bed and you guys could just talk about me and it would be no big deal, really."

"Sorry, Andi-chan," said Masa. "Too late for that."

* * *

With her increasingly complicated home life, school had become the easiest part of the day for Andrea. As long as she didn't run into Natalya in a deserted bathroom, she figured things were good.

One odd development was that Gaylen had joined Black Swan Brigade—or, as she explained—the *former* Black Swan Brigade. Natalya had decided to expand the concept with bass and drums, and the new band would be getting a new name.

Gaylen, Andrea was finding out, was more than just a cool girl playing a little bass. She felt stupid not to have known that Gaylen was considered the best bass player in school, working with a number of bands, and even playing clubs in Manhattan. Apparently, Natalya had actually been pursuing her to join the band for months but wouldn't add the drummer until she agreed.

It was Gaylen herself who had revealed the most interesting fact about Black Swan Brigade. They were the only band Gaylen had ever played with who got paid for rehearsals. It was a token amount, but with six players twice a week, the expense was more than token.

So *that* was what she did with the money.

It was hard to imagine what working for Natalya would be like, but she got a glimpse of it in the cafeteria a few days later.

Natalya would hold lunchtime band meetings there occasionally and it was quite a show: an Elegant Gothic dictator holding court. Today, the three string players huddled in respectful terror while, temporarily out of the line of fire, Gaylen, the keyboard player and drummer, all looked slightly bored and amused.

The string players were getting a savage review of their last rehearsal. Natalya was armed with both the score and the individual string parts. "So, again! We agree these are *not* legato eighth notes?"

A round of sheepish nods from the trio.

"As written, they are *staccato* eighth notes, yes?"

More nods.

"But when I listen to yesterday's rehearsal, I hear nothing like this. I do not hear '*dit, dit, dit, dit,*' do I? No! I hear '*dah, dah, dah, dah.*' Big, sloppy, barely articulated eighth notes!"

Having handed down the indictment, Natalya let the moment breathe, and then started in again, slower and softer. "And *why* do I need this? Who could possibly care about this?"

They all shrank back as she pulled out a well-worn notebook.

"These are lyrics, yes?"

Everyone nodded emphatically, not seeing the trap until it was too late.

"No! This is a *manifesto*. In lyrical form. I don't expect you to understand Russian, but I have given you the essential concepts in the supplementary materials. You all have the supplementary materials, yes?"

More frantic nodding. She began gesturing to different points in the score. "You are the tools I have chosen to express my will. And yet, *here,* when I turn to you to empower me with steely precision..." She looked around at the group. "To cut through a maze of lies..."

Afraid to meet her gaze, the band was staring fixedly at the scores on the table.

"To lay waste the apathy and cruelty of this world... In this moment of judgment, when I turn to you for the bone and sinew of the vengeance I have vowed to inflict, you give me..."

No one could work a dramatic pause like Natalya.

"*Pudding!* You give me a handful of *pudding!*"

Sitting behind Natalya, the rhythm section fell into soundless giggles. The string players, meanwhile, were too scared to react in any way at all.

Natalya stood up and swept the music into a folder, and Andrea's world collapsed into a black hole. For now she saw what Natalya was wearing.

Technically, it was a coat. Black. With a wide collar. Strange writing in intentionally tortured English in patches on the front and back.

Andrea felt as if she were having an out-of-body experience, watching herself approach the table.

Gaylen caught her eye, shot her a look. Waved to her. Looked at Natalya, looked back. Shook her head. Pleaded with her eyes. All to no avail.

Andrea wasn't really there.

Nothing else was really there. Just the coat. *That* coat. The coat that dreams were made of—or, at least, Andrea Melman's dreams since last summer.

Gaylen felt that she was watching a terrible accident unfold in slow motion.

Andrea reached the table.

Natalya looked at her.

Andrea looked back and spoke the words that would haunt the rest of her high school career. "Sex Pot Revenge."

Chapter 14

The entire cafeteria fell silent. One didn't just interrupt a Natalya diva moment—let alone with a line such as "Sex Pot Revenge"—and expect to get away unscathed. But Natalya just looked at her.

Andrea kept staring at the coat.

Finally, she spoke again. "The Anarchy coat."

And, a long moment later, "In black."

From Andrea's perspective, time was now frozen. She could contemplate her history with this coat and what it had come to mean to her. She had discovered the site last spring: SEXPOT ReVeNGe, a Japanese clothing company for girls with aspirations trending toward the punk side of cute.

The Anarchy coat was Andrea's dream, made manifest with a SKU number. The coat wasn't really designed for sexpots, vengeful or otherwise. The most notable feature was a high, wide collar that went almost from shoulder to shoulder. Utterly impractical. Graphic touches in English tossed on with no apparent rhyme or reason.

"STIMULATION BAILOUT," with a skull underneath.

"THE INSTINCT—IT SWIRLS."

And the one she couldn't get out of her head: "INPULSE THAT CANNOT BE CONTROLLED."

Andrea was utterly captivated by this vision of a world where she might run around Tokyo with a group of girlfriends wearing wild, fun clothes from labels with names like SEXPOT ReVeNGe.

A silly, outrageous piece of fashion nonsense from a company whose very name would give any parent fits. It existed at the very center of everything that Andrea Melman dreamed of doing and that, she feared, she would never be brave enough to experience. It wasn't an issue of price. The coat cost less than two hundred dollars. She could have ordered it through Dion and never had to explain to her parents the meaning of a credit card entry from Sexpot Revenge.

Only one thing was keeping Andrea from this coat, and that was Andrea.

She knew with absolute certainty that if she ever ordered the SPR Anarchy coat in black, it would never leave her closet. She hated herself for being such a coward, but the horrible truth was that there was no "inpulse" that Andrea Melman could not control.

Back on earth, these thoughts were interrupted by an unexpectedly soft "Yes."

All eyes turned to Natalya. If Andrea's intrusion hadn't been confusing enough, this defied comprehension.

Natalya didn't agree with fifteen-year-old girls. She made them cry.

Andrea floated back into reality, contemplating how Natalya's willingness to incorporate this edgier, irrational influence within the more restrictive tropes of her essential Elegant Gothic Lolita look indicated a rare mastery of fashion.

She looked Natalya straight in the eye. "It looks perfect on you."

"Thank you," Natalya replied solemnly.

Gaylen was fascinated. Trying to make sense of this whole exchange was giving her a delicious headache. It was like coming in for the final scene of an untranslated samurai movie: completely incomprehensible, yet heartbreakingly beautiful.

Had Natalya actually bowed slightly to Andrea's compliment?

What would drive Andrea to commit social suicide like this?

Gaylen had enough sense to figure out that Sex Pot Revenge was a clothing line. But she knew for sure that the headline for this bit of high school drama would be more along the lines of "Tween Calls Queen 'Sexpot' in Front of Entire School."

Walking to her next class, Gaylen was still pondering the meaning of it all when Natalya caught up with her in the hall and pulled her out of the flow of traffic.

Gaylen had had negotiations with Natalya and received orders and instructions, but she had never experienced anything approximating what people might call "talking" with her.

"Gaylen? I... may I request a favor of you?"

Gaylen noted with surprise the unprecedented lack of direct eye contact.

"It is a small thing, but I need—wish—to clarify something to... your friend, Miss Melman, regarding this coat that she expressed interest in. Could you please inform her that I bought the coat last summer?"

"Uh, okay. Is that all?"

This was getting more confusing by the minute.

"Yes. Oh, and can I beg your discretion in this matter?"

By this point, Natalya was actually looking down at the floor.

It was Natalya's good fortune that Gaylen happened to be a girl who enjoyed a bit of drama and mystery, particularly when it was happening to someone else. "Confidential go-between" was a job description she could relish. Rising to the role, she lightly touched Natalya's arm and said, "In strictest confidence then."

This prompted a disproportionately relieved smile and the oddly formal, "I am in your debt, Gaylen."

Oh, yeah, Gaylen thought. *Hands down, the two weirdest girls in the school.*

When she relayed the message later, she was dying to ask its significance. But Andrea didn't react in any discernible way, and somehow, it was all the more fun to be kept in the dark while being the trusted intermediary. She was disappointed there was no response, though.

* * *

"I don't get it," Andrea said during a training break that night.

"It's odd," Rei agreed.

"Yeah. Not going-catatonic-and-talking-to-someone's-coat-while-they're-eating -lunch kind of odd, but odd nonetheless," Masa remarked.

"Hey! Not supportive." Sumi piped up, but Andrea was already laughing.

"You really don't see it?" Masa prodded. "She gets that the coat is the object of your dreams. Her having it precludes your being able to get it. You'd look like a sad little copycat. But why 'last summer'? What's so special about that?"

"Andi-chan!" Rei said. "She thinks you believe she used the money for Kyle's egg to buy the coat. She needed you to know that those things aren't related, that she wasn't rubbing it in."

"Wait. You're telling me she *doesn't* want me to feel bad?"

"Well, I guess not *that* bad. Or, not *that* way."

Sumi looked puzzled. "For a nemesis, she's not being very evil."

"I thought *Illya* was my nemesis."

"Oh, no!" they all jumped in. Apparently, they didn't see Illya as nemesis material at all.

"He's more interested in trying to impress you than he is in doing his job," Masa said.

"Look at how Nyanka behaves," Rei agreed. "No focus at all."

"Natalya's the brains behind everything," Sumi said confidently.

"And the spine," Rei added. "It's a good thing *she* doesn't have a character."

* * *

The focus of the night's training was learning to use the heart baton accessory to immobilize dark eggs. In keeping with the cheerleader theme, the heart baton looked like a twirler's baton, only a little bigger – and predictably pink -, but it functioned more like a boomerang. You threw it, and it would encircle the egg with clouds of sparkly stuff and then return to you.

Rei and Sumi took turns being the "egg" and being immobilized. Apparently, one could immobilize any living thing, with the condition that if something flew or floated, it would float in place—which was a good thing since the two characters were seriously frozen during the training.

They still had time to cover the pom-poms. Basically shields, you held them up and they blocked all kinds of incoming low-velocity projectiles and what Masa vaguely termed "other stuff that might get thrown at you."

Walking home, they all agreed that Andrea was ready to get some more real experience. She had impressed them—not just with her basic skills—but with a tangible improvement in her aggressiveness.

There was one thing, though, that Andrea wanted that couldn't come from training alone. But she was working on it. A well-researched purchase online and she was feeling a lot more prepared for the big, bad world and her next encounter with Illya and Nyanka.

Chapter 15

Four nights later, they went out on their first official patrol, with the characters deployed in a wide circle around a bike riding Andrea. It was a situation that left her with conflicted feelings.

Technically, she had enough experience with flying now to allow her to take to the air with them.

The primary obstacle to doing that was Andrea's fear of being seen. Oddly though, the characters never appeared to take the issue seriously. And since it didn't bother them, they didn't see why it should bother her.

So she was on her bike. The safe, rational choice which should have settled everything, except for those conflicting feelings. Because, the truth was that Andrea was beginning to fall in love with the act of flying. Whether hovering cautiously or moving between treetops with Rei's constant guidance, Andrea Melman was going from reluctant participant to eager enthusiast with every additional second of air time. But tonight she was to remain earthbound unless absolutely necessary. Perfectly prudent and totally maddening.

Her thoughts were interrupted as Rei swooped down just long enough to check in for her regular visual-contact verification.

"Visual-contact verification"—that was what they actually called it. And anytime Andrea called it something else, one of them corrected her as if it were a big deal. Somehow, a shift in tone had occurred as the Dark Egg training proceeded. Andrea had first noticed it in the terms and vocabulary that had arisen.

She didn't want to read too much into the situation, but when you added up all the "procedures" and "protocols" the characters wanted to implement, it had a pretty strong militaristic feel to it. Lots of "reconnaissance" and "assessments" and "rules of engagement."

Honestly, they're like pixies with combat skills. Where does this come from?

Nonetheless, losing the Battle of Kyle's Egg had inflicted some painful lessons, and Andrea was fully signed on to the rules of engagement, at least in theory.

For the time being, they would seek out "uncontested" eggs. Too many questions about Illya and Natalya remained for her to risk a real fight. But the characters' abilities to sense out each other, as well as the presence of dark eggs, meant that an engagement was always possible.

Rei had conducted tests to establish the capabilities and limits of their "radar." Masa was twice as sensitive as Rei and Sumi. When focused, she could sense one of the others from almost half a mile away. They had no way of testing their dark-egg sensing, but it was probably the same. Hence the patrols. The theory was to find newly emerged eggs and Bright Heart them before Nyanka could detect anything. It was a good theory. Fortunately, none of them believed it, and they went out expecting trouble.

The first few hours were uneventful, with Andrea cycling down alternate streets along a predetermined grid. Rei and Masa were scouting a block out to each side with Sumi a few hundred feet out in front. Around midnight, the wind started picking up and the temperature dropped.

Andrea was getting tired of rolling past house after house. *I know I'd probably freeze to death but I wish I could be flying up there with them.*

Masa suddenly zoomed in, interrupting her train of thought. "I can feel one a block over."

Andrea had done her own scouting of the neighborhood a few years ago and knew that a park was over there—along with a shortcut to get her there in under a minute.

On arrival, the situation was suspiciously familiar to Kyle's: a kid, looking zoned out and sitting on a park bench slightly away from the street. She hid the bike and moved in with Rei to investigate. Masa and Sumi took up positions on the park's perimeter.

Andrea was on edge. If this wasn't a setup, it sure felt like one. She was the first to notice the swirly purple mist emerge above the kid, and signaled Rei to initiate the change to Crystal Bright Heart Lunation. She came out of the transformation, alert to the fact that time was now in short supply.

It seemed to take forever for the dark egg to emerge, and Andrea was already holding the heart baton when Masa zipped in front with her "serious business" look. "Character presence. About half a mile. Assume you have two minutes or less."

Andrea was oddly comforted by the information. She knew something about the likelihood of who, where, and when. And even conservatively, one minute was all she needed to save this egg.

The heart baton in her hands had a satisfying heft to it as the egg slowly rose into the night sky. Throwing it, she was gratified to see that the trajectory was solid. Even though it had a lot of self-correcting capabilities, it was still possible to miss or overshoot.

This egg hadn't shown any tendency to make a run for it, but immobilizing it gave her one less thing to worry about, and within seconds, Andrea had proceeded through "Dark Heart, lock on" to "Bright Heart" and was enjoying the show as the egg turned white and merged back into the kid who had almost lost it.

Rei allowed herself a single "Outstanding, Andi-chan." and got a thumbs-up and a smile in response.

"It's gone! It's gone! I don't understand. What happened?" a familiar voice squeaked from nearby.

Nyanka wasn't really the kind of character who could be expected to understand the concept of stealth, so the four of them were in position when Illya finally came into view.

Andrea was sitting on a nearby bench in plain view, Crystal Bright Heart Lunationed to the max, and pretending to file her nails as Illya sauntered up. "Ah, Miss Melman. Why am I *not* surprised to find you here?"

Andrea stood up and said, as casually as she could fake it, "Oh, hello there, kitty boy. No, wait. It's 'Illya,' isn't it? Nice evening, no? I mean, a bit chilly, sure, but it *is* that time of year. You know, I didn't really go for the leg warmers when I first got this outfit, but I've started to come around on that. You know, form-and-function is always a dialogue, but—"

"Where's my egg?" Illya said in what was probably as close to an intimidating snarl as he could manage.

"I'm sorry, *your* egg? Was it marked in some way? I mean, you were nowhere in sight, and I just happened to be going by and—"

"Enough!" Illya was getting flustered, but Andrea had no intention of letting him regain his composure.

"You know, lobstermen have a whole system for marking their traps and resolving disputes, and maybe—"

"Stop!"

Andrea knew she was treading on dangerous ground, but she was counting on a little bit of chaos to help her out, and right on schedule, her secret weapon began undermining Illya.

"You girls must be so cold out here. Maybe you need a hot Nyanka sandwich to warm things up."

"Oh, please! Has that kind of talk *ever* worked on anyone?" Rei threw out with just enough of a flirty spin to drive Nyanka out of his randy little mind.

Nyanka's only way of escalating a flirt, it appeared, was to get more suggestive in a smutty sort of way. It was utterly predictable, and the girls were counting on it.

Andrea and Rei began to react to Nyanka's nonsense by projecting reactions of mild shock and embarrassment while Masa and Sumi quietly disappeared.

Illya tried to calm Nyanka down and get something intimidating going on with Andrea. "Nyanka! Mind your manners," he said, locking eyes with Andrea and encroaching on her personal space.

"Our virginal little flower's ears must be burning with your inappropriate suggestions."

His hand went up to almost cup the side of her impassive face.

"Don't go there, Illya," Andrea said in an unusually still voice.

He moved his hand down her side, almost but not quite touching her.

"Are you disturbed by such close proximity to a man?"

"I'll let you know if one shows up. Now, *back it off*, Illya."

Nyanka seemed torn between trying to get a rise out of Rei and enjoying the vicarious thrill of watching Illya put the moves on Andrea. "She's so feisty for one so young. I don't know if you can handle her."

Illya's hand was a fraction of an inch away from touching Andrea's hip, but his eyes were still locked on to hers. "Maybe the question is more whether *she* could handle *me.*"

Andrea's look suddenly broke into disappointment. "Oh, Illya," she said sadly. Stepping back, she raised what looked like a rainbow-hued machine gun and said in a firm tone, *"Bad kitty!"*

The next thing Illya knew, he was soaking wet. Andrea had shopped well.

The ThunderTek-SuperSoak only looked like a very colorful MAC-10 machine pistol. But a real MAC-10 couldn't pump ten ounces of freezing cold water onto someone at up to twenty-five feet with any real accuracy.

Having gotten Illya's attention, Andrea had some prepared remarks to deliver.

"This behavior toward me is going to stop." *Squirt.* "And it is going to stop…" *Squirt.* "… right…" *Squirt.* "… now!" *Squirt, squirt.* "I'm willing to bet you weren't raised like this"—*squirt*—"were you?" *Squirt.* "Maybe you've gotten some mixed signals about how to treat women." *Squirt, squirt.* "You want to fight for eggs with me, that's fine. But this pathetic sex talk?" *Squirt.* "I can fill this thing up with something a lot more unpleasant than water!" *Squirt.* "Am I being clear? *Squirt, squirt, click, click.* "And as for your monkey…"

Nyanka must have made the understandable mistake of thinking that just because the ThunderTek-SuperSoak was out of water, that… well… it was out of water.

Hovering just out of arm's reach, he compounded his error by thinking it was safe to go and see what Masa and Sumi were doing near Andrea's free hand.

By then Andrea had popped out the empty water magazine and slammed in one of the fresh ones they were holding. This reloading capability was her favorite feature on the ThunderTek. Now Nyanka was going to learn just how accurate Andrea could be against moving targets.

* * *

One magazine later, Illya and Nyanka were two very cold, wet kitties. Illya was shivering as he made ready to leave. "Perhaps you are not entirely mistaken in this respect," he said. "We should be able to conduct ourselves as sworn enemies without rudeness or a lack of manners. My apologies if my behavior has been unseemly. In the future, I will restrict myself to trying to destroy your ability to interfere with our business."

"Thank you," she replied cordially. "That's all I ask."

Illya was turning to go when he paused and added, "Of course, I can't speak for Natalya."

Chapter 16

It took less than a week for the Sex Pot Revenge encounter to percolate through the school. Andrea, too embarrassed to attempt eye contact with another student much less actually speak to anyone, found herself dependent on Gaylen for status reports.

For her part, Gaylen seemed to be enjoying the process a bit more than Andrea would have liked. Never having been present at the birth of an actual meme before, Gaylen took it upon herself to conduct her own investigation into the matter. She performed experiments to see how much her own first-person testimony influenced how the story evolved. The answer: very little. Even when she explained the whole thing in detail, including reference photos of the coat itself, people preferred a spicy tale of confrontation with the word *sex* in it. Like it or not, the former Andrea Melman was now, and possibly for the rest of time, the Sex Pot Revenge girl.

An unexpected dividend that Andrea could have lived without was the looks of quiet admiration that she got in the hallway from many of the younger girls. Whatever version of the story they bought into, they thought she had somehow stood up for them, and it really annoyed her to be receiving unearned admiration from an ill-informed public.

"When does it stop, Gaylen?" demanded Andrea, slouching in sunglasses and a large floppy hat during lunch.

"My estimates are that the looks will last maybe another week, but the 'legendary defender of Tweendom' could become a big part of your backstory. Think of it as something on your permanent record, socially speaking."

"Ugh! Okay, firstly, Gaylen, I am not, and have never been, a *tween*…"

"Even when you were, like, twelve years old?"

"Never!"

"Okay…"

"And even if I had been, I am fifteen years old now. I am beyond any known definition of 'tween,' and I have checked *all* of them. Admittedly, I am a bit on the short side, but I am in no way *tween* short. And furthermore…"

The look on Gaylen's face seemed to combine suppressed amusement with an almost clinical level of concern. Andrea froze and took a moment to look within herself. Slowly she took a deep breath.

"I really need to get over this, don't I?"

"Bad associations with the term 'tween'?"

"Let's just say junior high school was hell."

* * *

Things were getting busy on the home front. Good to their word, Rei, Masa, and Sumi were presenting Andrea with a nonnegotiable self-improvement regimen.

Rei had gone through the house and found a small gym's worth of exercise gear. It now occupied a corner of the bedroom, and she expected to see a minimum half-hour workout pretty much every day.

Masa agreed to restrict herself to music for now. The visual arts campaign would begin later.

Sumi seemed to feel that she had a mandate to teach Andrea to cope with kitchen disasters and to feed people using scant resources. Andrea couldn't tell whether a simmering animosity lay behind it, or whether Sumi really took a survivalist approach to household chores.

Today's teaching scenario was typical. "So, Andi-chan, can we find a way to make pancakes without butter, eggs, and milk?"

"Why?" Andrea asked wearily.

The other two characters were in the kitchen floating around Sumi's seminar when a discussion broke out.

"How come the last kid was in exactly the same state and the same kind of location when his egg emerged?" Masa wondered.

"Yeah: outdoors, nighttime, spaced out, and ready," Rei said.

"I still want to know what role the music is playing," Andrea added.

"Well," Sumi began, thoughtfully wiping flour from her hands, "what if we accept as a given that the music triggers an egg to transform? Maybe it takes multiple exposures. Could Illya and Natalya be going through the neighborhood, playing their music near these kids' houses?"

"It doesn't seem very practical," Rei said. "Illya doesn't fly. He can't just bounce all over Brooklyn looking like that. How would they deliver this music to enough kids in a reasonable time frame? I'm thinking they must be getting at least three or four eggs a week."

"Maybe we need more intelligence," Sumi said.

"Or *different* intelligence," Masa added.

"How do you feel about a flying patrol, Andi-chan?" Rei suggested.

"Are you crazy? I don't know about you guys, but I'm *freezing* out there. I've kept my mouth shut about this till now, but who designs this stuff? And for where? Tahiti? I'm guessing your outfits aren't any warmer. And really, I'm supposed to fly all over Brooklyn and no one's going to see me? What about all the police and traffic helicopters? And power lines? And another thing…"

They just let her go on for a while. Much of it was perfectly true. But since most of it couldn't be changed, there wasn't much to say.

There would be one improvement, though.

That night Andrea took off wearing a World War II bomber jacket over her cheerleader outfit. It sort of ruined the look and didn't quite solve the problem, but it was better than nothing.

As for making a stealthier Andrea, that was a matter of exploiting the local terrain.

Since most of the houses in Brooklyn were attached brownstones, the center of each block was mostly backyard spaces filled with trees and foliage. The trick to keeping a low profile was pretty much a function of skimming over and weaving around the trees. The Star Lifters trailed out some pink sparkly stuff, but normal people couldn't see that. Andrea figured this solution wouldn't work once the Brooklyn roof party season got going, but it would do for now.

It was odd experiencing the world from fifty feet up. Fun, but odd. Andrea had to resist the temptation to stop and observe people through their back windows. A few hours of this was rather tiring, but as they approached an area of industrial parks on the edge of the neighborhood, Masa suddenly called out. "Singing!"

Instantly alert, Andrea strained to make out anything against the wind. She climbed a few hundred feet and out over the empty warehouses. Floating in place, she peered down to get a better view of the streets. "I don't see anything down there, Masa."

"Where are you looking?"

"The sidewalks. Where else?"

"Look with your eyes, not your expectations. Look everywhere."

She let her vision float over the scene. The twinkling Manhattan skyline. Planes taking off and landing at the local airports. The Verrazano-Narrows Bridge in the distance.

Then down again. Into the darkness between the streets. The trees and houses where she had just been hiding, and, yes, there it was. Exactly where she had just been. Flying down the center of the block, over the backyards. Blending in with the treetops. A dark figure, with… *wings?*

The singing was becoming clearer. Andrea was confused. *"Wings?"* Her mind was frantically trying to put things together when the singing abruptly stopped.

The silence hit her like a physical blow. *"They know I'm here!"*

Hanging there, fear overwhelmed rational thought. Suddenly realizing she was silhouetted against the bright city sky, Andrea panicked. Without thinking, she dove for the safety of the ground. It was the worst thing she could have done.

Her sudden motion caught the attention of the winged figure. It pulled up with surprising speed and accelerated toward her. Gasping, Andrea checked her descent and began sliding backward into the industrial park, trying to identify the fast-approaching creature.

Moments later she had her answer. Hopeless and overwhelmed, she stopped, frozen in place a hundred feet off the ground, facing her worst nightmare.

Natalya, silhouetted by an enormous pair of wings, flying straight at her.

Chapter 17

If not for the iconic blond ponytails, Andrea would never have believed it was Natalya rising to confront her. As the winged figure passed into the space above the deserted industrial zone, her flying transitioned to a slow, predatory stalking. Andrea gulped a lungful of air, temporarily relieved at not being directly assaulted, but dreading Natalya's next move.

She wanted to calm down and form a plan, but now that they were close enough to examine, she was transfixed by those wings. They were like bat wings, but *huge*. Leathery black, with a wingspan of over ten feet when fully spread. As Natalya hovered and drifted, the wings didn't so much flap as undulate gently. The effect was beautiful and menacing. Then, a flick of the wing tips and Natalya resumed her aggressive moves and Andrea returned to freaking out.

Natalya's control was on a completely different level than anything Andrea had imagined possible. Her positions changed unpredictably. She zipped in threateningly. Then hovered in place while sinking slowly. Or darted to a position above Andrea while sliding away backward.

If the Star Lifters let Andrea zip about like an airborne skater girl, Natalya flew like an angry hornet. Eventually she stopped tracking around Andrea but even then she kept shifting position, a few feet left or right, up and down, while maintaining a disciplined hover between shifts.

Andrea had seen an air show years ago with attack helicopters that moved like this, and the comparison was pushing her to the edge of hysteria. Many things were calling loudly for her attention, but they weren't the things that needed her focus right now.

For one thing, she couldn't get over the fact that Natalya was wearing a variant of her usual Elegant Gothic Lolita look, a pair of black leggings with a white webbing treatment that looked more stylish and considerably warmer than what Andrea had on.

Oh, what? She gets a bespoke outfit and I'm stuck looking like a cheerleader?

Any further resentments were violently interrupted when Andrea's foot unexpectedly touched the ground, and she almost fell over.

"Andi-chan, stay focused!" Rei shouted. "You're losing altitude. Stay in the air. Prepare for evasive action. Deploy pom-poms!"

All good advice, but Andrea had just observed a pair of guardian characters rising up to positions alongside Natalya, and the sight left her dazed. On the one hand, they were such a cliché, it was hard to take them seriously: a little angel in a frilly white dress and feathery wings beside a little devil, with wings resembling Natalya's and what looked like tiny horns on its head. Somehow it just didn't seem very *Natalya* to be represented by something so obvious and almost... cute. But when you really looked at them, any sense of cuteness quickly evaporated.

The angel was squinting and looked spaced out in a creepy, overmedicated sort of way, and the devil came off as really deranged— even psychotic. There was something so wrong, so cruel, and damaged about them. Andrea knew she had to regain some semblance of control. She forced herself to look away, trying to shift her focus somewhere else.

She became dimly aware of her characters yelling. Then she heard Rei.

"Masa! Sumi! Engage those characters. I want our girl out of here *now!*"

As Masa and Sumi moved to distract Natalya's forces, Andrea's mind landed on an unsettling fact. So far, Natalya had not said a single word.

No warning or acknowledgment, no banter, no threats. Nothing. And somehow, this silence scared Andrea more than anything else. It was the last thing she would have the luxury of considering for a while.

Raising her hands and splaying out her fingers, Natalya started producing clouds of a familiar swirling purple and black plasma. It looked like stuff that heralded an emerging heart egg, but the stylish wraith appeared to be shaping it into… *butterflies?* Something deep inside told Andrea this wasn't just for show, and when Natalya sent a cloud of the fluttering butterfly plasma toward her, she snapped back to her senses.

It was quite a transition, and she had a lot of catching up to do. For starters, Rei was going crazy: waving her arms, yelling stuff, flying back and forth. The instructions were pretty straightforward. Mostly, what she heard was "Pom-poms!" and "Evasive action!"

Andrea called for the pom-poms first, and this was almost a good thing since it was almost in time. As it was, she got a serious taste of angry purple butterflies served in a swirling dark plasma sauce which did do a wonderful job of refocusing her priorities.

The plasma burned like acid on contact with her skin, and the "butterflies" gave the distinct sensation of biting. *Really* biting—not like playful kitten nibbles, but like piranha teeth, drawing blood and leaving scars that the plasma seeped into with agonizing effect.

She had the pom-poms held up tightly around her face, so her hands and legs got the brunt of it. For a moment, she thought she might pass out from the pain. She had sunk almost to the ground again, and took this opportunity to jump away and out of range.

But moments later, she found herself two hundred feet up and a hundred yards back, and yet still looking straight at Natalya, with another cloud of plasma just about to hit. This time, she was ready.

Without any thought to where she might end up, she threw herself into a series of furious evasive maneuvers, trying to put altitude and distance between herself and this awful, elegant creature.

All this bought her was enough time to watch Natalya's exquisite flying technique as she quickly closed the distance and poised for another attack.

Another cloud of plasma, and still not a word.

Andrea felt somehow that anything she might say would just be seen as weakness, so she kept her mouth shut and tried to get a handle on the situation. The characters were nowhere in sight, and that was actually a relief. Worrying about them would only take time and energy away from worrying about herself, and the longer this went on, the more she worried.

She came out of another frantic evasion close up behind a stand of evergreens, breathing hard and hoping for even a moment's respite, but some inner sense told her to float back away from the trees—just as another wave of dark purple seeped through the branches to where she had just been.

"Ahem."

It was Natalya's first utterance of the evening, and it came from directly behind her.

Spinning and diving simultaneously, she caught a glimpse of Natalya floating so close she could have reached out and touched Andrea. Unable to think of anything better to do, Andrea started flying her evasive maneuvers facing backward to keep an eye on her pursuer. Perhaps she shouldn't have, for the view was very depressing.

Natalya's speed and agility were astonishing. At times she would zoom to a position, make a pinpoint stop with no overshoot, turn, and perform the mirror image of the same move.

Thoughts tumbled through Andrea's head, but nothing stuck that would help her cope with this insane situation. She began to realize that Natalya's efforts seemed designed not so much to cripple her as to break her spirit—to overwhelm her with technical superiority and run her out of the game.

It was a nice theory, but every time Andrea stopped, a cloud of hurt was waiting to make contact. She wasn't even sure how to surrender. But somehow, as bad as this was, she didn't really feel like giving in. She had this crazy idea that maybe, if she could get one good shot in, things might change.

The thought made no sense, though. *A shot of what? Where? Get it in how, exactly? Change to what?*

Time seemed to stop. Most of the attack-and-retreat sequences lasted less than a minute, but Natalya never let up. No talking, no respite; one attack followed by a reset and another attack.

Andrea finally realized that the only definition of "winning" that she could aspire to here was to continue taking fire and yet manage to escape. Survival was going to have to be victory enough. This attitude kept her panic at bay, but she was losing energy fast, and every few minutes a round of plasma would manage to get through.

The sheer relentlessness of it all finally caught up with her. Distracted for a moment, she couldn't locate Natalya anywhere. She knew that a new attack was only seconds away, but from where?

By the time she looked straight down and then straight up, it was too late. Natalya had shot a good three hundred feet up, directly over her, and hovered there, perfectly still. A hunter precisely targeting her prey. The plasma was masked by the night sky and tightly focused into a narrow beam. Almost impossible to see unless you knew it was coming.

Andrea got the pom-poms up over her head a little too late and a little off center. The left half of the bomber jacket was shredded. Her hands were blistering. Worse than any of that though, the steady, repeated application of fear and pain was eroding her situational awareness.

Finally, she let herself get backed into a loading dock with high walls on both sides. Natalya had somehow created a grid overhead out of bands of plasma to contain her. Andrea sank to her knees as it filled in above her head, trapping her.

For a long moment, nothing happened. Andrea was too exhausted to offer even token resistance. She wasn't even looking at Natalya. No tactical assessments, no appeals for mercy—just waiting for the next wash of pain.

Which never came. The plasma evaporated.

By the time Andrea looked up, Natalya had made the transition out of the wings and was standing there in her regular clothes staring at the ground. Andrea didn't get it.

Natalya looked depressed. Defeated even. Without looking up, she spoke with quiet resignation. "Just go home."

Then, louder, into the wind: "Malka! Gella!"

The two characters appeared with Masa, Rei, and Sumi following. They all looked beat.

Natalya looked up distractedly before she walked away. "Oh, I'd mix some vitamin E and aloe vera with an ointment and get it on those blisters before you go to bed tonight."

* * *

Nobody said anything until after they had visited the drugstore and were almost home. Andrea was beyond exhausted. "I don't get it. Why is her Excellion transform so powerful?"

"Magical-girl transform," Rei said.

"Right, whatever. But I mean... Wait, I thought the Excellion transformation was, like, ten times more powerful than a magical-girl transformation."

Something was sneaking up on Andrea, and she was having trouble breathing.

"Andi-chan," Sumi said quietly," we should talk about this tomorrow."

"Wait!" Andrea stopped walking. "That *wasn't* her Excellion transformation?"

Rei wouldn't look at her. "We're all trying to come to terms with it right now. Oh, and those offensive weapons. I don't know how..."

Andrea wanted to stop, but she was too tired. Things had been so desperate tonight, and she hurt so much right now. Between tears, she tried to get to the point. "So, that was a *tiny fraction* of what she can do? I mean, what am I going to do? Tonight was... I can't do any more. She wasn't even trying. I can't do this."

Masa floated up before the group. "We need help."

* * *

By the time Natalya got home, she was in a terrible mood. Natalya had lots of moods, and many of them appeared bad, but Illya knew that most of it was just for show. Diva tantrums were so easy for a girl of Natalya's talents, they were just too good not to use. This, though, was the real thing.

"I hate her."

"Good evening, Natalya. Did you run into Miss Melman during your travels?"

"She's now *flying* her patrols."

"Did you confront her?"

"I beat her up for… what… an hour?"

"And did that do any good?"

"I hate her."

"So, not really, I take it. Has she any special skills you couldn't overcome?"

"She won't give up."

"That sounds familiar. Maybe you're related."

Illya realized that this wasn't a good place to take things, even before Natalya sat down on the floor in front of him. "Oh, that's very funny. This isn't *cute,* Illya. This is Victor. Do you think he'll find her amusing? Do you think he'll take a special interest in her, or are you hoping he'll be merciful and just kill her? I just spent the evening trying to break this girl so we wouldn't have to go to her funeral, and I failed. And you can't stop flirting with her long enough to get a word in edgewise, so what options do we have left to us?"

"I'm sorry. Other than the option of trying to explain everything to her, which you're opposed to, I can't think of any way to make her stop."

"You like this girl," she said softly. "Would you involve her in our misery? Would you destroy her?"

"Of course not. So, you achieved *nothing?* Somehow, I doubt that."

"No. She was impressed—just not enough."

Natalya began doing stretch exercises on the floor. "Oh, and Malka and Gella interacted with her characters. That ought to put a good scare into everyone."

Chapter 18

A good night's sleep might have helped, but nobody got one. Fortunately, it was the weekend, so there was time to nurse all kinds of wounds.

The searing pain from last night's aerial battle, along with the story the characters brought back, kept Andrea's mind off her humiliating defeat in the face of Natalya's superior powers. She was sitting on the floor at the foot of her bed, daubing her arms with fresh ointment, as the characters drifted aimlessly about the room. "So, you guys think her characters are crazy?"

"Deeply disturbed," Rei said.

"I'd go with 'damaged'—maybe *severely* damaged," said Sumi.

"Absolutely freaking crazy," said Masa.

"Gella is simply unhinged," Rei said. "She goes on and on about how she's the goddess of love, and all this weird insane crap. I'd seal her in her egg just to shut her up. And she's the *angel*."

Masa looked troubled. "Malka, the devil character, is borderline psychotic. She bullies Gella constantly. There's something awful behind this. Every second with them was disturbing. Oh, and Natalya won't change or transform with Gella."

"But why?" Andrea wondered aloud. "There must be power there. Even with everything she gets from Malka, you'd think she wouldn't just *ignore* an asset."

"Maybe Gella's powers are damaged as well," Sumi said. "Remember, Illya has this whole cat-based aspect to his transformation, but he doesn't seem to have any flying powers. Maybe there's a connection. This angel/devil thing is just as strange. I mean, *we* haven't seen characters like that before."

"So, is Malka the reason Natalya has these powers?"

"Not just powers—*offensive* powers," Rei said. "We're still trying to understand it. No one has that. How did she get them? What are they even *for?*"

"Really," said Sumi. "What possible use could a guardian character have for that power? It just doesn't make sense."

Rei flitted over to a forlorn nylon string folk guitar, sporting an especially ugly sunflower decal, propped against the wall. Absently plucking a string, she said, "We have the names for Natalya's Excellion transforms."

"Go ahead," Andrea said.

"The Excellion transform with Malka would be called 'Psychotic Charm.' If she ever Excellion transformed with Gella, it would be 'Seraphic Nightmare.' What you encountered last night— her basic magical-girl transformation with Malka—is called 'Bitter Nightshade.' We don't know anything about Gella's basic transform except that Natalya won't even consider using it. And, of course, we have no idea what powers come with Gella's Excellion transformation."

"Except that they would be all about *Lu-u-uv*," Masa said derisively.

Andrea shook her head in bewilderment. "Bitter Nightshade, Psychotic Charm. I don't even know where to start. Guys? Anything?"

Rei was still plunking away on the cringingly out-of-tune guitar as they pondered the question. Masa flew over, backed herself up against the strings to mute the sound, and shot Rei a look of pure exasperation. Rei gave her one back and floated off.

"Andi-chan," Masa said, "we still haven't explored all your powers. You have a range of different immobilizing methods, but we haven't trained with them—at least, not for this kind of situation."

"Do you really think Natalya's going to let me get the heart baton around her? She's so fast." Andrea could feel her courage evaporate as she remembered how thoroughly outclassed she had been trying to outmaneuver Natalya.

"*Let you?* Not in a million years. But maybe we have more than one way of immobilizing her. For one thing, her characters are even more unstable than Nyanka, and he's been more use to us than to Illya so far."

Rei disagreed. "The dynamic is really different with Natalya. Malka and Gella are *really* afraid of her." Zipping over to Andrea, she hovered above the patchwork quilt. "Crazy as she is, Malka won't initiate a character change on Natalya without her permission. And Gella wouldn't *dream* of it."

"Moving on," Andrea said, giving the discussion a gentle nudge. "We do know something about the music and its delivery now. She must patrol on nights when she isn't rehearsing the band, and get to these kids when they're going to bed and more susceptible to—"

"Andi-chan!" Rei shot up in the air. "That's it! We know when she's working with the band—through Gaylen, right? That's when *we* work."

"Rei, that's brilliant."

A concrete plan for collecting eggs without confronting Natalya was the only good news Andrea had heard today. "Okay, Masa, Sumi—what aren't we taking into account here?"

"Illya," Masa said. "We know as little about his real powers now as we did about Natalya's before last night. We've always had the advantage of surprise with him, but that may be over. If you recall, we sort of encouraged him to 'bring it' when we took away his 'hot moves' strategy. I mean, Nyanka's cute and dumb, but Illya's only cute."

This triggered a passionate, four-way argument about how much cuteness and dumbness could or could not be assigned to Illya and Nyanka. Things settled down only with the making and eating of lunch.

"So," Andrea summed up later, "we have temporary immobilizing tools, and we can clean dark eggs. Our only significant 'weapon'— is surprise. We can sense Malka, Gella, and Nyanka half a mile away, and we know when Natalya is unavailable. They, on the other hand, can outfly us and can hurt us quite badly right now, with the possibility of hurting us even worse in the future. And, presumably, they have some sort of 'cat-based powers'—which could pose a problem."

Looking down at her red, blistered hands she said quietly, "Unless we can figure out a way to weaponize the power of friendship, I'm going to have to really stock up on ointment and aloe."

"That would seem to bring us back around to surprise, I guess," Rei suggested. "What do we have in the surprise file?"

"Well," Masa said, "I can think of one thing no one would see coming. Andi-chan, Natalya's rehearsing tonight. How do you feel?"

"Masa, no!" Sumi gasped.

"Well, let's see. I feel completely beat up and humiliated. I'm exhausted and so frustrated I could scream. I'm really scared and have zero confidence in myself and my skills. Why do you ask?"

"Oh, I was just thinking, maybe we could go out tonight and train really hard, learn a bit about my powers, patrol the neighborhood looking for dark eggs and maybe mix it up with Illya. See what he's got besides smooth moves and cute looks. How does that sound?"

"Ambitious?" Andrea murmured.

* * *

By nightfall, she had come around to the idea. If she was learning anything from this experience so far, it was that a decisive commitment to action beat a timid theoretical approach to life. In fact, surviving the First Battle of Natalya had actually boosted certain areas of her confidence, and her decision to immediately re-engage proved motivating for the group.

The leadership that the characters had all but given up on— what with Andrea's endless analysis and second-guessing— finally seemed to be emerging.

They could see it in her surprising decision to continue wearing the half-shredded bomber jacket. Although Andrea claimed that it was just really cold out and she didn't want to put another jacket at risk, seeing her in that tattered leather jacket reminded the characters that their Andi-chan had survived a desperate engagement with a terrifying nemesis without begging for mercy. It made the fact that she had never landed a finger on Natalya somehow heroic instead of hopeless.

The transformation with Masa that night revealed a number of things: first of all, that whoever was designing these outfits needed to look into a broader and more coherent range of options. Luminous Diamond wasn't so much a *bad* look as just sort of confused and unfocused.

What at first glance appeared to be a blue miniskirt was, in fact, culottes, which was just baffling since the long blue-and-white-striped stockings were attached with garters. This made the whole thing look suspiciously like a miniskirt with stockings and garter belt, or, as Andrea termed it, "Creepy Lolita Chic."

Completing the look was, in Andrea's opinion, an unnecessarily complicated light-blue blouse with detached sleeves, a ruffled front, and gravity-defying side-firing ribbons. All topped with an oversize pale-blue hat with a large, blue diamond-shaped decoration.

Her first thought, which she diplomatically kept to herself, was that it could have been worse.

Experimenting a bit, they found that she could transform directly from one character to another without going back to just plain old Andrea. It also worked out that clothing added after a transformation would stick around in the next transformation. Thus, once she transformed and put on the bomber jacket, it wouldn't disappear on her if she transitioned to a different outfit.

Luminous Diamond's main contribution to the cause was a giant paintbrush. It performed the function known as Sparkling Canvas, which projected a field of sparkly paint drops, providing a broad field of immobilization. It meant that Andrea could cast a wide net to hold multiple dark eggs simultaneously.

The big downside was that although Luminous Diamond could jump and float, unlike Luminous Heart, she could not fly. Transforming from Rei in midflight meant initiating a glide back to earth. *Not good.* The idea of trying to run away from any variant of a flying Natalya was simply a nightmare.

Andrea was just getting comfortable with her new powers when Masa got that look signifying a presence. "Masa?"

"Dark eggs."

"As in plural?"

"Yeah."

Transforming back with Rei got them all airborne. The trail led to a group of brownstones across the street from a school, and sure enough, they came upon three zoned-out kids, sitting on some steps at the back of the school yard.

"I need to try out Luminous Diamond," Andrea said to Rei. "I don't want to test-drive this on a Psychotically Charmed Natalya."

"Got it. Sumi, let's take the perimeter."

Changing back into Luminous Diamond, Andrea approached the kids with a jump-and-float combination, which was quicker than walking, and tried to assess how close they were to giving up their eggs. She got her answer almost immediately.

This was her first experience with multiple eggs, and she quickly learned that they had a completely different dynamic from single eggs. For one thing, they were social and playful, and right away they scattered to different parts of the school yard.

It took her a moment to realize they were playing tag, which was a problem since she couldn't get all three eggs in one place at one time. Not knowing what kind of time frame she was dealing with, she decided to settle for two out of three and called for Sparkling Canvas. The big paintbrush was actually easy to handle, and after a couple of tries, she had two eggs locked in a midair float.

Luminous Diamond's version of Bright Heart had a slightly blue tint to the sparkles but was otherwise familiar, and within minutes, two shiny white eggs were headed back to their owners. She was trying to locate the third egg when Illya suddenly leaped down from the school roof into the yard, not ten feet from where she stood.

"Whoa!" Masa was stunned. "But I never felt Nyanka."

"Oh, not expecting me this time?" Illya said, giving Andrea something between a smile and a snarl. "Don't worry, Nyanka will be along shortly. We're not unaware of how things work, you know."

He sniffed the air. "There's only one egg."

Then he noticed the half-shredded bomber jacket. "Nice look."

"Oh, thanks. Your girlfriend helped me style it."

"Oh, yeah… *Who?*"

"Natalya."

"What? Who told you that?"

Andrea gave him a skeptical look. "What do you mean? She was right there when it happened."

"No. Who told you she was my girlfriend?"

"Oh, you're denying it? Wow! Like *you're* ever going to do better. That's kinda pathetic, Illya. I've seen you two together, and—"

"Did she tell you that? Did she use that word?"

Andrea was taken aback.

"I don't know. Yeah. Or maybe I did, but… I mean, she never corrected me, or anything."

"Miss Melman, is it *always* your habit to leap to conclusions like this?"

"No! Wait, don't you guys live together or something?"

"Perhaps that would be yet *another* area that's none of your business, but suffice it to say, she isn't my girlfriend."

Andrea had more important issues to deal with, but now she was intrigued and becoming obsessed with trying to solve the riddle.

"So-o-o—you're just *friends*?"

"Miss Melman…"

"Professional colleagues?"

"Andi-chan? Maybe this isn't the moment?" Masa urged.

"She seemed to really enjoy the connection when I brought it up. Maybe you need to be a bit more demonstrative about your feelings."

"Miss *Melman*—"

"I mean, I don't claim to have any special understanding of these things, but—"

"My sister."

The words rang over the empty school yard, leaving behind an uncomfortably long silence.

"What?" Andrea said weakly.

Softly but with surprising intensity, he repeated, "My *sister,* Miss Melman."

"Wait!" Andrea said, recovering. "I didn't come up with this all on my own."

Masa and Illya looked unconvinced.

"No. Natal—*your sister*—never corrected me. Not once. And every time I said it, she got this big smile and…"

She looked pleadingly at Illya. "All that, just to mess with my head? Can she *be* that evil?"

Illya shrugged. "Well, her sense of humor can be."

Andrea looked crushed. "And you made such a cute couple."

Masa and Illya exchanged a disbelieving look.

"That can't really be your takeaway from this, can it, Miss Melman?"

"Oh, I guess not. So, it was all just a lie? The whole crazy 'I won't lose Illya to you, little girl!' thing?"

"No that's quite in character," he said. "That's just Natalya being Natalya. She'll throw down challenges like that over the last English muffin at breakfast."

Andrea glimpsed a blur overhead, and Illya's hand shot out. Transforming into a huge cat's paw, it reached out twenty or thirty feet to catch the third dark egg and bring it in.

"Wow! I had no idea."

"Yes. I'm not quite as useless as you seem to imagine," he said with a grin.

"I never said…" she started, but he was already leaping up to perch on a second floor window ledge.

"So today we will split these eggs, but I should hope that your recent experiences would be a painful lesson you might take to heart. From here on, Miss Melman, it only gets more painful."

He began to leave and then turned back. "Oh, and nice outfit."

"Wait, what do you mean by that?"

"Well, the culottes are an interesting choice."

"I didn't *ask* for culottes!"

"But the rest of it is nice. I guess the culottes make it a bit more 'age appropriate.'"

"*Age appropriate?* What are you, my *mom?*"

"I have to go find Nyanka. He gets easily distracted, you know."

Sumi and Rei flew in as Illya was bounding off.

"What did we miss?" Rei asked.

Masa laughed. "I'll tell you later."

Andrea was unusually quiet, prompting three inquisitive looks. She just shook her head. "Can you imagine what it must be like, living with a sister like that?"

The characters nodded in agreement.

Chapter 19

"I am disowning you." Natalya proclaimed.

Without looking up Illya replied, "You can't disown your brother."

"I can't live another second under the same roof with you. I'll move into the backyard. No, *you* will move into the backyard. For your treachery."

Illya was sitting in a sprawling old armchair, pretending to read by the light of a modern floor lamp. Everything else about their house was so old and gloomy the lamp came off looking like alien technology.

Natalya stalked about the living room, passing through pools of illumination into shadow. Illya sighed and looked up from his book. "Need I remind you again that it was *you* who created this drama by playing that foolish and irresponsible game with Miss Melman?"

"Oh! Oh, no! *You* do not get to speak to *me* using the words *irresponsible* and *Miss Melman* in the same sentence."

The argument had started the night before, when Illya came home and told Natalya what had happened.

"Our sworn enemy. And you just chat away as if you were on *a date*?"

"Did you expect me to pretend to be your boyfriend just so you could amuse yourself? She's not stupid, you know."

Natalya stalked out of the room, leaving Illya shaking his head. He had seen his sister do this transference trick before: ascribing her reactions about stressful situations to otherwise meaningless issues. Now it was about her game with the Melman girl. You would think he had committed some awful crime, when all he did was take away a favorite toy before she was done playing with it. All he could hope now was that this tempest would blow over as fast as it had come on.

When Natalya returned with two cups of tea, his hopes rose. There was no trace of her "battle aura." He decided to try out a test question. "So where's Gella?"

"What? Oh, I don't know. Malka was giving her a hard time. She may have quit again."

"Or disowned *you?*"

"Whatever. I mean, where's she going to go, anyway?"

* * *

It was starting to get dark. For over an hour now—the longest hour any of them had ever known—Andrea, Rei, Masa, and Sumi had been sitting on the bed, hostage to the nonstop ranting, lecturing, complaining, haranguing, gossiping, crying, praying, singing, and talking, talking, *talking* of Gella.

Andrea had suspected a slight, heat-of-the-moment, exaggeration in her characters' assessment of Natalya's little angel. Now she could see that—if anything—they had been entirely *too* charitable.

"And so now it is to be your divine good fortune to give shelter and succor to the angel of love in this, her darkest hour. Abandoned and in exile, discarded by those who should have cherished and protected her, nourished her dreams and given to the world the light that only I, goddess of all matters concerning the tender arts, can bring to this sad vale of tears, this wicked world... this... Did I mention that my halo works as a radar of love?"

"YES!" her captives shouted together. She had been looping interminably through the same half dozen topics, and they were desperate to finally shut her up.

"It senses love in all its many splendiferous forms and manifestations. I have already swept the area for signs of romance, and I am detecting a strong signal. Prepare your heart for an invasion. I declare signal strength to be overflowing. The angel of love brings you four bars of reception and hereby declares open season for the joining of hearts. Hark! I sense the universe speaking to me now... Andrea Melman, are you ready to accept love into your heart?"

"Uh, what?" Andrea answered. Not that it mattered especially what she said.

"Then open your heart to Angelic Dream."

And with that, Gella's egg suddenly reformed around her, and she did something that, as everyone knew perfectly well, couldn't be done: She forced a full-blown transformation on Andrea.

Andrea came out of the transformation breathless and in mild shock. She couldn't see most of Angelic Dream's outfit, but the openmouthed looks on Rei, Masa, and Sumi's faces told her to get to a mirror—fast.

What she saw looked like a second-grader dressed up for a Christmas play. Pink nightgown with red ribbons. Hair in pigtails. And on her back, a pair of totally fake-looking angel wings.

For a moment, Andrea really didn't know how to respond. Then she remembered that this bizarre getup had been forced on her, and she started using the anger welling up inside to try to take some measure of control. "What the hell is *this*?" she demanded.

Gella backed off, just a bit. "It's your connection to the universal love within all creatures?"

"How dare you just go and do that to me!"

"Oh, great. Now you're starting to sound like Natalya."

"What exactly does this transformation *do* Gella?"

"It…"

"In purely functional terms!"

"Oh."

"Do these wings even work? They look fake."

"Oh, no. Those wings will enchant the heart of any boy you encounter, and—"

"Gella! Do they fly? Do they provide propulsion and lift?"

"Well, not 'fly' in the physical sense…"

Andrea tried to find some upside—any upside—to this unwelcome gift. She was starting to understand why Natalya had cut Gella out of the loop.

"Gella, is there an *actual* power associated with this transformation?"

"Well, with Natalya there's Twilight Cradle. That's a lullaby that can put anyone within range to sleep. In your case, however—I mean, as a third-party transformation—you can summon the power of White Flag to pacify your opponents."

Okay, Andrea thought, *now we're getting somewhere.* "Do I just call it?"

"Yes. Just focus your heart on the—"

"White Flag!"

She found herself holding a pair of white flags.

"Okay, so how do I use them?"

"You surrender!"

Blank stares all around.

Gella looked immensely proud of her answer. "Pacifying your enemies."

Dead silence.

"Ending all conflict."

Nothing.

"Bringing peace?"

Rei rolled her eyes. Masa held her face in her hands and moaned. Sumi was too stunned to speak. Dropping the flags, Andrea was now beyond even the pretense of civility. "Here's how it's going to be, Gella."

Gella started to react, but Andrea's hand shot up to silence her.

"For the time being, you can remain here."

Her characters let go a collective groan that brought up the other hand.

"Provided you stop harassing us with your constant chatter, behave yourself as a guest, and never, *ever* take it upon yourself to force a transformation on me *ever* again, or so help me, I will stuff you with whipped cream, bake you in a four-hundred-degree oven, and serve you for dessert. Agreed?"

"Now you sound *exactly* like Natalya."

"AGREED*?*"

"Yes! Yes!"

* * *

The very next morning, Andrea was waiting outside K290 to intercept Natalya before she got to school. There was no subtlety to this ambush. She practically ran at her from a block away.

Natalya started laughing as soon as she saw her coming. Only one thing could cause that.

"Natalya!" Andrea gasped.

Natalya tried to compose herself. The best she could manage was a deadpan smirk. "Miss Melman, have you anything that belongs to me? Perhaps a thousand dollars' worth of dark eggs I believe you owe us?"

Andrea wasn't about to go into that discussion. "I have Gella."

"And you want to ransom her back to me?"

"What? No! You *have* to take her back."

"I didn't send her away."

"Natalya, please. She's driving us crazy."

"I'm sure the United Nations has a policy on the self-determination of guardian characters. Gella is free to make her own choices."

"Natalya!"

"Perhaps this would be a good moment to reflect on the wisdom of involving oneself in the affairs of others."

"Natalya, please. We can't take it anymore."

"Well, since you seem so desperate... hm-m-m... no."

"Oh, my God. What do you want to take her back?"

"Nothing. I don't want her back. I'm enjoying a nice moment of peace and quiet that's been very helpful to my creative endeavors."

"A-a-a-a-ah-h. Please!"

The pleading continued all the way up to and into the school, down the halls, and up the stairs toward Natalya's homeroom. Surrounded by the noise and chaos of hundreds of high school students in motion, they made a memorable sight: the normally reserved Andrea talking a mile a minute and gesturing wildly, and the imperious ice queen, Natalya, sporadically bursting out in uncharacteristic laughter.

Holding this over Andrea was great fun, and Natalya dragged it out to the door of her classroom, down to the last possible second. "Okay! Stop. Your begging no longer amuses me." Which both of them knew was a total lie.

"I will take her back…" Andrea's eyes lit up.

"… a week from today." A soft wail escaped Andrea's lips.

"*Providing…* you and your little gang leave the field to Illya and me for that entire week."

As desperate as Andrea was to lose the angel of love, this was a bitter pill to swallow. She tried a weak negotiation. "So… no contesting dark eggs?"

"No patrols whatsoever."

Andrea looked down. It wasn't much of a win.

"Oh, come on. You can focus on whatever sad little life you might have left these days. Your characters will be training your ass off to stop us, and who knows? You might even learn something useful from Gella."

Andrea looked up, beaten, but calm. "Okay. I mean, it's only been about a month anyway."

This seemed to startle Natalya. "A *month?*"

"Yeah. A month since I got my characters. My birthday was, like, a month ago or so and…"

Natalya didn't hear her. This little girl who had survived a sustained attack with nothing but pom-poms and a pair of sparkly flying roller skates had possessed her powers for only a *month*? Natalya had been flying with her characters for almost ten years.

Arrogant as she might appear to some, Natalya never dismissed anything that might prove a threat. Andrea wouldn't be the only one training this week.

Chapter 20

Predictably, the deal over Gella satisfied no one—except Natalya, of course. Still, within a day or two, things settled into a routine and life went on.

Gella had a disturbing habit of keeping a journal, which Masa sneaked a peek at and reported to be just more of the same inane ramblings about love that she normally spouted.

So they stopped worrying about it. Besides, there was work to be done.

Hanging over everything were Natalya's two powers. Andrea wasn't sure which one bothered her more.

Bitter Nightshade was pretty simple to wrap your mind around if you've ever been chased around by biting, stinging butterflies in acid plasma. It gave Andrea anxiety attacks just thinking about it.

On the other hand, Psychotic Charm gave her nightmares. Since encountering Gella and finding her to be certifiably nuts, the idea of an Excellion transformation based on Malka was simply terrifying. A major power-up from a sadistic sociopath was almost too much to contemplate.

Gella, as it happened, was around this week because Malka had been waging a campaign of abuse centered on the theme of "a character one never transforms with isn't a character worth keeping alive."

Andrea didn't really understand the theory behind what ended a character's life, but just the idea of it seemed akin to encouraging someone to commit suicide. It made her sick.

The only useful way to deal with any of it was to train, and so that's what she did. But a girl could not live by training alone. Natalya's little crack about "whatever sad little life you might have left these days" seemed to have been directed at Masa, Sumi, and Rei, and they made sure that she did more than just training and homework.

They planned out the week away from patrolling to include a couple of activities that might lure their Andi-chan into social settings. The most successful of these was getting her to a school dance.

Only the fact that one of Gaylen's bands was playing did the trick. If it wasn't likely to be an enchanted evening, knowing someone in the band would at least make it a lot more fun.

Gaylen had a wide circle of acquaintances and that night she made a point of dragging Andrea around to various groups of people. As it was, Andrea spent most of the evening watching Gaylen play in what she called her "funky dance band." It was amazing for Andrea to see someone so close to her own age produce such accomplished music and have fun doing it.

In the middle of their final set, the band went into a slow-dance medley, and Andrea took the opportunity to tear herself away from the side of the stage and take a walk around the gym. It was slow going. The dance floor was sparsely occupied by a few "real" couples, and even fewer individuals brave enough to make or accept a dance invitation. That left everyone else crowded around the periphery.

Although she was hardly the only person on her own, Andrea couldn't help but see that almost everyone was laughing and talking in small groups or pairs. It surprised her that most people would actually be comfortable in this kind of social situation. *God,* she thought, *they're really enjoying this. This is actually fun for most people.*

She eased her way into the crowd around the refreshments table. *What is wrong with me? Why can't I do this? How hard can it be to learn to make small talk?*

By the time she finally had a cup of tepid punch in hand, she was well on her way to making herself miserable. *Am I really that weird? No. No way. Natalya has to be at* least *as weird as I am. No! She's* twice *as weird. I mean, she'd never even come to something like this in a million years. But if she did, she'd probably handle it better than I am...*

The slow dance ended, and Andrea dropped her untouched cup of punch in the trash and started back toward the stage.

* * *

Meanwhile, Natalya, free from the twin distractions of Andrea and Gella, was having a great time with her program. Black Swan Brigade was now officially renamed Black Swan Revenge. And if Andrea thought the break was designed just to let Natalya and Illya collect more eggs, she was quite mistaken. Dark eggs were indeed collected in good quantities, but Black Swan Revenge worked in four rehearsals that week. Natalya was busy rearranging old material to work with her new rhythm section and writing new compositions to take advantage of the newfound power. The entire band was energized by the change.

Still, the end of the week left Natalya Volkova filled with longing. All she wanted to do was create, and she was weary of having to steal time to do so. But that was her situation, and she held no illusions about changing it.

* * *

Truth be told, Andrea's week with Gella hadn't been all bad. Aside from the endless ramblings, Gella actually seemed to find a place with them. Every once in a while, she would say something to make Andrea wonder. Some of her crazier comments could even be interpreted as strangely insightful.

The outside world held no terrors for the goddess of love. She came and went as she pleased, and yet always seemed to be around when any sort of discussion broke out. Masa seemed worried that she was spying, but Andrea could feel the loneliness beneath Gella's spacey demeanor. She just wanted to be part of anything that would have her. Still, her squinting eyes never lost their disturbing quality.

Sumi mentioned that Gella never flew very quickly, and wondered whether her sight was impaired somehow. She didn't want to ask, but it was just one more thing to make you wonder.

The other major activity of Andrea's week was supposed to be training with Sumi on her transformation, Luminous Star. But somehow, that kept being put off. Finally, late on the last day of the break, the four of them went into the backyard for a quick transformation and an even quicker rundown on Restoration Heart. Restoration Heart was difficult for Andrea to grasp. It was supposed to "repair broken things" and "restore what was lost," which seemed to mean everything and nothing.

Since everything seemed to require a giant something-or-other to function, Andrea wasn't entirely surprised to find herself holding a huge whisk broom, looking around for something to repair or restore.

They settled on a kitchen chair and did a credible job of restoring it. Then—realizing that Dion would notice the change—they had to mess it up again.

Andrea was so unfocused, she never really looked at Luminous Star's outfit, except to note that it was green and rather poufy.

* * *

As the only one not driven to complete distraction by Gella, Sumi ended up being her minder. At week's end, she accompanied Gella back to Illya and Natalya's house. Flying into the kitchen, they interrupted Natalya making tea. A potentially awkward situation was averted when Natalya invited Sumi to join her.

Gella flew off, and Natalya and Sumi had one of those odd moments when one sits down to tea with a sworn enemy and finds oneself having a rather nice time of it. Although conversational topics were necessarily somewhat limited, Sumi was impressed with Natalya's demeanor and sophistication.

After an hour, when both of them knew that this guilty pleasure had to end, Natalya made the unusual gesture of walking Sumi to the front door.

The door hadn't even closed when she called out loudly, "Malka, transform with me. I need to train with you!"

Sumi hung out across the street in front of the house for a minute, wondering what to make of it. Seconds later, the lights of a character transformation spilled out of the backyard, followed by the figure of Natalya, fully engaged as Bitter Nightshade and rising up past the roof. Suddenly, a thick burst of purple and black madness shot up into the night sky. It was a display of power with a clear purpose.

On her return, Sumi reported this to the group.

"Wow," Masa said. "She *really* wants us to back off."

The room went quiet as everyone contemplated what a confrontation might mean at this point. The week's training had gone well, but no one was under any illusion that anything had really changed, and a disturbing sense of pessimism started to set in.

* * *

The next morning, Andrea was awakened by small fingers poking her head and an annoyingly chirpy voice calling out, "Miss Melman? Miss Melman?" She sat up in bed suddenly, and found herself face-to-face with a new character.

Straight auburn hair, a yellow mini dress with white belt, and a white headband with an inverted triangle decoration. Hovering impatiently and beaming a smile made of weapons-grade perkiness.

As Rei had discovered, Andrea wasn't really at her best meeting new characters first thing in the morning, and something about this character's outfit and frozen smile immediately rubbed her the wrong way. "What? I'm sorry, who are you?" The question was meant for the new character, but the others were quick to jump in and answer.

"Our supervisor," Rei said, sullenly.

"Our commanding officer," Masa added, coldly.

"The bitch who's responsible for dropping us into this nightmare," Sumi said, with surprising hostility.

The newly arrived character seemed unfazed by their responses; she simply curtsied and smiled brightly at Andrea. "Hello, Miss Melman. My name is Janelle, and it's a pleasure to meet you."

Andrea, noting her characters' collective irritation, thought it best to withhold judgment. "We'll see about that, Janelle." It was the best she could manage.

The graphic theme of Janelle's outfit was an inverted triangle, which extended to her egg's decoration. Andrea was starting to find this reliance on cute icons tiresome, but then, it was still early in the day to be evaluating new things.

Either Janelle was one hell of a positive girl, or she was really used to people not liking her. Masa, Sumi, and Rei's overt hostility seemed not to have the slightest effect on her mood. "A little birdie told me that you might be having a few difficulties adjusting to the busy life of a magical girl, Miss Melman."

Andrea couldn't believe how much she could hate someone based on two sentences. With an effort, she kept silent.

"It can be a challenge trying to manage your new responsibilities and strike a balance with your high school activities, but I know that together we can find solutions to work with all of the—"

"Oh, God, shut *up!*"

Andrea had lost the battle to remain silent—or even civil—and was now fighting the urge to simply strangle Janelle. Still, she realized that if she didn't set the tone of the relationship, Janelle would, so she tried a different approach.

"Look, Janelle, I don't know why you're here or what your story is, but right now we're kind of busy trying to not get stomped into the ground by an opponent who outclasses us in every possible way. I don't know if you've ever been attacked by purple butterflies floating in acid plasma, but if you don't have anything useful to contribute to *that* challenge then I'd appreciate it if you would just zip it."

Janelle tried to jump on the end of Andrea's outburst with an attack of her own. "As it happens, Miss Melman, Masa's was the correct answer to your question. I am the commanding officer in charge of this operation, and—"

"Oh, so then, you *are* the bitch responsible for dropping them into this nightmare?"

"That is hardly the way I would put it…"

"Well, ignoring for the moment the fact that you're not *my* commanding officer, Janelle, I'm guessing that *you* have a commanding officer—maybe even a bunch of them—and that you're here now because they want to know why your people are in such a mess. How'm I doing, Janelle? Am I close?"

Suddenly Janelle was at a complete loss for words.

"Oh, okay, well, how about this, Janelle: Do you have *any* idea what's going on right now? Masa? I'm guessing it was you who sent out a distress signal?"

"Andi-chan, I didn't mean to go behind your back…"

"No, it's okay. I trust your judgment. Was there enough detail in it for Janelle to have any idea what's going on here?"

"Definitely not."

Andrea realized that she had let her emotions drive the situation too much and that she immediately needed to dial it back. "Look, Janelle, I'm a bit on edge here, but before they brief you on where things stand, you should know something. We've been through a lot in the last few weeks, and I've had my doubts about a lot of stuff. In fact, the only thing I don't doubt at this point is that my characters have had my back. I know there's a lot they can't tell me, but I have never felt for a second that they had anything but my welfare and the welfare of the mission as their top priorities.

"You may be their boss back where you guys come from, but over here, they've let me call the shots. And I've followed their training and advice, and we have come through some pretty scary situations in one piece. So don't think for an instant that your rank is intimidating to me. *Their* opinions are the ones I trust, and right now, they don't seem to have a very high opinion of *you*. So, unless you plan on doing this mission yourself, you'd better start worrying about what this team needs and how you can help supply it."

* * *

As she floated there, humiliated at having been dressed down by a child in front of her own team, Janelle consoled herself with one thought: *No doubt about it. That's a Morrighan.*

Chapter 21

The briefing that Andrea's characters gave Janelle was bad. Really bad. The description of Illya and Natalya, their tactics and their powers, appeared to be completely new to her. There wasn't supposed to be any serious opposition to the egg cleaning. Moreover, if everything they were saying was true, very little of the original mission still made sense.

That said, Janelle hadn't gotten to her position of authority by being sincere or self-effacing. She dug down deep, got in touch with her inner bureaucrat, and started nodding affirmatively without confirming or denying anything—and then proceeded to minimize and belittle everything they had to say.

Besides, even though it was obviously not going to address any of their issues, she did have something to offer them.

"Janelle, did you manage to bring *anything* with you for us to use against this?" Rei asked.

"Aw, Rei, you spoiled my little surprise!" she chirped.

Janelle floated over to her egg and pulled out something about two inches squared, covered with tissue paper. "This is something we recently developed especially for you." She pulled off the tissue paper to reveal what looked, to the untrained eye, like a cheap little H-shaped pendant with a tacky rainbow-themed surface.

No one reacted to the unveiling.

"Uh, what does it do?" Andrea asked flatly.

"Oh, Miss Melman, I'm *so* glad you asked! This is a working prototype of the H-lock. It allows you to combine within yourself the powers of four guardian characters into a single, new guardian entity with the sum of the original four characters!"

This revelation earned Janelle a wall of skeptical looks.

"H-lock?" Sumi asked.

"Prototype?" Rei asked.

"You do realize we only have *three* guardian characters available, right?" Masa asked.

"*Prototype?*" Andrea repeated.

Janelle wasn't about to lose momentum by addressing serious questions. "Now, I'm sure we can overcome *any* of your concerns with a little constructive problem solving."

"Okay," Masa said. "What part of 'only three characters available' can we overcome with constructive problem solving?"

"Well, now, contrary to your —I'd like to acknowledge—well presented and highly informative briefing, *our* projections indicate that there should be quite a number of guardian characters in this area."

Masa was fuming. "We were led to believe this area had *dozens* of characters."

"Recent developments have forced a reassessment of certain critical assumptions about the situation here. Still, our underlying methodologies are still believed to be sound, and I feel you are displaying a bit of unwarranted pessimism in this claim of—"

Rei threw down a topographical map of the New York metropolitan area. Grid markings, overwritten with dates and times, overlaid the entirety of Brooklyn, Queens, and parts of Nassau County.

Sumi took over. "On Rei's recommendation, we undertook a grid search of these areas over the last three weeks, working at night and around Andrea's schedule. Masa has estimated that this area contains over three million humans. Our character sensing, recently recalibrated and assessed at a nominal half a mile, point to point, indicates that other than the deranged Malka and Gella, that pervert Nyanka, and the three of us, there are *no characters in this area!*"

Janelle looked blankly back at her.

"*None!*" Sumi was starting to lose her temper. "Not a *single one!*"

"Has anyone tested this prototype?" Rei asked.

"Well, of course that would be impossible to do back home, but we have a high degree of confidence that—"

"Confidence based on what?" Andrea jumped in.

"Projections from both our simulations and our estimates based on past performance of similar systems."

"No, Janelle." Masa said. "Without real-world testing, I wouldn't even call a device a *prototype,* much less a 'working prototype.' And what, might I ask, constitutes a 'similar system'?"

Andrea cut in, "Janelle, what possible use would the device be with only three characters?"

"There's a theoretical possibility that you would merely combine the powers and strengths of the three characters."

"Any other theoretical possibilities I might be interested in?"

"Well…"

"'Nobody knows' is the answer," Masa interjected with mounting aggravation. "You would be at the mercy of a jury-rigged attempt to make a weapon out of a grab bag of theories, thrown against the wall and evaluated through a haze of wishful thinking."

Andrea smiled at Masa. "Oh. Okay. Thanks. Just trying to balance out any unwarranted optimism. I feel much better now. Do we have any other options? Even bad ones?"

Universal silence greeted her question. "Okay," Andrea continued, "So, unless we're prepared to give up right now—and for the record, I am not—I think we need to work out a plan for testing this 'H-lock' thing. If we're lucky, it won't result in any *completely* horrible consequences. Masa, a little birdie told me that *you* might have a passing acquaintance with simulating complex systems…"

Not that she would have shared it, but Janelle was relieved to see Andrea moving things forward.

* * *

When Natalya got home, Illya was waiting with a look that could mean only one thing.

"Viktor called." She sat down and faced him expectantly. "He wants to change the schedule."

Nothing Viktor wanted could be good, but this was an ominous request.

"He wants to—in his words—*formalize the procedure*. He says he now wants a fixed numbers of eggs."

Natalya felt a knot forming in the pit of her stomach.

"He's expecting more demand."

Only one question remained, and she didn't need to ask it.

"He wants ten eggs a week."

"That's ridiculous!"

"He suggested that he might move back in with us if we needed motivation."

These days, it took a lot to get Natalya to cry, but somehow Viktor could always find the right thing.

Chapter 22

As the days past, Janelle's unrealistic scenarios, unfounded assumptions, and relentless bureaucratic happy talk was getting under everyone's skin. She couldn't see it, but the kind of behavior that had made her a big star in her position at home was having dimensional translation issues.

Janelle would never admit it to anyone, but the team's assessment of everything was pretty accurate. This really was a nightmare, and the more she learned about it, the worse it got. Numerous facts used to establish other key assumptions had simply evaporated. Nothing in her experience had prepared her for this level of chaos and uncertainty.

Janelle was also scared on a whole other level. She had worked with these characters for a very long time, but their personalities were becoming completely different. When did Rei become efficient and disciplined? And Sumi calling her a bitch in front of the others? Just enough New York attitude seemed to have rubbed off on the characters to make dealing with them an entirely new situation. And Janelle didn't like any situation she couldn't control. This, she positively hated. But there was a mission, and right now, she was the only one here who knew what it was.

A few hours of hands-on testing with the H-lock left everyone frustrated. While nothing bad had happened, not enough good had happened to balance the disparity between Andrea and Natalya.

Basically, the only "shared power" was the pom-poms; one could use them with all the transformations. But it still left Andrea unable to fly when she transformed with Masa or Sumi. Based on recent experience, flying away in terror from Natalya seemed infinitely preferable to running away in terror.

* * *

But really, Andrea thought. *What difference would that make anyway?*

She had started to wonder about things. What was an aggressive power like Bitter Nightshade doing in this context? She was dying to ask Natalya what it was for—other than for scaring the hell out of her, of course.

At this point, the tendency was to blame Janelle for everything, but whether she was or was not responsible, the break initiated by Gella's arrival was still in place a week after she'd gone back to Natalya's. That said, no one was really complaining.

Still, it felt odd to be preparing to resume patrolling with Janelle around. It was obvious she needed to check out the situation firsthand, but her presence threw the group off, and they all wished she were gone.

* * *

Returning from the break highlighted a number of changes. Andrea's bike was a thing of the past. From now on, all patrols would be flown as Crystal Bright Heart Lunation. The plan was to resume on Friday, but then Gaylen caught her in the hall on Wednesday with some bad news. "I don't know what's going on, but BSR isn't rehearsing for the next few weeks. Natalya seems *really* bummed out about it."

Gaylen seemed to sense that Andrea held the keys to at least a few of Natalya's mysteries. She stopped talking for a long moment in hopes that Andrea might fill the silence with something interesting but when nothing did, she continued, "So, Friday night will be Latin night for me instead. Wanna come? It's a bunch of Dominicans playing salsa classics with a Cuban flair, and this funky Irish girl on bass."

Andrea laughed, but begged off.

* * *

No one knew what to make of this news, but that night something worked its way up through Andrea's subconscious as she slept. Something born in the first moments of her heroic defeat to Natalya on that awful night. A critical issue, quickly forgotten in the heat of battle and then buried by the distraction of dealing with Janelle. Around four in the morning, she woke from terrible dreams to find the characters clustered anxiously around her.

She couldn't tell them anything. It should have been obvious long before now. All she could say was, "I need to talk to Natalya right away."

Chapter 23

Natalya was dead set against it, but Andrea just persisted until she finally agreed to meet.

Andrea figured that a food court in a busy shopping mall with its noisy crowds would provide a good measure of privacy. Unfortunately, as she was well aware, Brooklyn didn't have any *real* shopping malls.

It had a few large indoor collections of national retail outlets, but by the classic standard of the American shopping mall, not even the huge Kings Plaza Shopping Center made the grade. Not for a girl raised in the Midwest at least.

So, on Saturday morning, she found herself walking cautiously through Brooklyn's closest approximation of an indoor mall on Atlantic Avenue. Cramped and malodorous, with intimidating groups of kids wandering about and a tone of employee rudeness unusual even by New York standards, it actually made her miss Ohio for the first time in quite a while.

Natalya was already waiting at the agreed-upon national franchise. They got some scalding-hot tea and sat down on the outer fringe of seating, almost in the walkway.

Natalya seemed to be on guard that she would be asked to do something impossible—or, worse, discuss something personal—but Andrea surprised her. "I give up."

Natalya didn't get it. "What? You give up what?"

"The eggs. I give up. I'm not going after any more eggs. You win. I give up."

Natalya regarded this surrender with deep suspicion. "*Really? And what prompted this sudden change of heart? You have been relentless up to now. Why should I even believe this, coming from you?*"

"I had a dream."

"That's... um, *interesting*. And what did this dream tell you?"

"That I can't protect my characters. I saw them in my dream, getting hit, and I knew they couldn't survive it. I don't know if you would try to hit them, but once things start, I can't protect them."

Natalya sat back in her chair. She seemed to sink into herself, different emotions playing out on her face. At one point, she looked up in annoyance at Andrea, but in time, an internal argument seemed to play out, and she relaxed as she accepted its conclusion. When Natalya finally started talking again, she seemed like a different person. "Thank God. I didn't think you were ever going to understand." She fixed her gaze down on her hands and said in a soft voice, "Years ago, Nyanka was fooling around while I was working with Bitter Nightshade. He flew right into the stream. It was horrible. He almost died. It took him a year to recover. He never trusted me again."

A harried mother dragged two screaming children past them, and the conversation paused until the howling blended back into the general noise. Natalya stirred her tea and looked up. "I never bring Gella out anywhere. She's so unreliable. And Malka—it was a gamble transforming with her and then letting her go off without me. She's capable of terrible things, but I couldn't think of any other way to engage your characters. I had no idea how I was going to get them out of the way next time."

Andrea wasn't sure how to respond. "Couldn't you have told me?"

Almost smiling, Natalya gave her a look that seemed to come from a much older person. "You trust people, Andrea. I trust nothing, and assume that my adversary will do the same."

Andrea pondered that for a moment. "Isn't that a kind of trust?"

Natalya laughed. "I trust my adversary will never trust me—is a kind of trust? Okay, maybe." Her seriousness returned. "Your characters trust you, don't they?"

"Well, yeah, I think they do."

"And you trust them?"

"Oh, sure, of course."

Natalya said nothing. Andrea suspected that Natalya's silences were never just dead air. Gradually, she understood the implicit challenge at the heart of this one. Their eyes met. Natalya was waiting for her to make a connection.

"God, Natalya! You are such a trip!"

Natalya smiled, but kept silent.

"So, let me see if I understand this. You have suspicions about the characters. Mine. Yours. Maybe the whole concept of guardian characters in general. But if I'm just young, dumb, happy little

171

Andrea running around in her dream world, you're *not* going to wake me up?"

Natalya took a sip of tea. "Dreams are precious luxuries. I have no use for them, but I have seen them casually destroyed, and I will not willingly disturb the dreamer or cause them to doubt their happiness."

An employee appeared nearby, sweeping trash from the empty tables with his forearm into a big plastic garbage bag. He shot them a dirty look for not being ready to discard the cups in front of them, and then moved off to the back of the store.

"Natalya, outside of you, me, and Illya, do you know of anyone else who has guardian characters?"

"No, I do not."

"Well, doesn't that make us the people most likely to benefit from a guardian character support group?"

"Perhaps, but our situations are very different, and the powers we each possess are being applied to very different ends. Sharing our knowledge could compromise a number of situations, now and in the future, for all concerned. Besides, to a great extent, our situation—Illya's and mine—is not ours to determine."

Andrea considered this for a minute. "Okay," she said, "but given that, there still must be certain issues that would be safe for us to talk about."

"Such as?" Natalya cocked a skeptical eyebrow.

"Oh, I don't know. Lots of things. What about these eggs, for a start? What are they? Why are people so anxious to possess them? What do they actually *do?*"

"Ah, yes. What do they do? We've pondered that for some time. The truth is, we have no idea what they're used for. For a long time, I assumed that, like most things with disproportionate value, the eggs either restored hair or enhanced virility, but I've never found any confirmation of that."

Shaking her head, Andrea looked down and laughed. "Really! Restored hair or... wow."

Natalya smiled. "Recent progress to the contrary, it's still very much a man's world, you know. So, do you know why your characters are so interested in preserving the creative potential of children?"

Andrea almost jumped on her answer, but the more time she spent around Natalya, the more she questioned anything that came too easily. A long moment passed with no hint of pressure from Natalya to move the discussion along.

When Andrea finally and carefully said, "No, I don't," it carried the seeds of a dozen other questions.

"You understand, I don't mean to make you doubt the sincerity of your characters. If anything, I would question what they themselves know about the situation."

"Oh there's a lot they don't know about things here—I mean, about what they expected to find. In their terms. They know lots about this world, but something seems to have changed on them. Oh, and there's a new character: Janelle. She was—well, is—their boss or commanding officer or something, and we all can't stand her and…"

Natalya's look stopped her midsentence.

"Maybe I should have mentioned that first?"

Putting down her tea, Natalya leaned back and stared in amazement.

"Andrea Melman, for ten years Illya and I believed that we possessed the only three guardian characters in existence. You now have *four?*"

"Well, strictly speaking, I don't think of Janelle as one of *my* characters. I mean, really? She gets on my last nerve and…"

Somehow, Natalya's presence was causing a shift in Andrea's understanding, and for the first time since Rei popped out of her shell a month ago, the sheer strangeness of it all was working its way into her consciousness. Fragments of memory floated across her awareness, each one leaving unsettling echoes.

The hum of activity in the mall was developing a discernible pitch, like a sustained chord on a pipe organ, or the low howl of an approaching storm. She felt again that original nugget of uncertainty and danger that she had so quickly dismissed, so easily traded for the fascination of engaging with a strange new world.

The rhythm of bodies in motion, flowing in and out of storefronts and along the walkways, seemingly random, yet inevitable. Predetermined. Why hadn't she considered all this in the same cautious way that she approached every other thing in her life? They hadn't even *tried* to convince her, and she had never asked for a shred of proof. Was that faith? Madness? Or just stupidity? A blurry co-coon of shape and sound drew in around her. Questions unasked, and lines of inquiry not pursued. Who were they? Fear arose and stole her breath. What had she done? Whom had she put at risk?

The noise of the mall was drowning out her thoughts. People walking by seemed to see nothing unusual: at most, two girls at a table—one self-possessed, the other a bit dazed, perhaps upset, her eyes trying to find focus on a distant horizon.

When she finally spoke, it was with the voice of a frightened little girl. "Oh, Natalya, what have I done? What do they want?"

Natalya took her hands and tried to make eye contact, but Andrea was sinking into an abyss of fear. "Andrea, listen to me. I'm right here. Find my voice, and follow it."

The words floated in and out of Andrea's perception, as if coming from a great distance over a windy field. "Our world is a series of dualities. Light and dark. Order and chaos. As above, so below. Order is nature, creating from the blueprints in our genetic codes. Chaos is an ocean; huge and terrifying, but beautiful and life-giving. From a distance, chaos appears threatening, but it is merely unknown."

Andrea felt like a camera lens going in and out of focus as she struggled to follow what Natalya was saying and to separate her voice from the background noise. "You need to step out of your fear, but first you need to look at it. Don't try to conquer it. Just acknowledge it. There is you. There is also the fear. You have the choice to view the one from the other. Don't view yourself from the fear. View the fear from *you*. You are the vessel. Find your center. Stay aboard. Ride it out."

Gradually, the food court came back into focus. The bored security guards, the endless lines of people in contrary motion on the escalators, the hum of music and talk forming a comforting backdrop of day-to-day reality.

Andrea realized she was gripping Natalya's hands. She let go and could see the deep red marks she had left there.

Without comment, Natalya took another sip of tea.

This isn't the first time she's talked somebody down from a ledge, Andrea realized. *What kind of life do you lead to get that sort of knowledge?* She suppressed a wave of sorrow at the thought.

"Who are they, Natalya? What do they want?"

"Yes, those are, of course, the central questions. But I suspect the answers are currently unknowable to us and that the real issue is more like 'What can we learn, and what are the first questions we should be asking?' I will tell you this: Before you came along, Illya and I were unable to see the most fundamental question."

"Which is?"

"Which is, 'Why can't we ask the most fundamental questions?'"

"Okay, is that some sort of Zen paradox?"

Natalya gave a quick smile, which vanished as a couple of guys decked out in licensed sportswear cruised by, checking the girls out with perfunctory glances. She paused till they were gone.

"No... Well, perhaps, but not intentionally. The question is, why is it so hard to ask questions about our situations regarding the world of the characters? We were introduced young, so we had believed it was familiarity that kept our analytical faculties at bay. But that certainly can't be *your* problem. You're too analytical for your own good, and yet, in no time at all, you were swallowed by this narrative your characters provided."

"You think they're lying to us?"

"No, that's not quite it. Again, it's not that I think they're being dishonest with us. I have a suspicion that they may be, oh, I don't know..." Natalya checked her watch. "I have to go soon. Why don't we walk back to the neighborhood?"

The way back passed from the hectic urban setting of downtown Brooklyn through long stretches of residential brownstones. They were halfway back, walking through a quiet area of local stores, when Natalya stopped in her tracks. "Okay, two things I may come to regret bringing up. Illya and I have been tasked to provide more eggs than before. The demand for more eggs was at the heart of my concern about further confrontations. Matters are no longer within our power to shape. I was actually contemplating making a direct appeal to convince you to back off. The forces compelling Illya and me are far more immediate and dangerous than anything a bunch of crazy pixies could ever come up with."

She held Andrea's gaze, as if to emphasize her next words. "Past this point, you, your family, and everything you hold dear are in grave danger, far beyond our power to protect or even help.

Your decision has lifted from my heart a burden that was destroying me. I am truly grateful you have spared me this."

Andrea was surprised by her seriousness. Not knowing how to respond, she said, "What was the second thing you're going to regret bringing up?"

Natalya smiled and continued walking. "Oh, I'm just thinking that there might be a connection between my increased demand and your visit from a higher authority."

Andrea pondered that as they passed a large park. The percussive squeak of a one-on-one basketball game off in the distance filled the air around them until she offered an ill-considered answer. "Well, actually, that started because we ran out of options for how to stand up to you, and Masa sent some kind of message to their headquarters and… Oh, I'll bet this is one of those things that might compromise future stuff and all."

Natalya gave a bemused sigh. "Well, yes. The fact that you've run out of options—that would be something you might not have wanted to tell me. But the really interesting thing is the idea that your characters are in communication with a home base and that they operate within a military-style hierarchy."

"Yeah, I was thinking the same thing. Pixies with military skills. What's that all about?"

Natalya didn't reply, and they fell into talking about Gaylen. Andrea learned that her mother had died when she was only five years old, and that her father had passed away a few years ago.

"Oh, that's so sad. But she's so strong and together. How does she do it? I'd fall completely apart going through something like that."

"It gets worse. Her stepmother is a hard-core born-again who is part of this movement—what is it, 'God's Dominion'?"

"Please tell me you don't mean Dominion of God."

"That's it."

"Oh, wow! Look 'em up. They're not just hard core; they're a bunch of violent psychos. They believe all sorts of insane things." Andrea got quiet. "They're, like, the only evangelicals left who actively preach the whole 'suffer not a witch to live' thing. To them, it's a biblical obligation to kill witches. There's all this discussion on Wiccan forums now about how far to go in the name of self-defense. People are really upset. I mean, there's all kinds of witches, and some of them raise animals for food and hunt, but, you know, arming yourself for protection from modern witch hunters is just *crazy*. I've never even touched a gun, but if someone is trying to kill you or your… well, anyway…"

Natalya sighed with deeper concern. "Really, Andrea. I hope you're a little bit more careful with other people about your personal business."

"What? Oh, right. Well, you're actually the only person I've mentioned this Wicca stuff to—except my parents and my characters."

She grinned; then the grin evaporated. "Okay, what's really kind of sad is the fact that my character friends currently outnumber my human friends."

Passing through a local business district, they were about to split up when Natalya eyed a nondescript car in the street. Curious, Andrea started to turn for a better look, but Natalya seized her hand and practically dragged her into a store.

Looking around in bemused disbelief, Andrea had to ask, "Really Natalya? We're going shopping *here?*"

"Uh, what? Sure, yeah, shopping."

Natalya was edgy and still looking out at the street.

"Isn't it a little early in our relationship to be mattress shopping?"

Natalya seemed suddenly aware of the dozens of beds surrounding them, and the tolerant but amused looks on the faces of the staff.

"Oh." She let go of Andrea's hand and went up to an older woman behind the counter. "Is there a back exit we could use? I think that's my ex outside, and I just don't want to deal with him today."

The smile vanished, replaced with a look of knowing concern. The woman ushered them past the rows of beds through to the back.

"Don't you worry, honey. If he comes in and asks, I'll say you're in the bathroom. Right down to the left. You'll come out on a side street that'll take you to the subway."

"Thank you so much," Natalya said.

"I know all about it, honey. Anytime."

* * *

They took the local one-stop without speaking. When they came out of the station, Andrea was surprised to see Natalya looking at her with real fear. It looked strange and out of place on her. More disturbing yet, a note of panic had crept into her voice. "Oh, Andrea, he's seen you. He knows you. Why didn't I act sooner?"

"Natalya, what *is* it?"

But she wasn't listening. "This changes everything. I'll tell him what we talked about. I'll tell him you won't be challenging him. I'll get extra eggs." She grabbed Andrea hard by the shoulders. "You cannot save so much as one single egg now. I can't protect you."

It was Andrea's turn to try to calm Natalya down, but she had no idea how. Helpless, she watched tears start to well up in the older girl's eyes. "*Swear to me!* Swear you won't save one single egg."

Andrea was nodding and agreeing, but Natalya seemed unable to accept what she was hearing. "Swear to me on the life of your family! Oh, Andrea, I'm *so* sorry. I can't protect you. Not one egg, you hear? He's noticed you."

"But *who,* Natalya? *Who* has noticed me?"

"Viktor. Viktor Lukov."

Andrea wanted to calm her down, but she was at a complete loss. "Natalya, I'm not going after any more eggs, okay? No one needs to be upset. Viktor can forget about me. He can have all of them. Really, nothing is worth getting you this upset. As of this moment, I am officially out of the egg-cleaning business."

Chapter 24

Andrea was so emotionally exhausted when she walked into her room, she didn't notice that her little collection of guardian characters had grown to five.

Janelle, ignoring her obviously frazzled state, took it upon herself to make the introduction. Pushing forward an impassive character with an almost military bearing, Janelle cooed, "Andrea Melman, this is my trusted assistant, Cami, and she's brought us something *very* interesting."

If Janelle's most annoying trait was her condescending perkiness, then Cami deserved credit for just cutting straight to annoying. Her outfit, like her egg, was a uniform industrial gray, with none of the cute primary colors and geometric themes that the other characters seemed so attached to. And for Cami, the opposite of cute was sullen. The look on her face said she didn't want to be here, didn't like anyone here, and wanted nothing more than to be done with the whole deal.

Andrea had to admit a grudging respect for her refusal to fake it. Still, Cami was in Andrea's house at Janelle's invitation, so Andrea found it in her heart to dislike her, at least on principle.

This didn't seem the perfect moment to tell everyone that she had just capitulated to Natalya and surrendered to a man named Viktor, whom she had never met. That could wait. Now it was time for making new acquaintances and trying not to hate them.

Janelle was twittering away about something Andrea couldn't even pretend to care about when Cami abruptly broke in. "When can I deliver the device?"

"Why, Cami," Janelle chirped, "what's the rush?"

"I'm due back in twelve hours, and you haven't given me a reconnaissance report on the situation yet."

Apparently, Janelle didn't inspire much civility even in her own subordinates. She appeared ready to launch into a long introduction of "the device," but Andrea was still reeling from the disturbing sight of a terrified Natalya. She was surprised to find her anger still building, and she was in no mood for a long preamble. Looking straight at Cami, she cut Janelle off in mid sentence. "What is it and what does it do?"

Janelle shot her a look of pure poison, but Andrea was past caring, and Cami appeared grateful to be that much closer to leaving.

Pulling the device out of a large plain gray egg, she set it on the area rug covering the floor at the foot of the bed. It was basically a tripod with a vertical center pole above, bisected by a crosspiece. Around a foot high, it had a small silver ball at the end of each tripod leg, and two slightly larger balls, one black and one red, at either end of the crosspiece. "It's a bi-variable inertial damper. It takes anything moving above a specified velocity and brings it to a halt."

Andrea thought about this. "It stops anything traveling above a certain speed?"

"Exactly. The black knob sets the lowest velocity it will affect. The red knob sets how far away it can affect the moving object. It hasn't been tested here yet, but the middle settings would probably stop a bullet from a hundred feet away."

"Thank you very much, Cami," Andrea said. "That was precise and succinct, and I very much appreciate that."

Cami nodded, and Andrea tried to think of what else she should be asking about. "Uh, Cami, how do I learn to use this? I mean, is there a manual or anything?"

Cami gave an odd smirk that Andrea couldn't interpret. "Oh, just play around with it and you'll figure things out. As I said, we've never had a chance to use it here, but I'm sure you're going to get all kinds of results with the device. Don't be afraid to experiment."

"Oh, okay." Andrea was still too overwhelmed by her day with Natalya to really focus on this new character and the unusual gift she had brought.

Janelle, on the other hand, was extraordinarily focused. Furious at being cut out of the inertial damper's presentation she seized the moment to push her demands. "Well, Andrea, now that that's out of the way, you simply *must* take me out on a patrol of your area so I can make my assessment of just what kind of operation you've been running here."

Andrea had been desperate to avoid going out on a patrol with Janelle. Beyond her personal dislike of the pushy little bureaucrat, she just didn't trust her. But now she could see no way around it. Since a patrol with Janelle was the only way to give Cami her reconnaissance report and get her out of the house, Andrea reluctantly agreed.

The wait for nightfall was endless and uncomfortable. Janelle and Cami were constantly engaged in tense whispered discussions at the far end of the room, and by the way Cami fired off questions and cut off Janelle's answers, any casual observer would have assumed that she was the superior.

Andrea and her group assembled on the bed and had their own whispered discussions about how to minimize Janelle's interference. They decided that they would restrict themselves to a limited circuit of the area, and expressly avoid any interactions with Natalya or Illya.

When they told Janelle and Cami, Cami appeared to greet the decision with suspicion, but Janelle seemed fine with it. Actually, she seemed more than fine with it, and even had a little smile on her face. This worried Andrea, but there wasn't much she could do about it right then.

Later, taking advantage of a particularly heated Cami-Janelle exchange, Andrea gathered her group in a close huddle. "Have you ever heard of this inertial damper thing before? And what about Cami? Do you know her?"

Rei and Sumi looked blank. Masa looked painfully confused, and answered cautiously, "We don't know. None of us can recall ever hearing about this machine, but then, we had never heard of that H-lock thing before, either."

Floating right up to Andrea's ear, Masa continued in an even softer voice. "But that doesn't make any *sense*. A device that complicated… that inertial damper thing—I *had* to know about it. And Cami. We're starting to get a certain sense, a certain feeling for suppressed areas of our memories. And I'm positive we have history with her. But none of us can seem to remember a thing."

Andrea pondered this. "Then, if you do have history with Cami and she and Janelle are hiding that from us right now…"

"Exactly," Sumi whispered. "We need to treat both of them as potential enemies."

Chapter 25

As the time for their patrol approached, Cami surprised everyone by electing to stay behind. Andrea was grateful not to have to contend with two new distractions out in the field. But once they got outside, her sense of relief disappeared when Janelle, despite her total ignorance of the local environs, decided to take the lead.

Brooklyn on an unseasonably warm Saturday night was just one brilliantly lit oasis after another, and Andrea gritted her teeth as Janelle ran around on what seemed more like a sightseeing tour than any sort of reconnaissance. As if unfamiliar with the whole concept of stealth, she kept moving them in and out of busy neighborhoods with barely adequate cover. At one point, she almost crossed over brightly lit Atlantic Avenue, and they had to backtrack and move Andrea with great care to avoid discovery.

Things came to a head when Janelle, spotting the swirling lights of Coney Island in the distance, insisted they go and "investigate." The ensuing fight between her and Andrea required physically separating the two on opposite sides of a warehouse roof.

Masa had the unenviable task of trying to calm Andrea down. "Look, I hate her, too," she said. "But you screaming at the stupid pixie doesn't help us keep a low profile."

Andrea had moved beyond the threshold of calming influence. "No! You don't get it! You guys are, like, six inches tall. You blend in with the background, and in any case, no one expects to see you floating around up here. I'm hanging up here, all five-foot-two inches of me, in plain sight, dressed in a *hot-pink* cheerleader outfit. Maybe, just *maybe,* that would be an ordinary sight back in Japan, but one single cell phone video of me up here, and my life is *over*! Do you really not see that? Don't you guys care at *all* about what might happen to me, or is it all just about your little mission and to hell with everything else?"

Masa couldn't answer. She was just floating, staring off to the side as if wrestling with some inner question as Andrea fought to keep her composure.

At length, Masa sighed. "Okay. I'm not supposed to tell you this—I mean, I'm not really supposed to tell you *anything* like this—but it's not quite as bad as it seems."

Catching the change in tone, Andrea managed to center herself.

"It's called a *glamour.* There's a mechanism in place. It's a kind of complement to how humans can't really focus on anything they're not expecting to see, and so they miss a lot of really obvious things. The glamour works a lot like camouflage, blurring the edges and randomizing the brightness and color of something. Most of those people down there, at worst, might perceive a shiny blur as you fly by. Someone actually expecting to see a cheerleader flying through the air, and focused on the task of doing so, *might* pick you out. Natalya and Illya, for example. But anything short of buzzing the crowds at Coney Island…"

Andrea absorbed this in silence.

When she finally turned to Masa, she said, "Okay. Thank you for telling me this. I can *kind of* understand that you could get in trouble for sharing that. But, *Masa…*"

188

Her tone of voice betrayed her anger, though she tried to keep some measure of control. "I have been terrified of being spotted and recorded since we started doing this. You really didn't *see* that? You didn't think my knowing this might have made things a lot easier for me?"

Masa was silent. Andrea nodded to acknowledge the others coming over to them. "Later," she said pointedly.

* * *

Gradually they made their way to the area around the Gowanus Canal. After more than a century as a toxic wasteland, Gowanus was finally succumbing to it's inevitable development and incorporation into the "new" Brooklyn. That said, the surrounding area was still a contested patchwork of artists' lofts, luxury condos and abandoned industrial sites.

Andrea began to suspect that Janelle wasn't just taking them on a joyride. She seemed to be searching out a particular sensation along a line of warehouses flanking the canal. She stopped short in front of an old-fashioned factory building with a pitched roof—part of a larger complex.

Without a word, she flew up and over, forcing the others to chase her to a line of ventilation windows just below the roof. Andrea's heart sank when Janelle whirled about to face the group. The look on her face made it clear that she was about to spring something. "Well, isn't this a surprise! I believe I may have come across something—or someone—that just might help us get this mission back on track. My special sense is telling me an old, um, *colleague* is in this building, and

I wouldn't be one bit surprised if he didn't have a few answers to some of those vexing problems you've been running into."

Sumi, aghast, interrupted her. "What, exactly, are you proposing?"

Generally the first to invoke protocol, Janelle seemed to be relishing her moment as the rule-breaking "bad girl" of the group. "Well, I tell you, I'm figuring to drop in on my old friend and see if I can't just go right ahead and hit the reset button on this whole situation."

Horrified, everyone started objecting at once while Janelle simply floated there, enjoying all the attention. Andrea was too stunned even to speak. Then, before anyone could stop her, Janelle zoomed through a half-open window.

The other characters eased cautiously up to the glass and found themselves looking three stories down to a harshly lit factory floor dominated by a long, wide table. There, a squat, heavily built man of indeterminate age stood, examining the contents of a series of cardboard boxes.

All eyes were on Janelle, who had flown up behind the man and apparently tapped him on the shoulder, making him spin violently around. The ambient noise level outside the window was too high for them to hear any more of the conversation than an occasional high-pitched Janelle chirp.

But the man didn't seem any happier to see Janelle than anyone else ever did. As it was, she appeared to be talking a mile a minute without ever pausing to hear whatever this "colleague" might have to offer in return.

Andrea noticed that he had begun absently tinkering with some plumbing parts, all the while keeping eye contact with the manic guardian character. She was just relieved that Janelle hadn't gestured up toward the window where they were hiding. Apparently, she was making the most of her moment in the spotlight.

Andrea floated back to survey their location. The warehouse ran about a hundred feet in either direction. Just above them, the pitched roof had a flat walkway on top, with what appeared to be lighting fixtures attached at regular intervals. Behind them, across a parking lot, were some dying, leafless trees and a series of storage sheds.

Andrea tapped Rei on the back. "I don't like this location. Check out what's on top of this thing and on the other side." Rei gave her a grim smile and took off. She addressed Masa and Sumi, "Check our perimeter. Anyone we've never heard of who knows about guardian characters is a threat until proven otherwise." They nodded, flew off to check the area and, finding nothing, quickly returned to watch the events below.

Rei came back, looking concerned. "I don't know what's in this crummy-looking building, but the roof has a brand-new lighting system and a *lot* of security cameras."

Andrea went cold. Gathering them around her, she said, "I hate this like poison. Anything happens, we all go straight up, two—no, three hundred feet—and fast. What the *hell* are you doing down there, Janelle?"

By the view from the window, Janelle seemed to be having the time of her life, yakking away like mad while the quiet man held eye contact and continued fooling with some sort of pipe-and-faucet assembly. Janelle was still chattering away when he gave one final twist to the thing, leaned back against the table, and, without a word, raised it and soundlessly blew Janelle into a puff of red mist.

The group outside stared, frozen in shock. The thickset man dropped what turned out to be a silenced handgun on the table, turned around and reached out for something.

Andrea reacted immediately. *"Go, go, GO!"*

The four of them had only just cleared the roofline when the entire area exploded in light. They were exposed for what seemed like hours while they clawed for altitude.

Oh, God, Andrea thought. *Don't let those cameras have some sort of automatic tracking. Please let them be slow or broken or… ANYTHING but seeing us now.*

By the time they stopped climbing, they must have been a thousand feet up, and still they felt exposed. Everything in the lot below them was now bathed in the harsh glare of high-pressure sodium lamps. A half dozen men were now patrolling the area. Andrea wished she had binoculars, but even from here she could see the men were carrying long guns. At this height, it was only a matter of time before someone noticed Andrea's silhouette, so the four of them moved toward a darker part of the canal district before touching down on a flat rooftop.

All Andrea could say was "Oh God, oh God, oh God." Then she threw up.

Sumi was crying. Masa looked catatonic, and Rei kept saying, "What happened? What happened? Where did she *go?*"

Chapter 26

It was over an hour before they had calmed down enough to understand what they had witnessed. For a long time, no one wanted to leave the safety of the rooftop and risk revealing themselves to the night. Around three o'clock in the morning, hunger and the thought of home finally pushed them into action, but it was a long, tense trip.

By the time they got home, everyone just wanted to fall down, but they still had to inform Cami. Andrea tried to take the lead, but everyone had a piece of the story, and it came out in a ragged jumble until they got to the moment of Janelle's murder. At that point, no one seemed to be able to come straight out and say what had to be said.

Cami was getting more and more impatient trying to follow the disjointed narrative. But what Andrea had at first seen as concern for their—or, at least, Janelle's—welfare began to feel like mere annoyance at them for not being able to tell the story clearly.

"So, then, where *is* she?" Cami snapped.

"She's dead," Andrea finally murmured. "He just shot her while she was talking."

"Dead?" Cami seemed at first to be puzzling over the meaning of the word, but her expression started changing.

Andrea was surprised to see a range of emotions play out on her tiny face. Confusion turned to rage and quickly broke into a smirk of smug triumph. The others didn't seem to be paying attention to it, but Andrea was becoming acutely aware of an underlying disconnect between Cami's apparent low status and the arrogance and cunning right beneath the surface.

To Andrea's mind, Cami was giving this a chilling level of calculation, weighing what options were now available to her by virtue of Janelle's death. Given that assessment, Andrea was the only one not shocked by her next statement. "So you killed her?"

At first, they were all speechless at the accusation. Then the characters all started babbling at once. But Andrea kept her eyes on Cami's demeanor. It was at odds with the seriousness of the charge. Instead of reacting in shock or anger, Cami seemed to be throwing out an almost casual provocation designed to intimidate them.

Cami noticed Andrea's silence and focused on her. "Was this your plan?"

This drew immediate outrage from the others, but Andrea could feel that a real battle was brewing here. And without really knowing what the terms were, she knew that she needed to respond in kind without losing control or giving anything away. "No, Cami. Was it yours?"

Dead silence as Rei, Masa, and Sumi looked back and forth, trying to figure out what was going on. Andrea wasn't sure how to continue, but she knew instinctively that retreating would hand Cami the advantage. "You don't seem all that surprised *or* all that upset. Did you know what Janelle was planning to do?"

Cami didn't take the accusation well, and her face contorted in rage as she lit into Andrea. "You stupid little *bitch!* You think to challenge *me?* Do you think you are somehow my equal? My better? Do you think I need to consider the opinion of a miserable creature like you or weigh the value of what your little band of traitors have been cooking up here? You are *nothing! I* will weave the story of what has happened tonight. Janelle's death is irrelevant. This sad little operation was destined to fail before you were born, and you know nothing about these worthless pixies."

She turned her fury on Rei, Masa, and Sumi. "All your scheming and cleverness, your 'long games' and 'big pictures'—all of that is *over*. You have already lost, and we will *annihilate* you when we take back our birthright. Janelle was a fool to involve herself in human affairs. She cheapened herself and our kind, but she was a useful fool, and I will weave her death into a greater story than she could ever have earned on her own. And as for *you!*" She turned again to Andrea. "You never learn, but *this* time you will pay nine times over for your meddling."

With that, Cami flew over to her egg and gave a parting shot. "Know this: We will make ourselves drunk on your suffering."

Andrea had never seen one of the eggs come or go. There was nothing to it. It just faded out, and the four of them were left sitting, stunned, in her bedroom.

The characters soon began to stir, but Andrea was lost in thought, and it was a long time before she turned to face them. "Okay," she said. "Events have been following a certain path up till now. But I think you know that has to change."

She paused and considered her next words. "Tonight is not the night to go into this, but you need to prepare an accounting of yourselves and the situation we're… well, actually, the situation that *I'm* in. And then we need to figure out what happens from this point on."

The characters looked stunned, guilt-ridden, and on the verge of tears.

Andrea didn't want to leave things this way. She looked at them another moment and then said, "I suspect that, for better or worse, we are bound together in a destiny not necessarily of our choosing. I doubt we can change that, but for me to be able to contribute wholeheartedly, the terms of our relationship will need to change. From now on, I will need you to be a lot more forthcoming about things, but we can talk about that later. The only question I need answered right now is this: Who *are* you?"

Sumi floated up in front of her, and the other two arranged themselves to the sides just behind.

With unexpected formality, Sumi announced, "We are the Fae."

Andrea just looked at them for a moment. "Um… okay…?"

The three of them looked expectantly at her. Andrea felt nervous, as if she alone wasn't getting something and everyone else was a little embarrassed for her. She figured she should say something or ask a question, but the day was really catching up with her and all she could think to ask was, "So… like F-A-Y?"

Sumi replied, "We prefer F-A-E."

Chapter 27

School was becoming a blur. Andrea could function on autopilot for only so long. Homework was going in late or incomplete, and her teachers were starting to notice. Andrea realized she was appearing more overwhelmed than usual, even for her. Indeed, at lunchtime, when she saw Gaylen heading over, Andrea feared that this was what she had come to talk about. But the girl was not her usual upbeat self. "Gaylen, you look totally stressed. What's up?"

Gaylen put down her lunch tray and flopped down in the chair across from her. "Oh, nothing. I mean, a lot of things, really. Home stuff and… you don't need to know about it."

Andrea knew a half-hearted dismissal when she heard one. She closed the history book she had been struggling to read, and focused on Gaylen. "Sorry, don't mean to pry. You just look so beat."

"No, no. I don't want to bother you with my stuff. It's, uh, complicated, and I don't think anyone can be much help. I did want to ask you one thing, though."

"Name it."

Gaylen took a tentative bite of what was alleged to be meatloaf, put down her fork, and sighed. "It's… it's a lot, really, and I totally understand if you can't do it or, you know, even if you just don't want to, because it's really not something I should be asking, but I just don't know who else I could ask, and—"

"Oh, my God. You need a kidney?"

Gaylen looked up and grinned. "Okay, no. Not a kidney. I need to store some stuff of mine, and I know you have a lot of space and all, and—"

"How much?" Andrea said, cutting her off. "Wait, is this like, your spider collection or your secret drug lab or anything I could do time for?"

She could see that Gaylen was suppressing a laugh.

"Okay. No drugs or chemicals, weapons of any kind, and... *Spiders,* Andrea? Really? It's just a small bass amp, two boxes of books, and two boxes of clothing."

"Oh. Well, that's nothing. I could store tons more than that."

"Oh, wow, thanks so much!" Gaylen looked as if she had just shed a huge burden. She paused a moment. "So, I guess you deserve to know why..."

But Andrea interrupted her. "No, I don't. Gaylen, I have a lot of things going on I would love to talk about, but I just can't. I trust you. Anything you want to talk to me about is great, but if you're not sure, that's fine. Just let me know when you'll be bringing your stuff over."

Just feeling that she could do something to lift the girl's spirits was a big boost in Andrea's day. "Look, I have to meet with Mr. Gertner about scheduling a bunch of makeup homework before fifth period starts. Just text me when you're coming over."

She started to grab her lunch tray and book bag, then paused. "Gaylen... do you know anything about the Fae?"

Gaylen looked puzzled. "The Fae? That's another name for the Faerie folk—you know, Celtic Faeries and all that. I mean, yeah, I do know a bit about them, but it's nothing you couldn't learn in an hour on the internet."

Andrea was only half-listening to her response as she stood up. "Oh, okay, thanks. I'm just being lazy."

A newly engaged Gaylen wasn't prepared to let the discussion end there. "Andrea, why are you asking? I mean, that's not exactly the sort of question I'd expect from you. You're not out consorting with the fair folk at night, are you? If you are, don't eat their food. Or let them take you to a Faerie fort for any reveling."

"*Reveling,* Gaylen?"

"You know, dancing and frolicking, or wild rides through the countryside on fiery black horses. If you eat their food, they'll have you forever. Or maybe you'll come home and find that a hundred years has gone by and your true love grew old and died awaiting your return."

Somewhat stunned by this flood of random information, Andrea tried to refocus the discussion. "What if *I* feed *them?*"

"Well, you can win their gratitude by leaving them a little dish of cream or some whiskey."

"How about ramen?"

"Huh?"

"They like ramen."

Fully alert now, Gaylen locked eyes with her. "Okay, Andrea, I'm not sure what you're doing with me right now, but let me just say this: Outside of the people into something called Faerie Magick, most everyone with an opinion on the Fae would be advising you to be really, *really* careful in any dealings with them. I know you're just messing with me, but the Fae were dangerous, vengeful creatures with no regard for human suffering. Don't think modern, happy Tinker Bell, hanging out with her friends and trying on cute outfits made of flowers. Think original, psycho Tinker Bell, trying to kill Wendy in a jealous rage."

Andrea was surprised at Gaylen's seriousness. Only now did it occur to her that the mere mention of the Fae might actually have repercussions. She had piqued Gaylen's curiosity and yet couldn't give her a genuine response. She wanted to apologize, but couldn't find the right words.

Evidently reading her confusion, Gaylen gave her an easy out. Rising to leave she said, "Just be careful and get thee to the internet, young maiden."

⚹ ⚹ ⚹

But Andrea needed a lot more than a quiet moment online. The events of that awful night were still eating away at her. Witnessing Janelle's death and the ensuing panic felt like a strange, terrible dream. Like tiny fragments of a nightmare, the memories kept sneaking back into her consciousness, and she would find herself in a cold sweat at random moments. By the end of her last class, Andrea was only barely paying attention to her surroundings and blanking out in the middle of simple tasks.

She appeared to be getting something from her locker when Natalya came up from behind her. "*Andrea!*" she hissed. "Snap out of it! I walked by here five minutes ago and you were standing here, spacing out. What is…?"

But Andrea wasn't spacing out. She was crying. Events had finally closed in on her, leaving her overwhelmed and paralyzed by fear. "Oh, Natalya, Janelle's dead. This man shot her, and I don't know if he saw us, and the characters… the characters are fairies—I mean Fae— and there was another one and she said we killed Janelle, but we didn't."

Andrea looked up at Natalya as if just now aware of her presence. "Oh, and the new character, Cami, gave us this thing that's supposed to stop bullets, but I don't know if it's true. And why do I need something that stops bullets, anyway? Why would anyone try to kill me?"

Natalya made a quick call to reschedule something, then took Andrea by the hand and led her from the school.

As they walked along, Andrea was slipping from catatonic to embarrassed. "I'm sorry," she murmured. "I didn't mean to cause a scene or anything."

Natalya's mind was elsewhere. "Where is this machine?"

"Oh, it's right here in my bag. I didn't know what to do with it."

"We need to test it," Natalya said.

"Well, sure, but how?" Andrea asked.

Natalya and Illya's house was only a few blocks from the school. A thicket of overgrown willow trees in the front yard hid a small house that was actually more run-down than Andrea's. A rusty wrought-iron fence surrounded the property, but the entrance was an incongruously modern iron gate with keypad access. An ancient brown station wagon sat in the driveway. Nothing about the place suggested that the stylish Natalya Volkova actually lived there.

Andrea was still in a daze as they went around through the back door, into the kitchen, and straight down to the basement. Around them was the usual clutter of a band's practice space: drum kit, cables, amps. Mismatched kitchen chairs and stools in front of mismatched music stands. The only thing slightly odd was a sharp smell that Andrea couldn't place.

Natalya went over to the back wall and hit a series of light switches. "This house used to belong to a gang," she said as harsh fluorescent lighting kicked in. A motor hummed, and a section of the wood paneling on the back wall swung up like a garage door to reveal a long passage, almost a hundred feet long. A cable on a motorized pulley ran the length of the passage. Midway down, a target was clipped to it.

As Andrea stood gaping, trying to make sense of things, Natalya busied herself at a nearby table. Moments later, she was standing in front of Andrea with a fully assembled AK-47 assault rifle. "Whoa! Where did *that* come from?"

"It's perfectly legal," Natalya said nonchalantly.

"Wait… It's *your* gun?"

"Well, technically, this one's Illya's, but we share it for target practice. My personal weapon is an M1911A1."

Andrea just stared.

"A Colt 45?" Natalya added, though it didn't seem to help Andrea's comprehension.

Putting the assault rifle down on the table, she zipped open a padded case and took out the classic pistol associated with the US military since before the First World War. "It's kind of a family heirloom."

Andrea pondered that a moment. "My family's heirlooms are mostly Christmas tree ornaments." Staring at the large, square-angled handgun made her uncomfortable. "This is the closest I've ever been to guns like this."

"Guns like this?" Natalya asked, putting away the pistol.

"Back in Ohio, my uncle's family did some hunting. You know, rifles and shotguns, but I never saw them up close, and I don't know anyone here in New York with military-style weapons."

"Hmm, you probably do, but people tend to be discreet around here."

Natalya picked up the AK-47 again. "So where is this magic bullet stopper?"

Andrea pulled it out of her book bag and put it on the table. "They call it a bi-variable inertial damper."

She couldn't remember which control affected which function, so they set both to halfway. Natalya handed Andrea what looked like a pair of red old-style earphones and put on another pair herself.

Then she turned to the firing line, slapped a longish curved magazine into the rifle, pulled back and released the charging handle. "Are you ready?"

Andrea centered the big ear protectors and nodded.

Natalya pulled the trigger.

A soft *thunk* issued from the gun. She pointed the weapon down, and a shiny copper-coated bullet slid out of the barrel. Slipping the safety on, she reasoned out the situation. "Okay, the velocity of the exploding gas from the charge gets suppressed; obviously, we get no speeding bullet. I'm going to assume there is just enough explosion to separate the shell from the case. Maybe there's a lag in the effect kicking in."

She yanked the charging handle, and a brass casing popped out of the side of the rifle as another round loaded. Turning back to the target, she disengaged the safety. "Now turn it off, just so I can satisfy myself that there's nothing wrong with the rifle."

Andrea turned the dials to fully counterclockwise and waited.

Even though she knew they were coming, and even with the ear protectors on, the three loud cracks made her jump. The detonations resonated in her chest.

Natalya looked at her. "I'm satisfied it does what it's supposed to." She released the magazine and ejected the round from the chamber.

Forty minutes later, they were sitting in the kitchen with the device on the table between them. Natalya had interrogated Andrea about the events of the past few days, her concerns growing with every new detail.

Andrea started playing with the "damper," as they had started calling it, and was twisting the knobs back and forth. Natalya was going over Cami's last comments for the third time when she suddenly stopped midsentence. "You probably shouldn't do that."

Andrea looked up. "What do you mean?"

"Did they tell you this thing is *expressly* designed to stop bullets?"

"No."

"Hold on. New test." Natalya went over to the counter and started up an electric blender. "Go. See what happens."

Andrea gave a twist, and the blender stopped. They could hear the electric motor hum, but nothing was turning.

Natalya was hot on the scent of something. "Out here!"

She ran out to the sad old station wagon and started it up. Standing just outside the kitchen door, Andrea gave the knob a twist, and the car stalled out.

Natalya sat with her hands on the steering wheel, staring straight ahead. Without looking up, she said, "Turn it off, Andrea. Turn it off and do not turn it on until we've had a chance to determine the range and effectiveness of the device."

Andrea turned off the damper and sank down onto the back-door steps. She stared at the device as if for the first time. "It takes anything above a certain velocity and damps it down to nothing?"

Looking up, there was real fear in her eyes. "This could stop jet engines passing overhead, couldn't it?"

Natalya walked over and sat down next to her. "Planes, helicopters, trains—this thing could cause an unbelievable amount of mayhem. And I thought it might only be dangerous to *you*."

"Me? I thought this would somehow, you know, *protect* me."

Natalya angled toward her on the stairs. "Andrea, I don't like having to tell you this, particularly in light of your tendency to react strongly when confronted with scary news…"

"Yeah, I do that sometimes, I suppose."

"But there are people—a *lot* of people, actually—who would kill to get a device like this. It's a game changer, and I don't mean that in a good way."

Andrea gave a weak smile. "So I guess this isn't the first step to a world of peaceful coexistence?"

"The ability to stall any engine makes it a terrorist's dream," Natalya said. "God, I can think of dozens of horrible uses for this thing. In fact, I'm struggling to come up with anything *good* you could do with it."

"So why did Cami and Janelle want me to have it?" Andrea asked.

Natalya pondered the question and Andrea took the opportunity to look around.

The Melmans' backyard wasn't exactly well kept, but Natalya's yard was a mess. Broken tools, empty packing crates, and rusting fifty-five-gallon drums, strewn about on the toxic dead zone that had once been the lawn. It was hard to reconcile such elegant people as Illya and Natalya with a backyard like this, but there it was.

"Cami called them traitors?" Natalya asked, interrupting her thoughts.

"Yeah. Oh, and pixies. I have a feeling that's meant in a bad way. But who was that man? And what was going on in that building? He knew Janelle, and she knew him. Why did he kill her?"

Natalya hesitated. Finally, she sighed and said, "The man you saw was Viktor—our uncle and—technically—our legal guardian."

Andrea froze. She tried to speak, but the words wouldn't form.

"Janelle must have led you to him. I can't imagine why, but he may have killed her to make sure no one found out about their connection."

"I don't know if he saw us," Andrea whispered.

"From what you told me, I would think not. He's prepared for a lot of things, but Andrea Melman flying around in a pink cheerleader outfit with her band of Faerie companions is almost certainly not one of them."

Andrea laughed in spite of herself. "I guess we showed him!"

Natalya smiled as she rose. "It's getting dark. I have to go to work."

"What? Now?"

"The eggs. We were tasked with obtaining many more of them, and I need to do so tonight with Illya. I have no choice."

"But what about all this Faerie business? And the damper? What should I do?"

"Andrea, we need to have a very serious talk about this new information. But before we do that, I need to tell you about us—Illya and me—and our circumstances. You are involved in matters too deeply to remain ignorant any longer. Go home. Hide this crazy machine, and tell no one else about it. We will come over tonight after we finish."

"Okay."

"I would like to reassure you and tell you not to worry, that everything will work out fine. But I am afraid I cannot. You need to be careful of what you say, and who might approach you. I wouldn't suggest you doubt the sincerity or intentions of your guardian characters, but be aware that what you tell them may be monitored by others without their knowledge. Can you handle this?"

Andrea held herself back from giving an automatic affirmative. She had almost suffered a complete breakdown twice in the past week, but this felt different. Someone who could understand the situation had heard her out, agreed that things were every bit as serious as she thought, and was prepared to offer support. Andrea wasn't sure what she could offer in return, but the least she could do was keep herself together.

Her voice was surprisingly strong when she answered. "Yes, I'm okay. I'll hide the device, keep my eyes open and my mouth shut for the time being."

Natalya smiled. "Probably a good approach to life in general."

Chapter 28

It was nearly midnight when Illya and Natalya arrived at the Melman residence. Andrea was glad that Dion was out for the night. Her first impression was that it felt odd seeing Illya without cat ears and a tail. She brought in a pair of armchairs from her parents' room and set them in front of a low table. A handful of candles in the center provided the main illumination. After serving everyone tea, Andrea sat down across from them. The Fae seemed comfortable just floating in place.

Natalya was staring at the cup in her hands. "Do you think I'm pretty?"

Andrea blushed and looked away. "Uh, yeah, of course."

Natalya scowled. "Beauty is a curse. It clouds the judgment of the girls who possess it. Our mother was an exceptional beauty, but vain and foolish. Her reckless self-indulgence was the root of our suffering."

Illya interrupted. "Natalya? You would speak of her so? To strangers?"

"They will come to their own conclusions, but they must know the facts."

He gave her a look. "Very well, then. Spare no one, and continue."

Natalya put down the cup and sat back in her chair. "We come from a land near the Arctic Circle. It is like no place you have ever known: the area north of St. Petersburg, known as the Kola Peninsula.

Life there is hard, and survival a desperate thing, but for years those very conditions were what protected us. Our mother, Marina, however, would have none of that.

"Actually, calling her our mother sounds strange. For all of her life, she was known as 'precious Marina,' 'dancing Marina,' 'Marina of the haunting voice.'

"She grew up knowing that her destiny would be found on the arm of a powerful man who would shower her with luxuries. Common girls got pregnant and grew thick with responsibilities. Marina would have the world at her feet, enthralled by her beauty. So, on her sixteenth birthday, she was off to St. Petersburg.

"After a few years, Marina established herself—but at the expense of her innocence. Within the privileged circle where she had installed herself, everyone knew that the sweet little girl from the north was now a polished performer, quick with a lie or a kiss—anything to move matters in more profitable directions.

"Marina came to learn that time doesn't favor the beautiful. Her opportunities were fading when she happened upon our father. She later claimed that she came to love him, but by then it was impossible to believe her."

"But we agree that her concern for him was real when he disappeared?" Illya interjected.

"Yes, of course. But we have also agreed that the marriage in which she ensnared our father—against the pleas of his family—was a cynical ploy, driven by greed."

Illya said nothing.

The Fae, meanwhile, had moved onto the table and distributed themselves among the teacups.

"By the time we were born, our father was sure he had made a terrible mistake. But now he had a son and a daughter to protect, and he did his best to do just that."

"Our father was a good man," Illya said. "He was a violin prodigy and brilliant in mathematics. Fluent in philosophy and poetry and…" Here the young man's voice cracked.

Natalya drew herself up and seemed ready to argue, but she interrupted him with tenderness. "He was a good father, and he did all he could."

She turned again to Andrea. "But he could never protect us from the crimes our mother subjected us to, and of all those crimes, the worst was to consign us to the care of our uncle, Viktor Lukov."

Natalya seemed unsettled at merely having spoken his name. Illya shifted forward protectively but she raised her hand to stop him before continuing. "Andrea Melman, I beg you to forgive me for what I must now involve you in. We have done all we could, but matters are no longer ours to influence. Believe me when I tell you that I would have done anything to avoid this."

Natalya took a breath and centered herself. "I should begin with two facts that must be known if you are to understand Viktor. First, we Russians are a deeply superstitious people, susceptible to all sorts of nonsense. Curses, spells, predictions, and what have you.

One of the oldest of these beliefs is the myth of the strong man possessing mystical powers and protections.

"Second, Viktor is a witch from a long line of Karelian witches. Now, do not indulge in any foolishness about this, for I assure you, there is no one on this earth who believes less in the powers of the witch than Viktor Lukov. The history of the Karelian witches is one of blackmail and extortion. They inflict curses and spells on the gullible for the purpose of removing them—at a price.

"How our family lines came to cross is a story for another time, but the drive for status and power was a common link between Viktor and Marina. Viktor, of course, was never burdened by delusions of morality."

"You praise him with diplomatic niceties?" Illya exploded. "Speak plainly! He is a monster."

He turned to Andrea. "Viktor is a murderous psychopath. He has killed hundreds. His crimes are horrible even by the standards of the Russian underworld. They say of him that while other bosses torture and kill in the name of business, Viktor Lukov conducts business precisely to create such opportunities."

Andrea must have looked shocked, because Natalya slid her chair over, closer to Illya. Laying a hand on his shoulder, she said softly, "Do you wish to inform her or terrify her?"

He sank back into his chair. "I'm sorry."

"Let me try to tell the story as best I can."

Illya nodded, and she sat back in her chair.

The Fae were being unusually quiet. Andrea thought they looked like little kids listening to a story around a campfire.

Natalya settled herself and returned her attention to Andrea. "My brother is quite right. Viktor deserves no euphemisms. But I am so used to playing a careful game that I've learned to stifle directness in favor of prudence.

"Viktor had based himself in St. Petersburg with great cunning. Do not misread him, Andrea. A psychopath he is, but in no way irrational. He ceded the rich pickings of Moscow to gain a free hand in his hometown.

"There he became the 'Specter from the North,' the fearsome spawn of witches. He let people refer to him behind his back as 'Viktor Grozny'—'Viktor the Terrible.' Hard men broke under his gaze, believing he could read their intentions through some magical insight. That is his way. People believe what they will, and he reaps the harvest of their ignorance.

"Viktor was always aware of Marina's little adventures, of course. But the lure of lawless Chechnya was enough to occupy most of his time. He was constantly recruiting men and running operations there under the guise of patriotism.

"Profitable years passed for Viktor. Meanwhile, Marina tried to stifle the disappointments of motherhood with affairs and shopping trips. Upon his return to St. Petersburg, Viktor had a notion of doing something to destroy or shame our family, if for no other reason than the fact that he could.

"He has always harbored an unusual hatred for my grandmother, and nothing would have given him greater pleasure than to drive her daughter into drug addiction or prostitution. That Marina had essentially prostituted herself in all but name thwarted his preferred course of action, and our father's family was too insignificant to be worth humiliating.

"For years they had travelled in parallel circles. Aware of each other but without making direct contact. Then one day they met at a party. Viktor was used to women submitting to him in fear and, preferably, terror. Marina, however, was smitten. It was as if her entire life had led up to the moment when she would win the heart of a psychopath. Within days, they were inseparable. Within weeks, he had rearranged everything to revolve around being with her. Needless to say, the scant time and attention she had given us disappeared completely.

"Within months, Viktor's crew was beginning to worry about his wavering focus on the organization's priorities. And yet, for all his apparent obsession, Viktor had a clear idea of what he wanted to do and what he needed to achieve it. And what he needed was us."

Illya interrupted. "We are speculating somewhat with this next part, Miss Melman, as I'm sure you will understand."

Natalya acknowledged this with a nod and continued. "We have come to believe that Viktor had—at one time—a guardian character of his own."

Andrea was too astonished to react, but around her the Fae exploded in a chorus of denial.

"That's impossible!"

"Why? To what purpose?"

"We would have known about this!"

The Fae had launched themselves off the coffee table and were buzzing about, indignant at the thought of Viktor having had a guardian character. They managed to collect themselves eventually, though clearly simmering over the accusation as they hovered above the teacups.

Natalya studied their reaction with a certain interest, and then went on. "What is more, we have reason to think that he may have—accidentally or on purpose—killed his character."

Andrea glanced over to see how Rei, Masa, and Sumi would take this, but they seemed numb to any further input. *And why not?* she reflected. *They've already seen him kill one character.*

Natalya continued. "We don't know how, but Viktor was familiar with the essential knowledge of guardian characters. He somehow knew that we were suitable to host them, and within a few months, he began implementing a plan to make it happen. The first thing he did was to get rid of our father."

Andrea sat up abruptly, almost spilling her tea. "He killed your father?"

Illya took over for a moment. "We are moving through this story so quickly that a great deal has been left out. Viktor is too clever to ever be tied to any action. Our father came in one day and told us he was going away, that we would be safe, and that he would always love us."

"We believe that his physical safety was the price for our mother's agreement to his exile." Natalya added.

"And you believe this?" Andrea asked carefully.

"It's hard to say," Illya replied. "Our mother was different that day. Everything else she did was done thoughtlessly and without consideration. This was different. We've discussed it for years, and remembrance is a fragile thing. But still…"

"More to the point," Natalya said, "it appears to have also been the price for her to allow Viktor to introduce us to our characters. Prior to that we had been little more than an annoying obstruction to their time together. Viktor acknowledged us for the first time that day and everything changed. Illya received Nyanka that day, and the next morning Gella's and Malka's eggs were on my bed."

"Wait," Sumi interrupted. "I don't understand. How old were you?"

Natalya looked at Illya. "I was six, maybe seven, and you were nine?"

This visibly shook the Fae.

"That's too young," Sumi said. "*Way* too young."

"It's perverse," Masa said. "Even with normal characters."

"Who would make a seven year old contend with two deranged characters?" Rei asked.

"Well, Viktor *is* evil, you know," Natalya said with a hint of a smile.

"No." Rei insisted. "One of the Fae did this. Only Fae of the highest standing can assign a character."

Sumi just looked at Natalya. "How did you manage?"

The gentleness of her tone seemed to take Natalya by surprise. Her features softened noticeably, and her voice took on an openness and vulnerability that Andrea would never have imagined coming from her. "It was odd and terribly stressful. By that time, I had learned to trust no one but Illya. He and Nyanka got along well enough, but Gella and Malka just seemed creepy to me. I mean, I was seven. What did I know? It was like having someone else's imaginary friends. Our mother couldn't see them, but Viktor could, and he always seemed to be pushing them to extremes. I couldn't understand most of it. We spent the better part of two years with him trying to train me to do things, and me pretending I couldn't while I tried to work things out on my own."

"Just you?" Andrea asked. "What about Illya?"

"He seemed to give up on me almost immediately," Illya said. "It always felt like he knew that everything depended on Natalya's characters and their development."

"Viktor was always trying to separate us," Natalya said. "But I learned to be—shall we say—'difficult' when Illya wasn't around. Much of the time we were up north, living with our grandmother. He had a place nearby, and we would go there for training, but

Babushka Tasha always made sure we came home every night. For some reason, Viktor would never set foot on her property."

Andrea had to ask. "Why not?"

"Yes, why? We never could understand it. I know I said Viktor didn't believe in... well, anything, but our grandmother is famous in her own way. Actually, our family was, for many generations... How would you say it, Illya? The shamans of last resort? The last magicians you might consult before finally surrendering to your fate."

"Wait! You're from a witch family, too? You guys are family traditional witches?" Andrea's wide-eyed reaction made them both laugh out loud.

"Oh, now you've figured us out, haven't you?" Illya teased. Natalya pondered the question as she poured herself more tea.

Eventually she responded, "Um, perhaps. That's a modern term, 'family traditional,' a Wiccan term. Babushka Tasha would merely say that she has 'listened and learned.' I wouldn't go trying to engage her in a conversation about witchcraft, certainly. In any case, unfortunately for Illya, the 'gift' seems to pass through certain generations of daughters in our family, so no scary witch stuff for him to impress the girls with."

Illya blushed, which made Natalya grin, and she continued. "One thing, though: Our grandmother could see our characters. That may be a part of Viktor's cautiousness around her. She swears she never had anything like that in her childhood or during Marina's upbringing, but Viktor always respected and feared her, even to this day.

"Meanwhile, he was trying to train me to summon up what he would call 'directable energies.' I don't know where he got his ideas from, but the brutality of his teaching methods had the benefit of forcing Gella and Malka to throw their loyalties to me."

Andrea looked skeptical. "Their loyalties… ?"

"I mean, I never really trusted them not to turn on me, but they understood that at least I wouldn't be the one to get them killed. In any case, they were different back then. Not so extreme, not so crazy. Gella was a bit silly and unreliable, but nothing like she is now. And Malka was—I don't know—mischievous? They would even watch out for each other and try to stand up to Viktor when he pushed too hard."

Natalya looked down, and her voice seemed to grow both sadder and harsher. "Malka used be Gella's protector back then." Her eyes hardened. "But they met their own monster, and everything changed."

"*Natalya!*" Illya gasped.

She turned to him. "Did you think I would neglect my own crimes?"

She nodded toward the Fae, who had regrouped back on the low table.

"They need to know what I did to Malka and Gella."

She set her cup down, folded her hands in her lap, and began. "It started with the phone call…"

Chapter 29

"We were home alone, as usual. Illya was practicing the violin upstairs, so I picked up the phone. I didn't recognize the voice. Later, I found out it was Yuri, one of Viktor's lieutenants.

"He recognized who I was, and he kept telling me to 'put someone on the phone.' I kept saying, 'I am someone,' and finally he gave up and said, 'I have very bad news, Miss Natalya. Your mother has died, and they're sending over the coffin.'

"I didn't realize that he was under express orders not to say any more than that, and I kept asking him questions. Finally, he said, 'I'm sorry, Miss Natalya, but no one can tell you anything.'

"We kept expecting someone to send over an adult, but by late afternoon, no one had called or come by. The first knock on the door was the undertaker and his assistants, rolling in this huge white coffin.

"Nothing made any sense. The undertaker wouldn't look us in the eye, and the assistants cleared out as soon as it was placed in the front room. It was our first encounter with Viktor's power. He had decreed that no one could speak of any aspect of Marina's death. And, of course, no one would defy him.

"The last thing the undertaker said as he was leaving was that the coffin was sealed and that it could not be opened under any circumstances. He said that this was Viktor's order, and it was final. We kept asking how she died, and he just kept saying, 'No one can say. No one can say.' And I kept going, 'Why? What's wrong? Why can't we see our mother?' All the while, Illya was trying to call our relatives, but Viktor had warned them all to mind their own business and that he would attend to everything.

"You must understand, by this time, our father's family hated everything about us, and Marina had crossed so many people in St. Petersburg that no one felt the slightest interest in helping her children, much less incurring Viktor's wrath.

"The light began to fade, and things started to sink in, but everything felt like a dream. This gleaming white casket in our front room became the center of our world. I grew obsessed over what might have happened. Had he tortured her? Was she horribly burned? Was she even in there at all? As night fell, I began to lose my mind.

"Anytime Illya left the room, I would panic. I began constructing all these crazy rules. I decided that we couldn't leave our mother alone, even for a second. Someone had to be with her at all times, or they would come and take her away. Eventually I wouldn't let Illya leave the room at all.

"Finally, around midnight, I became hysterical about looking inside the coffin. They had sealed it with all these screws going up into the bottom edge of the lid. I made Illya find a screwdriver only it wasn't the right size. It was too small, and it kept stripping the screw heads. Still, I wouldn't let him look for another one. I thought that if he left the spirits of the dead would take him, and I wouldn't be able to lift the coffin lid by myself.

"Eventually, I let Illya go into the basement for another screwdriver, but first I had to cast a spell to protect him, and call on the angels to keep him safe. I made him swear on his soul that he would come back and not disappear and not die, and if he did die, he had to come back for me so I wouldn't be the only one left alive.

"After he returned and resumed working on the coffin a furious thunderstorm brewed up. I can remember seeing so many screws lying on the floor. But even after he undid the last one the lid wouldn't budge. The thunder and lightning were so intense and I was having difficulty understanding what the problem was. Illya finally came over and yelled in my ear that he thought they had sealed the lid with some kind of glue, and that was when I just lost it.

"There was this really big glass ashtray of my mother's, and I grabbed it and tried to smash it up into the edge of the lid and every time I managed to hit it, the ashtray would ring like a bell, but I kept missing it and hitting my fingers. I began to scream with each clap of thunder, all the while smashing away at the coffin lid until the ashtray became slick with my blood and I couldn't hold it anymore.

"Suddenly, a motion by the doorway caught my eye. Viktor was there. Looking through the side windows. He seemed to be studying us. I tried to call out to Illya but my voice was gone. Finally I just pointed and Illya saw him and Viktor began laughing. Laughing at our desperation.

"He quickly disappeared, but a few minutes later the door burst open and he marched in with a half a dozen men. I can still picture him, arms folded and silent. He let his men address us just to make it clear how insignificant we were. They announced that my grandmother wanted to see Illya, but that she didn't want to see me. It was such an obvious lie. My expression must have been highly amusing. They all burst out laughing. Illya began yelling, but they just lifted him up like a doll and walked out, leaving me alone.

"Up to that point, Illya had been my connection to reality. Without him, the boundaries between the worlds fell. I kept touching things just to prove to myself that they were really there. That *I* was really there. But never the coffin. The coffin had become the gateway to the world of the dead and I was sure that to touch it now was to be pulled into the beyond.

"Gella and Malka came out from wherever they'd been hiding and I could see that they were really scared. I took a step in their direction and they pulled away. I suddenly realized that it was *me* they were terrified of. *Me!* My first impulse was to try to calm them down. But something about seeing their fear unleashed a torrent of rage within me. Even though they had nothing to do with our mother's neglect or Viktor's brutality, they were complicit. I couldn't help but see them as agents of our misery. The fear I had lived with for so long… this new state of insanity had given me the means to turn it around and make it *their* fear.

"A rush of incredible power surged through my body. If I could inflict my fear upon them, I could do *anything*. Without realizing it, I was now seeing existence through the eyes of a psychopath and I became intoxicated by the clarity to be had by giving in to my rage. A world that could kill my mother and leave me to wrestle with a monster could only be moved by summoning the darkest of forces. I began creating a ritual to curse Viktor.

"Unburdened by compassion my focus was now perfect. All of a sudden I wasn't worried about leaving my mother alone. Everything had become cold and procedural. All that mattered was my will and the means to execute it. With no more thought than one might give to chaining up a bicycle, I cast a binding spell on my mother and went to work.

"Without hesitation, I now knew exactly what to do. What forces to summon. What spirits to invoke. I went out into the garden and gathered up wolf's bane and nightshade and long strands of dark ivy. I collected a bowl of the dark soil that had given life to the plants. Finally, I set out to obtain a source of blood and breath.

"I patiently waited by the bird bath. Eventually, a grey dove landed for a drink and I caught her up in my net. She beat her wings frantically but I eased her with soothing words. I whispered that everything was going to be okay and not to be frightened. I swore that I would not hurt her. Lying was so easy.

"I came back in through the kitchen and selected the sharpest knife we had. As I brought my supplies into the front room I could see Malka and Gella huddling together in the corner. Once again, a shock of exhilaration ran through my body... Huddling because of *me*!

"I no longer feared my mother's coffin. What I had previously viewed as the gateway to hell was now merely a worktable to lay my materials on. I lit a pair of candelabras from the dining room and placed them at the ends of the coffin and set more candles around the perimeter. Then I wove a garland of dark ivy for my mother's casket and wove a second one for myself. Setting the bowl of earth from the garden before me, I grabbed the knife and made a deep cut into the palm of my hand. A stream of sanctifying blood flowed onto the moist soil and I prayed for vengeance as I kneaded the mixture together.

"Offering up the bowl to the powers that be, I took my potion of earth and blood and cast it into a circle around the coffin. As I did, I began calling upon the occult forces to attend me. To bless my efforts and lend me their power.

"Focusing on the hate within me I began burning the wolf's bane in my mother's, still bloody, ashtray as I called out my revenge. I was too young to have a lot of specific spells or formulas to chant, but as I stood before my dead mother's coffin and summoned up the face of Viktor, the words flowed freely from some dark place within.

"Suddenly, I realized that Malka had crossed into my circle. She looked hurt and terrified and she was trying to tell me something, but all I could see was her weakness. Swept up in the torrents of hatred I was summoning I wanted nothing more than to slap her away. She must have read my intentions because she quickly darted back.

"I set fire to the nightshade and let it smolder on top of the coffin. With every step I could feel my rage building. By the time I noticed Malka again she was pointing frantically over to the couch and mouthing something I couldn't possibly hear. It broke my concentration and interrupted my chanting and I wanted to kill her right there.

"Finally I just screamed '*WHAT?*'

"'Gella' she said, pointing to the couch. 'You're hurting her. You're hurting her eyes.'

"I threw a glance over to Gella and even in my state I could see something was very wrong. She was on top of the sofa with her hands over her eyes and shaking. Somehow I knew that what I was doing was causing her suffering but I didn't care. No, more then that... I *hated* her for showing me her terror. She was mirroring my hate and all I wanted was to smash that mirror.

"I threw myself back into focusing on Viktor and called on the powers of fire and air to aid me in my spell but Malka kept begging me to stop. I can't remember much after that. I could hear Gella crying out in agony and it just infuriated me and fed my anger. At one point, I recall slashing at Malka with the knife. Trying to shut her up. She kept pleading with me to stop. Telling me that Gella's eyes were burning and that I was blinding her but by then, the dove was in my hands, swaddled in one of mother's scarves and I could feel her heart beating in panic but I just kept telling her it would be okay even as I raised her up with my hands and pledged her blood and her breath to fuel my ritual.

"Gella was wailing continuously at that point and Malka kept trying to intervene but I was now beyond caring. I called upon the wolf and I offered her blood and sustenance. And I called upon the raven and I offered her breath and vitality. Then I laid my offering on my mother's coffin, and I called upon my hate and I gave my hate a name, and my hate was named Viktor, and my offering was trembling, and my ears were filled with the keening of the dying, and my mother's coffin was bleeding and I felt the life force pass from my hands into the beyond and the beating in my hand ceased and then... a long time afterwards, when the room finally fell silent, I heard my grandmother come into the house.

"It was light out by then and the storm was over but I was still shaking. For a long while, she simply stood beside me without speaking. I can't imagine what was going through her mind at the sight of me and my handiwork. The sacrificial blood and earth smeared across her daughter's gleaming white coffin. Her granddaughter's mad spell, all for nothing. I finally asked her if my mother was really dead and when she said yes I wanted to cry, but there was nothing left inside. I think she was afraid to touch me at first. But finally she embraced me and moments later I passed out."

Chapter 30

Andrea's room had never seemed so huge and empty. The candles on the table had burned down low, and outside that fragile circle of light, the walls seemed to recede into the distance. A soft voice broke the stillness.

"He wanted it that way, you know." Natalya was calm now, but she had dragged them all into the world of her tortured childhood to tell her story, and Andrea was still shaking from the experience. She looked around the room. The Fae had floated over to the window and were staring out at the street in silence. Illya looked drained. He sat straight up in his chair with his hands on his knees, eyes focused on the floor in front of him.

Andrea pulled herself out of her own inner darkness and realized that she hadn't understood Natalya's last statement. "What do you mean, 'he wanted it that way'? Wanted what?"

"My rage. My hate. It led to my special ability. The power, Violet Miasma—it would become mine after that."

"The... *what?*"

"I don't know where the term comes from. It's not an appropriate use of the word miasma, but it's what he called those clouds of life forms that Malka provides me with when we merge."

"Oh! The purple butterflies in black plasma?"

"You make it sound like alien Chinese food."

"Not really—it hurt like hell!"

"Yes, I know… Oh, right. Sorry about that. I tried not to be too accurate, but a little bit packs a lot of hurt."

Remembering the experience, Andrea shuddered. She was reaching for her tea when the realization hit her. "Wait—Viktor *wanted* you to curse him?"

"He wanted Malka and me to go through a violent transformative episode in hopes of enabling that power."

"He *killed your mother* to do that?"

Illya coughed. "We don't know what happened to our mother. What we believe is that however she died, he took the opportunity to force the development of Natalya's powers."

Natalya continued. "We don't know why he knew of this power or how it could be summoned like this, but there is a chance that Viktor may have been trying to do that at the time of his character's death. There is much we don't know."

Andrea lit a few more candles. When she sat back down, she noted that the Fae had returned to the circle but were now floating next to her chair. She wondered if that meant anything. Looking up, she caught Natalya giving them a quizzical look before she resumed her story. "With the death of our mother, Viktor moved quickly to gain custody, and we disappeared from the world. Our grandmother tried to prevent it, of course, but Viktor is a genius at acquiring legal results by illegal means. I mean, he's our uncle. You'd think marrying his niece would have raised questions. But somehow Marina's marriage to our real father was annulled and, as if from nowhere, the paperwork appeared to show her wed to Viktor. So technically, he is now our legal stepfather though it makes us sick to think it."

"He bought a house in St. Petersburg, moved us into it, and immediately began trying to exploit my powers. He had determined that there was a link between the rage he could instill in a character and the degree of power that could be summoned. Part of that involved ensuring that the host and the character existed in a constant state of conflict."

"I can't imagine what that must have been like," Andrea said. "And the authorities didn't catch on to *any* of this?"

"You must understand that Viktor is far too smart to have done anything to alert anyone. Still, he lives to flaunt his transgressions, and nothing can change that. His inner circle lived right in the house with us, and from the first, they made no effort to hide their operations. And yet, we witnessed nothing illegal. We never saw a kidnap victim or a body. We knew about the girls, but we never saw them. Instead, they would describe the process of breaking them in, where they were destined, and the preferences and perversions of their future owners. Very matter-of-fact—routine descriptions of routine horrors.

"Viktor did this for a few years, and then, when we had come to believe, to hope, that we had seen the worst, he began to expose us to his 'punishments'—the retribution dealt out to any who defied him. Illya is correct that this was the real reason he ran his business. There would always be a few punishments a year, and over time, he saw to it that the victims were closer and closer to people we knew: a business partner we had once met, a merchant we knew, a relative of someone we went to school with. We stopped making friends—it was just too dangerous."

Illya picked up the thread. "It was a gradual process. At first, we would hear about something at school: a mysterious killing in the neighborhood, violent and senseless. No one would know. But we would suspect. Or at home, they began to let things drop in passing. They'd say 'That shopkeeper needs to be disciplined,' and a shop would close in the neighborhood. No one would say why. Finally, all pretense was dropped, and we would know who and when, what was to happen, and what they had done to deserve it. Then they started showing us the souvenir photo books…"

"Illya!"

"You wanted them to know."

"No!" Natalya was on her feet. "She doesn't need that!"

Illya gave her a look of surrender, and she sat back down and continued.

"The last thing you need to know," she said, "is that we, at the center of all this, were completely safe. It was Viktor's genius to make it clear to us and everyone in our circle that under no circumstances were we to be touched. Surrounded by animals with monstrous appetites, we lived in a bubble of perfect security. Men disappeared for the crime of simply looking at me the wrong way."

"This may sound stupid, but why hasn't anyone killed him by now?" Andrea asked.

"Oh, it isn't for want of trying. It's one of his favorite games: to reduce a decent person to a state of murderous rage. Particularly an innocent—that's a special treat. You can't believe how good he is at playing this game. On a certain level, we represent the essence of this. He knows we would love to see him dead. He used to call us his 'little vipers' in front of the crew. Keeping us so close at hand was another way to display his power.

"But whoever might someday succeed in eliminating him will see their loved ones pay a terrible price. He doesn't fear death, but he has created an elaborate web of arrangements and interlocking schemes that guarantee he will be avenged many times over in the event he is killed. His insurance policy. It was one of the few things he fully reconstituted when he shut down his St. Petersburg affairs and moved us to Brooklyn."

At this, Natalya fell silent. Illya stared at the candles, and the characters floated together, stunned.

Finally, Andrea broke the silence. "God, I hate him."

Natalya stared toward the window. "He is capable of destroying the lives and dreams of people who have never had any direct contact with him." She turned to Andrea. "You cannot allow this to happen to you. He wins when he destroys goodness. I told you this ugly tale not to make you hate him, but to prepare you—perhaps, *inoculate* is a better word."

Then she turned to the characters. "Is it true that you are of the Fae?"

Sumi moved forward from Rei and Masa and bowed slightly. "We are."

"And our characters as well?"

"Yes."

Illya exchanged a look with his sister. "We know nothing of the Fae."

Sumi simply smiled. "Then you will have less to unlearn." She turned to Natalya. "I will say one thing to you that you deserve to know. Your characters are not—and have never been—normal by any standard, even for the Fae. Perhaps we will know more about this soon."

Without looking at anyone, Andrea interjected. "And perhaps, while you're at it, you'll let us know what is really going on here?"

She had said this without any malicious intent—really without any inflection at all. But it hit the characters like a slap in the face, and they looked down.

Eventually, Sumi answered for them all. "Andrea, I won't pretend that we haven't obscured a lot of information about our situation here. We have and will continue to, but on our word, we have never consciously lied to you—"

"*Consciously?*" Natalya pounced on the word.

Sumi seemed at a loss for words, and Masa stepped in. "Yes. Consciously." She looked to Sumi and Rei and continued. "There is a lot more to our dealings with you than you know, and we are not innocent of certain evasions done to preserve that. But in order to avoid an excessive amount of… evading, we arrived here with certain parts of our memories suppressed."

"You knowingly blocked out certain memories?" Natalya asked.

"Our circumstances at home are rather complicated," Masa replied. "A significant part of the decision that led to our coming here ourselves, rather than sending anyone else, required that we be capable of immersing ourselves in this experience. Remembering the details of all the ongoing conflicts we are involved in would make it impossible to focus on being here with Andrea. The point was, we had confidence in the individuals around us. Perhaps, we were playing too clever a game."

"*Perhaps?*" interjected Rei.

"Not everyone wanted to take this approach," Masa said. "The idea was not to be withholding too much of a very complex story from you, Andrea."

Sumi continued. "We thought of it as weaving a new narrative from within the four of us, with all the facts arising and being experienced together. We chose to become pieces in a game with you rather than manipulate you as some sort of game masters. Unfortunately, we are starting to fear that opponents—"

"Enemies!" Rei hissed.

"Yes," Sumi said wearily. "That's clear now. Enemies at home have taken advantage of our decision, and we are unsure even of how much we *don't know* about our situation."

"You say that rather calmly," Illya observed. "I would think that represents an existential threat."

"You don't know the half of it," Rei said.

Sumi went on. "Janelle's death and Cami's behavior afterward are disturbing enough on their own, but we fear that a conflict—a political situation that we had believed to be tense but stable—may be unraveling. Before this, as far as we remember, Cami was unknown to us. Her very presence here is alarming." She looked around at Andrea, Illya, and Natalya. "We need to return home to find out what's going on, but we're afraid. We don't know what awaits us."

"We need to sneak back to our home and contact those we can trust," Masa said. "It will take some time, maybe even weeks."

Rei looked up at Andrea. "We have no intention of abandoning you, and you deserve a proper accounting of what is going on, but right now we can't even trust our own picture of what brought us to this point."

As these statements sank in, Natalya poured herself another cup of tea, which never made it off the table. She turned abruptly to Sumi. "This ability to selectively delete memory—can it be done to humans?"

"Oh, no." answered Masa. "It's an extension of another process, which simulates cultural experiences so we can learn how to behave and speak languages. It's how we learned Japanese. We spent a long time in Japan."

"We *think*," Rei muttered.

"We don't understand human physiology nearly well enough to do that," Sumi said. "Besides, we spent years in the simulations."

"We *think*," Rei repeated. "The problem is, right now, we don't 'know' *anything* for sure."

* * *

Natalya and Illya left for home, and Andrea's characters, the only sentient creatures she had ever felt really comfortable around, were preparing to go, too. Andrea couldn't focus. She was still numb from absorbing Natalya and Illya's story, and now Rei, Masa, and Sumi were just taking off—maybe for good. "So, this is it? You're just *leaving?*"

The three characters settled down on the bed. It occurred to Andrea that they were sitting precisely where their eggs had first appeared the day after her birthday.

Sumi spoke first. "Andrea, we're not planning to stay away for long. Try to understand. We need to do this to give you a better accounting of who we are and why we are here. Also, we've put ourselves in a terribly dangerous position by trusting others back home to guide us in a scenario that we thought we had created and controlled. Now we fear that it may be someone else's plot. And more than anything, we need to find out what that could mean for you."

"I know we've given you good reason to question our motives and your decision to help us," Masa said. "I'm afraid that for our kind, hiding things is a defining character trait. But so is loyalty. You have been loyal to us, and we must return that loyalty. If we are alive and able, we will come back."

"*If* you're alive?" Andrea asked.

"The conflict at home has been framed as a battle for the soul of the Fae," Rei said. "It has forced all to take sides, and the most extreme have gained influence beyond any they might normally have possessed. Many would find our deaths cause for celebration."

It was all becoming more than Andrea could handle. She loaded them down with as much food as they could carry, and when the time came, their parting moments were wrenching.

But it wasn't until her last glimpse of them as they flew off, silhouetted against the setting moon that she really broke down.

Chapter 31

The next day, Andrea arrived at school in a bubble—a rather uncomfortable one.

Too many things were happening already, and over breakfast she had received an even bigger shock: Dion was going away. Actually, she should have seen it coming, but her focus hadn't been on family issues. Her parents had been bugging him to come visit them at the site in Turkey. They seemed to think he might "get his priorities straightened out" by working with them, and since Andrea seemed to be doing "just marvelously" at school, they felt that a few weeks on her own wouldn't hurt.

She wondered what they would think when they saw her next report card. If there was any upside to surrendering to Viktor and saying goodbye to her characters, it was the possibility that she might regain control of her school situation.

Andrea wasn't watching where she was going when she literally bumped into someone from the past.

"Ow, watch it, moron!"

A girl with an aggressive sense of fashion to match her utter lack of manners stood in front of Andrea in the hall. She wore faded black work pants tucked into heavy black boots. The presence of a long black trench coat seemed appropriate but the reference was off. It seemed out of place in a school where—whatever else might be going on—no one was about to give you a hard time for not being a jock or for listening to thrash metal.

The girl's face was hard to read. She was wearing makeup, but it was applied in a style designed to play down the natural beauty of whoever was behind it. Her eye was drawn to the girl's earrings. Big hoop things, two—no, three—to an ear. It just didn't make any sense.

Then it did.

"Marion!" Andrea said, a little too happily to hide her discomfort. "How's it going?"

Marion, it seemed, had found a new attitude along with her new look.

"Melman," she sneered. "What do you want?"

Andrea was suddenly confused. She hadn't bumped into Marion intentionally, and she wasn't sure how to answer her rude challenge.

"Uh, how's it going?" she said, before realizing she had just said that.

Fortunately, Marion wasn't paying much attention to what Andrea was saying. Unfortunately, she did appear to have something to say to Andrea. "Listen, Melman, I'm not listening to any more of your fashion-whore propaganda."

"Um, okay?" Andrea was having trouble making the shift from her own issues to whatever Marion was so upset about. "They were just suggestions, you know?"

"Don't you try and weasel out of this with some lame-ass apology. I'm not having any of that."

"You *don't* want me to apologize?" Andrea wasn't sure what to apologize for, but she was now prepared to confess to anything to get away from Marion.

"No. You just need to know that I'm not letting some stupid fashionista bitch make me feel bad about myself."

"Marion, didn't you ask me...?"

"Don't try and change the subject... bitch!" Marion seemed to find the word "bitch" empowering. "I'm dressing for *myself* now, and you can just keep your stupid loser rules about... everything... to yourself!"

Marion's words were being launched with a lot of force, but they weren't landing with much impact. Other girls might be "fashionistas" or "whores," but calling Andrea that was like calling her a Zoroastrian or a manatee—it just didn't connect. Still, being yelled at was being yelled at, and she wanted to get out of this—fast.

"Marion, what do you want? I'm sorry what I said... didn't work for you. I didn't mean anything bad by it, and seriously, I would never say anything to make someone feel bad about themselves."

Marion's face turned red and she crowded up on Andrea. Apparently, by making a gracious apology for something they both knew she had never done, Andrea had put Marion in a spitting rage. "Don't think I'm going to forget this! You think you're so... good and so... special, with all your fashion crap and your friends and everything. You think you're all perfect and you can go around telling people what to wear and what to think, but you're not. You're just a stupid fashionista whore bitch, and you better stay out of my face if you know what's good for you!"

Marion seemed to realize she wasn't going to do any better than this. Stepping back, she shot Andrea a withering glare and stormed off into a nearby stairwell.

Andrea was relieved, but puzzled, trying to sort out *what* exactly was not going to be forgotten and who these mysterious "friends" were. The one who was going to store some boxes at her house, or the one with the crazy backstory and a personal sidearm?

* * *

The first-period bell rang just then, and it wasn't until much later in the school day that Andrea had a moment to consider anything beyond averting academic disaster.

With the end of her last class, though, she remembered that she was going home to a life without her guardian characters, and she felt close to tears as she sat waiting for the room to empty. By the time she made it into the hall, she was deep in her own thoughts and barely aware of anything around her.

What got her attention was a loud, taunting singsong, immediately identifiable as the bullying whine of an aggrieved high school jock. It came as no surprise to Andrea who that might be.

Ronald Mankey was the closest thing K290 had to a big man on campus. At almost six feet tall he towered over practically everyone and he had the sports mojo to make him the alpha male of the senior class. As such, he had come to expect as his due a certain amount of

241

flirtatious tribute from any girl superficially attractive enough to catch his eye.

Any girl except Natalya, that is. Over the years, her unwillingness even to acknowledge Ron's existence—much less smile at him—had built up a certain tension between the two of them.

On this particular day, Ron was hanging out at the door to the boys bathroom with a half dozen of his crew, picking targets of opportunity from the passing throng.

Andrea couldn't hear what he was saying, but she knew the gist of it: comments along the lines of "Nice hat!" and "Hey, loser, what are *you* looking at?" It didn't matter what Ron said; it was all just an excuse for his crew to burst out in braying laughter.

Like everyone else in the hallway, all Andrea wanted was to slip by unnoticed. A sharper, more alert version of herself would have summoned up her long experience at disappearing into a crowd—and done just that. But nothing was sharp today. She let her thirst draw her to a water fountain across from the boys' bathroom, and before she had finished, Ron was announcing his next target. "Hey, Nata-a-alya!"

Andrea froze. Natalya was coming from the opposite direction, minding her own business and unaware of the scene around the bathroom. She had been toning down her looks recently, minimizing the accessories and keeping her hair in a less horizontal orientation. By Natalya's standards, she was disguised as an ordinary girl.

Under normal circumstances, the boys would have hooted, Ron would have said something stupid, Natalya would have insulted him, and Andrea would have used the moment to escape. But over time, Natalya's icy Russian dismissal of Ron had evolved a bruised male ego into a festering one. Ron was out for payback and Natalya wasn't in the mood to deliver the kind of tart put-down that would satisfy everyone's need for entertainment.

Andrea was starting to hyperventilate. She caught Ron's eye, but he apparently didn't recognize crazy when he saw it, and must have thought she was trying to flirt with him.

Natalya, however, saw the crazy brewing in Andrea's aura and failed to pick up on the situation with Ron's crew. When Ron moved out into the hall to block Natalya's way, Andrea was equidistant between them on the opposite side of the hall.

The jock's opening salvo had no effect on Natalya, but it threw Andrea back into her fight-or-flight moment from the encounter with Marion. "Oh, here's our little fashionista, Princess Natalya."

It was beneath contempt, and Natalya treated it accordingly, but Andrea felt her blood rise.

Not getting a response, Ronald went right for the big gun. "Hey, Natalya, why ya gotta be such a bitch?"

Natalya stood there, giving him nothing to work with. But all Andrea heard was the word *bitch* being thrown down for the second time that day, and it just wouldn't go away.

The Andrea who could walk away from a bully calling *her* a bitch was being confronted by the Andrea who wasn't going to stand for anyone else being called a bitch.

The irony was, Ron had actually given up. He was starting to turn back to his crew when he threw out his last line, a stupid bit of nonsense he had given no thought to. "God, Natalya, is your mom a bitch, too? I mean, does it run in the family, or—"

Wham!

Before anyone knew what was happening, Ron was flat on the floor, with Andrea sitting on his chest, simultaneously trying to beat and strangle him. The sight of the five-foot-two girl flailing away at the six-foot guy was almost funny, but nobody was laughing.

Ragged and piercing, Andrea's screaming could be heard all the way down the hallway. "Shut up! You don't get to say that! You don't know anything! Leave her alone! How *dare* you talk about her mother! You don't know *anything! Nothing!*"

Ron couldn't seem to get her off of him, and it felt as if the scene went on for hours until, finally, two teachers and the school police officer managed to separate them.

As Andrea was being led to the disciplinary office with Ronald and Natalya, she noticed Gaylen off to the side. She hoped she hadn't seen her like this, but the more she thought about it, the less it seemed to matter. She was pretty sure she was going to be expelled—and quite possibly arrested.

Chapter 32

Police Officer Linda Petrossian's career with the NYPD was going nowhere. You didn't get assigned to be the house cop at a low-crime school like K290 if you were going places. Most of the kids had no idea she was even there, and the biggest issues she usually had to deal with involved faculty parking.

Still, Officer Petrossian was a good cop, and she had done her homework. Ronald Mankey was on her radar. He fit the jock-bully profile: mostly harmless, but under a bit of peer pressure, capable of something stupid.

Natalya Volkova was a different story. A little digging on her made for interesting reading. In her three years at the school, there had been only one incident. Early in her first year, a girl gang at the school had got her in their sights and decided they didn't like her.

The worst thing to expect from something like this at K290 was maybe a ruined outfit and some nasty gossip. Apparently, no one had informed Miss Volkova, and she put one of the girls in the hospital. Another girl was upset enough to file a complaint of harassment, which was dropped when it turned out that the girls—all four of them—had cornered her in a restroom and threatened her with a box cutter.

Nobody messed with the pretty Russian girl after that, but it did make Officer Petrossian curious, and over time, she managed to tease the name Viktor Lukov out of the system as her legal guardian.

And *he* fit a whole other profile. Still, Natalya had walked the straight and narrow at K290, and that made her and her Russian mob boss guardian somebody else's problem.

As for this Melman girl, the alleged perpetrator in today's little scene, there was nothing. It being the end of the day, Petrossian just wanted to wrap this thing up—read somebody the riot act and send everyone home without generating any paperwork.

Unfortunately, Linda Petrossian was a second-generation cop. It was in her blood. Her mother had been one of the first women to join the NYPD.

"Linda," she used to tell her, "your problem is you won't let things go. Honey, not everything can be a big investigation. Either get your detective shield or take early retirement, because your idea of doing the job is gonna piss off a lot of people."

So now Officer Petrossian was about to piss herself off by asking one simple question: How, exactly, did this happen?

The teachers had left it in her hands, so she brought the kids into the hall and made them lay out who was where, and when. The problem was, when you broke it all down, the story made no sense.

The kids were no help. Mankey was clueless and defensive, and Volkova was evasive. The alleged assailant, Melman, was still a bit out of it, but facts were facts. The fountain was where it was, and the boys' bathroom was where it was, and there was no way she had done what was alleged unless she literally flew there.

Finally, Officer Petrossian had to let it go. She put it in her notes for future reference. But the fact remained that for little Miss Melman here to hit Ronald Mankey high enough to knock him over, she would have had to rise a few feet and cross at least eight feet of school hallway. Even if she took two steps before launching herself, the force needed to knock down someone of Ron's height and weight was more than she should have been able to generate.

Finally, Petrossian gave in and tried to wind things up starting with the victim. Item one: Did Mr. Mankey want to press charges?

The only advantage to an otherwise useless investigation was that Ron was starting to calm down. Petrossian knew the angle to work with him. She made as if she were checking her notes, talking casually to him.

"I probably shouldn't go into this with you, Ronald, but…" She looked up at him. "… the mother's dead, you know."

He shook his head, "Wait. The little one…?"

"No. Miss Volkova—uh, Natalya. And Miss Melman—the little one?—she just learned about it."

Ron actually appeared shocked. "Oh, God! I didn't know that. I didn't mean to…"

"Ronald, Ronald, how could you know? You walked right over a line you knew nothing about."

She was glad to see his reaction. Ron wasn't evil—just dense and incredibly self-centered. Time to wrap it up. "So, Ronald, look, it's up to you. You're the victim here, and it's your choice about pressing charges. I mean, the only possible downside might be the media thing."

Ron didn't get it. "What media thing?"

"Well, you know, once there are charges, then *everybody* can work the story."

Ron still had a look that said, "What story?"

"Oh, come on, Ronald," she continued, "you've got to admit, it's pretty funny, right? I mean, this little girl gets lucky, and you and I both know, this was a one-in-a-million, crazy-ass lucky shot. Am I right? I mean, 'Cheerleader Sacks Quarterback'? There's your headline. Just the kind of thing to go all—what is it—viral? You never know, right?"

Ron's look said "*Oh, holy crap!*" But his statement, as taken down in Officer Petrossian's notebook, went, "I am unhurt and I prefer not to press charges," with a little "RB+C" next to it—Officer Petrossian's shorthand for "read back and confirmed."

One down, two to go.

Andrea Melman got off with a stern warning, but Petrossian felt like an idiot delivering it. Even though she sprinkled in a bunch of legalese and managed to keep a straight face, she was warning a scared little fifteen-year-old girl not to beat up any more football players.

They both were glad to be done with it.

She left Natalya for last. Even though the girl really had nothing to do with it, the cop in Linda Petrossian wanted to try to open up a line with her—not to pry or to interrogate her, just to communicate.

From what little she knew about the tightly controlled, serious girl, Petrossian guessed that Miss Volkova was dealing with much more than she let on. The problem was how to approach her.

Her veteran-cop mother had a saying: "When in doubt, let them do the talking."

So, she waited.

At last, Natalya started. "Thank you for not punishing Andrea. She's rather high-strung, but she is a good person. I don't think she'll do that again."

Officer Petrossian saw an opening. "I hope not, for Ronald's sake."

They both laughed, and Natalya added, "I actually feel sorry for him. He never knew what he was dealing with. Andrea is one of those quiet ones."

Petrossian shifted her focus. "Natalya, Ronald didn't know about your mother. I felt I should let him know which land mine he stepped on. Was that okay?"

Natalya waved her hand. "Oh, that's fine. He's not really such a bad guy. I mean, it's not his fault he's an idiot."

They laughed again, and Petrossian tried to make her move. Without thinking, she pulled out an official police business card and laid it on the table.

"Natalya, just in case you ever need any help with anything—you know, maybe just a question answered—I'd be happy to respond. Just in case."

Something was wrong. The card was lying on the table, and the room was suddenly ten degrees colder.

Natalya looked the same, but only because her previous look was frozen in place.

Damn it Petrossian! What did you do? You just lost her! What?

Her eyes locked on the card.

Standard police card. Got my name... phone... e-mail... embossed NYPD logo, and...

Victor finds this and I'll be fishing this girl out of the harbor.

"Crap," she said out loud.

Natalya smiled.

"Well, that wasn't exactly a trust builder, was it?" Petrossian said.

Natalya's smile grew as Petrossian took back the card and fished in her pocket for another card. A worn-out card from K290, with a recently retired guidance counselor's name on it, and Officer Petrossian's private number written in pencil. "You asked about music schools, and I got some brochures together for you. I always answer this phone with just plain 'yeah.' Never my name and never in the station or in a radio car. Otherwise, leave a message, and I'll get back to you as fast as your tone of voice tells me I need to."

Natalya put the card away and rose.

"Thank you, Officer Petrossian. I appreciate your discretion. I'm sorry I'm not a more open person. My experience with authorities has not been as positive as one might wish. Do understand, though, if I don't call you, it won't be because of trust issues."

* * *

When Andrea and Natalya left, it was dark, and no kids were outside the school.

They had not spoken a word since they left the school office. Andrea could feel tension emanating from Natalya, but a part of her was still giddy with relief that she wasn't getting expelled or going to jail. They didn't even try to call Dion. Maybe things were going to work out. With some serious effort, she could still get her grades up to high averages and slip through the term.

They were just reaching the point where their routes would diverge when Andrea finally turned to Natalya. "I'm sorry for making such a—"

Whack!

Andrea was amazed to be still on her feet. It took a moment to realize that Natalya had just slapped her as hard as anyone had ever hit her in her life, and it stung like hell. She turned to confront her, but the older girl's face was a mask of rage and tears. "Don't you *ever* do that again!"

Andrea was mystified, but she was pretty sure an apology wasn't going to help. Natalya could barely speak. She was sobbing and furious. "*That* is how girls die. *That* is how girls disappear."

Andrea still wasn't getting it. "What? What?"

Natalya grabbed her by the shoulders. "They are *men*! You don't humiliate their leader in public. You don't make him look bad in front of the others. *Girls die, Andrea!* Girls die all the time. Every day, they die for less than what you did."

Andrea wanted to break through, but she could see that Natalya wasn't talking about Ron or his friends or K290 or America. She was talking about the rest of the world—the world she came from, where the law was just another tool for the powerful to achieve their ends, and where justice stopped at the gates of their compounds. Where status came from the direct application of violence, and girls had the rights and protections granted by the men who owned them, and nothing more. "You would be *dead!* You would be dead, and it would be *my* fault. You stupid girl! Is that what you want?"

"Natalya, it doesn't happen that way here. Ron's not going to have me killed. He just won't talk to me. And I'm really okay with that."

Natalya smiled through her tears, but she continued. "You don't know, Andrea. You're so innocent... so naive. We are always a careless word or gesture away from the violence of men." She seemed to be collecting herself. "You think I'm crazy, don't you?"

Andrea thought for a second. "No. Not more than usual. I mean, not just for this. I mean, *this* may not be as crazy as..."

Natalya failed to suppress a smirk as Andrea thrashed about for the right response.

"No, not crazy. Not at all."

Natalya started laughing. "Okay. It's okay. But never again. Don't you ever put yourself in a position where your actions could justify violence against you by wounding a man's pride—especially by threatening their status within the pack."

"Okay, Natalya. Got it. I wasn't planning on making a habit of challenging every alpha male I see. I still don't understand how that happened, anyway. I just got a little crazy. You should understand that."

Natalya smiled and waved goodbye. She turned to go and had started down the street when she stopped, ran back, grabbed Andrea, and kissed her on the forehead.

It was more astonishing than the slap. "What was that for?"

Natalya had already turned away. Over her shoulder she said, "No one has ever stood up for me before." Then, louder, as she walked off down the street: "Don't *ever* do it again."

Chapter 33

Days went by, then a week. Dion was going to Turkey. Then he wasn't. A flurry of messages went back and forth. Finally, her mother called just as she was leaving for school one morning. Andrea was already distracted at that hour, but her mother's rambling explanation/apology confused her to the point that she could barely remember the conversation later.

Her parents were sorry to be taking Dion away, but they were "worried" about him in some way they didn't want to share right now. Just for a few weeks. Maybe a month. How was she? Grades good? Sorry to be doing this, but they were counting on her to take on the extra responsibility.

Andrea was all positive reactions and affirmative responses, but the call ended so quickly, she came away feeling dazed and abandoned. For the first time she could remember, she actually wished she could share some of her problems with her mom.

* * *

Moving on from "the incident" was something she resolved to do. Really, it was to calm down Natalya, but Andrea figured that everyone would benefit from the gesture.

It was part theater, part ritual. The setting was the school cafeteria at lunch period. The cast was Ron, his crew, and Andrea. She gave a lot of thought to her outfit, knowing that it—more than anything—would set the tone. She wanted something that would identify her as "girly" without being provocative.

What would they picture their little sister wearing to school? she wondered.

It turned out to be a cardigan sweater.

The hard part was timing the approach. Ron had to be there. And they needed to be done eating and not engrossed in some important sports topic. Near the end of the period, she steeled herself and made her move. Crossing over to the north wing, she could hear her own footsteps.

Predictably, Ron's table was in the center of the wing. He was sitting at the head, with his back to the aisle. His crew noticed Andrea's approach and nudged him.

Coming to a stop at Ron's right elbow, she cleared her throat and prepared to launch into her performance. Right away, she almost blew it. He looked up and displayed a flicker of fear, and she very nearly burst out laughing. But the hostile looks from his crew stifled that. Since the idea was to look flustered, it helped that she now really was.

Knowing he wouldn't remember her name, she made sure to put it in her intro. "Uh, hey, Ron, it's me, Andrea... Melman. About that whole thing the other day..."

Looking up at his crew and then back at him made her appear nervous saying this in front of them—even though, in fact—they were the real audience. "I don't know what to say..."

Ron tried to jump in. "No, hey, it's cool. I mean—"

She pushed on. "No, really Ron, I was anything but cool. It was bad enough going off and ranting all that stuff, but... I don't know how I blindsided you and caught you off balance like that. I'm so embarrassed, and you were really great about it. I mean, I'm not usually so... crazy about things, but there was a bunch of girl stuff I was dealing with, and... anyway, thanks for being so understanding about it."

She had taken great pains to make sure the boys took away two main points: (1) she had caught Ron off balance; and (2) "crazy girl stuff" was to blame.

That was the end of Andrea's prepared remarks, but it seemed Ron had something to get off his chest. He moved his chair in close to her and lowered his voice. "Andrea, you gotta know, I had no idea about her mom. I mean, you know, I like mixing it up with Natalya, and all, but I wouldn't go there."

To her great surprise, it turned out that Ronald Mankey had a set of previously unsuspected human feelings—and now she was going to have to respond to them.

She threw caution to the winds and went with her preferred option: the truth. "Ron, I know that, and I'm pretty sure she does, too. I was the one who had just learned about it, and when it came up in the hallway, I just lost it. I was way out of line."

Ron considered this for a second and looked at her. "No, Melman. You thought I was taking a cheap shot, and you threw down. That makes you a good friend. You're okay."

Andrea left the cafeteria in a state of mild shock, but she hadn't gone far before Gaylen grabbed her and dragged her into an empty classroom. They had talked sporadically, and Gaylen had given her support, but she also respected that Andrea just wanted to hide for a while.

Now she was due the whole story, and Andrea gave it up, right down to the Ron moment that had just occurred.

Gaylen pondered the meaning of it all. "Wow, 'crazy girl stuff'? You realize you've given them all a lifelong complex about menstruation? Good for you!"

"Gaylen, that's not what I meant. But yeah, I probably did. Hm-m…"

Gaylen changed her tone and approached the next topic cautiously. "You know, Andrea, I was standing right there behind Ronnie and his boys when you flew at him."

Andrea laughed. "Well, I wouldn't say *'flew.'*"

She couldn't remember ever seeing Gaylen look this serious. "Oh, yeah, *flew*. You didn't jump, leap, or hop. You flew. Everyone else was looking at Ron and Natalya, but you had this certain look. And at this point, I kind of know that look, and I was watching you to see what you might do. Andrea, you left the ground and headed straight for him. You didn't just rise; you even accelerated in the last few feet. What's going on, Andrea? Tell me this isn't related to what you were asking me about the other day."

She didn't really want to lie to Gaylen. She wasn't even sure she could. But the lesson she had been learning over and over from Natalya was that involving outsiders in her personal problems could have consequences. It wasn't about trusting Gaylen; it was about protecting her. Still, what could she say? Honesty was the last place she wanted to go, but what else was there? "Okay, Gaylen, I need you to trust me about this. Right now, I can't give you the story behind that. I didn't even realize that had happened until you just said it, but yes, you may have seen something that's… uh, hard to explain."

When Gaylen kept silent, she continued.

"I'm afraid to get you involved in anything. Things have been moving so fast, and I don't know what to do. Things are so crazy right now…"

"Crazier than you flying across the hall to knock over a guy who's got almost a hundred pounds on you?"

"Actually, yes. Quite a bit crazier. Gaylen, you could be in real danger, in a bunch of different ways, if I involve you."

"I'm not involved already?"

Andrea felt a shiver of fear. "Oh, God, I hope not. Not you. Oh, no, you don't know anything. How could any of this be…?"

Perhaps sensing an Andrea Melman meltdown, Gaylen backed off. "Look, you don't have to tell me everything right now. But you're going to need to decide if keeping me ignorant is going to protect me any better than giving me a bit of warning. I'll try to act cool about this for the time being, but you do realize it's becoming a minor obsession with me, right?"

"Yeah," Andrea said. "I'd be the same way. I'll try to give you as much of the story as I can, as soon as I can. Just understand, the more you know, the less you may like it."

"And now I'm *dying* to know." Gaylen laughed.

Andrea's look stopped her. "No, Gaylen. Please. It's just... there's nothing funny here."

Andrea couldn't handle any more. She spun around and hurried out of the empty classroom, leaving Gaylen to wonder exactly what was going on.

* * *

This time of year, the walk home was always dark. Andrea was in no rush to get there, though. She stopped off at the Japanese supermarket and picked up some ramen and mochi ice cream.

Why am I still doing this? she wondered. *I never used to eat any of this stuff.*

Dion's absence was even worse. They had barely interacted in the past few months, but she had felt comforted knowing he was just down the hall or a phone call away. Maybe she wasn't really as independent as she imagined. Whatever. This was the moment to shake it off and get her act back together.

She had loaded herself up with makeup work, and it was possible to picture, a few weeks from now, a return to the status quo. "Boring is good." she said out loud.

Approaching her house, she barely noticed a nondescript man in a brown coat, standing on the sidewalk. The sort of person one passed every day without a thought.

She had already walked past him when he addressed her in a pronounced Russian accent. "Miss Melman?"

She stopped.

"Miss Melman?" A command, posing as a question.

She didn't know what to do. She wanted to run. To scream. To do anything but stand there frozen, awaiting her fate.

"You don't *know* me, Miss Melman? Oh, now, I think perhaps you do. Didn't I see you over my property a few weeks ago? Yes, yes. Oh, now, I'm not here about that. Nothing at all about that. Please turn around, Miss Melman. You have nothing to fear. We should at least have the formality of a face-to-face meeting, don't you think?"

Andrea couldn't move. Her heart was pounding, and her breathing shallow and ragged. The man moved himself around into her field of view, but she was too scared to move her head and look directly at him.

He didn't seem to care. "There, now. That's better, no? A bit late for you to be getting home, isn't it? Oh, a little shopping. Of course. Such an independent young lady, aren't you? Yes, yes. You remind me of my daughter, Natalya."

Andrea gasped involuntarily. It was her first acknowledgment of anything she was hearing, and she prayed it didn't betray the disgust she felt hearing him claim Natalya as his own.

His burst of laughter told her that this was exactly what had happened. It was a cruel, victorious laugh, expressing the joy of drawing first blood.

Andrea felt something shift inside her. A small flame of hope died and left a cold cinder in its place.

"And your little friends—where have *they* gone?"

Andrea was slowly coming out of her panic, but without a plan, the best thing she could think of doing was to maintain the picture she presented: a girl paralyzed with terror and beyond rational thought. But inside, she was wondering, *How do you know that?*

He pushed on, apparently not expecting any response. "Perhaps my son, Illya, might provide some companionship? They frown on the age difference here, but in a few years? Maybe someday you could produce your own little ones."

He paused and seemed to study her. "Perhaps he is not to your liking? But you are an American girl. You don't believe in people interfering in your decisions, do you, now? No, of course not. You believe yourself to be above all that, don't you?"

Andrea was calming down, but her assessment of the situation wasn't good. He was breaking her down, killing her slowly with small cuts. All she could think to do was to stay silent and give up nothing.

"You're a very interesting girl, Miss Melman. A one-in-a-million girl, in fact. My girl, Natalya, has two of these characters, but they are—how would you say? —quite damaged. But you have more than that, yes?"

She stifled a spark of hope. *He doesn't know! He won't say? Does he know of Cami? Is he just fishing?*

"Of course you won't say. A very willful girl, aren't you, Miss Melman? And yet, you give up to my Natalya. You surrender. Why? To protect your little ones? Yes, I think so. A noble gesture and a very wise decision. But then there you are, over my place. Doing what, Miss Melman? Looking for what? I have asked myself this for some time now. My curiosity gets the best of me, and I think, perhaps Miss Melman will tell me what I wish to know."

Andrea's leg was starting to cramp from holding the same position for so long. She took a small step backward.

"Oh, no, Miss Melman, don't move away. I have something to show you—something I would have you verify for me. If you please. No pressure, of course. I just need to know if a few of these facts are correct."

With that, he pulled out a small electronic tablet. It took Andrea a moment to focus on the page being displayed. When she did, she could see that it was filled with Dion's complete itinerary: flights, hotel, transportation—everything.

She shuddered when he swiped to another page, with her parents' hotel information, and another page with what appeared to be a daily transportation log of their trips back and forth to the excavation site.

"I believe this is all accurate, but you would know for sure, no?"

Andrea's world began breaking into pieces, each one a bit of her sense of home and security. And as each piece fell away, it left another cold shard in its place. On the surface, she appeared the same, but a new perspective was growing inside her—a perspective older than civilization, older than humanity.

"Ah, perhaps I have caught you at a bad time, Miss Melman? Perhaps some other occasion? Do you think that might be possible? I hope so. You don't know me, Miss Melman, but I can be very persuasive, and I think we have more to say to each other. Take care, Miss Melman. Take very good care."

She didn't see him leave, didn't remember going in the house. Didn't remember anything after the words "Take very good care."

When she started to regain awareness, she found herself sitting at her desk, staring at a blinking cursor in an empty search field. She couldn't focus, couldn't think clearly about what she needed to do. Eventually, she looked down to find a notepad in front of her.

At some point, she had written the words *fight or flight*. That was the moment when Andrea Melman realized that flight was no longer an option. She drew a line through the last two words and stared at the result.

Chapter 34

Natalya was having tea by the kitchen window when a frantic Gella flew in. "She's going to kill him! She's going to kill him!"

"Calm down, Gella. Who is going to kill whom?"

"Andrea! Viktor! He approached her in front of her house, and now she's looking for ways to kill him. You have to stop her."

"Okay, Gella. Thank you." Natalya calmly put her teacup down and called out, "Illya, where is my cauldron?"

"Where you left it: in the basement," he shouted back from the living room. "Do you need help moving it?"

"I can handle it."

The rest of what she needed was already in a duffel bag under her bed. She was almost out the door when she remembered. "Oh, do we have lingonberries?"

"They're not in the fridge?" Illya said. And then: "Lingonberries?"

Coming out of the kitchen, she looked at him. "For pancakes— if everything goes well… when we're done."

"You're very confident," he said.

"This one is different. She's a witch."

"Good luck all the same."

* * *

She parked the station wagon off the street at the back of the driveway and texted Andrea: *downstairs – coming up*.

When she came in the room, Andrea was sitting at the computer, flanked by an ink-jet printer and a paper shredder. The corkboard that had previously held school schedules and whimsical paste-ups was now covered in printouts about sniper training and the specifications for the Dragunov sniper rifle.

Andrea didn't look up or speak. Natalya took a deep breath and centered herself. "The Dragunov—a good choice."

Andrea kept working.

"Accurate, affordable. You'd need practice, but there are ranges nearby."

No reply.

Natalya moved closer behind her. "It has a bit of a kick, you know." She held her hand above Andrea's shoulder. "If you're not careful, you can break this bone... here."

She touched Andrea's collarbone, making her flinch. "You know the particular model you're looking at is four-feet long, right? You'll need the right case to make that work with any of your outfits, or you're going to look pretty funny with it on the bus."

An involuntary smile appeared on Andrea's face. Seeing it, Natalya silently gave thanks to everything she prayed to, and moved to reel Andrea in. "Viktor would be proud, Andrea."

Andrea stopped typing without looking up.

"You forgot what I told you."

Still silent, Andrea's hands hovered over the keyboard.

"You may be his proudest accomplishment. He has a low opinion of Americans, but to get you to take him on—a good, decent American girl driven to murderous intent..."

Andrea finally turned around to face her. There were no tears. No fear. No emotion of any kind. All she said was, "He's after my family. I have to kill him." Then she turned back to the screen.

Natalya took a moment to assess the printouts. She was impressed. In a few short hours, little Andrea had gotten a good head start on the world of military-level sniping.

Even more remarkable was her approach. The other girls had tried to get close to Viktor with a pistol or—even sadder—a knife. With guys, it was always a pistol or an assault rifle, but they never got in a position to fire at him. Andrea had already realized she needed to trade passion and proximity for distance and patience. The Dragunov was an inspired choice. A semiautomatic rifle with a ten-round magazine—accurate and reliable.

Natalya touched Andrea's shoulder again. "I need to talk to you face-to-face for a minute. Please." She pulled over a chair and waited until Andrea turned around.

Natalya began with the tone of voice she might use to critique the solution to a design problem. "Let me say this first. This is impressive—really impressive. Of all the people I know who have made attempts on Viktor's life, I think you might have the best chance of any of them. Put him in the sights and empty the magazine—you'd probably get him."

A faint smile betrayed Andrea's pride in Natalya's assessment.

"But, of course, it isn't that simple. It's not like his 'insurance policies'—the vengeance he takes from beyond the grave—would come after just you. It wouldn't even stop with your family. Viktor spreads the horror around to relatives and friends. Trying to kill him usually results in at least a dozen victims. That means Gaylen, for one. You need to think about her, too."

Natalya had chosen her words well. Andrea was starting to melt. "But he has to die. What other way is there? What else can I do?" She began tearing up.

Natalya didn't have an answer to that. But she hadn't set out this night to destroy evil; she had come here to save goodness. In her mind, a battle was on for the soul of Andrea Melman, and by everything she held holy, Natalya Volkova was going to win that battle.

"So, do you accept that your plan will kill a lot of innocent people?"

"Yes."

"For the time being, can we agree that a good harvest cannot be grown in poisonous soil?"

"Yes, but—"

"Then would you agree you need a different plan, from a different perspective?"

"Uh, yeah, I guess."

"Then I need you to trust me, Andrea Melman. More than person-to-person. I need you to trust me witch-to-witch."

At that, Andrea seemed surprised. She brushed away her tears. "Okay."

"Viktor believes in nothing. Yet, he himself is a witch, and he knows that it gives him a special power over the witch who *does* believe. His main weapon against you is to make you believe that his way—the way of violence and death—is the only way. To make you abandon everything that you know to be good or decent, in hopes of destroying him. Your soul in exchange for his annihilation.

"Andrea, his tone with you may have been casual, but every word, every threat, implied or stated, was designed to make you deny your own goodness and to put you in a state of terror. Essentially, he cast a spell over you to enlist you in his game. We need to counter that spell."

Leaving Andrea to consider this, Natalya stepped out into the hallway and wheeled in a handcart holding a most impressive item: a black iron cauldron filled with various ritual implements. As she had hoped, Andrea, even in her current distress, was fascinated. "You have a real cauldron. That's amazing."

"It weighs a ton, but you know what they say: When you need a cauldron, you need a cauldron."

Andrea's eyes grew wide as Natalya started pulling things out of the big cast-iron pot. Natalya knew she was going to need every trick in the witch's tool kit tonight, and she had brought just about everything she possessed: oils and incenses, candles, salt, and charcoal. Ritual dolls and manuscript paper and special chalks for inscribing sacred circles and sigils. Wands and pentacles and bundles of sage and things Andrea couldn't even identify. But the most intriguing thing she set out was a knife. It had a blade seven or eight inches long and two or three inches wide, and a bone handle bound with strips of animal hide.

Andrea had seen a lot of ritual knives—mostly athamés for Wiccan rites. But those were delicate by comparison and always immaculate, in keeping with the concept of their cutting nothing but energies. No one would dream of using one for practical work.

This thing looked like a farm tool—something with a long history of hunting and cooking, with some hand-to-hand combat thrown in for good measure. "What is *that*?"

"Oh, that?" Natalya said, as she began clearing the center of the room. "That's the Good Knife. It's been in my family for as long as anyone can remember."

"'Good' as in 'good versus evil'?"

Natalya laughed. "Oh, not really. Good as in 'the one we reach for when we need our best knife for the job.'"

"Is that blood on it?" Andrea asked, eyeing the blade carefully.

"Probably. It has…" Natalya stopped in her tracks. "Oh, right, I forgot. You Wiccans tend to be a bit more, um…"

"Precious?" Andrea suggested.

Natalya looked apologetic. "No, no. I don't mean to criticize. A lot of Wiccan craft has these ceremonial roots with specialized tools that only get brought out for rituals. What you call 'family traditional witchcraft' tends to be a bit more, uh, frugal. I mean, basically no one can afford to have special clothes and tools and all. I hope that doesn't bother you."

Andrea considered this for a moment. "No, it's just different. It's fine. My comfort zone has more important challenges just now."

Natalya went back to setting up. "One could make the argument that a ceremonial athamé hasn't been charged with the experiences of life the way a practical knife like this has. It has served us for generations. This knife has harvested our food, given protection, cut umbilical cords, taken life to sustain life. In a sense, I'm here because of it."

Andrea found herself absorbing Natalya's words and opening herself to the power of the Good Knife. It was a connection back to a life common to all humankind for... well, the entire span of human history, except maybe the past hundred years. It also reminded her that she had grown up a member of the lucky part of the world who didn't need to think about killing their own food.

Natalya tied up her hair and began working faster. She used a compass to establish true north. From then on, all her ritual activities relating to the cardinal points began from the north. A large central area was inscribed, with three overlapping circles drawn in chalk. Candles marked the quadrants. They were blessed with incense, anointed with oil, and sprinkled with water and salt, each with its own incantation.

Some of this was familiar, but with a twist. Andrea's circles were oriented to the east. She never drew an actual circle and always pictured it as a single boundary. But most of it was completely different from anything she had ever known.

Natalya filled the center of her circle with a large chalk pentagram and then filled the pentagram's internal spaces with symbols—some astrological, some in the Cyrillic alphabet, and others unrecognizable. The cauldron went—not in the center of the circle—but in the topmost section of the pentagram. Then, after placing candles around the cauldron, she commandeered a low table, placed it near the center, and loaded it with ritual implements and materials.

From time to time, she would task Andrea to fetch things, such as water or cups. "No chalices, though—something hard to knock over." But mostly, Andrea felt like a passenger on a strange journey. On this night, she was receiving a vision of a very different world of magic.

Andrea's experience of magical ritual was a polite, respectful "thank you for these gifts," "please, if the universe allows" sort of approach. She was amazed at how matter-of-fact this magic was. Natalya didn't seem to make a big distinction between the sacred and the secular. She crossed over the circle boundary without any "making a doorway" or so much as an "excuse me" to the occult powers that be. Beyond that, Andrea was quite unprepared for the adversarial way Natalya approached her magic. Her opening statement was anything but polite.

"Powers of earth and sky, I *demand* that you hear my voice. In Aradia's name, I will assault you without mercy. No sleep will you know. No peace to your days. I am the storm at your door, and you *will* heed me and surrender the aid I seek. Awaken, Aphrodite! Attend me, Astraea! Love and justice *demand* vengeance. My voice be heard!"

This went on for long stretches, and Andrea was amazed that Natalya had no Book of Shadows—no notes, manuscripts, cheat sheets, or reminders of any sort. As far as she could tell, Natalya was summoning up this entire ritual from within herself as they went along.

As striking as its spontaneity was the *physicality* of Natalya's magic. The circle she had cast was almost twenty feet wide, and she stalked her way around it, gesturing and storming and pleading, demanding and cursing and imploring, drawing down the moon with her bare hands.

Andrea hadn't really known what one actually used a cauldron for in a situation like this.

But Natalya knew: You burned things in it.

Symbolic images, parchments inscribed with oaths, poppets, sage—all sorts of things. You threw them into the cauldron and then threw more things on top of them: frankincense, oils, sparkly dust that erupted into clouds of flame and smoke. On more than one occasion, Natalia snipped locks of Andrea's hair, adding it to a bundle of stuff headed for the cauldron. The swirl of sights and smells lifted them into another world.

Andrea's consciousness of where she was and what was happening crossed into a floating dream. Sharply focused on the smallest wisp of smoke or the sound of the wind outside, she felt her awareness being pulled out of her body and up through the room, the house, and the world beyond. Words and phrases floated into and around her. Little by little, things began to shift.

As she worked, Natalya began a low droning chant in a strange language. Andrea could sense a door opening within herself. Unbidden, she began to intone her own contribution, her words a counterpoint to Natalya's steady rhythmic intonations.. "Great Mother, protect me. I am pledged to the Goddess, but the evil before me is beyond my power to resist. Sweep the fog of fear from my mind. Give me clarity." Andrea's voice grew stronger. "Break the chain of fear that enslaves me. Bind the will of my enemy, and destroy his power."

Still chanting, Natalya tied a branch of sage to another package. Rising, she held the offering over the cauldron, and anointed the bundle with oil. In it went, igniting immediately and filling the room with an explosion of light and smoke. The chanting ceased, and Andrea's voice, strong and clear, was the only sound in the room. "Let love be strong and justice merciful, but empower me to protect and avenge the abused. Light of the Goddess, sustain and preserve me."

She looked up to see Natalya holding the Good Knife with both hands. Raising it over Andrea's head Natalya declared, "Isis, I beg. Ransom me this soul."

Andrea felt a spark within her catching fire as Natalya continued. "By your grace and within your grace."

With the knife, Natalya described a circle around the rim of the smoldering cauldron, saying, "Life for life. Death for death. My blood my bond."

Lifting a large bowl of water, Andrea went to her side. Without hesitation, Natalya brought the knife down and pierced the tip of her own index finger. Letting the blood drop into the bowl, she intoned, "We summon the power from within us and beyond us. As above, so below."

Exchanging knife and bowl, Andrea did the same. Drops of her blood fell and mixed in the water. Raising the knife over her head with both hands, Andrea said, "By my blood, you will know me."

Natalya offered up the bowl and repeated, "By my blood, you will know me."

They drank, the moon rose on the eastern horizon, and soon it was dawn.

Chapter 35

By the time they woke, Saturday was half over. But any concerns over the appropriateness of eating breakfast in the afternoon melted away in the aroma of Natalya's pancakes.

The lingonberries made a big impression on Andrea. "These are fantastic!" she said. "Why haven't I heard of lingonberries before?"

Andrea had more important questions than that but she wasn't sure which ones to be asking, so she decided to go with a broad approach. "So why do you know so much about this stuff, anyway?"

Natalya seemed to consider her answer as she worked on the food in front of her. "Well, most of the ritual stuff—oh, and the pancake recipe, too—is from my grandmother."

"Oh, not that. I meant the weapons and the breaking-and-entering stuff."

Natalya paused as a ripple of annoyance passed over her countenance – leaving a knowing smirk in it's wake. "Andrea, that back door is practically cardboard. *Anyone* could break into this place."

Andrea frowned at the response, or possibly at her empty plate. Helping herself to another stack, she continued. "Okay, okay. Your freakish knowledge of guns and tactics, then. Were you always like this?"

With a sigh, Natalya applied another glaze of lingonberry to her pancakes. "I don't know any more, to be honest. Probably not. The other night, we didn't go into any detail about our day-to-day life with Viktor's crew, but it was a strange dynamic. Most of them were former

Spetsnaz—a blanket term for a bunch of different types of Russian Special Forces. They all had been in Chechnya with Viktor. Every one of them was hard core, and almost certainly some kind of war criminal by the time he was done with them.

"But it was odd. Under Viktor, we all were equal. Anyone there could be eliminated at any time, and that was that. One day, you would come down to breakfast to find Boris gone and his room reassigned, and you would just stop referring to him and no one made a big deal of it. Illya and I knew that any one of them would die protecting us—or cut our throats—on command.

"We came to accept that it was nothing personal. Gradually, Viktor's men came to see that we understood the rules and we didn't blame them, and it changed the dynamic. They started to train us in all the different skills they had. It became a kind of game. Illya wasn't so into it, but it gave me something to hold on to. Every weapon, every technique of tradecraft, each strategy or scheme I learned, made me stronger by giving me leverage in that world. And besides, everyone thought it was really cute training this little girl to fieldstrip and reassemble an AK47 blindfolded in under a minute."

Andrea laughed, and Natalya blushed. "I'm out of practice, but I really can, you know."

"I don't doubt it. I'm laughing because you're still so proud of it."

Natalya rolled her eyes and poured herself another cup of tea. "Viktor even approved of it, though he never personally taught us anything. There were restrictions, of course. Any details about his operations were totally off limits—that would get you killed. But the nuts and bolts of running operations—finance, tactics, equipment, communications, and a lot of computer stuff—that was all fine."

"Did they know about Malka and Gella?"

"Oh, no, that was all up north. Viktor was off running operations during much of that period. We spent a lot of time at our grandmother's, learning."

"Pancakes and rituals?"

"I remember a lot of algebra and Russian literature, but yes, pancakes and rituals, too."

Andrea stared down at her plate, distractedly running her finger around the edge to get the last of the jam. "Natalya, I feel like you broke Viktor's hold on me last night, but you know he's not going to give up. Also… not that Viktor isn't enough to worry about, but I've been trying to get my head around this whole Fae thing. And honestly, I'm scared."

"Yeah, I know. I was minimizing it the other day, but I've been around three of these Faeries for a long time, and when I think about how little I know about them—personally or as a group—I'm not sure which to be more worried about: Viktor or them. One thing I can worry less about is collecting eggs. Viktor told us we were 'caught up,' whatever that means, and that we're off egg duty until further notice."

Andrea brightened. "Really? Well, that has to be good, right?"

"Maybe not. With Viktor, any little change in the wind usually bodes ill. We'll see."

* * *

It was getting late, and shadows were stretching across the yard outside when Natalya's phone rang.

"Hi, Gaylen. What? No. *What?* Wait, slow down. What's going on there? No. Of course. Gaylen? *Gaylen!* Wait… Who is that? You tell her I… *What!* What are they doing there? Okay, Gaylen, listen to me. Listen. I'm with Andrea… Yes… Yes… Alright we're coming over there. Yes, right now. Stop talking to them and get your stuff together. All of it. We'll be over in fifteen minutes. Just hang in there and stop talking to them. You're *what?* We're coming over *now!*" Natalya looked up. "Gaylen's in trouble."

Five minutes later, they were in Natalya's old barge of a station wagon, lumbering through the streets of Brooklyn. When they hit a red light, Natalya turned to face Andrea. "Okay, level with me," she said. "You knew Gaylen was a witch, right? I mean, I'm not mad or anything, but you had to know, right?"

"*What?* No! She is? You're kidding. If anything, I would expect *you* to know. She's over at your house all the time. She's never even *been* to my house."

"Well, I think that's about to change."

"Um… huh?"

"Okay, a few things. Her stepmother found her Book of Shadows last night. And instead of confronting Gaylen directly, she called in her friends from Dominion of God, and they showed up an hour ago. About a dozen of them. And as we speak, they're conducting a combination intervention-exorcism-eviction on her. We need to get her out of there."

"Absolutely! Wait, can we *do* that? Doesn't her stepmother have some power?"

"Okay, next thing. Did you know Miss O'Reilly turned eighteen three days ago?"

"Natalya, I didn't even know Gaylen's last name *was* O'Reilly. Did you?"

"I've written checks to her, so yeah, but the rest is news to me. But it does mean that she can—make that *probably has to*—leave her stepmother's house."

"She had her birthday, and no one knew about it?"

"Uh, Andrea? Sumi told me you did the same thing."

"Yeah, but it's so sad when someone else does it. God, that girl *is* a book of shadows."

It was almost dark by the time they pulled up to Gaylen's house and right into a crazy scene. A half dozen big black SUVs and pickups were parked in the driveway, in front of the house, and across the street. Andrea noted that they all had license plates from places considerably south of Brooklyn. And every one of them tricked out with elaborate searchlights and gun racks. *So, this is what Suburban Tactical Chic looks like,* Andrea thought.

Natalya seemed to be taunting them with how close she came to scratching their paint jobs as she pulled in. One of the trucks had its lights trained on the front lawn, and what looked like a pile of junk turned out to be clothes and a few dozen books.

The front door opened, and Gaylen's stepmother, accompanied by two tall, angry-looking men, came outside and threw another armful of books onto the pile. A woman in a long dress and a bonnet followed with a suitcase, which flew open when it landed.

Andrea was about to jump out of the car when Natalya motioned her to wait. "We need backup."

Andrea shot a look at her. "We *have* backup?"

Natalya already had her cell phone out. "This is Miss Volkova. I'm at my friend's house, and we have some questions about the separation of church and state in America. If you can't make it tonight, could you send someone over? Thanks."

She repeated the address twice and hung up just as Gaylen came out the door, wrestling with her stepmother, Millie, over a guitar in a padded carrying case.

Andrea was out of the car in a shot, and reached the sidewalk just as the gig bag sailed out over the lawn. It hit the ground, and out slid Gaylen's bass guitar.

"Bernadette!" Gaylen screamed, running over to kneel beside it.

Andrea was puzzling over what she should do about any of this, when a huge pair of hands on her shoulders gave her a new problem to consider.

"Pass not judgment on the ways of the Lord," a voice behind her drawled. "Be meek and submissive in the presence of his—*Ow! Crap!*"

Andrea basically knew one trick for escaping someone: the old stomp to the instep. She whirled around and found herself face to chest with a man wearing suspiciously well tailored camouflage and a cowboy hat. Right at Andrea's eye level was a hand stitched "name tag" in the style of a real Army uniform proclaiming that she was dealing with *Big Jim Rankin*. As only Andrea could, she took an immediate dislike to "Big Jim" based on his outfit alone. As it happened, his next utterance confirmed her judgment. "Listen here, girlie girl. This is a serious matter you're interfering with, and if you don't want the wrath of the Lord raining down upon—*Ow! Damn it!*"

Andrea was glad she was wearing boots. Her second attack on his foot was better aimed, and she hoped it would buy her enough time to grab Gaylen and get the hell out of there. But Gaylen was on her knees in front of her bass. Andrea couldn't tell whether the instrument was damaged, but its owner was definitely a wreck. Andrea felt a familiar anger building up inside. One more provocation, and someone was going to be dealing with more than a sore foot.

She felt another hand on her shoulder and turned around, ready for a fight, but it was Natalya. "We need results here. This is too much for us to handle alone. Right now, we have to buy time. Go to Gaylen."

As she knelt next to the sobbing girl, Andrea could hear Natalya engaging Gaylen's stepmother in a tone of low-key compromise. "Mrs. O'Reilly, if you could just let us gather up Gaylen's—"

"Because you have rejected the word of the Lord, he has rejected you," Millie O'Reilly snarled back.

Andrea could barely hear Natalya's words, but the intent was clearly to slow down the tempo of events. "Yes, Mrs. O'Reilly, but perhaps…"

But Millie was in no mood for any Pagan reasonableness. "Those who practice the magic arts, their place will be in the fiery lake of burning sulfur."

Kneeling on the lawn with Gaylen, Andrea was feeling a little overwhelmed. The truck lights were blinding, Gaylen was beyond reach, and Millie's shrill preaching was unnerving.

Natalya was buying them time here, but for what? The jarring lights and sirens of an NYPD radio car were her answer.

Natalya stopped talking to Millie in midsentence. Big Jim, limping now, looked enraged. The Dominion of God posse exchanged looks and stood up a little straighter as Officer Linda Petrossian got out of her radio car.

This would have been the perfect moment for the group to back things off. Make some fatuous apologies. Show a little Southern charm. Just shutting up and pretending to listen would have improved their chances significantly.

Instead, they began to sing. "A mighty fortress is our God. A bulwark never failing…"

Then Big Jim decided to double down on the condescending. "Hey, there, little lady, we're just doing the Lord's work here. Nothing you need to worry about. It's all in God's hands."

The choir picked up the reference and went with it. "He's got the whole world in his hands. He's got the whole wide world in his hands…"

* * *

In the time it took Officer Petrossian to walk from her radio car to the center of the lawn, she made several observations.

First, she saw a female student, known to her from K290 as Gaylen O'Reilly, kneeling on the lawn in obvious distress. Next to her was another student, a Miss Andrea Melman. An unidentified woman was spouting scriptural hellfire, apparently toward the person known as Natalya Volkova. A number of other unknown persons, including a tall male wearing military camouflage and in an apparent state of agitation or injury, were arrayed near the O'Reilly girl. SUVs with matching tactical trim options, and the enthusiastic singing of traditional hymns might be a common occurrence elsewhere, but in Brooklyn, New York, it fit the profile of a "situation." So, following standard procedure, Officer Petrossian called for backup, and this being New York City, a significant police presence was on the scene in very short order.

When the parties were physically separated, Officer Petrossian got a rundown from Miss Volkova that seemed to fit the facts at hand.

Gaylen's birthday simplified things considerably. If she wished to leave, she could collect her belongings and go. But she seemed beyond caring. Whatever had happened had left her in pieces. "Let's go!" she said between bursts of crying. "I just want to go. They can have everything. I can't go back in there. I don't care. I just want to go."

Recent events had alerted Officer Petrossian to certain issues that might arise from anyone picking on a friend of Andrea Melman, and she didn't need to be a cop to see that Miss Melman was ready to blow.

She wisely sent Natalya to talk to Gaylen, and then took Andrea aside, ostensibly to get her story, but mostly to keep her from starting something. Eventually, the cops decided to have Natalya accompany Gaylen and an officer inside to collect Gaylen's things. Millie insisted on going along "so the witch doesn't steal anything."

* * *

Andrea began loading the things piled on the lawn into the car, and was relieved to find "Bernadette," Gaylen's heretofore anonymous Fender Precision Bass, apparently undamaged. Things were almost settled when Gaylen suddenly ran out of the house ahead of the others and over to the car in a fresh state of shock. "Oh, Andrea, my book."

Andrea swallowed her fury and tried to focus on what Gaylen was saying. "What book, Gaylen?" But Gaylen seemed unable to say much beyond "my book."

Natalya came over and took Andrea off to the side. "I don't know what to do."

"What is it?"

Natalya was really mad now, and Andrea was wondering what could still get to her at this point. "They took her Book of Shadows. It's in the toilet. I'm pretty sure one of them pissed on it."

Andrea felt a rush of blood shoot to her head. Every cell in her body wanted to start screaming at the Dominion of God bunch over on the other side of the lawn, but that wasn't going to help Gaylen. And Natalya was obviously drained from the stress of dealing with Millie and the police.

A deep sense of guilt washed over Andrea. So far, her contribution to the situation had been pretty close to nothing. She had let Natalya handle the adult interactions and responsibilities. No, it was worse than that. By being a known risk for panic attacks and freak-outs, Andrea had *forced* Natalya to handle all the adult responsibilities.

She took a deep breath and grabbed an empty garbage bag. "Let me do it."

Andrea quickly explained the situation to Officer Petrossian, and the two of them entered the house. Millie, apparently sensing what they were going in for, decided to sit this one out. The object of their quest was in the guest bathroom near the kitchen, half-submerged in the toilet. Someone had definitely urinated on the book.

As they stood there, Petrossian looked a bit perplexed. "So, tell me, Miss Melman, a Book of Shadows has *what* in it?"

Andrea had to stop and think about how best to describe it. "Well, it's kind of a diary of a witch's progress. No, that's not the right word. Maybe *workbook* is better. Rather than have one book that everyone reads the same prayers from, each individual witch starts their own sacred book. You write down the rituals and spells and everything that you do as you go along, and over time you sort of build your own personal…"

"Bible?" Petrossian suggested.

"Hmmm. That would suggest that every witch has the same stuff in their Book of Shadows."

"Recipe book, then?"

The suggestion made Andrea laugh. "Well, maybe. How about personal like a diary, practical like a cookbook, and sacred like a Bible?"

"Okay." Petrossian smiled. "Let's go with that for now."

Andrea was about to pick it up with her bare hands when Petrossian offered her a pair of latex gloves. As she was putting them on, she decided to take advantage of the shower in there and give the already wet book a rinse down. It took about five minutes and made some of the ink run, but she figured Gaylen would have to recopy the stuff anyway, and it was definitely worth minimizing the smell.

As she was putting it in the garbage bag, she couldn't help venting. "So, this is *okay?* This isn't a hate crime? Disrespect a Bible or a Quran and everyone's outraged, but piss on a witch's Book of Shadows and it's just a big joke?"

She wasn't even raising her voice, but the words resonated with anger and frustration.

"No, Miss Melman, this is not all right, and it's not a joke. As far as I'm concerned, yes, this should be considered a hate crime. But I have to tell you, Gaylen out there isn't up to it. She's not up to putting her whole life out there. The media reaction, these Dominionist assholes, the whole circus. We can't make that decision for her."

Andrea sighed. "You're right, we can't."

As they left the house and crossed the lawn, a thought occurred to Andrea. "Officer Petrossian, don't we have more stringent concealed-weapons laws in New York than in lots of other states?"

Petrossian started to smile. "Why, yes, Andrea. Yes, we do."

When they reached the station wagon, Gaylen hugged her and Natalya gave her a grateful look. As they were pulling away, Andrea could see Officer Petrossian and two other cops approaching the Dominion of God people to ask about concealed weapons.

She could have sworn she caught an evil eye from Big Jim.

Chapter 36

"I still don't get it," Natalya said to Gaylen between spoonfuls of mochi ice cream. "How could you not have known? I had a *cauldron* in my basement where we practice. How many people do you know with a cauldron?"

"You said it was a planter."

"In my *basement?*"

By midnight, they were exhausted, but the night's events had made them edgy. On the way back, Natalya had insisted on stopping off at home "for some more lingonberries," but Andrea was sure she had also picked up her gun. Normally, she might have had objections. Tonight, she was grateful to have something more substantial than her boot heel to put between herself and Big Jim.

So, they dragged another bed into Andrea's room and were just about to turn in when Gaylen thought she saw something at the window.

"Probably a bird," Andrea said, yawning, but Gaylen opened the window to check.

And there they were.

"Oh, hello." Gaylen said.

"Oh… Hello?" they answered.

"Who are you talking to?" Natalya asked from where she lay on the couch.

"I'm not sure," Gaylen answered. "Who are you?"

"We're friends of Andrea," one of them said.

"They're friends of Andrea," Gaylen repeated.

"Are they Faeries?" Natalya asked.

"Oh, Natalya. You know Gaylen can't see Faeries," Andrea said.

"Oh," Masa said, flying into the room, "I think she can."

As reunions went, this one was pretty intense, considering they had been gone less than a month. But Andrea was just glad to see them and didn't much care whether she was being too emotional. For their part, the characters looked thinner and considerably more careworn.

Gaylen got the condensed version of their history together, with the promise of a more detailed picture to come.

It was a while before Natalya got around to asking, "So, how is it that Gaylen can see you?"

No one spoke at first. Sumi finally broke the silence. "I'll answer that." Rei and Masa floated over next to her, as if to lend their support. "We'll go into a lot of things tomorrow when we're all rested, but, Andrea, what we learned at home has changed everything. From now on, you will be getting a lot more information about us. Not everything. Never *everything*—we are the Fae, after all, and that is our nature—but much more, I can promise you."

Sumi turned to Gaylen. "The reason you can see us is that you have the blood of the Fae. 'Faerie Blood,' as they used to call it."

She looked at each of the girls in turn. "You all three have the blood of the Fae."

Masa addressed Natalya's skeptical look. "It's not just a cute expression. You share a number of genetic traits—chromosomal possibilities, if you will—that can be activated to enable the abilities we give you."

"Is it restricted to witches?" Andrea asked.

"Oh, hardly." Rei smiled. "But in any case, it's not common."

The characters were as exhausted as the girls, but Andrea kept talking while Gaylen sat, dazed and smiling, happy to be in the presence of real Faeries. Natalya watched carefully but said little. Eventually, everyone fell asleep.

* * *

When they woke, it was already getting dark outside. Everyone had ramen, and then settled down in Andrea's room.

The girls arranged themselves in a row of chairs in front of the bed. It seemed almost formal to Andrea. The humans assembled to receive an official presentation by the Fae.

As the Faeries floated up before them, other things felt different as well. Maybe it was just repetition softening the edges of the fantastic, but somehow the Fae's cartoonish outfits were beginning to feel less like caricatures of human designs and more like the clothing of an alien race.

Even Rei's absurdly cute pink cheerleader look suggested a second interpretation—one closer to the fancy-dress military uniforms of a bygone era. Andrea couldn't find an analogy for Masa's costume, but Sumi's green flowing outfit now seemed to confirm an earlier impression of leadership—one of being "first among equals."

Sumi positioned herself before and slightly above Masa and Rei and began. "We are the Fae. Our world is best understood as a dimension or membrane existing synchronously but separately from this place, which we refer to as the Green World. It lies across the void we call Parallel Space. Parallel Space both joins and separates us. It exists as a buffer zone between the worlds.

"It has some very useful characteristics. For one thing, there are ways of storing items in Parallel Space. Those items can then be summoned and returned there, or exchanged for some designated item of yours. Items connected to you will travel with you in that space and can be called back."

She turned to Andrea. "This is where your clothes go to and come back from."

"Finally!" Andrea said triumphantly.

"How much stuff can you park like that?" Gaylen asked.

"Can humans enter this space?" Natalya asked.

Masa moved to the front and answered the questions in order. "Congratulations, not a lot, and no."

She looked at Galen. "We have to designate items specifically to be associated with you and then create a linkage to Parallel Space. The procedure is neither quick nor simple."

Next, she turned to Natalya. "Any living thing we've tried to pass though Parallel Space into our world dies. If you'd like, we could put some living stuff in one of the eggs and pass it through and back to show you. Everything ends up looking like gray goo."

Masa went on. "Which brings us to an important point. We are really not like you in a lot of ways. Basically, our world shares the same laws of physics, but the values are very different. For example, in this world, electromagnetism is the dominant force; in our world, gravity is. As a result, where here you have creatures using the planet's magnetic fields for navigation, many species in our world can manipulate gravity."

Rei came forward to speak as Masa settled back next to Sumi. "There are many other differences, but the main thing to understand is that we do not come from a parallel Earth. The other important thing to understand is that most of the questions you might want to ask about our world are off limits."

"Really?" Natalya said flatly.

Gaylen was nodding her head. "Yeah. That's the Faerie nature *I* was raised to expect."

Andrea sighed. "What is *with* all this secrecy?"

The usually cheerful Rei looked exasperated. "There's a lot more to our situation than you could possibly understand. We are the Fae. Our nature is our nature, and it is not open to discussion. In the past, asking questions about us would have brought about painful consequences. We were feared, and with reason. If you have cause to interact with other Fae in the future, you should be exceedingly careful."

Sumi edged in front of her and continued. "You also need to know the broad arc of our story. For many millennia, we observed your world from across Parallel Space. At first, the Green World was deemed too dangerous to visit, but it proved too interesting a place to ignore. The colors and sounds. The earth, sky, and water, and all the creatures within. Eventually, by the grace of the Living God, we developed certain methods that allowed us to interact with your world and your kind.

"From the beginning, of all the many wonders here, it has always been humans that most fascinated us. In fact, learning your human language was an important breakthrough in our own development. We began returning to observe the generations of humans that lived here and we became increasingly obsessed with following their stories.

"The making and telling of tales is at the very heart of the Fae, and we created legends about what we witnessed. Mind you, at the time I'm referring to, perhaps ten thousand years ago, you were very different from how you are today."

"*Ten thousand* years ago?" Gaylen asked, incredulous. "How far back does your history go?"

"How long do you live, anyway?" Andrea asked.

"Oh," Masa said, looking to the other Fae. "Important details?"

Sumi wasn't thrilled with the interruption. "Hm-m, okay. Our life spans average about two hundred years. Without going into too much detail, we 'arise' in a single, unified birth moment and so are always roughly contemporaneous to each other. The other rather important point I must reveal is…"

She hesitated. Rei and Masa moved closer. "Go ahead," Rei urged gently. "We all agreed to this."

Masa then looked at the girls individually, her eyes coming to rest on Andrea last. She spoke directly to her. "We are about to reveal enough to merit the fate of traitors. You need to appreciate that." Andrea nodded slowly in acknowledgment.

The Fae floated side by side now, as though their shared complicity had somehow removed any difference in status.

Under her breath, Sumi spoke. "Protection and mercy of the Living God."

"Forgive us," Rei and Masa murmured together.

"We call it 'persistence,'" Sumi continued. "You might call it a soul memory or something else. It is that ability that lets us retain our 'selves'—the sum of our personalities, memories, all that we identify as who we are—beyond the end of our physical life cycles and into those that follow."

"Like reincarnation?" Gaylen suggested.

"Perhaps," said Masa.

"You're immortal?" Natalya asked.

"No. Not our bodies, in any sense. But as the cycles of physical life rise and fall, we—our true selves—persist. The substance of our bodies renews with each cycle, but we continue and are sustained through time by persistence."

A long silence greeted this revelation.

Andrea eventually spoke up. "How old are you, then?"

"Persistence arose in a time long before we discovered Parallel Space and your world. That time—maybe thirty thousand years ago—is when we date our persistent selves from.

"Mind you, we don't remember every event of every day any more than you remember exactly what you did a year ago. What persistence allows is for the emotional bonds of kinship, the important lessons of life, and the great stories of our people to inform each life cycle. We don't start life at zero and relearn everything. We build on what we already are."

"So, your society should be perfect by now?" Gaylen asked.

The Fae burst out laughing. "Not quite," Rei said. "While, on the one hand, you learn a lot of stuff, on the other hand, nobody ever forgets a grudge."

"That's an understatement," Masa said softly.

Sumi floated up higher to get everyone's attention. "There is much to tell. Over time, it became apparent that human development was stuck. You had language, but almost nothing was being passed down. All the wonderful stories we had of your past deeds were completely unknown to your descendants.

"So, we sought to change that. In time, we introduced an artificial form of persistence to your culture. We added rhythm and meter to the stories that would otherwise be forgotten. They became more entertaining and much easier to remember. It's basically how we tell our own tales."

The Faeries seemed quite pleased with themselves, and Andrea wondered if they expected to be thanked for graciously sharing this with humanity. She looked over at Natalya. The girl seemed to be puzzling over what had just been revealed.

"Wait. You mean poetry?" Natalya asked.

"Oh, yes." Sumi smiled at her. "Poetry. Verse. All that. It worked better than we ever could have imagined. It seems to focus the human mind in useful ways. Based on that, we became bolder in our interactions."

"And more arrogant about our prerogatives," Rei added.

"Yes," said Sumi. "We began to take certain um… liberties with your kind. Most of it was quite harmless. Simple play. Confusing games. Lead a man to a field at night and hide the gate till morning light."

The other Faeries nodded in amused recollection. "Or sweeten the milk of a good woman's cow as you turn her stingy neighbor's sour," Masa added. "Just good fun, really. But there were no restrictions on who could come to the Green World and what they might do. Our kind has a limited sense of what you call morality."

"So I've heard," Gaylen said.

"And then we discovered a delightful new trick," Rei said. "We called it 'overshadowing.'"

Sumi continued, "With a willing human—or, in some cases, not so willing—it is possible to hitch a ride on their consciousness by crossing into Parallel Space right at the physical boundary of the person's body. We think of it as *overshadowing* their will. It works best with mutual participation, but that isn't required.

"Andrea, you and Natalya know the two variations of this as the basic magical-girl transformation, where you summon control, and the magical-girl Excellion transformation, which would be initiated by one of us."

Sumi seemed ready to leave things there, but Rei turned and prompted, "An-n-nd…?"

Reluctantly, she continued. "Yes, I should tell you, even though we found humans to be such fascinating and wonderful beings, we didn't think of you as that much different from… many other creatures."

"*Livestock,* Sumi," Rei snapped. "We thought of them as, treated them like, and *called* them livestock, and we used them in exactly that way."

Sumi shot her an angry glance, then sighed. "I'm sorry. Yes, livestock. We were very free with taking individuals out for a night of dancing, fighting, riding, sporting games—everything. It became a bit of an obsession. You should know that there are certain perception limits on our physical manifestations here, but a Faerie riding a human feels all that the human does. We can significantly enhance the experience as well. A good trick was simply to bring all the humans involved in an activity to a lower gravity. They can't get hurt as easily while fighting and sporting. Their dancing improves immensely, and, um, other things are… more fun."

"Other things?" Andrea asked innocently.

"*Sex!*" Gaylen and Natalya said together, and burst out laughing over Andrea's embarrassment.

Sumi continued. "You were very different back then. Life was short. And brutal. You were lucky to survive childhood and reach breeding age. Yours was a world of endless sorrows. I must tell you, if we were guilty of imposing our will on you, there were few complaints. In those times, the lot of you would beg for the privilege of joining us for a single night's ride—at least, before the age of the priests."

"Not just the priests," Rei said.

Sumi agreed. "No, they were only part of a larger change, which we refused to acknowledge. Changes for the better, perhaps, but the end of our time of dominion."

"Dominion? *Must* we use that term, Sumi?" Masa protested.

Sumi ignored her and continued. "Toward the middle of your nineteenth century, we were coming to the end of a life cycle, but your kind was entering a new phase that threatened to end our times here forever. We were so focused on the priests as the big threat, we paid little attention to the rise of science and technology. But your world was changing in ways we would never have thought possible…"

"Wait!" Gaylen interrupted. "I'm getting overwhelmed. This is *way* too much information. I must have brain stimulants."

"Tea?" Natalya suggested predictably.

"Give me a moment," Andrea said on her way out the door.

Chapter 37

Twenty minutes later, an array of brain stimulants—two kinds of ice cream, and green tea—had been administered, and a slightly more focused trio of girls was sitting on pillows across from the Faeries, who were on the floor, finishing off a bowl of ice cream.

"Okay," Gaylen said. "End of Faerie good times, no more human pony rides, world changing beyond your imagination… And then?"

Masa threw her a look—equal parts amusement and annoyance—and continued. "I know that some humans think we fear metal or bells or… well, all sorts of stupid things, but what changed everything was the advent of artificial light. People tend to view Faeries as being magical and powerful, but the fact is, aside from a few tricks and escape techniques, we are very much at risk here. Almost all of our protections depended on the dark, and we began to see how, in the coming age, there would be no night to shield us. Much as we hated it, our time here had come to an end. But the loss of the Green World was only a part of a much bigger crisis."

Sumi appeared to be lost in thought. As she rose up to speak, she seemed to be shaking off a fog of memories. "The crisis we call the Closing of the Green World made us question the foundations of our own society. It ultimately fell into two opposing camps. We are of the faction known as the New Fae. We believe that it is the destiny of the Fae to evolve and that lessons gleaned from others can be applied to us. For the last century, we have controlled the agenda, and I can tell you, our accomplishments have been significant and benefited our entire society.

"It was our decision to abandon the Green World completely and focus on our own needs. We pushed to discover the principles behind our powers and develop them into technologies. We also introduced certain political changes—a shift away from our traditional ways. The greatest of these changes centered on the role of our queen, the Living God. I use the term 'queen,' but that's not really adequate. The Living God is not merely a symbolic political figurehead. She is our genetic archetype, not just for what we are now, but for all that we can become."

Masa took over. "Before we could fly, it was she who mastered the ways of manipulating gravity and taught them to us. It was she who first pierced Parallel Space to break through to the Green World. She who reads the emotions of all creatures.

"Our society is—by its nature—a chaotic thing, and she has always been the center that held everything together. But after the last Arising at the beginning of the twentieth century she was nowhere to be found. We still don't know why. Her disappearance and absence is still the central fact of our current crisis. It's forced us to change everything. And, let me tell you, Faeries do *not* like change."

Sumi jumped back in. "As you might imagine, there was a huge backlash to this. Many of the Fae hold these changes to be treasonous. They demand the return of the queen, as though *we* were the ones hiding her, and the return of the world they once knew. They call themselves the True Fae, and what we learned is that they're basically running everything now."

"In fact, " Rei said, "by positioning their agents to run our training and imprinting—particularly memory suppressions—they have blanked out vast amounts of our histories. We still don't know the full extent of what we don't know."

"It appears that the True Fae have managed to destroy almost everything we've achieved," Masa added. "They've even seized control of an important resource."

Looking to Sumi, she asked: "Can I tell them about the dark eggs now?"

Sumi looked weary. "Go ahead. At this point, we're all going to be cooked in our own eggs anyway."

Gaylen raised her hand and waved it.

Sumi smiled weakly. "Yes?"

"Okay, for the record, I'm enjoying every second of this. Having said that, I have had a lot of tea tonight, and I was wondering…"

The Faeries looked baffled as Andrea and Natalya cracked up laughing.

"Bathroom break!" Andrea announced.

"Seconded." Natalya said.

The luxury of having three bathrooms on the second floor made it a short interruption. The girls met up in the hallway outside Andrea's bedroom.

"Don't Faeries have to pee?" Gaylen asked.

"Maybe that's covered in the next lecture," Andrea suggested.

Natalya shook her head. "Do we really need to know that?"

"Only if it's going to be on the test," Gaylen said, opening the door.

The Fae were clustered together above the window seat. Not talking, just staring out the window into the night. Something in their posture evoked deep despair. Sensing the mood, the girls quietly returned to their pillows and settled down.

As the Faeries floated back over, Masa shot them a rare tolerant smile. "Not too much more." Then she looked from Natalya to Andrea. "But I would think you'd want to know a bit more about the eggs you've been fighting over."

Suddenly, the girls were fully attentive.

Masa went on. "So, the dark eggs... Let me begin by telling you something about the state of human science. In many respects, you are more developed than we are. You don't really *know* as much as we do, but you do more with the knowledge you have. Still, certain... preconceptions have prevented you from acknowledging a lot of types of energies, asking what they really are, and what might be done with them. The dark eggs are an example of this.

"Until a few hundred years ago, practically no human young had what you now think of as a childhood. The conditions of human life meant that no one really invested much time, energy, or love in individual children. Most of them didn't survive long enough. When that changed and more of them reached maturity, it changed the very nature of childhood.

"What you haven't noticed is how this is affecting your evolution. Since it doesn't show up in something you can already test for—like genetics, say—you don't see it. Specifically, you remain unaware of a certain energized particle stream, a unique byproduct of the developing creative energies of your young.

"Under certain circumstances, this particle stream forms an egg-shaped coherent mass. We can perceive it and collect it. And unlike most everything else from here, it can be transported through Parallel Space back to our world. When it gets there, it becomes a very different substance, and that substance was found to have a profound effect on the psychology of the Fae.

"Faeries are not the most stable of creatures. You smile, but yes, we are aware of this. Ingesting even a tiny amount of trans-formed dark-egg material counteracts a variety of antisocial and destabilizing tendencies in our kind. It improves our focus, reduces aggression, and allows a more objective view of the world. It has basically allowed us to evolve from a somewhat touchy group of what you might call sociopaths, into more rational and cooperative creatures."

Sumi shook her head in exasperation as Rei interrupted Masa, "Not a lot of Fae would necessarily agree with that last part—you know, about us all being sociopaths."

"Exactly," Sumi said, staring unbelievingly at Masa, whose take on the topic seemed to be one side of a long-standing dispute. "It's just the sort of characterization that's contributed to our being the hunted 'traitors' you see before you today, *Masa*."

Masa ignored her and continued. "The thing is, a little bit—and by this, I mean a *tiny* little bit—goes a long way. A single egg, or maybe two, would cover the normal needs of all the Fae for an entire life cycle. The problem is, as larger doses are administered, the effect turns back on itself. Given a big enough dose, a Faerie will revert in personality to behavior that has not been seen for a millennium or more.

"The most recent patterns of more moderate behavior are suppressed, and a *traditional* mind-set takes over." Looking towards Gaylen she emphasized, "Exactly the kind of Faeries your ancestors rightly feared. Needless to say, when the True Fae discovered this, it became their holiest sacrament. For a time, we controlled access to the substance, which everyone commonly refers to as 'Sparkle'—everyone but me, that is, since it's a slang term…"

Rei laughed. "It's called 'Sparkle.' By everyone. Get over it, Masa."

Masa sighed. "Anyway, we had strict control over Sparkle until relatively recently. Then it began to appear at True Fae gatherings."

She looked at Natalya. "We now know that it was Cami who was working with Viktor to build a stockpile of eggs outside our control. Our primary mission here was to stop you and Illya from obtaining those eggs."

Natalya looked down and sighed, "Sorry?"

"No, we owe *you* the apology. Our plans were totally unrealistic. We had believed that we could dry up the supply of eggs by returning them to their host children. Actually, that was originally Janelle's idea. It never had a chance of succeeding. Maybe that was actually the point. In any event, it's now obvious to us that Viktor has always known what we were up to."

Looking as though she couldn't bear to go on, Masa shook her head and flew over to the window.

The sky was turning gray in the east. Sumi looked at each of the three girls. "There is more we need to tell you, but the night is gone and we must travel a great distance. We are hoping to receive a delivery, but our situation is such that we can't really say what we'll be getting, if anything. We should return in a day or two."

Without turning from the window, Masa spoke. "Everything has changed now. We don't want to worry you, but we want you to be ready to handle whatever might happen. You may be called upon to... *do* things."

Rei glided over to them. "We're not going to abandon you, but you may be on your own for a long time, depending on how things develop."

No one had a response. With the briefest of goodbyes, The Fae slipped out into the dawn. It was Monday morning, but the girls were too exhausted to think about school. They came up with plausible excuses for why they wouldn't be there, and fell asleep.

Chapter 38

Andrea and Natalya were in the kitchen, making the last of the pancakes for Gaylen. The still-sleeping girl was beginning to worry them. Almost a week had passed and she hadn't breathed a word about the traumatic experience at her house.

Andrea was confused. "I mean, I get the deal with meeting Faeries for the first time. It's magical and all, but it's like the whole Dominion of God thing never happened. What am I not understanding?"

Natalya was at the stove, pouring batter into the skillet. "Gaylen may be a much more troubled person than we've understood," she said. "Think about it. She's had to live three completely different lives. High school musician Gaylen, closeted witch Gaylen, and whatever awful home life with the crazy stepmother she's had to endure. She's learned to compartmentalize those lives, and we're part of two of them. Maybe she doesn't want us in the other one. I don't really blame her."

Gazing out the window, Andrea eventually asked, "Natalya?"

"Yeah?"

"When was the last time you got to fly?"

"About ten days ago."

"Do you miss it?"

"Yeah. I mean, I've always been a bit conflicted about what I'm flying around *doing,* but the flying part is always good."

"Yeah. I haven't flown in weeks now, and I'm, like, really depressed about it."

"Really?"

"Oh, God, I miss it so much. I really do, and now I don't know if I'm ever going to fly again."

"But is it not better to have flown and lost, than never to have flown at all?" Gaylen said from the doorway.

"Oh... hi!" Andrea said nervously. "How long have you been standing there?"

Gaylen smiled. "Since just before the part about me being more troubled than you thought." Natalya laughed out loud at this, and Gaylen continued, "You can actually hear things clearly from the top of the stairs."

"Well?" Natalya said. "Are you going to talk about any of it?"

"You don't have to if it's too weird," Andrea rushed to add.

"No, no, the weirdness is the best reason to talk about it," Gaylen said, while loading her plate with pancakes at the stove.

"Believe it or not, I thought I had learned to cope with dancing around Millie's insanity. I mean, I still have trouble forgiving my dad for marrying her and putting me in that situation, but I'm pretty good at managing crazy. You don't play in as many bands as I have without developing some effective social management skills."

Sitting down, she took a few bites. "Wow, loving these lingonberries!"

"Tell me about it," Andrea said, licking preserves from the jar lid.

"Anyway, I knew I could leave after I turned eighteen, but my dad was a musician, not a rock star. If there's a trust fund hiding out there, I haven't found it. I figured I'd finish out the school year, get the diploma, and maybe go on tour with someone. I still don't know how she found my witch stuff. It was literally under lock and key. You saw it, Natalya."

"It looked like she used a crowbar to open it."

"Someone must have told her about it. You wouldn't believe how careful I've always been around her. *Years* of hiding. Sneaking around, always missing Samhain because she'd get extra vigilant around then. But the funny thing was, during all that time, I always thought I was doing a super job of handling things—the clever little witch using her wits to survive."

"But it sounds like you were," Andrea said.

"I thought so, too." Gaylen said. "But when this confrontation happened, it all came apart. *I* came apart. I really thought I was going to stand up to whatever came my way, and just be all awesome and everything. Instead, I just caved and fell to pieces."

"In front of *that* gang of thugs?" Andrea asked. "I mean, really, what else could you do?"

Gaylen sat back for a moment. "Apparently, not much. I went into a complete free fall. Even after you guys came to save me, all I wanted to do was run away. I was ready to leave absolutely everything just to get out of there. Even with the cops there, I could barely handle going back in the house.

"I had this picture of myself as being so cool and together, and it was such a lie. I would have walked away from all my stuff and everything I believed in, just to save myself. The truth is, every second I've been out of that house has felt like heaven. It's just that I betrayed everything to get here, and that's not so great."

"You were alone," Natalya said. "There are limits to what anyone can do on their own. What's more, you had no training. Experience is the only way to cope with fear. Trust me, I know a lot about it."

"Still," Gaylen said, "I think I'd go through the whole thing again if it came with flying lessons."

"It's so cool!" Andrea said.

Natalya smiled. "Incomparable."

* * *

The rest of the week quickly passed. Andrea set Gaylen up with a room but never took the spare bed out of her own room. Natalya made herself at home on the couch and suddenly Andrea found herself with a pair of human size roommates. Most nights they would talk till they passed out, then show up late to school together.

The Fae came back Thursday night, but they were so stressed and exhausted on arrival, they all agreed to wait until the next evening to share what they had learned.

After school on Friday, as they walked back to Andrea's house, Natalya dropped a small bombshell. "I think I may be out of the flying-witch business no matter what the Fae brought back. Viktor came over last night."

"I'm guessing that can't be good," Gaylen said.

"It never is. What's more, he seemed to be in a good mood, which is always a bad thing. He told me he was finished with the egg-harvesting business, and that since I no longer needed any of the powers derived from Malka, he was 'repossessing her.'"

"What?" Andrea exclaimed. "Can he even *do* that?"

"Can and did," Natalya went on. "Malka was unusually quiet about the whole thing. I wouldn't be surprised if Viktor made a deal with her."

"Wait… So you can't fly anymore?" Gaylen moaned. "But I never got to see you fly. I never even got to see your outfit with the wings. This is terrible!"

Natalya gave her a sly smile. "I'm sorry to have disappointed you. But I must say, any point of contact with Viktor I can escape from makes life a little bit less stressful."

Andrea stopped short, bringing them all to a halt. "But do you actually escape from Viktor in any real way? He's taken away a major power of yours, yet you're still under his effective control, and if you don't communicate with him, you've lost a way to monitor him and his moods."

310

"Wow, Andrea!" Gaylen laughed. "You sure know how to keep things on the sunny side."

But Natalya was thinking in a similar vein. "No, she's right. With someone as dangerous as Viktor, distance only gives the *illusion* of security. Yes, Illya and I have lost a means of reading his intentions. I'm beginning to fear that darker plans are afoot."

"What about Gella?" Andrea asked.

"Oh," Natalya sighed. "She's never around anymore. Viktor didn't even ask. I need to check on her."

They resumed walking. Andrea threw out another question. "Can he use Malka's powers with another host?"

Natalya seemed surprised at the idea. "Another host? With Malka? I mean, in theory? Yes. But in practice, I can't imagine how. The host needs to be able to control her to an extent, and yet needs to be in an adversarial relationship to engage Bitter Nightshade. It took me forever to get the balance right. What else could anyone do with Malka?"

"What if you didn't care about control?" Andrea asked. "What if you just wanted to cause mayhem by subjecting an unqualified person with a lot of their own rage to a character transformation?"

"A terror weapon?" Natalya asked. "Oh, *Andrea!* I see why Viktor likes you so much. Yes, that's just the sort of thing he would think of."

Gaylen regarded Andrea with a mix of admiration and concern. "You are a much darker and edgier girl than I gave you credit for. Remind me never to piss you off."

* * *

When the girls got back to the house, the Fae were flitting about Andrea's room in a panic. They had good reason.

"We have to go!" Masa said. "They've been coming through Parallel Space all day, harassing us. They may try to grab us." A flurry of motion shot by the window, startling the three Faeries and driving them under the bed.

"Wait! Masa! Sumi! Guys!" Andrea tried to reason with them. "They have always known about this place. Why is this happening now?"

Sumi poked her head out from under the dust ruffle. "Faeries don't usually make direct attacks. Before now, it was good enough that *they* knew that *we* knew that *they* knew where we were. Actually, from a Faerie perspective, it's *better*. It makes a prison of anxiety. It's the worst!"

"So then this is better?" Gaylen said.

"No! We were wrong," Rei said from under the bed. "Having them pop into the room or outside the window and try to grab one of us is much worse. I can't take this."

"We need to get all of us to a location at least twenty or thirty miles from here," Masa said. "Somewhere we can do some flying without people around. At least for this weekend."

"Tonight?" Andrea asked.

"Flying?" Gaylen practically swooned.

"I'll get the car," Natalya said on her way out the door.

Chapter 39

Forty minutes later, the ancient station wagon was cruising along the Southern State Parkway. They were on their way to a little-used safe house of Viktor's, bordering the Long Island State Pine Barrens Preserve.

Sumi was sitting on the dash, with her back to the windshield, looking like some sort of animated dashboard ornament. "There is a lot going on right now, and we've lost most of our sources of information," she said. "What about Nyanka? I wonder if they'll try to grab him, too. Why didn't Viktor take him?"

"He's not much of a weapon, you know," Natalya answered. "Viktor would only want him for leverage over Illya. And I don't think Illya figures into things right now, but we have emergency protocols just in case."

"How about it, Andrea?" Gaylen asked with a grin. "You and Dion have your protocols in place?"

Andrea looked at her blankly. "Our family isn't big on protocols beyond 'Don't do anything that might embarrass the family,' and I'm not even sure if that's really a protocol."

When they arrived, everyone except Natalya got to see their first honest-to-goodness safe house. While perfectly understandable in a "form follows function" sense, it was still pretty underwhelming. Other than being isolated from any nearby houses, the place was remarkable only in its unremarkableness.

As soon as they unpacked and made a quick meal, Sumi began the discussion, right there in the kitchen, while the girls sat around the table eating. "We have learned—I guess 'relearned' would be more accurate—a number of things about the powers, and had some misinformation cleared up. It turns out that we had been imprinted to believe a number of things to keep us from fully powering you up, Andrea.

"For one thing, you would have been able to fly with any of our transformations. I mean, Rei is still a much better flier than Masa or I, but that was always possible. We just didn't know it.

"What's more, all the different varieties of the immobilizing powers are essentially the same. The different cleansing and restoring powers? Also basically the same. They were just made to *look* like separate powers. We're not sure why. Oh, and they don't require the props we thought they did."

"No more giant paintbrush?" Andrea asked, with just a hint of disappointment.

"No. Oh, and, Natalya, we now understand a lot about you and Illya. Well, we understand a lot *more,* anyway.

"The information on your development is an almost completely suppressed area of our memories, but we do know this: Your powers are all early prototypes. Especially Illya's and Nyanka's. In fact, it appears that they are the only one of their kind. The whole cat-ears-and-tail thing on Illya was abandoned long ago."

"Illya gets *cat ears and a tail?*" Gaylen sounded giddy at the prospect. "*I* want cat ears and a tail. Are there pictures? Why didn't you tell me this?"

"I never suspected this side of you," Natalya teased.

"What else don't we know?" Andrea wondered.

"Why on earth did you stop doing that?" Gaylen asked Sumi in a faintly accusing tone.

"Uh, well, it kind of freaked people out, you know, and it didn't really *do* anything. It just, you know, gave you cat ears and a tail. That's not exactly a *power* or anything."

"It's the power of *awesome*." Gaylen was obviously coming at this from a completely different direction.

"Gaylen, why do you even have an opinion about cat ears and… that sort of thing?" Andrea asked.

"It's all over the Japanese anime and manga universe. It's just one of those standard transformation options when a magical character gets powered up, right?" she said, looking at Sumi.

"Uh, well…" Sumi looked distinctly uncomfortable at being asked for an opinion on the subject. "I think it's really important that we stay focused on *your* powers right now, actually."

Gaylen was over the ears and tail in a heartbeat. "Really? Powers? *My* powers? Now?"

Sumi could see that she was losing control of things. Andrea and Natalya were giggling over this previously unknown side of Gaylen, and even Rei and Masa were barely suppressing their own amusement. Looking down at them all from her perch over the stove, she tried to restore some order. "Okay, we'll get back to all that later.

There is a reason we need to stay focused here. The True Fae have a lot of crazy ideas, and virtually all of them will never get beyond the talking stage. But the connection with Viktor allows them a number of very scary possibilities—possibilities that could end up on this side of Parallel Space.

"You need to understand how the True Fae see things. The foundational delusion of their movement is that the Green World— your world—belongs to the Fae by right of historical possession. They believe themselves entitled to dominion over this world, and they appear to be ready to act on that in the very near future."

Sumi seemed satisfied that no one was laughing now. "We are of the opinion that a full-scale invasion is simply out of the question," she said. "What you call 'command and control' aren't really Faerie concepts, even under the best of circumstances. The battles of old that they love to sing and brag about were basically riots between clans. No, the things we are mostly worried about are targeted mayhem attacks."

"Like dropping Malka into an unstable host," Natalya suggested, nodding to Andrea.

"Oh, please!" Sumi gasped. "Don't even say that. The only upside to that is that we've never encountered another Faerie like Malka, and one lunatic Faerie can do only so much damage. No, what has us concerned is something being whispered about at home, which we could never verify. Masa, explain the kyne-darath to them."

"Okay," Masa began. "So, the next item in the series of things we should never be telling you about is that—unlike you humans here—we are not the apex predator in our world. That distinction goes to a nightmare called the kyne-darath. The name essentially means 'the horrible thing that eats Faeries,' and all the Fae live in terror of it because, once it has fixed on you, you're dead. Now the bad news. The whispers among the True Fae are that a way has been found to transport the eggs of a kyne-darath to the Green World. Needless to say, we think Viktor must be involved."

"Not to minimize any of this," Gaylen interrupted, "but how worried should we be about something scaled to eat Faeries?"

Masa nodded, "A good point. Unfortunately, the kyne is incredibly flexible in how it copes with changing circumstances. It continues to evolve inside its egg until it has a suitable set of features to survive in whatever environment it is being released into. A kyne released in your world would be much larger from adapting to the rich conditions to be found here. All this oxygen... it would be more than big enough to hunt humans."

"Okay," Gaylen said. "Sorry I asked. So how does one kill this thing?"

"There is only one way we know of to kill a kyne-darath, and it's um... a challenging procedure."

Sumi gave Masa a brusque nod and turned to the girls. "This possibility—more than any other threat—is why we have to get the three of you enabled."

"Um, what exactly does 'enabled' mean in this context?" Andrea asked.

"We had hoped it was going to mean using Natalya's powers while you and Gaylen immobilized the kyne from a distance, but Viktor seems to have eliminated that option by grabbing Malka. So, basically, we're going to teach you to kill the kyne-darath the way we do it at home: up close and at great personal risk."

"I'm going to do this *alone?*" Andrea gasped.

"Oh, no. This time, you get to do things the *right* way. You three are about to become Project Magical Girl."

"Really?" Andrea said flatly.

Natalya shot Sumi a skeptical look.

"Yay!" Gaylen cheered.

Chapter 40

If Project Magical Girl had any kind of coherent philosophy, the Fae were not about to share it. Instead, everyone just moved into the backyard to get things going.

The first task was to determine which Faerie to assign to which girl—yet another thing that appeared to require no input from the girls themselves. After a quick huddle, the Fae announced their decision. Natalya would pair up with Rei, Andrea with Masa, and Gaylen with Sumi.

Natalia transformed first, and in the process revealed that the outfit was actually paired not to the character, but to the girl. To Andrea's disappointment, Natalya would not have to suffer the indignity of flying around in hot-pink cheerleader regalia; she came out of her transformation with her Goth Queen of the Night look intact. Without Malka, she couldn't summon Bitter Nightshade, but she still had her wings.

Gaylen was thrilled. "You've been able to do this the entire time I've known you?" she asked, indulging in what some might consider inappropriate wing fondling. "How could you possibly transform back into a normal girl? Even *your* idea of a normal girl? These *wings*… I would sleep in these."

Upon transforming, Andrea was not happy to find that she was indeed stuck with her original costume. To her further annoyance, Gaylen's first reaction to the cheerleader outfit was a fit of giggling.

"I didn't have a choice in this, you know," Andrea said. "I asked—no, *begged*—for something more appropriate, but I was *forced* to wear this."

"I see…" Gaylen finally managed to gasp. "But I think it's exactly what you *needed.*"

"What?"

"Andrea, you're *way* too serious for your own good. This, um, ensemble, it's just the thing to bring out the pink cheerleader within."

"I do not have a pink cheerleader within!"

Trying to head off a heated and unproductive argument, Masa turned to Gaylen. "We hadn't really anticipated needing a costume to fit your measurements. And on rather short notice… well…"

Apparently Gaylen's outfit came with a lot of disclaimers, which her new partner, Sumi, started ticking off. "Okay, this outfit was never supposed to be worn by an actual guardian. It's a prototype—an *early* prototype. We borrowed from existing Japanese outfits, and the outfits themselves were somewhat dated when we began working with them. You must understand, there was no time for development—this was all we had available. Again, an older prototype, from an earlier period that—"

Gaylen couldn't stand it any longer. *"Give me my outfit!"*

Sumi gave a deep sigh, then dived into and through Gaylen. And after the usual light show, there it was: a sleeveless Japanese-schoolgirl sailor blouse with a huge blue bow at chest height; a blue micro miniskirt that would give an Ice Capades performer pause; blue high-heeled boots reaching to her knees; and white gloves that went up to her elbows.

Natalya had thoughtfully brought out a full-length mirror for Gaylen's benefit and propped it against a tree. Everyone held their breath while she took in her new look. Long moments passed as a stunned Gaylen considered the image in front of her.

"Sumi," she finally choked out. "This outfit…"

Sumi threw a worried look to Rei and Masa.

"This outfit…"

"I took a while to get used to mine, you know," Andrea offered weakly. "It does grow on you. Maybe…"

"This is *amazing!*"

Gaylen jumped up and launched herself twenty or thirty feet into the air. "Oh, my God! It does *that?* No, wait. Did *I* do that?"

She leaned sideways and was rewarded with a lateral movement and another few feet of altitude. "Wait, how do I do a loop?" Bending backward, she managed to achieve a passable back loop and then descended to earth, one leg bent at the knee, landing legs akimbo, and arms in a heroic posture. "Oh, yes-s-s. I am *here!*"

Still watching herself in the mirror, Gaylen hopped up and made another descent, this time hitting her mark with more authority. She arranged her hands in a certain iconic pose, and announced to no one in particular: "Flowers on the earth. Love to the people. Defender of love and justice, Sailor Gaylen has arrived! Bow and be chastised. In the name of the moon, I will punish you!"

Natalya couldn't stop laughing. The Fae were beaming.

Andrea managed to find something troubling. "So, guys, was this how you thought I was going to react?" She looked apologetically at them. "I'm sorry. I'm not really very…"

Rei laughed. "Certain individuals," she said, indicating Sumi and Masa, "were more confident in the universal popularity of Japanese manga and anime culture."

They finally waved Gaylen back down to earth. "Okay! This is it," she said. "So what are we called?"

No one had a response.

"We fight evil, right? Okay, so what's our name?"

"Um, we don't have, like, a name or anything," Andrea said. "Do we actually need one?"

"Who's going to address us?" Natalya asked.

"Our *enemies*!" Gaylen shot back. "Our nemesis, or nemeses! Nemesai? Is there a plural? Wait! You only get one nemesis, right? God, there's so much to learn. Are there special moves? We should practice landing together and announcing ourselves. It really helps to show a united front with a strong introduction, don't you think?"

Natalya started laughing again.

Andrea was just confused. "Why do you seem to know more about this than we do, Gaylen?" She turned to the Fae, who were perched atop the mirror. "What is she talking about?"

Sumi mumbled something about "cultural models" and "previous assumptions."

Masa was a bit more direct. "Project Magical Girl was based on existing archetypes of Japanese popular culture. We spent almost all of our time in Japan working on a system for collecting and cleaning children's eggs. That's where we expected them, and that's where we figured we'd be. What can I say?"

Rei floated over and addressed Gaylen. "You might have to modify some of your ideas about this. We borrowed a few things here and there, but this isn't a cartoon show. The threats you will be facing are not going to let you announce yourself and shout out a challenge."

"Oh, all right." Gaylen said. "One last question: Do I have to go back to my old clothes?"

"You mean, go back to them *ever*?" Andrea asked. "You *really* want to sleep in that?"

Gaylen's look suggested she did, but she must have seen that everyone else wanted to move on, so she let it go.

Any spark of fun was quickly extinguished as the Fae moved the group away from the island of light around the house into the surrounding scrub pine forest. As they formed a circle in the center of a clearing, Andrea sensed an unusual tension emanating from the Faeries.

Masa began. "We managed to obtain only one useful item from home to help you against the kyne-darath. It's a very dangerous device, and you will need to treat it with great care. Basically, you are receiving a weapon. We call it an *ice dart*. It looks like a silver arm band on your wrist and you get one for each arm. It uses your skin to filter and absorb carbon dioxide. Then it collects and condenses it into a very dense cylinder of dry ice, tapered to a needle-sharp point.

"When you position your hands and fingers in a certain, precise way, a small CO_2 charge is decompressed, and the dart is launched. It can penetrate almost anything. When it stops moving forward, the dart goes from a solid to a gas almost instantly, with a very high expansion ratio. Pretty much anything you shoot this into is going to explode."

Andrea looked skeptical. "How do you keep it from giving us frostbite?"

"Good question. If I told you it uses polarized gravitational fields, would that mean anything to you?"

"Okay, no. But you've checked it out?"

"Yes. Also, the whole process only engages when you initiate launching. You can't go walking around with a dry-ice dart inside your wrist, or anything like that."

"How long is the lag time?" Natalya asked.

"About one second between initiating and firing. Then there's a recharge time of about twenty seconds. That's the reason you get one for each wrist."

With that, Masa disappeared into Parallel Space.

Moments later she returned, accompanied by six gray eggs almost twice the size of normal Faerie eggs. She then removed what appeared to be six silver metal bracelets about two inches wide, each connected to a six-inch-long tube. They were installed on the girls' arms by moving each bracelet into Parallel Space and then back.

The effect was essentially to fuse the bracelets into their forearms, leaving a smooth-edged ring around the wrist, with the tube apparently embedded inside. Being associated with Parallel Space meant they could be called into being and then returned without leaving any indication of their existence.

The next step was the firing sequence: thumb and pinkie tips touching, with the other fingers pointing straight forward. The hand had to be held palm down and raised slightly since the dart left the bracelet from the bottom of the wrist. Any variation on the procedure that might put a dart through ones hand was effectively locked out.

Natalya got comfortable with it first, firing a few darts into the sky. "It's not really any more dangerous than a gun," she said. "But you guys aren't used to that. You need a lot of focus and discipline."

At first, only Natalya could accurately hit an upended piece of wood with any consistency. But gradually they all began to get a feel for the aiming procedure, and after a while, the sound of exploding wood filled the air.

"This is a really nasty weapon, Masa," Gaylen said during a break. "You're trusting us with an awful lot of lethal responsibility."

"Yes, we are. You will kill anything you shoot this into, so make sure that is your intention. The firing sequence is such that it should be almost impossible to fire one accidentally. The weak link in the sequence is your state of mind when you are making the decision.

If you have any doubt at all send the bracelets back and figure some other way out of your problem."

It was almost midnight when they decided to call it a night.

"We'll talk about hunting the kyne tomorrow," Sumi said as they walked back to the house.

Andrea and Natalya wanted to pick up a few things from an all-night convenience store nearby, but Gaylen begged off, and they left her and the Fae in the kitchen to clean up.

* * *

With the first stage of Project Magical Girl complete and the threat of interdimensional kidnapping significantly reduced, the Fae were almost feeling relaxed. Gaylen was washing up at the sink. She had been unusually quiet since the girls left, but the Fae hadn't seemed to notice. Eventually she finished up and was carefully drying a very large knife when she turned around to face them.

"You know, it's interesting to me that we share a penchant for secrecy in dealing with the world," she said casually, looking down at the blade in her hands.

The Fae floated together above the kitchen table in front of her.

"What do you mean?" Rei asked.

"Well, as you've said before, it's in the nature of the Fae not to be open about yourselves. I imagine I'd do the same in your situation. You know, with most people, I'm very careful about saying anything

326

that might reveal my true intentions—certainly nothing that might provoke any unnecessary questions."

The Fae shifted uncomfortably, but kept silent.

"In fact, I'm guessing we even use some of the same tricks. I mean, I don't usually lie outright unless I absolutely have to. I prefer to just leave out certain information and let people come to the wrong conclusions. I mean, it's not really lying if I simply don't correct them, is it?"

Sumi and Masa exchanged a look.

"Mind you, my relationship with Andrea and Natalya is different—very different. Over the next few weeks, I'll be telling them everything there is to know about me. They've earned my trust, you see—and not just by saving me from my stepmother and her crazy friends, you understand. Every interaction I've had with them has been completely straightforward."

The knife was completely dry by now, but Gaylen seemed intent on polishing it with the towel in her hand.

"But *you*... I'm having to withhold judgment about you. Partly because Andrea trusts you, and partly because Natalya doesn't completely *distrust* you. Not to mention the fact that, in finding myself swept up in this crazy situation, I realize I may need your goodwill to survive. But *most* importantly, to protect Andrea and Natalya."

At this, she lowered the towel to her side to better examine the gleaming blade in her right hand. "But the question that keeps nagging at me is, do I need to worry about protecting them…" she looked up and pointed the knife in their direction, "from *you?*"

The three silent Faeries followed the blade with their eyes.

"So, here's the thing: I'm going to let you know a few things about me, as a kind of trust-building exercise. And then, over time, I'll be looking for something from you in return. How does that sound?"

The Fae were starting to look alarmed. This was not any Gaylen they had ever seen. The fun-loving, easygoing nature associated with the Gaylen O'Reilly they knew was gone. The person in front of them was calm, focused, and still holding the knife in what now appeared to be an ominous manner.

Her next words unnerved them even more—less by what she said than by its delivery. She spoke quietly and seriously, in an impeccable, surprisingly authentic Irish brogue. "So you might be surprised to know that whatever amount of Faerie blood you'd be crediting me with, the fact is that I am—pure and for sure now —one hundred percent Irish. Irish blood from before the standing stones. Me mother right from Eire, and me father but a generation out. I'll be telling the girls that information right soon, mind you, but I have a special message for you regarding that.

"Before their passing, I was blessed with two of the wisest grandmothers you might ever hope to have. Good Christian women, but neither of them above a spot o' 'special help,' and I'd not be surprised if they both had some of your Faerie blood to them.

"Now, they could never agree on a single thing in this world, but wouldn't you know it? Between them, they were of one mind on the subject of the Good Folk—or the Fae—or whatever it is you wish to be known by. And that was that you brought *nothing* but trouble, and were not to be trusted under any circumstances *whatsoever*.

"Now, so far, the rewards I've seen for getting mixed up with you and your kind haven't been all that good. Natalya's life has been one long nightmare, and Andrea has changed from a nice girl with some self-esteem issues into a weapons platform to go fight somebody else's dragon."

Gaylen leaned toward them and abruptly switched back to speaking in the breezy cadences of an upbeat American girl, born and raised in Brooklyn. "So just to be super clear about this, while *I* am prepared to believe your, shall we say, ever-evolving story and sign up for whatever happens, those two girls are more precious than sisters to me. More precious than my own blood, in fact, and *vastly* more precious to me than *your* blood."

Holding the knife inches away from the Fae, she summed things up. "So… if you *ever* hurt them, betray them, or subject them to any of your Faerie shenanigans, you won't have to worry about Viktor or Cami or any Fae—True, New, or otherwise. Even that Faerie-munching kyne-darath will be the least of your worries. Because you will have *me* as your enemy, and I swear to you on the last drop of *my* blood that you will pay nine-fold for any suffering you cause them."

Outside, they could hear the car was pulling into the driveway.

Gaylen immediately softened her features and tone of voice. "I'm hoping we are going to be really good friends and maybe even do some good stuff together, I really am. But you need to keep your little Faerie minds focused on the fact that their safety will always be my top priority. And if you *ever* betray that trust, I swear by the Goddess, I will cut off your Faerie heads and drink your Faerie blood. Okeydokey?"

The door swung open with a bang, and the Fae darted to the back of the room as Andrea and Natalya came in bearing groceries.

"Whatcha doing?" Andrea asked, putting down her bags.

"Oh, just getting acquainted," Gaylen said cheerily, putting the knife away in a drawer.

Natalya glanced slowly from the Fae over to Gaylen, but said nothing.

Chapter 41

They began Saturday morning with low-level flying maneuvers, followed by a brief period of instruction on immobilization and restoration techniques.

On the plus side, immobilization no longer depended on the use of giant props, but the downside was that they now had to stay concentrated on what they were immobilizing using what the Fae termed a "focusing hand gesture." Essentially, the field of immobilization was directed and contained within the area indicated by the practitioner's two hands. Sweeping the hands together made the field more tightly focused and increased the intensity.

Eventually they all learned to summon up restoration, but Andrea still didn't really get what it was supposed to do. "What, exactly, on a human or Fae, actually gets restored?"

"We're not entirely sure about that," Masa admitted. "If you hit an older person with it, you see some kind of aura around them. With kids, it's less noticeable. There may be more to it, but everything we know about it is related to restoring a child's egg."

"Restoring it to what?" Andrea persisted.

Masa tried to remember. "Something like 'an unstressed state of equilibrium, the neutralizing of occluded scar tissue in the acquired memory.' Sorry, I can't really remember the statement. It's supposed to remove certain effects of memory and restore... something."

"A cleansed aura?" Andrea suggested.

"No. The aura is some kind of indicator, but who knows what it means. Restoration is supposed to give you a more accurate picture of certain past events, like wiping dirt off a window. You might see the reality of things more clearly. That's what I remember of it, anyway. Honestly, once we saw that it did the job with the eggs, we moved on to other issues."

"Masa, tell them about the H-lock and the Trinary lock," Sumi said.

A cloud of annoyance passed across Masa's face. "We've come to believe that the *H-lock* was introduced to waste our time trying to figure out a fake device. It did something, but the fundamental configuration of a single guardian and four characters is just not compatible with any known power multiplication formulas.

"We *have,* however, managed to obtain information on reconfiguring the *H-lock* into a dual trinary configuration that would superimpose a triangle of guardians against an inverted triangle of Fae—basically, making a six-sided star of alternating guardians and characters. That has the advantage of proven mathematical correspondences."

"Meaning…?" Gaylen asked.

"Meaning it might actually do something useful. But we'll need to test it and see what happens."

"Okay."

The primary lesson of the day, though, was "How to Kill a Kyne-Darath, Faerie-Style."

Masa ran the class. "Not to make this too overwhelming up front, but the reason we don't just go kill these things ourselves is that a kyne hatched here will have fed on your high-oxygen environment and will be much larger and more powerful than the ones we're used to."

"Starting to feel a teensy bit overwhelmed already," Andrea said. "What does this thing look like?"

"Okay, I looked around for something that looks like it, and the best I could find was an armadillo, but with the sides pushed in and up to form a kind of A-frame. Flat sides that peak on top of its back. Avoid the teeth and claws. Oh, and the tail can act like a metal whip when you're on its back, so that's something to keep an eye out for. You can expect your kyne to be about the size and weight of a small car."

The three girls exchanged looks.

Masa tried to reassure them. "Now, you're not just going to fly up and engage this thing. There's a procedure that we've used successfully a number of times, and we're confident you guys can learn it with a little practice."

A grim-faced Gaylen raised her hand. "How, exactly, do we practice this technique without a kyne?"

"Yes, yes, that *is* a problem, but we're going to give you *really* precise instructions on what to do."

Natalya raised a flaxen eyebrow. "So our first real test of this will be when we're locked in mortal combat with it?"

"Well… yes."

Masa, never the sort to sugarcoat things, was apparently starting to doubt the likelihood of success herself.

Sumi took over. "The problem is it's impervious to almost everything. Once it curls up on itself, fire, explosions, puncture and impact weapons—almost nothing is going to stop it."

"So it's practically invulnerable," Andrea said glumly. "And we're just going to talk it into committing suicide?"

"Not quite," Sumi replied. "There is a way, and we have done it many times."

She nodded toward Rei and Masa. "It just requires a certain *finesse*. The weakness of a kyne-darath is that under very specific circumstances, it can be distracted. Usually, a kyne is totally focused on the single thing that it's hunting. If it's presented with too many things at once, it goes into a berserker mode and tries to slash and tear up everything in sight. But if two roughly equivalent items of interest are presented to a kyne, it falls into a state we call *fascination*. It can't figure out which thing to attack, and becomes locked into a frozen state. This allows a third party to drop down onto the kyne's back and fire a dart into its neck."

"Dibs on *not* being the one to drop on the kyne's back," Gaylen said.

Masa picked up the instruction. "The invocation goes 'The seeker seeks it to be seen. The dancer twirls it into a dream. The hunter drops and kills it clean.'

"The seeker is the one who finds the kyne, but more important-ly, she must let the kyne see her and select her as its prey. That takes a minute, and during that time, the dancer twirls down from above and provides the second point of distraction. Those two are usually directly in front it and about ninety degrees apart, from the kyne's perspective. Once the kyne is fascinated, the hunter drops down from above and behind—*always* above and behind—and lands on the kyne's back. They can't feel you, but if they see any part of you, they'll pop out of their state of fascination and slice you in half with their tail."

The girls showed a definite lack of enthusiasm as they watched the Fae perform a run-through.

"We're really going to *do* that?" Andrea asked. No one answered.

The lessons went on all day, with each girl trying each position. After a while, it appeared that Natalya would be the most distracting dancer. Gaylen's lack of flying time disqualified her from the hunter position, putting her in the seeker slot. This left Andrea to contem-plate the idea of dropping onto the back of an alien death machine and shooting an ice dart into its neck before being cut to ribbons.

They dutifully spent the whole day learning the drill and trying to absorb the lessons regarding exceptions and emergency procedures. But by dinnertime, no one was too happy about any of it, and it was a painfully quiet meal.

Chapter 42

The next day was more of the same, but the pressure was getting to everyone. Sumi was doing a good job of keeping up appearances, but Rei and Masa weren't handling the stress well. They seemed to be constantly bickering over trivial issues, and at one point Sumi had to order Masa to suppress her dark predictions and endlessly gloomy speculations.

Andrea and Natalya noticed that the Fae were staying clear of Gaylen, though they couldn't understand why. Gaylen, for her part, was proving to be a quick study and—more importantly—a team player. More than once, as they flew in a group, it was Gaylen who would swerve, lag, or stop to avoid accidents with the other two.

In a way, it made sense. Natalya had always been the queen of her own airspace. Andrea had developed a certain sense of situational awareness from her experience with the characters, but they had never coordinated anything.

Gaylen, on the other hand, was a natural at formation flying, always seeming to know where they were, where they were headed, and what she could do to adjust. After a while, they fell into the habit of forming up with her in the middle.

Meanwhile, Masa had reconfigured the H-lock into the Trinary lock. Everyone got a medallion to wear, and to their surprise, when they arranged themselves in a circle the whole formation glowed and gave every indication that an actual enhancement of their powers was taking place.

The problem was, they had nothing to immobilize or restore.

They managed to stop some birds in midflight which was satisfying enough, but in the process learned that, while immobilized Faeries continue to float in place, immobilized birds drop like a rock. After that, a proposed test on a larger flock was canceled on humanitarian grounds.

Restoration proved as difficult to test as it was to define and with the vastly more compelling concerns about facing the kyne to worry about they just moved on.

In the end, it did appear that they were getting an increase in the individual powers, as well as the ability to combine them. But without something to try it on, well—who really knew?

* * *

During a break in the late afternoon, Natalya got a call from Illya's phone. Answering, she visibly shuddered at the sound of Viktor's voice. As the others gathered around, she held the phone up.

"Natalya? Yes, it's your stepfather." Her face registered disgust at the word. "You heard about Illya's little character Nyanka? He seems to have simply disappeared. Yes, a shame. Perhaps. Not that they were ever very effective together, but what can you do? Yes. Listen, Illya's feeling a bit down about it all, and we agreed this would be a good time to fly back to St. Petersburg for a little vacation. Illya *insisted*. We're at JFK right now, waiting on Aeroflot flight one-oh-three, leaving at five after seven. Here, let me send you a picture of us."

Taken at arm's length, the image of Viktor and Illya in front of the Aeroflot departures desk flashed onto Natalya's phone.

Viktor looked pleased with himself. Illya was looking at his feet, and it wasn't hard to guess his mood. "I'm expecting us to stay for a week or two, but you never know. Illya's not feeling well now, but he promises to text you later, when we're on our way. And we'll call when we arrive. Mind you, with the stopover in Moscow, we are talking about a twenty-eight-hour flight, so don't worry about us. You just have fun with your little friends and we'll talk soon. One more picture, and I'll let you go."

Another image filled the screen, this time with Illya at the bottom of the frame, with the departure board showing the flight number and scheduled departure time. The screen went black, and the call ended.

Natalya looked grim. "This is very bad."

"Did Illya reveal anything in the pictures?" Gaylen asked.

"No. He's probably been under their control all day." Natalya looked at the pictures again, more closely. "He may be drugged."

"This may not be the moment to bring this up, but are you sure we can really believe what we're being led to believe?" Andrea asked.

Natalya smiled. "Exactly. Almost certainly not, but which parts? They're not at the airport? They're not going to St. Petersburg? Viktor won't get on the flight? It's really more a question of what might be *true* about what we've been told."

Andrea hesitated before continuing. "We're being pressed on all sides and losing our sources of information. I know this is a bad moment any way you look at it, but our new number one priority seems to be the issue of whether we're going to be performing Swan Lake for a flying death monster. Is this our only chance to get a look inside Viktor's warehouse and see what's been going on there?"

Natalya didn't answer at first. Her face suggested that she thought a visit to Viktor's workshop would probably end with them all in a shallow grave, but by the time she spoke, it was with the voice of someone resigned to their fate. "Okay, I will go and determine what I can and…"

Gaylen caught Andrea's eye and then interrupted Natalya. "Oh, no. *That's* not going to happen. Whatever awesome purple clouds of acid you used to be able to shoot out of your hands are gone. You aren't even *close* to being able to handle anything you're likely to find in Viktor's place. Besides, you've already made the case that we're *all* dead if he decides to start handing out punishments. Oh, and to quote you, 'There is no safety in distance.' "

Natalya rolled her eyes at having her own assessments thrown back at her but kept silent.

"Anyway, I say we take our Faerie-certified kyne-darath extermination experts along, and if the opportunity should arise, we might get the satisfaction of seeing *them* served up as appetizers before we become entrées."

"So say we all!" Andrea declared.

"So mote it be!" Gaylen threw in for good measure. Then she turned to the Fae. "Any objections?" She asked in a tone suggesting that none would be welcome.

"We are sworn by our sacred honor to help you at any cost," Sumi said. "You are right to hold us accountable for the failings of our kind. We need to prove ourselves, and we will."

* * *

The sun was setting as they headed back to the house for dinner. Masa flew over to Rei and whispered something in her ear.

Rei flew up ahead of the group and turned around to speak. "Um, I know this isn't the best moment, but, Sumi, are we going to do the... you know?"

"Oh! I almost forgot. Masa, are they ready?"

"They've been ready all day," Masa replied.

The girls formed up at the bottom of the kitchen steps, eyeing the Fae with justifiable suspicion.

"Another *treat?*" Natalya asked.

"Another wardrobe option?" Gaylen asked.

"Do we have to kill anything with it?" Andrea asked.

"Yes, yes, and no," Sumi replied, smiling. "Okay, if you will simply repeat after me, 'Magic Hat!'"

"Magic Hat," the girls called out in unison.

And lo and behold, upon each girl's head appeared a perfectly proportioned, big pointy hat. Andrea's was a deep midnight blue, Natalya's a smoky red, and Gaylen's a dark emerald green. Out came the mirror, and there were oohs and aahs all around.

"The colors are perfect," Natalya noted approvingly.

"It's floppy but not *too* floppy," Gaylen added.

"It's just what I always wanted," Andrea exclaimed, her voice edged with emotion. "It's got the soft wizardy thing going on, but it definitely skews witchy."

Gaylen took her hat off and regarded it with a mixture of awe and suspicion. "So what do they do? Can we expect anything useful out of them? Magical powers maybe?"

Still admiring herself in the mirror, Andrea added, "And what *else* do they do that you don't want to tell us now."

As Gaylen went back to trying out different angles in the mirror, Natalya turned around and gave a the three Faeries a hard look, "What – *exactly* – do they do?"

Sumi looked hurt. "You're so *suspicious*…" she said, prompting a slew of accusations rooted in recent historical events delivered in a simultaneous jumble from the three girls.

"Okay, we're not perfect you know." Sumi said to three nodding heads. "They're pretty much just decorative. Just for fun really."

"Really?" Natalya said in a tone of flat disbelief.

Sumi just ignored them and moved on. "So, powers… let me see… what do the hats do? It will stay on your head at any speed and any angle. And best of all, it will never eat up valuable closet space. If you will repeat after me, 'Hat Magic!'"

They did, and just like that, the hats disappeared.

Gaylen turned to the Fae.

"Oh, you guys are *good*. First, I get the outfit, then the flying lessons. Then I find out that the cost for the flying is to take on your Faerie hell-beast, and just when I'm so over all of this, the magic hats come out of the closet. *And*, it's a magic closet."

The Fae looked proud of themselves. "You spend a few millennia tempting humans, you learn a bit about tempting humans," Sumi said.

It was amazing how much more fun preparing dinner was in a kitchen full of girls wearing magic witch hats. Low ceiling height presented a bit of a challenge, but even the act of returning them to the Parallel Space "closet" when passing through doorways created another opportunity to call the hats up again, and that never seemed to get old.

At one point, Gaylen turned to Andrea and Natalya, who were prepping vegetables on the kitchen table while she sautéed onions at the stove. "So, no one wants to hear this, but I'm just going to lay it out. If we don't come up with something to call ourselves, someone's gonna end up doing it for us, and I guarantee, you won't like it."

"Is this our most pressing problem?" Natalya asked.

"What's the worst that could happen?" Andrea asked.

"Maybe not," Gaylen said to Natalya.

Then, turning to Andrea, "Firstly, you've got to stop saying that, okay? Nothing good has ever come from someone asking,

'What's the worst that could happen?' And secondly, the worst would probably be a toss-up between Fox News and an adorable five year old on YouTube."

"*Really?*" Natalya said.

"Oh, *Gaylen*." Andrea said.

"You've been warned."

Chapter 43

The ride back to Brooklyn the next day was quiet and tense. All anyone wanted to do at this point was to check out Viktor's warehouse and go home. Natalya insisted on going to Andrea's first and picking up the inertial damper. They had established certain settings that they believed would protect them from gunfire at reasonable ranges without taking out local air traffic. Ultimately, it was their only real protection from Viktor's weapons.

They parked just off the main entrance to the compound as night fell and the streetlights blinked on. Everyone but Andrea got out of the car.

"Are you okay?" Gaylen asked.

"I can't breathe. This is bringing back Janelle... Just give me a moment."

Natalya walked around a part of the perimeter fence and looked in a ground-floor window of the main building. "Looks like he's emptied the place out."

Rei came down from the roof. "The lighting system and the cameras are still there, but nothing is powered up."

Andrea slid out of the car, walked over to the bushes, and threw up. After a moment, she steadied herself. "Okay, let's go."

Everyone transformed, and they floated over the front gate. The compound contained a number of different structures surrounding a wide central courtyard. They let the Fae fly a sweep through the area to make sure they really had the place to themselves. That done, the main building awaited.

Natalya had been inside only once, but that was enough to get in the door and find flashlights to snoop around with. The beams skittered around the cavernous interior, revealing a second-floor balcony against the back wall, with a row of small offices underneath.

"Is this *too* easy?" Gaylen asked.

"I'm afraid it would be like this whether we were walking into a trap or not," Natalya replied.

Andrea was still nauseated and in a cold sweat as she walked along the long center table where she had first laid eyes on Viktor. Where Janelle had met her end.

She peered up into the rafters, trying to figure out which window they had looked down from that night. Her vision blurred as her knees momentarily weakened, and she fell back against a waiting Gaylen. For a second, she felt a little embarrassed. "Oh, I…"

Gaylen pushed her up straight. "It's okay."

Andrea nodded in sheepish acknowledgment.

Gaylen leaned in and added, "That said, you've got to stay focused, Andrea. We all need to keep it together tonight." Stung by the implicit criticism, Andrea quickly brushed off her shame as an unaffordable luxury and resumed searching.

The Fae were examining the upper level when Rei let out a gasp. "Oh… oh, no. Sumi, Masa. They're here. Hurry!"

By the time the girls flew upstairs, the Fae were gathered around a large cardboard box full of the split shells of numerous Faerie eggs.

"There they are," Rei whispered. "Sumi, can you count them?"

"No. I can't look in there. How many were missing?"

Masa was circling the sides, looking down without getting too close. "Twenty four—six groups of four. I don't know, but I think there's enough room for all of them. Oh! The blue one with the crescent—that's Rani, isn't it? Isn't that her egg? So, where's her team? Wait! Green with crescent, red with crescent. Yellow? It's the whole group."

Natalya moved closer to look inside. "What are these, Sumi?" she asked.

"Characters. Fae. Dead Fae," Sumi said without emotion. "I mean, the eggs of dead characters. The remains would have fallen back through Parallel Space."

"Right back to the *bastards* who sent them here to die," Rei snapped. "They *knew*! They sent them and sat there waiting for the bodies to come back."

Gaylen had to interrupt. "Call me dense, but what's going on?"

Masa floated over. "One mystery we've been trying to solve since we got here was whatever happened to these guardian characters. Our memory of it was that they should have preceded us here. They were supposed to be establishing six other groups around the area, rescuing eggs. It's one of the only memories the three of us agree on. We never got a straight answer at home. Some said it was a false memory we'd been given, but others were positive the eggs had been sent here but never checked in after arriving."

Sumi seemed unable to take her eyes off the box as she added, "Andrea was never supposed to be operating alone.. It appears that all these characters were sent here to Viktor, and he killed them. But that could never happen without the involvement of Fae of the highest rank."

Turning to the girls, Rei was beyond furious. "We may kill each other for all kinds of reasons, but always in hot blood. You die fighting in a battle. You perish for your honor. You might even kill or be killed over possessions. But always in a fair fight—well, okay, *our* idea of fair. Even killing humans, you would be expected to have a passionate motivation. To lure the unsuspecting to their deaths, to murder them *this* way…"

"It might seem arbitrary to you, but it is unthinkable for a Fae to commit cold-blooded murder," Sumi said. "It's especially perverse for the True Fae to consider such a thing. It suggests that their leadership is becoming unbalanced."

"More like insane," Rei said.

Andrea was scared. The box really unnerved her. She knew nothing about these particular Fae, but she felt as if she were standing before a mass grave. "They were like you? They would have had guardians and gone out saving eggs?" No one answered. "Their kids never knew them?" She struggled to keep her head clear. "What is Viktor getting from this, Natalya?"

347

"I don't know. This could be anything. A message to Cami or anyone else foolish enough to think Viktor actually works for anyone but himself?"

"No," Rei answered coldly. "This is a crime of the Fae against our own."

They spread out and continued searching. Most of the building hadn't been used in a long time. Other sections showed dusty outlines where crates and boxes had recently been.

On a table inside a corner office, Natalya and Gaylen found a four-foot square Plexiglas box with a rubber tube leading to a small canister labeled 'Liquid Nitrogen.'

"The execution chamber," Natalya said softly.

"You think he froze them?" Gaylen asked.

"Oh, no. They came out of their eggs, and there wasn't any oxygen to breathe."

It wasn't until they got down to the basement that they found what they had hoped not to find.

Andrea discovered it with her foot. "Oh! What was that? Guys, what does a kyne-darath egg look like? Please tell me it's not light brown with dark little spots and three feet tall, because this one's already hatched."

As Sumi and Rei rushed over, Masa took charge. "Okay, you three, out of the building right now! You can't fight a kyne without room to maneuver. Out! *Now!*"

Chapter 44

By the time they reassembled outside, the girls were already starting to panic. Two days' training about the theory of how to take down a monster had also planted in their minds terrifying images of a violent death.

Even though the hunter was the only one who could possibly get a kill shot, they all had called up their ice darts. When Masa saw three pairs of silver bracelets, she was furious at their lack of focus. "What are you doing? Gaylen! Natalya! Put those things away. At this point, you're more likely to shoot each other than the kyne. Andrea! What are you doing down here? Get up in position and start circling. Establish visual communication with the seeker and the dancer. We went *through* all of this! Gaylen! Start seeking! I told you, the kyne has sensed you already and is hunting *you*. Find a position to be seen from. Where's your dancer? Is she in position? Look at your hunter. Eye contact! Your dancer and your hunter have to pivot on your direction. Do you remember the signals?"

Rei and Sumi were keeping out of it and doing their own search for the kyne. The only good news was that the egg was freshly hatched. The creature would be about a third of its mature size—bigger than the girls, but not by much. Of course, on the downside, this one was already bigger than anything the Fae had ever hunted at home, and it was still genetically predisposed to feed on Faerie meat.

Masa was still trying to get the girls back into the game. "How does it find you? The same way you find it: smell. Calm down.

Smell the air. *Taste* the air. You're searching for a cooked-meat smell with an acidic finish. Andrea? Are you with me? You might smell it first up there. Where are your seeker and your dancer? Good!"

The endless repetition had a special magic to it. As brief as their instruction had been, the girls were trained for this. More to the point, they realized that for the first time, they had now placed their lives in each other's hands. If any one of them failed to perform, they would all pay for it.

Andrea broke through her fear first. Looking down on Gaylen and Natalya, she found a cold resolve to do her job for the sake of protecting them. The thought of how often she had lost her composure in the past weeks, and how often someone had to rescue her made her cringe. Whatever else might happen, they were not going to die tonight because of an Andrea Melman meltdown. Her flight circles became more even, and her eye contact more regular. She began to function like the clock that Masa had talked about. The dancer was floating up in a fixed position, waiting, and the seeker was on the ground, focused out to where the kyne might be lurking.

Andrea focused on her timing and consistency. Smooth motion was the key to keeping the kyne fascinated. Anything abrupt or uneven would provoke an immediate attack. The seeker and the dancer couldn't afford to move even their heads, so Andrea could make eye contact only when she was out above and in front of them—practically on top of where an approaching kyne would be.

When it eventually showed up directly below her, she was supposed to stop circling and then curve around in the opposite direction.

The long, lazy S curve would bring her around to the back of the kyne without startling it, and when she didn't appear in front on the next expected circuit, the dancer would begin a graceful twirling descent.

There! There it was: the smell.

Andrea almost lost her rhythm, but managed to stay sharp and indicate to the others that she had picked it up. On her next cycle, Gaylen slowly blinked twice. She had it, too. The game was afoot.

Gaylen began moving out from cover, preparing to expose herself. Andrea wondered if she was still happy with her job responsibilities as seeker as she turned to face the direction the kyne appeared to be coming from. Masa hadn't said anything about what a kyne-darath sounded like, but hoarse, ragged breathing made them all look over to the left as the thing floated around the corner of the main building.

This was it. No more Masa, no more coaching. They were on their own now. Any distraction would send the kyne into a rage.

Andrea completed her last cycle and made final eye contact as Gaylen moved directly into the kyne's line of sight. The creature gave a loud snort of recognition and came into the light, where it could be clearly seen.

Masa's attempt to liken the creature to an armadillo had been dangerously misleading. There was nothing cute or familiar about the thing. It was a massive alien predator more akin to a dinosaur. The skin was silvery with a rough, pebbled texture. The eyes had the glassy, dead stare of a shark, and the teeth rose and fell in an impossible circular motion, like a meat grinder. The claws—three on a foot and curved like a raptor's talons—had their own creepy rhythm, rising and falling as if waiting for warm flesh to savage. The tail seemed deceptively lazy and harmless.

If not for the Fae's warning, the girls might not have given it a thought.

Perhaps the only thing reminiscent of an armadillo was the line of overlapping armored plates running down the kyne's neck. Masa had described how they would separate to leave gaps when its head was extended in hunting. But any small disturbance meant the head would retract. After that, nothing could get through, and you were as good as dead.

Gaylen moved to keep herself in the kyne's line of sight, and Natalya began a slow spin with her wings pulled tightly in and arms raised overhead, like a ballet dancer in a music box. Andrea began ever so carefully to circle around, always keeping her movements even and regular, until she was in position behind the beast.

Unfortunately, the most important lesson Masa had tried to drill into Andrea's head was the one most easily forgotten at this point. Instead of focusing on the target below her and preparing for the kill, she looked up one final time to see Gaylen and Natalya out in front of the kyne.

Below her waited the hellish creature. Before her were her friends, hanging there like edible Christmas tree ornaments. Suddenly, Andrea's mind stopped believing in any of the facts at hand. The kyne was too terrifying to be real. Moreover, anything that horrible couldn't possibly be entranced by the sight of two cosplaying high school girls floating around a deserted Brooklyn parking lot.

Any second now, the kyne would charge them, and they would all die. And what was supposed to prevent all this? Some crazy ice rocket shooting out of her wrist? Delivered by her? By dropping down on this monster's back? No way. None of it made sense, and someone needed to come into this situation right now and put an end to all this nonsense. She wanted to call a time-out and discuss everything—all her objections, all the ways this didn't add up, how this couldn't possibly work.

Eyes locked on the girls. Mind spinning with rationalizations. Heart racing in terror. From a million miles away, the tiny fragment of rationality left within her could see that she was paralyzed. And with that came the clear understanding that her friends were about to die. Natalya and Gaylen, dead. Because of *her*.

It was the shock she needed to reassert control. She hadn't been frozen for more than a few seconds, but when she looked down, she could sense the kyne beginning to stir.

Panic replaced paralysis. Suddenly, time was of the essence. Andrea needed to drop down onto the top edge of the kyne's back, and she needed to do it *now*.

She dropped quickly—too quickly, without a clear picture of where she was trying to land. Her timing was off, and she alighted too far down the back, almost on the base of the tail. The landing almost bounced her right off the kyne and onto the ground.

The kyne sensed something was off, and started sniffing to identify the disturbance. Worse, the head began slowly retracting back into the armored back plates. In seconds, it would be protected against any weapon the girls possessed.

Andrea was on the verge of flying off, but the absolute certainty that Gaylen and Natalya would never survive fixed her resolve. Time seemed to slow down. Her choices were now very limited. Very clear. She was still too far down the kyne's back and would have to adjust. Taking a deep breath, she pushed up and slid down. Not enough. Another breath. Another push and slide.

There… right behind the neck. The head was still moving back under the armored neck plates, but she was beyond fear now, and felt no real hurry. Andrea carefully positioned both wrists just above and beyond the edge of the back, and just before the sheath closed in on the back plate, she triggered two ice darts directly into its neck.

Then—in what felt like a leisurely dismount—she floated off and above the kyne-darath just as the two highly compressed spikes of dry ice exploded, decapitating the creature.

Andrea kept floating upward, surveying the scene below. Gaylen, dazed and standing on the ground; Natalya, gracefully landing and calmly walking over to the two pieces of what—seconds ago—had been one ferocious predator.

The Fae floated out of hiding to take in the scene for themselves.

As Andrea landed, the remains faded out, back through Parallel Space. She entertained a momentary sense of triumph, picturing the shocked, enraged faces of her unseen enemies in that world as their secret weapon returned in mangled pieces.

Masa brought her back to reality. "Andrea! What happened up there? You could have gotten them killed with that hesitation."

"I'm sorry, Masa, everyone. I…"

"Good recovery, though. Just don't do that again. An older kyne wouldn't have given you that much time."

Natalya and Gaylen were still pretty shaken.

"I don't *ever* want to get that close to one of those things again," Gaylen said.

"That isn't going to get any easier, I'll bet," Natalya said. "Good shot."

In all the excitement, no one had noticed a group of armed men spilling out of two cars at the back gate. By the time they had taken up positions around the central courtyard, it was too late.

With a loud bang, the area lights came on, blinding the girls, but Viktor's voice was all they needed to hear. "Oh, look what you've done, Miss Melman. You've gone and killed my little pet. You're going to have to pay for that."

Chapter 45

The girls instinctively ascended a dozen feet and hovered. The Fae had disappeared. Viktor walked into the center of the courtyard, flanked by two men carrying AK-47s. He seemed in no rush. Finally, he looked up at them and gave a short, harsh laugh. "Look at you with your cute little getups. I could find work for you in Moscow. You'd be a big hit."

Then he focused on Natalya. "Ah, there you are. Have you been a good girl Natalya?" Her face was a mask. "No, I think not. In fact, I think you have been working against my interests. A little birdie told me you may be deploying a system against me right now—a system that should have been brought to my attention as soon as it appeared. Let's see if that's true."

He turned to the gunman on his left and pointed up at Gaylen. Without hesitation, the man brought his weapon to his shoulder, took aim, and pulled the trigger.

Andrea heard a click. A soft *poof…* and then nothing happened. The gunman ejected the casing and pointed the muzzle downward, and a bullet slid out and dropped to the pavement. He looked up in confusion. Viktor merely nodded at this confirmation of Natalya's treachery.

Andrea was shocked. With no more concern than a man checking his watch, Viktor had just ordered someone to fire an assault rifle at Gaylen, merely to verify an assumption. Had the Fae not gotten the inertial damper activated… She couldn't even think about it.

"Yes, quite an act of disloyalty to her own father, don't you think, Miss Melman? Or was I not supposed to be aware of this device? Interestingly, I happen to have a little tool of my own for locating devices. Malka!"

The creature floated up from behind his shoulder. "Find it!"

Malka immediately took off for a nearby stand of trees. A short commotion in the upper branches ended with the little devil-costumed character emerging victorious, carrying the inertial damper. Masa, Sumi, and Rei followed her down from the branches.

She put the device in Viktor's hands. He examined it and then placed it in his coat pocket. "That may prove quite useful in due time," he said to no one in particular.

As he was talking, two more gunmen came around opposite corners of the main building. From where she was floating, Andrea could count six of them now positioned around the girls. *How many more? And where?*

"So now, what possible use are the three of you to me at this point?" The threat was explicit, but Viktor seemed to be savoring the moment. They were his now, and he seemed in no hurry to lose them. "For that matter, what use have I for any of your little friends?"

Rei, Masa, and Sumi had stationed themselves next to the girls, and Andrea could sense their fear. *Can't they just fly away? Can't we all?* She glanced over at Natalya, who seemed oddly calm. Was she planning something? Or had she simply accepted her fate?

Natalya surprised everyone by asking Viktor, in a normal conversational tone, "How is Illya?"

He chuckled at that. "Oh, he's fine. Quite well at the moment." A moment later, his face hardened and he dropped any pretense of civility, "Do you expect to distract me with a bit of family chitchat now? To pique my curiosity and buy time? Do you really think there is anything you can possibly do to save your friends?"

He moved toward them, keeping his eyes fixed on Natalya. "I know all your tricks, my little viper. I know everything there is to know about you. I even know which ploys you believe to be your own that actually came from your mother. You think you are better than her, don't you? You think you are different. That is your sad delusion, little girl. You are *exactly* like her. *No* different. *No* better."

Natalya held her tongue. Andrea wasn't sure, but her lack of a response seemed to provoke Viktor. "Illya will be in St. Petersburg in a few hours, and you will never see him again. Consider that!"

Andrea suddenly felt a spark of hope. Viktor had been careful and disciplined up until this point, but the last piece of information was unnecessary. And his "Consider that!" comment felt like the taunt of a schoolyard bully. Natalya was definitely getting him riled up.

A cold, rational Viktor was unbeatable, but a hot, angry Viktor might make mistakes—hopefully before he got around to killing them all.

"Time to wind up my affairs here." He looked around for Malka. Indicating the back of his hand, he ordered, "Here! Now!"

Malka flew over and landed on the back of his wrist. Andrea tried to read her face, but she was too far away. Viktor stroked the character's head. "There are no loyalties in this world but those you command through fear," he said.

He seemed to be talking to them all, but it was obvious who he was directing his words to. Andrea saw Natalya twitch when he touched Malka. "You couldn't reach our little Malka here. You tried all sorts of things, didn't you? Love, reason, common causes. All for nothing. As long as you have known her, Malka has always been mine. Every appeal you made to her, the things you and your brother would scheme, everything you shared in confidence—all mine. Everything, every word. None of it for love, nothing for a greater good. Not for reason or justice or anything but the hard, brutal reality that fear conquers everything. All her loyalties have been mine to possess for one simple reason: the fact that failure to recognize me as her master would result in *this*…"

Malka gave a single faint gasp. With such a small body, there was no slow, dramatic penetration. One moment she was perched on Viktor's wrist; the next, she was impaled from behind on the blade of his knife.

Viktor lowered his hand, leaving Malka in her death throes, hanging in front of him.

As Andrea tried to absorb this senseless murder, a flash of light crossed her peripheral vision and made a line for Natalya.

The next few seconds took an eternity to play out.

Gella's anguished face and her screaming out Malka's name. Natalya's attempt to suddenly refocus from the dying Malka to the tortured Faerie diving toward her. Her pleas to Gella, even as she tried to wave her off.

Gella pulling up just before hitting Natalya, and then diving into her, triggering the Excellion transformation whose name Andrea could just barely recall: Seraphic Nightmare.

What did it do? She racked her brain. *Did we ever find out?*

Natalya's back arched, and she seemed to be in agony. Andrea and Gaylen instinctively moved over toward her and heard desperate fragments of speech. "Gella, no! You can't..."

An aura of white light was starting to emanate from Natalya, beating softly at first, and then with increasingly sharp, intense pulses. She strained to make out what was around her, and then croaked out a warning. "Get away. Get back. They're dangerous."

Gaylen crossed in front and grabbed Andrea, pulling her out of the way as the pulses of light accelerated to a harsh strobing and Natalya's dark, leathery wings began a violent transformation.

Rows of white feathers pushed their way through the skin as the wings grew outward and upward, doubling and tripling in size, pushing Natalya skyward. The points of contact on her back began to look tiny and inadequate to the task of supporting the increasing mass. Although her own body remained at it's original size, she appeared to grow smaller and smaller against the expanding wings.

As an Excellion transformation, Seraphic Nightmare carried its own unique costume. As if to counter the massive wings, Natalya was now clad in a delicate, all-white, full-length lace dress.

Andrea had the presence of mind to check out how Viktor's men were handling this. It was gratifying. Apparently, he had prepared them for the sight of a few girls flying around in scanty outfits, but this was another story entirely. As Natalya's wings approached a total height of forty feet, they stood there, guns at their sides, staring up in open-mouthed horror at the awesome spectacle. Even Viktor looked stunned.

Then the wings started to beat.

At a distance, it might have looked graceful, even beautiful. But up close, it was terrifying. Perfect white angel wings, the height of a five-story building, moving enormous volumes of air with each beat. Andrea and Gaylen got themselves up and out of the way, but the gale-force wing beats knocked Viktor's men over.

The noise was even more frightening, like a hurricane or the sound of a huge engine tearing itself apart. Gaylen tried to talk to Andrea, but she had to time her comments between the pounding thrusts of the wings as they swept through their cycles. "What is this?"

"I think it's called Seraphic Nightmare."

"What?"

"SERAPHIC NIGHTMARE."

"Is this all it does?"

Andrea shrugged and waited for the next null point between beats. "We never found out what it does, but I don't think this is all."

Rings of intense white light were emanating from the wings and shooting straight up, spreading out and dissipating into the night sky. Gradually, the wings slowed their cadence, with smaller cycles and less overall intensity and sound. The gunmen picked themselves up, but seemed unsure how to proceed. Two more had come around the side of the warehouse to see for themselves what was happening. Viktor wasn't giving any orders, so they stood by and waited.

Natalya's eyes were shut. She looked peaceful now, but also completely out of it. The wings pulled back slowly and relaxed forward, almost as if they were inhaling a deep breath and letting go a sigh, as the aura of light swelled and subsided.

Then Natalya began to sing. Not in any form recognizable to anyone, or even with a voice that anyone would have known as hers. She was singing a lullaby that itself was a dream. Her voice seemed not a product of vocal chords and air, but the pure essence of singing, beyond the medium of sound, manifesting directly in the soul.

Andrea was spellbound. She couldn't turn away. She knew this was the moment to make plans, to evaluate the situation and try to save her friends somehow, but that voice was too beautiful, the song too heartbreaking.

Long minutes seemed to go by—and nothing, it seemed— could break the spell. When Andrea finally pulled herself away from it to see what had happened, Gaylen and Viktor were entranced, and the eight gunmen were lying on the ground, apparently sleeping. Looking around her, Andrea saw Masa close by. "Masa, what is this?"

"I don't know. I mean, I think I do, but this isn't supposed to exist. This form is using a power based on sleep. It's very old. It's part of our rebirthing procedure. It sedates predators while we are being born. But it's not supposed to exist in the form of a... a weapon? It doesn't work on any with the blood of the Fae, but those other guys are going to be out for at least eight hours."

"Is Natalya in any danger?"

"I don't know. Those wings are insane. No wonder she never wanted to transform with Gella."

"Masa, this light, the pulsing—it's so different from the usual lights. It's so white and pure. No one but us can see this, right?"

Masa shot her a look. "I don't know. Gella's so out of control. You're right, though. This is really different. I hope it isn't visible."

Gaylen caught their attention and pointed to Natalya. She was starting to look exhausted, and her song seemed to be coming to an end. Andrea and Gaylen wanted to try to get to her, but those huge, crazy wings were too treacherous to risk getting close to.

They were trying to position themselves over Natalya when she abruptly stopped singing and her wings began to collapse into themselves, disappearing faster than they had come. Diving down to catch the falling girl, Gaylen and Andrea almost crashed. As Natalya settled onto the ground, Gella materialized out of her and fell to the parking lot pavement. She was in bad shape. Her breathing was labored, and she seemed to be in considerable pain.

Natalya reached over and touched her. "Why Gella? You knew you couldn't survive. Why did you do this?"

"He killed Malka. She didn't deserve that. Y-you're next. You have to fly. His blood isn't pure. He'll be… affected. You can get away."

Andrea didn't understand, but when she looked over at Viktor, he seemed drunk and was obviously struggling to stay awake. She wondered what they could do to take advantage of the situation, but when she turned back, she could see that anything like that would have to wait.

Gella was dying. Natalya was holding her tenderly and whispering in Russian. She started singing the lullaby, softly, in her natural voice. Gella was glowing with a violet-tinged radiance. Her eyes were closed, and she lay perfectly still for a while. Then her body jerked once, and she settled back into Natalya's hand and dissolved away.

When Natalya looked up, her face was a mix of personal grief and tactical concern. "Check on Viktor," she said urgently.

Andrea spun around just in time to see him stumble toward the nearest sleeping gunman and grab his rifle.

Hovering right by Andrea's ear, Masa hissed, "Immobilize him now!"

Andrea brought her hands out and together, channeling her immobilization with such power that she forced the gun straight up in Viktor's hands and knocked the breath out of him. That settled matters for the moment. They used the next few minutes to calm down and recover. Eventually, though, they had to face the fact that the situation was unsustainable.

"We can't leave him with that gun in his hands." Gaylen said.

"What do we do, then?" Andrea asked, not daring to take her eyes off her captive.

Gaylen thought for a minute. "Natalya, can you put a secondary immobilization on him?"

"Of course, but I don't get it. What am I going to do different?"

"If we put you to his side, we could free his hands while you hold his body and make him drop the gun."

Natalya considered this. "I'm sure I can hold everything but his hands, but what makes you think he'll drop the gun?"

"Oh, I think I can handle that," Gaylen said.

They approached Viktor as if approaching a dangerous animal, and Natalya got into position on one side.

"I will make you all pay for this," Viktor spat.

"Oh, you can still talk," Gaylen said with feigned casualness. "Well, that's a mixed blessing, but we'll just have to live with that."

"You will die last and suffer the most," Viktor said.

"One thing at a time, Viktor. By the way, I'm Gaylen, the girl you tried to kill before." He eyed her with hatred, but she managed to meet his gaze. "So, you seem to know a lot about all this Faerie stuff, Viktor. Do you know about *this*?" Gaylen called up her ice-darts and the silver bracelets appeared. From the surprise on his face, it was obvious that Viktor had never seen the like of them before. "Oh, I guess not. Okay, let me show you what this does."

She turned and launched a dart into the middle of one of the larger trees bordering the lot. A moment later, the dart exploded with a sharp crack, and the top of the tree fell over, smashing into a maintenance shed. Gaylen turned back and came within a few inches of Viktor's face. "Ice dart. Compressed carbon dioxide. Explodes after impact. So, here's the deal: You let the gun go when we free your hands. Otherwise, I put a dart in your hand, it explodes, you drop the gun, same result. Honestly? I don't really care which way this goes."

Viktor said nothing, but Gaylen got into position, and when they switched from Andrea to Natalya, he dropped the weapon. Gaylen picked it up as Natalya widened the field to secure him, and they walked back to where they could talk without being heard.

"So now I have the wolf by the ears," Natalya said, eyes locked on her captive. "How do I let go?"

"I understand that we can't just kill him," said Gaylen. "Am I wrong in assuming that a few hours in police custody will just delay the inevitable?"

Natalya nodded. "Neither option is favorable."

"Wait," Andrea said, holding up her hand. "Listen."

From their quiet, remote location near the Gowanus Canal, they could pick up the sounds of dozens of sirens. They seemed to be coming from all directions.

Gaylen finally asked the obvious. "Did something happen?"

Chapter 46

Across the canal, an NYPD radio car had been sitting quietly for the past five minutes. That made it an unusual radio car on this particular evening. Half an hour earlier, all hell had broken loose in the New York metropolitan area when huge pulsing rings of white light of indeterminate origin had lit up the night sky.

Police Officer Linda Petrossian had been on a break nearby when the incident began. In attempting to get to the location, she had arrived at the opposite side of the Gowanus Canal from the warehouse complex.

Viktor's security lighting had lit up the courtyard like a sports arena, effectively blinding everyone inside to Petrossian's approach. The whole situation was already unusual enough but when she pulled out a video camera to use the zoom lens, she was astonished at how many people she recognized.

She began recording immediately.

* * *

The situation across the canal wasn't resolving itself. Gaylen had taken over holding Viktor. Natalya had decided to fly all the guns she could find to the roof of the main building in case Viktor got free or the men awoke. The Fae were still in shock over watching two of their own die in front of them.

Andrea was thinking. There wasn't a lot to think about—at least, not in the sense of useful options that could keep them alive once

Viktor regained his freedom. Finally, she gave up. "I don't know. The only thing we've got left is to hit him with restoration."

"What will that achieve?" Natalya asked.

"No idea. I just don't know what else we can do. I mean, what have we got to lose?"

* * *

Officer Petrossian was just about to stop recording and call in a report to the precinct when the scene through her viewfinder got considerably more interesting. A building had blocked her view of Natalya bringing the guns to the warehouse roof, but she had relocated to a higher, less obstructed location just in time to see the three girls rise up in front of the unidentified individual whose back had been to her since she arrived on the scene.

Petrossian found it oddly comforting that, even though the levitating appeared to violate the laws of nature, it did make the Melman girl's ability to fly up and knock over a high school jock more plausible. She made a mental note that Miss Volkova was at the bottom of an equilateral triangle with Misses Melman and O'Reilly across from each other at the top. They appeared to engage in a short discussion. Subsequently, the unidentified male began glowing.

* * *

The main thing Andrea didn't like about Masa's T-lock was that the dual trinary configuration put her on the opposite side from the Faerie she needed to consult to make the thing work.

Natalya was back on immobilizing duty. It required a lot of focus, and the stress built quickly and wore her out.

Gaylen and Sumi initiated restoration, and at first, it seemed that nothing was happening. Gradually, though, a red glow began to appear as a fringe around Viktor.

A few minutes into the operation, Andrea looked over to Masa and indicated that they should join Gaylen on the restoration. Because they had only barely tested combining the powers of the T-lock beforehand, the first thing they learned about applying a double dose of restoration was that the power didn't double. It increased exponentially.

This came as a shock. The change started with a blinding ring of golden light that built up around the edge of their circle and then shot toward Viktor, illuminating him before dispersing outward in a cone into the sky. Then the light around him modulated down to more of a deep-red aura, and gradually, the hue began to shift.

Andrea couldn't be sure anything useful was happening yet, but she took comfort in the fact that Viktor's aura was shifting along the color spectrum – through orange and then to yellow. She would have felt a lot better knowing what the color shift meant.

As it was, if Andrea could have found a moment to take a look behind her, she would have felt a lot worse.

* * *

Officer Petrossian had scored a ringside seat to some world-class strangeness. What had begun as a localized phenomenon over the skies of New York City was now beginning to arc across the strato-sphere and, unbeknownst to her, circumnavigate the globe.

As it did, the population of the world began working itself into a collective frenzy, and with good reason. The night sky had begun pulsing with enormous bands of green light. People would later compare it to the aurora borealis, but those were people who had never actually *seen* the aurora borealis. This phenomenon had a violent intensity completely un-like the northern lights. Arcing like a Tesla coil, parallel bands of green snapped together sharply and then separated while random bursts shot across the sky like green lightning. Internet servers started crashing left and right as people searched for information about what was happening.

The media, as baffled as anyone else, couldn't contribute any-thing more useful than a name. Perhaps too shocked to indulge in the usual clever branding given to an important story, they called it what everyone called it that night: "The Lights in the Sky."

The good news was that the light show seemed to be electromag-netically neutral. Air traffic control radars, satellite transponders, comput-er links—nothing appeared to be affected by what was going on. Beyond that, though, it was becoming apparent that the weird light display wasn't conforming to any known standards of measurement, meaning that no one could analyze or explain what was so clearly visible in the night sky.

* * *

Petrossian was cursing the fact that she didn't have a tripod. She had finally decided the situation needed to be called in, but trying to hold her camera shot while operating her radio was tricky. And the dispatcher wasn't making matters any easier.

"Seven six Henry, the captain is *not* available to talk to you. You *are* aware that the whole freaking world is exploding?"

"Dispatch, you need to inform the officer on duty that I believe I am at ground zero for the disturbance."

"Seven six Henry, this is *really* not the night for this. File your report like everyone else, and we will get to you ASAP."

"Dispatch, listen to me. Pulsing white lights and green wave lights are originating directly across the Gowanus Canal from my position. I have identified three girls from K290, Brooklyn Prep. My regular assignment. They're involved in something here. It's complicated. Request backup."

"Seven six Henry, no backup available. Continue surveillance, and resources will be diverted to you when and *if* they can be spared. You're *really* pissing people off with this, Petrossian. Cut the crap and do your job. *Over!*"

* * *

If the shift in Viktor's aura along the light spectrum was an indication of the restoration's progress, then they were finally getting somewhere. Over time, it had shifted through green and was now moving into blue. The only problem was that holding Viktor immobile was obviously wearing Natalya out. Yet Andrea didn't want to risk interrupting the restoration process to take over the immobilizing for her.

She passed a question around the circle to Masa. "What if we use all three of us in restoration? Would that hold him?" Masa looked up and indicated that she didn't know.

371

Andrea realized she was going to have to make this decision for the group but trying to think her way through the problem was rough going. After all, what the hell could even *be* restored in someone like Viktor? Might they end up with a refreshed and fully recharged monster, ready for a new round of terror?

The doubling part had worked well and yielded a big energy boost. Viktor wasn't reacting to anything, but it was impossible to tell why. He might still be exhausted from Seraphic Nightmare, or he might be waiting for the opportunity to make a move.

Or maybe, just maybe, something was happening inside him.

A decision coalesced within her. Natalya was fading. The restoration was at least doing *something*. And from somewhere in the back of her mind arose a saying she had heard and remembered, even though it was the last thing anyone would have ever associated with Andrea Melman: "*Fortune favors the bold.*"

"I want to go to full power." She surprised herself with the force and clarity of her voice. The words came out like a command, and even more surprisingly, the circle of girls and Fae acknowledged her and readied themselves to comply.

* * *

Officer Petrossian was torn between frustration at the NYPD's institutional stupidity and fascination bordering on delight at the scene unfolding across the canal. Plus, her camera work was improving.

Resting the lens against a tree branch helped stabilize the tightly zoomed-in shots. It also allowed her to make a provisional ID of the previously unidentified male as Viktor Lukov. But what the hell was *he* doing there?

Speculation ended, however, a moment later when Andrea gave Natalya a signal.

A variation of the first power-up began with significantly stronger golden pulses emanating from the girls' circle. But after bouncing back off Viktor, the rings of light continued into the sky and appeared to interact with the waves of green light already there.

After a moment or two, the golden pulses began alternating cycles of faster, more compressed waves, with slower and wider bursts. Shortly afterward, the golden cycles appeared to be coming in from the opposite direction and interacting, making increasingly complex combinations.

Petrossian had to wonder: Were these things really traveling all the way around the world and circling back on themselves? Whatever was going on the scene up in the night sky looked scary as hell.

Chapter 47

Viktor was fully awake now. He could tell he wasn't being restrained by anything anymore, but something else was preventing him from walking away from whatever they were subjecting him to—something new and quite unexpected.

He felt *good.* Not that he would ever, in a million years, admit such a thing to anyone. But there it was: good. Not pleasure. Not ecstasy or stimulation. There was really nothing in his experience to compare it to. The sensation was one of utter completeness. He felt no need to explore anything beyond the immediacy of his existence— right here, right now.

The thing was, his whole life had been dedicated to establishing iron control over situations—dominion over all the people and things that came within his reach. But from this new perspective, he couldn't figure out what he wanted. Everything was already there.

* * *

The sirens were getting louder, and it occurred to Andrea that even by Faerie light-show standards, this had to be kicking out a lot of energy. Stealing a glance upward, she was quite surprised at the commotion going on above, and motioned to Masa to check it out.

Masa's stunned look was not reassuring, but since there wasn't much that anyone could do about it at this point, they just kept on restoring Viktor to whatever he was turning into.

* * *

It wasn't clear to Viktor whether he was still under the influence of Natalya's lullaby, the immobilizing, or the ongoing process the girls were putting him through, but something wasn't quite right. Something was shifting—something fundamental.

Viktor's existence had always been motivated by a series of transgressive power-ups. You saw something; you took it. *Wanting* the thing didn't even enter into the equation. Basically, you wanted it because the act of taking it—especially if it involved taking it from someone against their will—gave you power. The greater the humiliation, the greater the power.

Everything Viktor did was designed to reinforce that feedback loop. And now something was interfering. He was having difficulty getting in touch with the rage that powered him. Maybe it was this process they were running. He had stopped talking, to keep the girls from sensing anything about this change. But more than that, he had stopped talking, because he didn't know what to say.

The shell of light surrounding him was turning a soft purple now, and with each color shift, he felt less powerful. Less aggressive. *They're stealing my power,* he thought.

A satisfying blast of anger followed this realization. They were humiliating him, and he would have his revenge, starting with the destruction of Marina's little bitch in front of her companions.

* * *

As the aura around Viktor moved through the end of the violet spectrum, Andrea started to get worried. Unless there was some alternative Faerie color spectrum to explore, they were almost done. Somehow, she had expected an explanation to pop up out of the process of restoration, letting them know what they had achieved.

Another bad sign, Viktor still wasn't saying anything. It suggested that he had endured whatever had happened to him, and still had the discipline to hold his tongue.

Whatever the situation, a few minutes later the light around Viktor was almost pure white, and everyone was exhausted. The girls stopped the process by breaking the circle and floating to the ground.

At first, Viktor looked as though he wanted to say something, but he caught sight of the crazy night sky, and for a time, he seemed mesmerized by the spectacle. Finally, he brought his attention back to the group.

The girls and the Fae were positioned a dozen feet away, trying to get some idea of what—if anything—had changed. Their hearts sank when his first words seemed to indicate that the answer was nothing. "So, this is it? You're done? What was that little trick supposed to achieve?" He watched them for a moment. "I'm guessing you didn't know, and you still don't. So, it's my turn now?"

* * *

He was silent for a long time. It might have looked as if he was savoring the moment or considering his options, but the truth was, Viktor was stuck. He couldn't say why, but he didn't know how to deliver the next part of his speech. He knew what he wanted to say, and he knew how he should express it, but he couldn't find the core of anger that had to empower him for his words to be effective. Still, he had to try. "Ah, Natalya. You've finally found yourself a little coven to worship you. Do they believe in you? Have you put them under the spell of your personality?" He nodded at Andrea. "This one certainly. The adoring acolyte you always dreamed of, isn't she?"

Looking at Andrea, he said, "You're quite smitten with the beautiful and talented Miss Volkova, aren't you? Oh, you don't have to answer. It's all over your face."

Turning to Gaylen, "And you... You see yourself as what—the aide de camp? The trusted lieutenant? Oh, well done, Natalya. Well done. Marina would be proud to see you building up a nice reserve of people to use."

He wanted to move around, but his feet wouldn't respond. Worse, he couldn't tell how his words were going over. The girls weren't giving up any response. He just had to keep pushing on.

"But they don't really know you, do they, Natalya? They don't know what you really are. The little games you've played with Illya. The hatred you feel toward your parents. The many ways you've flirted with death. Did she tell you about what she did to her characters? The little angel she blinded with her rage? The devil she created in the process of cursing me? Oh, you girls are quite brave to be associating with such a damaged and dangerous individual. Does she still refer to me as a monster? She should know, after all. If Gella were still here, we could ask her all about monsters."

Nothing.

He could see that his talk was doing nothing—all words and no effect. Without even looking at them, he could sense their lack of fear. All he could do was keep talking. "Do they know, Natalya? Do they know how you've harmed yourself over the years? Oh, yes, Miss Melman. The long sleeves are much more than a fashionable affectation. But that's just the kind of harm that you can see, isn't it, Natalya? You've cut yourself up much worse than that on the inside, haven't you? You've actually managed to achieve some real permanent damage. Am I right?"

At this, Natalya's trembled. Instinctively, Andrea and Gaylen shifted toward her.

"Do you know what Natalya's greatest fear was, growing up with me? She had many, of course, and not all of them unwarranted, but the thing that terrified her *most*? At some point, she became convinced that I was going to impregnate her, to create a more powerful guardian to bring about a more powerful character. A breeding program with her as queen of the hive. Mind you, I had considered that for a long time, but she didn't know that. She simply kept feeding on her own panic, year after year, until finally, you know what she did? Last year, she went out and had herself sterilized. Yes! That's how much my little princess hates me. She had such a strong picture in her head of me creating a version of herself to experiment with, she found a doctor who would perform the procedure on an underage girl—for a considerable sum of money, of course.

He paused to unleash a triumphant leer in Natalya's direction. "Yes, Natalya, I've always known. But there is so much *you* don't know. Let me tell you something. A little secret. I didn't need your body or your eggs. All I need from you I can obtain from your *hairbrush*. My second-generation guardian requires no more than a sample of your DNA and my own sperm. And I have plenty of both. It was for *nothing*, Natalya. You have ruined yourself for *nothing*!"

* * *

Viktor was obviously waiting for a response to his revelations. So were Andrea, and Gaylen. Natalya's face remained impassive. What should have—at the very least—enraged them was falling oddly flat. Andrea had to wonder whether, after all that had happened, they were simply too tired to react properly, but that didn't quite seem to fit.

The words were horrible enough on their own, and Viktor's intent was as evil as ever. But somehow, the underlying emotion—the hate—wasn't there.

* * *

Meanwhile, the sky had become a chaotic wash of light. Even though no new light was being added to the mix, the existing streams appeared to be accelerating, and the green wash was developing its own pulse. Finally, the elements seemed to find a resonating point where everything coalesced into a single bright event that washed across the whole sky. From directly above the warehouse site, a point of pure green appeared and began to spread out in all directions, absorbing and extinguishing the gold light as it traveled.

In moments, the sky was a luminous green as far as the eye could see, and then it all began to dissipate into the night air.

379

Within minutes, the stars were back in the sky as if nothing had ever happened. But that wasn't the case. Something had indeed happened. Restoration was now beginning.

For as long as the light of the Fae was present, whether from the side effects of restoration or from the scattered glow of its application, Viktor Lukov was protected from the full impact of what had been done to him. With the last glimmer dying above, he became a new man.

Not only had the connection to his inner rage been broken. Not only had he lost the joy of dominating and humiliating others. But the very core of his ability to ignore the suffering he had inflicted on his victims was no longer functioning.

As he stood there, waiting for them to react, a response was building up inside him from a long-suppressed aspect of his being. Events—beginning with the memories of earliest childhood—surfaced briefly and sank back into darkness, each with its own distinct emotional imprint. Like flowers with their own singular scent.

But these emotions were anything but sweet. Each derived from an episode of bullying and brutalizing behavior in Viktor's past. Events that had once carried the triumphant thrill of conquest: the infliction of punishments, the brazen theft of cherished treasures, the domination and destruction of other human beings—everything Viktor had ever lived for was there for him to see.

But instead of reveling in his accomplishments, he felt the clear, unblinking eye of conscience breaking down his ability to enjoy the life he had made. Faces long forgotten swam into view and took him back to the moments of cruelty he had cherished, only to turn the tables and force him into a state of empathy.

It was as if he could no longer distinguish between "me" and "them." Every artful nuance of terror and sadism he had ever inflicted was being inscribed on him, body and soul. The faces continued, unabated. The memories grew worse as the crimes they reflected became more perverse.

Viktor had no idea where he was in this monstrous chronology when he began to fear for his sanity. The years were passing more slowly, even as the volume and tempo of his crimes were picking up. By now, it was clear that he would have to feel, in meticulous detail, not only the specific pain of those he had wronged, but also the weight of personal responsibility for having committed those acts.

He was losing the ability to focus, but he could tell that he was approaching the period when torture and murder had become a regular part of his existence, and the thought left him terrified.

Chapter 48

"What's going on?" Gaylen asked. Everyone was wondering the same thing, but no one had an answer. Viktor was still standing in front of them, but he no longer appeared cognizant of their presence. His eyes seemed to look inward, and his hands were shaking. Andrea looked over to Natalya for a clue, but she seemed just as confused.

When tears began forming in Viktor's eyes, Natalya spoke up in a tense whisper. "He's never done that. He can't even fake it. Sumi, no one has ever tried this on a human?"

"Not that I ever heard of. Mind you, no one has ever used restoration for that long or taken it up to that level of power."

By now, none of them could take their eyes off of Viktor's strange performance.

"Oh, that reminds me," Andrea said, "What exactly does restoration use for power?"

"I don't know," Masa replied.

"Yes, you do," said Rei. "You invented it."

"No, she just invented the stuff that distributes it into the Green World," Sumi pointed out.

"I don't remember any of that," said Masa. "How does it work, and what's the power for?"

"All I remember is that you made it work," Rei said.

"I think it was a big deal, but I can't recall anything else," Sumi added. "It had a name, I think."

Rei nodded, still unable to take her eyes off Viktor. "Yeah, it had a name. I think it was important."

"I hope not *too* important," Masa replied. "I'm guessing that all that stuff we did tonight would probably break a system like that."

* * *

Fifteen minutes after the skies cleared, Officer Linda Petrossian was reassigned to guarding an intersection in a nearby neighborhood. Nothing further seemed to be going on across the canal, and she had lost the will to argue with the system, so she packed up and headed to her posting.

Along the way, she remembered two things. The first was the warning her mother had given her on her graduation from the Police Academy. "Listen, Linda, I'm damned proud of you for joining the force, and I wish you the best in your career. But I'm gonna tell you something, and don't you ever forget it. No matter what anyone else tells you about how it's all one big happy family of cops, all that big-blue-wall stuff is true—up until something goes wrong. And then, you mark my words: It's every cop for himself. If you *ever* find yourself in any kind of position where the department might be embarrassed and they could blame it on you, you better do everything you can to cover your ass. Because, honey, *no one* is going to cover it for you."

Linda Petrossian's entire career had borne out that bit of advice, so the second thing she remembered was that her media-geek nephew Richie's house was on the way to her assignment. A lot of things could get lost in this world, and securing a backup copy of tonight's feature presentation showed both prudence and initiative—two things the department always claimed to value in an officer.

Whatever was going on back there between the girls and Viktor, the girls seemed all right, and Viktor couldn't be too badly off.

* * *

Viktor was in hell. By now, he was on his knees, begging for the memories to stop. But the images would not stop. One after another, they surfaced. Things forgotten for years. Every possible variation of depraved behavior. And every single instance was coming into his awareness, fresh as the day it occurred—every blow, every word, every decision. He couldn't stand another second of this self-inflicted torture, and he longed for the release that he had always held to be his trump card in the game of life.

Death had always been Viktor's best friend. Once you understood that there was a place where nothing could get you, where you couldn't be held accountable for your sins, all things became possible.

Death was always the place he helped his own victims see as their final release. When they begged for death, he had won, and they now saw things his way. But a man unafraid of death didn't need to be persuaded to see that. On the contrary, Viktor was fearless precisely *because* he had death in his corner.

In his life, he was never without a variety of escape options, either on his person or within arm's length. He should have been able to end his suffering in seconds, but for one problem: the terms of the sentence imposed on him by this terrible awakening put the highest value on human life. Even the most evil, miserable life was now precious beyond measure, and what had been the easiest of decisions was beyond consideration in this new reality.

He could no more kill himself now than transform into a bird and fly away from his past. Or lie. Or withhold information. Or fail to atone for his sins against those he had wronged. And right there, not ten feet away, was the single most abused victim in Viktor's long criminal career.

The realization that he must begin to undo some of the damage he had so savagely inflicted on Natalya was the beginning of Viktor Lukov's salvation. And when he finally made the connection, when he came to understand that from now on, the only thing that could lessen the pain of his existence within this terrible ocean of remembrance was the path of atonement—he wept.

* * *

When Viktor called Natalya over, the group was suspicious, even though he was still on his knees. The ice darts came out, and Gaylen and Andrea were ready to take him out if he so much as breathed in a threatening manner. But Natalya could sense the change, and asked them to give her a moment alone with him.

* * *

By the time they got back to Andrea's house, it was dawn.

For hours, Viktor and Natalya had sat huddled in front of a computer at his place while he dismantled the web of hired killers who were to avenge him in death. Then he had transferred the vast network of accounts that constituted his financial empire over to her control.

While this went on, Andrea and Gaylen mostly watched television. Not that they were bored, or anything of the sort. On the contrary, they found it quite instructive to be at the center of a global incident beyond human comprehension and see how the media handled it.

On balance, they decided, not well. People were taking ignorant speculations, reporting them as fact, and then speculating on those same "facts" to create yet more ignorant speculations. It all had the air of a fantastical movie, a magical-realist creation that they had played a part in.

Now it was over, and they had gone home, but it seemed that no one else had left the theater. There was also the whole question of whether anyone had seen them or was looking for them.

It appeared not, but the thought of being somehow tied to this was getting scarier by the moment. People were acting crazy, saying crazy things, threatening to take crazy actions. Any connection to having created the, now universally branded, "Lights in the Sky" was going to become a nightmare.

But right now, they were just tired. Before passing out in Andrea's room, Natalya gave them the short version of what was happening. "Okay, firstly, Illya is not in any present danger." She looked pointedly over at Andrea who looked pointedly down at her feet, avoiding eye contact. After a glimmer of amusement, Natalya continued. "Russia is vast and things are easily lost within it's vastness. Illya intends to become such a thing for the time being. We are uncertain, but it's prudent to believe that Viktor's former associates and rivals would find him a valuable acquisition. He intends to deny them that pleasure. It is unclear how he could return to America at this point. Too many law enforcement agencies here will want to grab him once his connection to us is established."

"You think the authorities already know who we are?" Gaylen asked.

Natalya frowned. "You need to expect the worst here. Our present anonymity, if in fact we have any, will be short lived."

Looking up, Andrea asked, "So what's the deal with Viktor? Is he still a threat?"

"Yes, that is the main issue isn't it?" Natalya said. "I don't know what a Faerie "Restoration" is supposed to do normally but the Viktor I knew seems to have disappeared. Without his underlying rage, it's hard to see what is left of him. I don't think he even knows what to make of himself."

"Has he turned "good?" Andrea asked with air quotes.

"That seems too much to ask." Gaylen said.

"Indeed," Natalya said. "Without any experience of being anything but evil he seems to be an empty shell. He is experiencing considerable suffering over his crimes but it appears to be related to an enforced empathy rather than some improvement in his values. Honestly, while this hasn't revealed any inner goodness, the Viktor I see now would be incapable of committing the crimes he's now suffering for. He's a broken man living with the razor-sharp memory of every depraved act he's ever committed. The simultaneous restoration of both memory and conscience was a cruel kind of paradox, really."

Noticing the two girls looking at her uncertainly she added, "Which I could not be happier about it." Triggering a round of laughter.

"Spending the rest of his life enduring the guilt and maintaining an empathic link to the suffering of his victims?" Andrea said. "It couldn't happen to a more appropriate monster."

"Would that be poetic justice or ironic justice? Perhaps both?" Gaylen wondered. "So, does that mean we don't need to worry about Russian mobsters anymore?"

"Hardly," Natalya said. "While Viktor's organization is gone it's legacy will be around for a long time. Dangerous things have been unleashed. For now, they'll evolve into smaller criminal organizations. Unfortunately, all of them will be searching for Viktor's loot and that means they'll be searching for me and that means they'll be searching for you."

"So my dream of being popular is finally coming true." Andrea said, earning a laugh. "Is there a good side to any of this?"

"Only in the sense that the burden of acquiring Viktor's resources includes the use of those resources. We have access to money in a variety of forms as well as a number of safe houses and cars. In our current situation, that could prove to be very useful."

"So what's going to happen to Viktor now?" Gaylen asked.

"He asked for and received a small amount of money to travel." Natalya replied. "Where he'll go is anyone's guess. Given the threats now facing him, I would expect him to find a deep hole in a distant land."

It was a comforting image but the girls were too tired to care. Andrea barely had the energy to turn off the lights before she fell onto her bed.

"So, all things considered, I thought today went pretty well," Gaylen murmured as they began drifting off to sleep.

That got everyone laughing again. When they settled down, Natalya spoke up. "Okay, but let's never do that again."

"I just hope we wake up tomorrow and no one remembers the whole Lights in the Sky thing," said Andrea. "That would be nice."

Everyone agreed. They went to sleep. And the next day, no one had forgotten anything.

Chapter 49

"This endless stream of denials can only confirm the vast government conspiracy…"

"Leviticus, Revelations. It's all right there, people. Open your eyes and…"

"But how could a reversal of the earth's magnetic field result in such a display?"

"Clearly the signs of an alien technology, you merely have to…"

"God's stern judgment upon Satanism, homosexuality, and the liberal arts…"

"Terrorist attack? Alien invasion? Or the first sign of the apocalypse? Tonight on…"

"Gaylen!" Andrea shouted. "Pick one, or turn it off! You're making us crazy!"

"Oh, uh, okay," Gaylen said, turning off the television and putting down the remote. "But it *is* crazy. I just want somebody to talk about it like a grown-up. What's the big deal? I mean, nothing really happened… I think. Right?"

Everyone was still exhausted. Six hours of rest wasn't even a down payment on the girls' sleep deficit, but no one could relax with the idea that a fear-crazed world might be coming with torches and pitchforks, looking for a scapegoat.

Natalya was the only one who seemed unaffected, but that was because she was fully absorbed in the details of redistributing Viktor's assets to a new series of international bank accounts. She had been at the computer for hours. There was a lot to do.

Aside from the unlikely notion that Viktor might return to his old self and want his fortune back, the rapid demise of his enterprise was already becoming common knowledge throughout the criminal world.

Hackers, like flocks of vultures, were circling the spoils. Moreover, since no bank could expect sympathy from the authorities for the kind of money Viktor had stashed, no one could complain if it all suddenly disappeared. Natalya's best ally was speed, and the vast, dense maze of channels that made up the global financial system.

The Fae were on edge. Since their return to Andrea's house, Cami's Faeries had put in no further appearances, but that was of no comfort to them. They were engaged in constant arguments, with breakdowns and tears a common occurrence.

After a while, Andrea decided to go food shopping and take Masa with her. She was almost out the door when Natalya dragged her back.

Tired as she was, Andrea couldn't quite summon the energy to complain, but she simmered with annoyance as an ugly beige overcoat, sunglasses, and a floppy hat were layered on top of her existing outfit.

"Of course you hate this. Yes?" Natalya asked as she assessed her work.

Andrea's silence was all the answer required.

"This is our new world. We leave no impression. Display no identifying characteristics." She opened the door. "Go. Be unremarkable."

Andrea sighed, "I'll do my unremarkable best."

Since no one could see Masa, she tended to float near Andrea's shoulder as they walked around, and the worst likely scenario was somebody thinking Andrea was talking to herself.

As they approached the market, though, Andrea started feeling weird. People seemed to be staring at her. They had just reached the store entrance when a young boy with his mother pointed up at her and announced, "Look, Mommy, a fairy!"

Andrea froze.

Masa froze.

The mother froze.

The little boy started pulling on his mother's jacket and demanding, "I want a fairy. I want a fairy. Can I get a fairy? Can I Mom?"

Andrea did an abrupt about-face and started heading back to her house as fast as she could, but the boy had broken some sort of social barrier, and people began pointing to Masa and trying to ask Andrea questions.

She broke into a run, and to her surprise, a half dozen people lit out after her, cell phones out, trying to get pictures of "the Brooklyn Fairy," as Masa was to be known from that point on.

In no time at all, the crowd grew. People spilled out into the street, running against traffic trying to outflank her. The volume of noise kept rising and the tone became even more threatening.

Andrea came to a busy intersection and had to wait for the light. Hyperventilating and confused, she looked around for her companion.

Masa was flitting about, a few feet above her.

"Masa! Get out of here. Get yourself home and warn them," she tried to whisper, but a cluster of people had caught up with her.

"What did she say?"

"I couldn't hear it. Did you?"

"'Go home and warn them,' she said. 'Go home and warn them.' That's what she said."

"Where's the fairy going?"

"We should split up. I'll go after the fairy; you stay with the girl."

"No! You stay with the girl. I'm going after the fairy. That's where the money is."

Masa floated up, looking down at Andrea as the group pressed in on her.

Andrea was losing control of her fear. The crowd, fired up by the sight of a "real fairy" and determined to find out her connection with it, was in a frenzy, and she couldn't shake them. She still had enough presence of mind to lead everyone away from her house, but she had no practical way of losing them on the streets of Brooklyn and she couldn't outrun them forever.

She considered stopping and trying to reason with them, but that was just the desperation talking. Worse, with every passing second, they were alerting even more people. For the next hour, she was pursued by the group as it swelled into a mob.

Furious and upset, she would have given them a real show and flown away, if just for a moment's peace. But without Masa to transform with, there could be no escape.

With the constant barrage of questions and cameras, Andrea became increasingly frantic. She soon found herself unable to orient herself in the section of town she had fled into. The buildings had gotten more run-down and industrial, and she knew she was hopelessly lost when she came out on a wide avenue dominated by auto body shops and junkyards.

Behind and around her, the crowd was taking on a wilder edge, the excitement of the chase drawing fuel from the still-fresh terror of last night. There were still shouts for autographs and pictures, but more and more often they were mingled with accusations and threats.

Running through a small park and finding herself on the curb of an unfamiliar boulevard, Andrea was ready to throw herself into oncoming traffic when her eye caught something in the distance. Something dirty, dented, and brown. The unmistakable lumbering of the world's ugliest station wagon.

It was the most beautiful thing Andrea had ever seen.

She stopped and bent over as if resting, waiting for the right moment. Dozens of cell phone cameras recorded her breathless pause. With her last reserves of focus, Andrea tried to judge the right moment to charge through traffic and get to the car, approaching in the opposite lane.

She appeared to get the jump on her pursuers when she launched herself into the road. Either that, or no one was crazy enough to follow her as she dashed into traffic, running across the boulevard.

Natalya didn't even pull over. Right in the middle of the street, she stopped dead as Gaylen opened the back door and Andrea fell into the car. Horns were honking and drivers were swearing, but Natalya calmly pulled away as Andrea's stalkers spilled into the road, trying to capture the final images of the Brooklyn Fairy Girl.

Lying on the floor of the car, Andrea wanted to be all brave and funny. She tried to think of something clever. But when she looked up at Gaylen, the ordeal suddenly caught up with her and she simply broke down in hysterics.

* * *

After the second hour, Linda Petrossian was starting to worry. What had started as a debriefing had evolved into an interview. Now, to all intents and purposes, it was an interrogation. And the worst thing was, she had brought it on herself.

Insisting on showing the video to the precinct commander seemed like the right thing to do at the time. To her, it was an explanation. A crazy explanation. But the events of the previous night were quite crazy, so her video seemed in line with that.

And she had names. Three girls she had documented interactions with. It meant nothing. All her precinct commander could see were three girls in cartoonish outfits floating around in a parking lot lit up like a disco. He kept coming back to the only reference that made sense to him.

"This is some kind of Cirque Du Soleil thing, right Petrossian? Like, performance art?"

"No, sir. Again sir, this is the video I took last night. The time stamp is right there on the image. And the lights? *Those are the lights.* You can hear my voice reporting in…"

"Where did you get this Petrossian?"

Nothing was getting through. He could not and would not accept the possibility that this was anything but a setup.

Finally, he left her in his office as he checked the dispatcher logs. His expression upon returning told her everything she needed to know about her future on the force. Whether she was out of her mind or telling the whole truth and nothing but the truth, everything Officer Linda Petrossian was bringing to light here made the department, the precinct—and him—look very bad.

After demanding her silence and threatening dire consequences, she was put on indefinite leave and barred from the station house pending further investigation.

* * *

They gave Andrea a few hours to sleep, but everything was closing in now. It was evening when Natalya shook her awake. "We need to get out of here. Tonight. Masa wasn't the only Faerie to be spotted today, and the footage of you is all over the internet. For the moment, we can go to my house, but I don't think even that will be safe much longer."

Andrea felt scared and lost. "What can we do?"

"It's not all bad. We have Viktor's assets, and that gives us options. There are safe houses available to us, and a number of vehicles in position for unforeseen circumstances. But, Andrea, I need you to pull yourself together and consider your situation before we go any further."

"What do you mean?"

Natalya sat down on the bed. "Andrea, this may be the last moment when you can still make a real decision about your future. We are all deeply drawn into this involvement with the Fae. The authorities are going to be looking to take us into custody, and I fear there may be a mob looking to get to us first.

"You need to decide whether you will submit to the protection and judgment of the state, or join Gaylen and me in flight. I'm sorry, but the choices are limited, and time is of the essence. I believe I can still contact Officer Petrossian and secure your safe passage into—"

"Never!"

"What?"

"I'm not putting myself at the mercy of the state *or* the mob. People are so crazy right now, I'm not sure there's even a difference."

Natalya looked unconvinced. "The path will be dangerous. You still have family, Andrea."

Andrea shook her head. "How could they help me? I'm more likely to drag them into danger. I appreciate what you're trying to do, I really do. But I'm afraid the time for backing out is over."

Natalya was looking down, still worried.

Andrea took her hands in her own. "I know you feel responsible. We can argue about that some other time. But we are in this situation now because of our choices. I don't regret any of mine."

Natalya looked up, still skeptical. "Okay, that's pretty much what Gaylen said. Pack two bags to put into storage and one to travel with." She stood up, walked to the doorway and turned back. "And Andrea, I'm sorry, but you need to assume that you are never coming back here. So, choose accordingly."

"Okay. Where's Gaylen?"

"Getting us a new car and securing food."

"And the Fae?"

"Still borderline hysterical and trying to make a plan. One thing they've managed to do is piece together a plausible explanation of what we saw last night. The 'glamour' they told us about? The thing that keeps Faeries hidden? They believe we may have tapped into the power supply for some kind of planetary-wide 'glamour' last night and overloaded it."

"You're kidding."

"Masa thinks they may have been using some property of the earth's atmosphere as a battery. She thinks the trinary thing she set up was tapping into that, and when we added a third escalation of the restoration power, it just blew the whole thing out."

A text alert interrupted Natalya. She sighed as she read it and shook her head. "Still nothing," she said to herself. Then, to Andrea, "We leave soon. Try not to forget anything."

* * *

For the rest of the evening, Andrea wandered around the house, trying to collect her thoughts, pack what she expected to need, and keep successive waves of fear and anger from paralyzing her. She was just passing the stairs to the basement when Gaylen emerged with a roll of gaffer tape. She held it up with a hint of triumph and a smile. "Always have gaffer tape Andrea. Most of life's problems can be fixed, at least temporarily, with gaffer tape."

Andrea knew it was a bit of bravado for her benefit, but it did coax a quick smile out of her. Then a new realization cut the moment short. "Gaylen. Where are the Fae?"

"Your room, I think?"

"Text Natalya. We need to talk. Now. *No Fae*." At that, she grabbed Gaylen's arm and dragged her back into the basement.

* * *

Five minutes later, they were standing around an ancient workbench under a single bare light bulb. Andrea was obviously agitated—yet strangely focused—which seemed to amuse Gaylen and worry Natalya.

"You seem to have found a second wind," Gaylen teased. "Wanna share?"

Andrea waved her words away. "Not now Gaylen." She took a deep breath and began, "Okay, why are we here?"

Natalya blinked her surprise and threw out, "Because of our choices?"

"No!" Andrea practically shouted. The two girls looked up in surprise. "Because of the choices we've been *handed* by the Fae."

"Yeah, well, Faeries aren't exactly trustworthy. But we've known this all along, haven't we?" Gaylen asked.

Andrea shook her head impatiently. "No. I'm not talking about the individual actions or information or decisions. The whole story. The whole situation. This isn't about good Faeries and bad Faeries. Or our Faeries and their Faeries. This is about everything we've been presented with. Every scenario, every power we've been given. It's all been leading us to irrevocable decisions. Once we accept any component, the rest just falls into place."

She turned to Natalya. "I agree to save the eggs I end up fighting you." Next, she pivoted to Gaylen. "We learn about the kyne, get armed up to fight it. What else were we going to do? We *had* to fight the kyne."

Gaylen looked confused. "So what does that mean?"

Natalya thought a moment and asked, "What do you think we need to do?"

Andrea sighed, "It means that everything they bring us, no matter which Faerie brings it, draws us into their intentions. And we will never know what that intention might be until it's too late for us to have any say in it. What we need to do now—at a minimum—is to stop believing everything we're told."

"Every time we've accepted their story, we just got pulled in deeper," Gaylen said quietly.

"But we're going need their help at this point," Natalya observed. "It will be a delicate balance to maintain their support while rejecting… what? Their advice? Their picture of events?"

Andrea slipped into a moment of regret. "This is all my fault. I trusted my three Faeries. I led you two into this."

Natalya drew herself up with a hint of anger. "We don't have time for this now. We'll indulge in recriminations later. Right now, we need to do what? Specifically *what*?"

Andrea looked uncertain. "We… withhold belief? At least we make our own assessments of what they present to us?"

"All of the Fae?" Gaylen asked. "Yours included?"

"Mine especially."

Andrea looked over to Natalya. "I think you were right. I'm starting to think they don't really have any idea of what's going on. They're sincerely clueless and I focused on the sincere and ignored the clueless. But now we're in it. Is there any chance that the people currently trying to hunt us down and imprison or kill us are going to listen to our story?"

No one said anything. Natalya checked her phone. "We need to move."

"So, what did we decide to *do* about this again?" Gaylen asked.

Andrea sighed. "We just have to watch out for the next piece of the story and not accept it as inevitable. We don't buy in without at least discussing it."

Andrea shrugged.

Gaylen shrugged back at her.

"Good enough for now," Natalya said. "Let's go."

Chapter 50

Around midnight they finished loading the car. Natalya kept checking her phone. "They're going to ID us any minute. I don't think we can go to my house again."

"You have everything, though?" Gaylen asked.

"Yes. I don't know. It's stupid. It's just that that was the only place I've ever lived without someone constantly monitoring me. I know it wasn't really mine, or anything, but it always felt like it belonged to me. I just wanted to… say goodbye."

"Maybe we can drive by and you can at least wave," Andrea suggested.

Natalya laughed. "Okay. If it's not surrounded by police cars, that would be nice." She checked an alert on her phone. It wasn't what she was expecting, though. "We need to go back inside and watch this."

The three Faeries floated into the living room as the girls dropped to the couch and turned on the TV. In addition to the "breaking news" banners, the graphic read, "Stand by for an important announcement." The newscaster seemed unusually agitated.

"Good evening. We have two breaking stories for you tonight, which may or may not be connected to each other and which may—I repeat, *may*—be related to last night's dramatic events.

"The first comes to us from the Westchester County Airport. A small single-engine aircraft with two passengers on board was attacked in the air by some sort of creature as it was attempting to land about an hour ago. In a highly unusual turn of events, we have video of the attack to show you. You won't see anything of the passengers being injured, and authorities have yet to release their names or their conditions, but we warn you, the sheer violence of this attack by this... creature is really quite shocking. We're going to roll that for you now."

The video was very high quality. Whoever took it had to be aware of what was about to happen. They had to know which flight was going to be attacked. They had to be prepared to hold framing and focus on what must have been a terrifying thing to observe.

As the plane glided in for a landing, a creature half the size of the plane itself—looking something like an armadillo with its sides flattened into an A-frame—descended on it from the right side of the picture. It flew straight for the tail section and—in a shower of metal—ripped the back of the plane to bits with a combination of teeth, claws, and tail. As the plane burst into flames and fell to the ground, the creature hovered over the wreckage a moment and then headed back the way it had come.

Back in Brooklyn, the world's three leading experts on the subject of horrible Faerie monsters concurred in their opinion.

"It's a kyne!" Gaylen said.

"And it's *huge!*" Andrea exclaimed.

"This is bad," Natalya said. "Viktor told me he had only the one kyne. That means someone else is working with the Fae. Sumi, what do you..."

The Fae were frozen with fear. A kyne-darath of that size was the stuff of nightmares. The girls weren't sure what to say, but that concern disappeared with the second piece of news.

"In addition to the video we have just shown you, we have what appears to be some kind of statement relating to this attack. This video was released on a website that goes by the name childrenofda-nu-dot-net, which we are trying to verify. It may be related to some aspect of fairy lore, which could tie this to the rash of alleged fairy sightings reported in the past twenty-four hours. I'm just going to play this, and we will try to put it in context afterward."

The image changed, and before a single word was spoken, Andrea gasped. "Cami!" Showing her from the chest up in front of a neutral blue background, the lens was pushed in far enough to give the impression that Cami was human size. Her demeanor was businesslike but imperious.

"We are the Fae. We are of the living god Danu, and she is of us.

Before your time, the Green World was our birthright. It remains so.

We have returned to reassert dominion over these lands.

In submission, there is harmony.

Your existence will be tolerated. Your opposition will not.

Resistance brings retribution. The kyne-darath brings terror.

Who resists… dies.

The sky submits to our will. This is our power. Remember it. Fear us.

The price of peace is compliance. Our dominion resumes.

We are the Fae. We are of the living god Danu, and she is of us."

The screen went to black, and then back to the studio. The newscaster was speechless.

Gaylen turned off the television, and everyone sat for a minute, digesting what they had just seen. The Fae, floating in a tight cluster to the side, looked shattered.

Natalya turned to them. "So it is to be war?"

"If what they're saying about dominion is serious, then yes," Masa replied.

Drained of emotion, Rei spoke up. "Damn them. They will destroy us all. We will never win a war against humanity. These idiots will destroy the Fae—and just when survival was becoming possible."

"There is no one to oppose them in your home?" Gaylen asked.

"No," said Masa. "*We* were the active leadership of their opposition. Too active. We should never have come here, but we did."

"Who else could we have sent?" Rei snapped.

"Not now, Rei." Sumi was exhausted, and her voice was barely audible. "Our decisions stand. We have lost, and badly. All that remains is to escape and fight again. Well, that and the girls."

Sumi floated out before them. "We have failed you. We have misread events and the True Fae's intentions. In addition, in our ignorance, we allowed you to use Masa's power-summing technology to cause major damage to the source of power that has kept our physical presence here invisible. Cami appears to be taking credit for that as a Fae weapon. I just can't believe they were ready to move so fast. Were we set up, Masa? Did they know we would overdrive it?"

Masa scowled. "Whether they set us up or were able to take advantage of the situation on short notice, it's all the same. They have been sharper and stronger than we ever gave them credit for."

Sumi drew herself up to her full five inches. "Andrea, Natalya, Gaylen, we need to go. We need to get home again. It will take longer than last time. We will provide you with whatever protections we can. But our leaving is going to deprive you of everything but the ice darts. No flying, no immobilization, no restoration."

"Oh," Rei said. "But they do keep the hats, right?"

"Yes." Sumi smiled weakly. "You do get to keep the hats. In fact, the hats are a little more important than we let on."

The girls tried not to react too suspiciously.

"Knew it." Gaylen said. "What's the catch?"

"No, no." Sumi said. "It's just that when you call for the hats, we—just the three of us—can locate you. Since you won't be here anymore, we need a way of finding you. When we return, we'll be able to sense where they are, anywhere on earth. So at least one of you should call for your hat once a day."

407

Rei looked impatient. "We have to go. There's a world full of humans out there hoping to catch a pet Faerie. Sumi, what about...?"

Sumi looked uncertainly at her, then—understanding the question—glared in annoyance. "*That?* What's the point, Rei? They don't have enough to worry about? They need another..."

She was heading for a breakdown. When Masa and Rei moved in to comfort her, they actually touched her. Andrea realized it was the first time she could remember seeing a Faerie touch another Faerie.

"Let me try," Masa said, moving away from Rei and Sumi. "There's little enough to say about it. Do you know anything about something called the Morrighan?"

Andrea and Natalya shook their heads. Gaylen seemed to be searching her memory. Eventually she came up with, "Something from Irish history? Celtic goddess, goddesses, something mythological...?"

"Yeah," Masa said. "That's what we figured."

Sumi had recovered enough to contribute. "All we have is the name. The last trip back, we kept asking, but no one would tell us a thing."

"Like they didn't trust us," Masa said. "We tried to narrow down the possibilities. It might be a human, a clan, a weapon, or—"

"Anything," Rei interrupted. "It might be *anything*. We have no idea, but we're absolutely positive we once knew and that our knowledge has been suppressed."

"So we should be looking *into* the Morrighan? Looking *out* for the Morrighan?" Gaylen asked. "Should we do some deep internet search for clues?"

Masa frowned. "I've been trying that. There's a lot there about the Celtic goddess Morrighan. But it's a mess. One goddess? Three? Ten? A dozen different names. Every conceivable family relationship. You dig down and The Morrighan is the patron goddess of pretty much everything. War, peace, earth, sky, water, fertility. She's associated with almost every creature except frogs, and I probably just didn't look hard enough. All we can tell you is to keep an eye out for anything about the Morrighan, especially if it involves the Fae."

Masa stopped talking and the room fell silent.

Gaylen had a blank expression.

Natalya was avoiding eye contact with everyone.

Andrea knew she should follow their lead, but she couldn't. Unable to keep silent, she threw out her next words with a big fake smile and practically shouting. "Oh, *wow!* So maybe *we're* The Morrighan. How cool would that be? Maybe there's some whole *other* set of traps for us to get snared up in."

The anger in her voice shocked the room. At first no one moved. The Fae exchanged glances. Finally, Sumi summoned up the courage to address her. "Traps, Andrea?"

Andrea didn't know how to respond. She didn't trust herself to speak.

Masa floated over. "Andrea, any 'trap' we've encountered has snared us as badly as you. I know this is a particularly bad moment…"

Andrea completely lost it. "Oh! Yeah! You could say that. Not a good moment? We're about to go into hiding from angry mobs and god knows what else and… the moment? Yeah. Not so good. And how did we get here? Is this our fight? Our monsters? Oh, wait! Yes! *Now* they are. *Our* monsters to kill. *Our* enemies to fight. *Our* own world hunting us down. But these were all *your* enemies and monsters. How did *we* get so mixed up in *your* disaster?"

She was gasping for air and close to tears. Gaylen looked slightly afraid. Natalya leaned over toward her, but Andrea waved her off. "No! I'm fine! But this? This Morrighan thing? Are you kidding? Another setup? Another path for you to lead us down? More of this, being…"

"Pixie led," Gaylen said quietly. "That's what they used to call it."

Agitated, Rei jumped in. "What are you talking about? We're trying to *warn* you. All we know is that The Morrighan is hated by the Fae and that you three are connected to it. Do you *not* want to know that?"

"All I know is that every time we get a new piece of information from a Faerie, it costs us." Andrea said. "Every new bit of your story ends up dropping another link onto the chain that's binding us to this nightmare. So, you know what? No. No, we don't want to know any more. We don't want any more of your information. Keep it."

Natalya addressed the Fae. "We all have to figure out our immediate needs. This declaration of war, on top of a new kyne threat…"

"Always *something* new," Gaylen said pointedly.

"Everything about this relationship needs to be reconsidered," Natalya continued. "Anything further you might want to tell us will have to wait." At that, she rose and walked to an open window. "Are you ready?"

The stunned Fae glided over wordlessly. Gaylen followed. For a moment, nothing happened. Natalya looked impassive, the Fae uncertain.

Gaylen broke the silence. "For better or worse, this does not end here. We are bound together. Our mutual survival depends on us having some kind of working relationship. And that means trust. You need to think about that."

Beyond words, the Faeries drifted out and upward.

Closing the window, Natalya sighed and refocused on the matters at hand. "We are within a half a mile of one of Viktor's safe houses. I'd rather put some distance between us and Brooklyn, but we can't risk being on the road right now. Hopefully they won't be expecting us to stay in the area. Go get you bags. We leave in fifteen minutes."

* * *

And fifteen minutes later, a perfectly anonymous car pulled out of the Melman's driveway observed by no one—save a trio of Faeries sitting on a nearby rooftop.

"Is that it?" Rei asked. "Have we lost them?"

"We've lost Andrea, that's for sure," Masa said.

411

"For now," Sumi agreed.

"Should we have told them more about home?" Rei said. "Would that have…?"

Masa sighed. "You're not getting it, Rei. We can't trust *them*, either."

Sumi looked at Rei and addressed her with quiet hopelessness. "Telling them about the collapse of our world, about our desperation… Do you really think that letting the humans know we're probably the last generation of the Fae is going to move them to kindness now? Would you expect them to offer us sanctuary here?"

"But Andrea… she'd come around." Rei said.

"After unleashing a kyne and declaring war on their world?" Masa asked. "Their natural allegiance is to their own kind. I would expect them to tell the authorities—sooner rather than later—and the authorities to just wait for us all to die."

"It wasn't supposed to be like this," Rei said.

The thought seemed to hang in the air when a hard voice from behind them demanded, "How else could it have possibly turned out?"

Spinning around the three were faced with an unusually tall Faerie, almost half again larger than they themselves and dressed in a shimmering gray garment made of a single piece of fabric. Her most striking feature though was the long silver streak that ran down one side of her long black hair. The effect was aristocratic, even regal, but her face was a mask of harsh judgment.

"Thea!" they exclaimed at once. Sumi looked flustered and scared. "Why are you here?"

The elegant creature floated there radiating disdain. The three Faeries blurted questions out over each other until, finally, she raised her hand to silence them.

"Do they know who they are?" she demanded.

The three characters shrank back. Finally, Sumi said, "They won't listen to us."

Thea wasn't looking for explanations. "So you've failed at the single task you were given?"

The Fae responded by exchanging frantic looks. "They're too suspicious." Masa offered up.

Thea answered with contemp. "You're too incompetent."

"They need more time." Rei pleaded.

"They need more *suffering*." Thea spat back.

Sumi visibly stiffened in reaction to that before calmly saying, "They've suffered for over a thousand years. Isn't that enough?"

Thea nodded, her suspicions apparently confirmed. "I see… you're weak. This is why you three no longer lead. No one trusts you."

"But we trusted *you*." Masa said.

Ignoring her, Thea looked pointedly away from them. "Perhaps you've lost sight of what is at stake here? In the absence of the living god it is our responsibility to secure the Green World for the perpetuation of the Fae. The survival of our kind rests upon us engaging the Morrighan and providing the motivations they need to act in accordance with our plan. Now…"

"But we don't know what the plan is." Sumi dared to interrupt.

"Honestly, we don't know what anything is anymore." Rei said

"Why won't you tell us what we need to know?" Masa asked plaintively.

Thea was moving from disdain to anger. "Have you forgotten your status? Are you under the illusion that you still hold the positions you once held? Must I remind you that you and your entire clan are held in disgrace? Do you not remember why you were banished to Japan?"

Her words cast a web of silence and shame over them. Looking approvingly at their degradation she said flatly, "You know what you need to know."

"But we don't know anything," Sumi said.

Thea broke into a smile of pure cruelty. "Yes. And how many centuries did it take for you to learn *that* lesson?

"We want to go home." Rei said on the verge of tears.

"Yes. About that…" Thea said, adjusting to a businesslike tone of voice. "Aside from your unfinished tasks here, it is no longer safe for you at home."

"We can't go home anymore?" Rei cried out.

Thea was reaching the end of her patience. "Do you not comprehend how *hated* you are at this point? Besides, your work is here now. None of us commands their own fate anymore. We are all headed for either annihilation or survival. Do your part as best you can understand it. It is all you can offer the Fae. Your success or your lives."

At that she held up her hands to signal the end of their meeting. "I go now."

Masa wasn't letting go however, "Wait! Who's Cami?"

Seeing their shared confusion brought a huge smile to Thea's face. "You really don't know?" She scanned them for confirmation. "None of you? Good!" And then, turning to Masa with satisfaction she said with sarcastic enthusiasm, "Congratulations Masa! You managed to do one thing correctly."

And without another word, Thea dissolved back into Parallel Space, leaving the three guardian characters alone and in exile on the now hostile place they called the Green World.

Chapter 51

Andrea woke up the next morning in a strange house. There were unfamiliar hums and clicks. Even the sunlight coming through the windows seemed harsh and artificial.

"This is a safe house?"

She got up and wandered about. There wasn't far to wander. The basement was the only point of interest. It was occupied by stacks of provisions. Boxes of dried foods. Water in big plastic jugs. Paper products and cleaning supplies.

Gaylen had secured enough fresh food yesterday to make for a pretty good breakfast. But eating in the generic kitchen felt like being on a stage set. Andrea wanted to ask whether there were interior designers who specialized in safe house décor, but no one seemed in the mood.

No one brought up the Fae.

Natalya seemed to be wary of overwhelming them with the new rules for living like a fugitive. She fed them little bits of tradecraft about avoiding detection as if she was feeding baby birds from an eyedropper. Basic principles now. Details for later.

One little surprise.

At some point, she had ransacked the Melman family closets to create a most unfashionable fashion collection. Two bags filled with the least interesting clothes a person could possibly wear. All guaranteed to "reduce our silhouette from a surveillance standpoint."

Somehow, the idea that they would all be dressing to be invisible hit Andrea as particularly depressing. Still, Natalya's insistence on disguising her the other day was probably the only reason they weren't already in custody.

* * *

Natalya's precautions were well justified. If nothing was showing up on police scanners and social media, it was because the New York Police Department was no longer running the show. The Department of Homeland Security was now in charge of the "Brooklyn Incident," and they weren't interested in sharing.

By nightfall, they had descended on Linda Petrossian's precinct, viewed and analyzed her video, and reinterviewed Officer Petrossian herself. By the following morning, DHS felt it had a clear enough picture of who was involved, if not exactly what they were involved in, but by then, events were drifting out of their control.

For one thing, the "persons of interest" were not at their "places of residence." As the girls lingered over breakfast, warrants were being executed at the now-empty houses of Andrea Melman and Natalya Volkova. Meanwhile, at Gaylen O'Reilly's former residence, Millie defiantly stood her ground, haranguing the federal agents at her door about government tyranny and illegal search and seizure. Once she understood they were looking to arrest Gaylen however, she settled down and became quite cooperative.

Bringing in the Department of Homeland Security had other consequences. By the time the girls finished doing the dishes in

Brooklyn, detailed information about them was starting to reach a wide range of organizations back in Washington.

One such group—a lobbying organization dedicated to the proposition that a Christian nation needed a Christian military supplied by Christian weapons manufacturers—was alerted by a concerned congressman who may or may not have inadvertently revealed certain restricted information to a particular individual there.

In what may have been a divinely inspired coincidence, that individual also happened to be a member of another group of patriotic Americans committed to establishing the word of God as the basis of governance for the country—a group known as Dominion of God.

A short time later, he was on the phone with Big Jim Rankin. "It's the same girls, Big Jim. Same as attacked our intervention at Millie's. A coven of witches, and now they've summoned up these fairy demons. Flaunting the laws of heaven and earth, they are. Flaunting 'em!"

"You got that right, Brother Bobbie. Consorting with fairies? We know who they've been consorting with, don't we now? We know what's behind these 'fairies,' don't we?"

"Satan, Big Jim. It's Satan."

"The devil himself, Brother Bobbie. But the Lord is on our side, brother. Our Lord has provided us with this information for a reason."

"Broke the laws of God and man, didn't they now, Big Jim?"

"That they did, brother. That they did. But we know that the laws of God always transcend the laws of man. Which means we are honor-bound to serve up his righteous justice."

"What are we gonna do, Jim?"

"It's all right there in the Bible, brother. *Exodus* 22:18. 'Thou shalt not suffer a witch to live.' We're gonna hunt these witches down and smite them in the name of our Lord. By the grace of God, we are going to show these harlots what it means to attack God and country. I am formally activating Blood of the Cross. We need to have boots on the ground in Brooklyn by sundown today."

"I'm on it, Big Jim. You wanna give the operation a name?"

"As a matter of fact, I do, Bobbie. We're calling this 'Operation: Payback's A Bitch.'"

* * *

Viktor may have been a psychopath, but he was quite rational when it came to safe house design. One could never truly appreciate the value of an attached garage until one had to load a car while avoiding a federal dragnet.

The small square windows atop the garage door gleamed with the final rays of sunset as Gaylen and Natalya got into the front seat. Natalya was visibly calm, but her voice betrayed deep tension as she started the car and spoke to Andrea. "This shouldn't take more than two hours. We're going to put the stuff in long-term storage lockers near JFK and come right back. You're sure you don't need anything from your bags? I can't guarantee you'll ever see them again."

Andrea tried to be upbeat. "Stop trying to sugarcoat everything, Natalya. No, I don't need any of it. Just a few bags of hopes and dreams. Plenty more where that came from."

Gaylen rewarded her with an appreciative cackle, but Natalya just sighed. "You're clear on the procedure if we don't return or text you by midnight?"

Andrea held up a couple of pages of notes. "Clear as day."

"And you'll burn those notes before leaving the…"

"Natalya!" Gaylen interrupted. "It's go-time. Andrea? Don't do anything stupid. See you soon."

* * *

The view of the world as the garage door opened was brief but moving. It was twilight, and the world was doing the same thing it had done at the end of every day of Andrea's life up to now: growing dark and quiet. Dark enough to reveal the stars that had lingered, hidden, all through the busy daytime sky, and quiet enough to let the sounds of birds and insects be perceptible to a discerning ear.

But it wasn't the same. Andrea wasn't the same. A single day in the dead world of Viktor's safe house had left her depressed beyond belief and desperate for the small pleasures of what had—so suddenly—become her former life.

The garage door hadn't quite closed before she began crying. She wanted to take a walk. To sit at her window seat in her bedroom and read. To go to school and shop at the Japanese supermarket and argue with her brother over nothing and a million other things that were now beyond reach.

Finally, she had to act. To her mind she was empowering herself, but she knew it was an argument she wouldn't dare make to the others.

It's a simple plan, she thought as she arranged the coat, hat, and sunglasses. *Twenty minutes, tops.*

She opened the front door and stood on the threshold of this newly forbidden world.

Here we go. One last look at my house and right back.

The moment the front door closed behind her, she knew it was a mistake.

It's like ten minutes away. I can do this.

Trying to walk inconspicuously made her tense up and look more conspicuous than ever. She had to force herself to stop twisting her head around.

I must look like I'm casing houses.

It only made her more agitated.

If the point was to enjoy the evening quiet, then this was already a failed mission. Now that she was out on the street, every calming impulse was lost in a storm of anxiety. She saw clearly that what she was doing was a complete betrayal of the group's security. She was ignoring or violating every lesson Natalya had been trying to teach them.

I should just turn back now. This is crazy.

It was perfectly true. But objective truth was a slender candle to put against the blazing sun of longing and loss driving Andrea. Nothing could quench her aching need to see her home one more time before... before what? Before a life on the run? Before exile? Jail?

The last leg of her journey went through the park behind Kyle's house. It was dark now. The park was empty as she made her way to the hedge-lined walkway in the rear that led through the block to her street.

She began to see reflections of flashing colored lights on the foliage above her. At first she thought someone had turned on their Christmas lights out of season. But as she came to the end of the path, she gasped.

A dozen official vehicles were parked out in front of her house, each one sporting an array of flashing emergency lights. Lines of yellow crime tape were stretched across the front lawn, and portable light towers bathed the scene in a harsh white glare while their generators contributed a low throbbing growl.

For all the vehicles out there, only a handful of police officers were standing around. Andrea realized they had probably been there for hours and that she was showing up long after what must have been a major assault on the Melman compound.

It was so unexpected, the only thought she could muster was, "*Mom and Dad are going to kill me when they hear about this.*

Her eyes were fixed on the house as she edged as close to the street as she dared. Drinking in the familiar sights of home as if there would be no tomorrow. The windows to her room. The peaked roof over Dion's wing. Her grandmother's big, shabby, crazy witch house. Her house. Trying to grab an impression to last her—what? The rest of her life? It didn't seem possible.

A muted clang from inside Kyle's house brought her up. Somehow, an encounter with Kyle at this moment seemed more awful than the possibility of being arrested. She had to get out of there.

As she turned to head back, the shift from the brilliantly lit crime scene to the dark path made her slip the sunglasses off and into her coat pocket. By the time she got to the park again, she had to sit down on a bench and try to recover. Unfortunately, at the moment she most needed it, Andrea's situational awareness simply vanished.

She took no notice of the two black SUVs parked and idling across the street from her.

* * *

As Christian warrior missions went, Blood of the Cross was having a decidedly bad mission. 'Operation: Payback's A Bitch' had run into a particularly challenging environment. They had almost gotten arrested at the Volkova house when they rolled up with their tactical light racks blazing. Then they tried to call Millie as she was sitting in her kitchen chatting with "some nice boys from the Bureau of Alcohol, Tobacco and Firearms." By the time they'd gone by the Melman house, it was looking like the forces of righteousness were going home empty-handed.

A low key drive by of the Melman house had prompted them to retreat one street over to reconsider their options. With the possibility of total failure in the air, no one paid any particular attention to the individual who drifted through the park across the street to a pathway partially hidden by foliage. But something about that same individual returning a few minutes later caught Brother Bobbie's eye. When they sat down on one of the benches, he realized he was looking at a girl. The outfit had obscured that fact and there were other things about it that just didn't feel right. The coat seemed a few sized too large. The hat was too big. He had almost dismissed it as some kind of Brooklyn hipster thing when the girl removed the hat and laid it on the bench beside her.

"Jim! Jim!"

The mood in the "command vehicle" was pretty somber by this time, and Big Jim was in no mood for nonsense as he checked his cell phone for messages.

"Not now Bobbie. I'm assessing some options here."

"Where are the glasses Jim?" Bobbie hunted through a duffel bag next to him on the back seat and pulled out an enormous pair of binoculars. Training them on the girl on the park bench, he let out a whoop. "Praise the Lord!" Pushing the binoculars to Big Jim in the front passenger seat, he could barely contain himself. "Looky! Looky! Who's that, Jim? Anyone you know?"

Holding the glasses in one hand and a picture of the three girls in the other, Big Jim gave a low whistle. "Well, son of a bitch," he said. "Boys, let's go hunting."

* * *

Andrea sat in a daze. Too many things were racing around in her head. The sight of her family home—lit up, taped off, and occupied—was impossible to shake off. In a far-off corner of her mind, something was trying to make a connection to the hat sitting in her lap and the endless concerns about safety Natalya had been lecturing them on. But she blew it off and went back to grieving over her lost home.

She barely noticed as two men, quietly walking down the street, moved past her line of sight. A police siren floated in from far away. Andrea finally shook off her state and stood to leave.

Suddenly the evening quiet was assaulted by the aggressive gunning of the SUV's engines as they pulled out to position themselves right in the middle of the street directly facing the park on either side of Andrea.

She froze. Physically and mentally, Andrea was totally unable to process what was happening right in front of her.

Run!

She looked about frantically. In front of her, the growling SUVs were bouncing slightly in place. Agile hunting animals on the balls of their feet ready to pounce.

The police are nearby! I should scream!

But she had no desire to bring herself to the attention of the invaders in her home. As terrifying as the situation was, no sound escaped her throat, and she kept uselessly grasping for a better strategy.

Kyle's house! His family. They can…

She couldn't finish the thought. They would probably just call the police. The same police who were already right outside her house. And she wasn't about to drop this dangerous mess on Kyle's family.

Any notion of rational decision making disappeared in a blinding glare as the tactical lights kicked in. Everything dissolved into a wall of white agony. Suddenly Andrea realized that the SUVs were crawling up onto the sidewalk and into the park on either side of her.

In a frenzy, she turned and ran back, looking desperately for the walkway. All she could consider at this point was escape.

As the vehicles roared about threateningly behind her, Andrea finally saw the entrance. Another dozen steps and she'd be safe within the tall hedges. Whether she forced her way into Kyle's house or turned herself in to the cops was of no consequence. The dark corridor beckoned and she lunged toward it.

And there they were. Not moving. Just waiting. Right where they knew she would go.

She pulled up short, momentarily unable to believe that this could be happening. A confused notion of turning around to run evaporated as she saw just who it was who'd stalked and trapped her.

Big Jim stood there with his arms crossed, and a big smile on his face. He looked down on his prize with a chuckle of satisfaction.

"Well, hello there, little missy," he drawled. "Looks like we just caught ourselves a witch."